JACOB BLACKFORT WAS A VERY DANGEROUS MAN . . .

Something in Jacob's gaze had shifted. He reminded her of a wolf scenting the air before fixing on his prey.

"What's the matter, Macon? You stopped yelling."

Macon drew in a deep breath, wishing she didn't like the clean soapy scent of him as much as she did. "You're insufferable."

"Undoubtedly." He leaned closer.

"Incorrigible." She was having trouble concentrating.

"That, too."

"Pig. . . . Pig-headed." She swallowed when he exhaled, and his breath fanned her eyelashes.

"Definitely." He brushed his lips over hers in the barest whisper of a caress. "But you still haven't told me why you're so mad."

"Because you lied to Chap. You let him think we're romantically involved." Great way to explain herself, she thought. She could feel herself blushing.

A warm smile curved Jacob's lips. "Are you always so proper?" When she didn't answer, he slid his lips over the arch of her eyebrow. "I let him know I'm hot for you, Macon Stratton. What's so bad about that?"

"Because you're not," she wailed.

Jacob's smile turned lascivious. "Wanna bet?"

D1464365

RESTLESS

NEESA HART

PINNACLE BOOKS
KENSINGTON PUBLISHING CORP.

PINNACLE BOOKS are published by

Kensington Publishing Corp.
850 Third Avenue
New York, NY 10022

Pinnacle and the P logo Reg. U.S. Pat. & TM Off.

First Pinnacle Books Printing: May, 1996

Printed in the United States of America
10 9 8 7 6 5 4 3 2 1

For the crews at RDI and ECG who know that fact really is stranger than fiction,

For Maureen, who could have taught Maylene Porter a thing or two,

For Libby, who will appreciate Macon's grammar fixation,

For Deanna, who really could figure out how to print all that money,

And for Amy, colleague and friend, who knew exactly what Isaac Asimov meant when he said: "If I only had six days to live, I'd try to type a little faster."

Prologue

Thule, Greenland.
Sometime on September 5

The top of the world was a god-forsaken place. The man they called the Black Arrow had been there for the past sixteen days. Every one of them had been miserable.

Black Arrow leaned back against a rock as he exhaled a deep sigh. His breath formed a crystallized billow of mist against the glare of the winter sky. A biting gust of the cinder-dry air cut through the insulated layers of his thermal clothing, and he pulled his heavy, fur-lined thermal coat tighter around his body. He knew he couldn't afford to wait longer than five more minutes outside the protective confines of the small outpost he used as a combination shelter and base of operations. He'd checked the temperature before he'd left the outpost. It was -47° Celsius. At that temperature, prolonged exposure for longer than ten to twelve minutes, even when he was protected by heavy thermal outerwear, threatened his body with severe hypothermia.

He scowled as he checked his watch, then strained his eyes into the boundless, glistening white distance for a glimpse of his contact. It wasn't, he supposed, the location that hid soured his mood so completely. As the northernmost city in the world, Thule had a stark, silent beauty that was slightly overwhelming in its magnitude. The naked expanses of untouched ice stretched into the horizon, and here, well within the Arctic Circle, only the ever-shifting flow of ice masses marred the barren silence with the haunted creaks and groans of the mercurial base. No, it wasn't the solitude, or the silence, or even the harsh conditions, that fired his temper. It was the knowledge that the weeks he'd spent at the outpost had been as largely unsuccessful as before, yielding little new information, and taunting him with operations he'd been too late to intercept. During his periods of solitude in the grave, frozen beauty at the top of the world, menacing suspicion had begun to form and take root. He knew that a mere communication from the coming messenger could not, and would not erase his suspicions.

He moved restlessly when he saw a dark shape emerge in the distance on the bleak expanse of ice. The distant whine of an engine heralded the approach of a snowmobile. Black Arrow unfolded from his crouched position to mount his own cruiser. He cranked the polar-equipped engine, grateful for the blast of heat it emitted into the frozen air, and he sped across the frozen plain toward the darkening figure on the horizon.

Black Arrow leaned low over his cruiser as he approached the other rider. His eyes shifted beneath his dark glasses, searching, watching for a glimpse of the tiny metal cylinder that held the information he wanted. He was within three feet of the other rider, when a silent communication passed between them. The cylinder whistled into the frigid air. Black Arrow shot a gloved hand out and wrapped his fingers around the precious cargo, tucking it safely into his pocket. The other snowmobile was already fading in the distance. Black Arrow cast a casual glance over his shoulder as he swung his own cruiser to the west. A blast of ice and snow billowed in its wake. He paused, waiting for the rider to disappear from view. before he raced in the direction of his shelter.

The tiny outpost was uninhabited, and he had used it twice before, when his investigations had taken him to Thule. From the upper floor, he could see the shadowy outline of the U.S. Air Force base in the distance, and the remote Danish fishing town on the coast. The outpost, once an aid station for fishing vessels caught within the merciless wedges of ice, was always under surveillance. Its proximity to the Air Force Base guaranteed its protection. He had known it would be too dangerous, too visible to meet his Danish contact there. Sliding his cruiser into the small shed, he turned on the tiny heater that would prevent the engine fluids from freezing, then walked through the short passageway into the anteroom of the outpost.

He stripped off his gloves and rubbed his hands together, thinking for the hundredth time since he'd reached Thule that he'd long ago grown far too old for his line of work. As he checked the temperature in the anteroom, he smiled wryly when the zero-degree air caressed his face like a tropical breeze. The piquant smell of hydrothermal heat draped the room in a blanket of humid warmth. He patiently waited until his body began to tingle unpleasantly from the ebbing cold, before he shrugged out of his heavy thermal outerwear. Five minutes later, convinced he wouldn't be plunged into thermal shock by the abrupt change in temperature, he slipped the small cylinder from his coat pocket, then carried it into the living area of the small outpost.

The warmer temperature inside felt like a furnace blast against his still cool skin. He waited a few more minutes for his body to adjust before pouring himself a cup of coffee. He sipped it tentatively. The first time he'd come to Thule, his partner had taken great pleasure in warning him that men had shattered their teeth by drinking warm beverages too soon after emerging from the extreme cold. The coffee tasted like hell, bitter and strong, but it went down easily enough. Finally feeling began to return to his fingers and toes in the form of an unpleasant prickling sensation. His hand reached automatically for the cylinder.

He broke the wax seal with his fingernail, then slipped off the cap. The tiny scrap of paper fluttered out onto the table. Carefully, Black Arrow spread it open and studied it. His mind deciphered the cryptic message. He frowned as the words formed sentences, and the sentences grew into a paragraph. There was obviously a mistake.

Senator Gordon Stratton was his target. Black Arrow had been focused on the man for nearly six months, ever since new evidence had turned up linking him to the international counterfeiting ring that had consumed the past four years of the Black Arrow's life. Why, then, was the Service recalling him to Washington to seek the help of Stratton's stepdaughter? If she was the powerful political player the message suggested that she was, Black Arrow suspected she was a typical Washington hoyden. Unapproachable, cold, and mean as hell. It was insanity to think she would cooperate.

But the Black Arrow needed her. His partner, working from the Washington office, had uncovered new evidence and Macon Stratton could unlock the hearing-room doors and the smoke-filled rooms in the power center of the world. She could place Black Arrow in a strategic position to build his case. She could betray her stepfather.

The Black Arrow leaned back in his chair. He studied the permanent layer of frost on the window of the tiny outpost. A grim smile tugged at his mouth. Washington; D.C. might not be the top of the world, but compared to Thule, it sounded damn close to heaven!

One

Washington, D.C.
Seventy-two hours later

It was well after eleven-thirty in the morning when Macon finally hung up the phone. She leaned back in her chair, wearily rubbing her eyes. The award she'd received that morning from *Electioneering* magazine had generated an inordinate number of phone calls from well-wishers and reporters alike. She hadn't had a break all morning. She looked up as May entered her office with a fresh cup of coffee. Macon managed a tired smile. "You deserve combat pay for today, Maylene."

Maylene Porter, Macon's personal assistant and self-appointed substitute mother, patted her hair with a plump, ring-bejeweled hand. "Well, you didn't expect anything else with that article coming out today, did you?"

Macon glanced at her picture on the front of *Electioneering*. She felt quite a sense of pride. "It was a good piece, I thought. It should be good for business."

May rolled her eyes. "Go ahead and gloat, Macon. You know you want to."

She did. She really did. She paused only briefly

before she scooped up the magazine and flashed a bright smile at May. "It is pretty wonderful, isn't it?"

"You get named Washington's Most Politically Powerful Woman by *Electioneering* Magazine, and the best you can do is 'pretty wonderful'?"

Macon laughed. "All right, it's fabulous. Mind-blowing. Absolutely the best day of my life. How's that?"

"You're starting to get the hang of it." The phone rang again, and Macon settLed back in her chair with a cup of coffee while May efficiently handled the call. The older woman set the receiver back in its cradle, then looked at Macon, "Between that article and the usual election-year rabble, it's going to be one hell of a week."

Macon sniffed the pleasant aroma of her coffee. The smooth, mocha almond scent of the gourmet coffee soothed her jangled nerves. She took an appreciative sip of the butter-soft liquid as she leaned back in her chair to cross her feet on her desk. She looked pointedly at the large stack of pink messages in May's hand. "Is there anything in that pile that needs my immediate attention?"

May speculatively flipped through the messages. "I don't think so. Jeff Parker called." She gave Macon a pointed look.

Macon ignored it. May never bothered to disguise her dislike for Jeff Parker and his relationship with Macon. "Who else?"

"Ateon called twice," she said, referring to a pesky vendor Macon occasionally used as a subcontractor. "There are a few calls from reporters who want an angle on the *Electioneering* story. The only thing that sounds halfway interesting is the bedroom voice."

Macon raised an eyebrow. "The bedroom voice?"

"Um-hmm. He's called three times and won't tell me what it's about. All I know is, he's got a voice to die for, and if he looks anywhere near as sexy as he sounds on the phone, he's bound to be dangerous."

Macon shook her head. "My luck doesn't run that way. What's his name? Maybe I'll know who he is."

May pulled out the three messages. "His name is Jacob Blackfort. Here's his number."

"Jacob Blackfort?" She took the messages.

"Yeah. Do you know him?"

"Never heard of him." She tapped her upper lip with her fingernail as she studied the pink message slip. "Jacob Blackfort. It sounds like one of those half-naked guys on the front of a—" She broke off the sentence when a prickling sensation at her nape sent a shiver of warning down her spine. She didn't have to turn around to know someone had entered her office.

"I'd be happy to strip my shirt off if I could get ten minutes of your time for it." The deep rumbling voice came from the door.

Startled, Macon swiveled in her chair with a curious sense of embarrassed dread. She felt an apology lodge at the back of her throat at the sight of the man in the doorway, the man she knew, without even the slightest smidgen of doubt, was Jacob Blackfort.

Well, hell's bells, she thought, it wasn't just his name that belonged on a book cover. Uninvited, an irreverent thought popped into Macon's head.

As she stared at Jacob Blackfort, she had to stifle the urge to giggle. When Macon had been in college, her roommate had been a budding professional model. Dorothy had a theory that all male models were locked away on some island in the South Pacific where they couldn't procreate and overpopulate the planet with nice-looking men. She would have agreed, Macon figured, that Mr. Jacob Blackfort was most certainly an escapee.

His physical appearance was arresting, she decided. He wasn't so much handsome as he was dangerous-looking. He was tall, at least six-three. The fashionable cut of his black suit, contrasted against the starched white of his linen shirt, certainly could have added to the impression of his height. His blue-black hair, a bit long for her taste, and a crisply knotted black and white tie, framed an angled face with a full mouth that made her think she wouldn't ever want to find herself on the opposite side of a frown. By far, though, his most arresting feature was the almost unnatural blue of his eyes. And the way they seemed to look right through her.

He wore contacts, Macon thought cynically. He had to.

Under the impaling gaze of those eyes, Macon fought the urge to run a hand through her cropped light brown curls to see if they were as unruly as usual. She lowered her feet to the floor instead. Resolutely, she met his aquamarine gaze. "I assume you're Jacob Blackfort?" Her voice sounded strangled. She couldn't decide whether her embarrassment, or his obvious lack of it, was causing the odd tone.

He nodded. "The same."

Macon swallowed. "I'm sorry, Mr. Blackfort, you must think I'm terribly rude."

With a brief wave of his hand, he crossed the room to stand in front of her desk. "Not at all, Ms. Stratton. I'm the one who barged into your office uninvited. I can certainly afford to overlook a good-natured jest. Although," he paused as he held her gaze with a knowing look that made her toes curl inside her shoes, "with a name like Macon Stratton, well, you know what they say about people in glass houses."

She thought it might have been a joke, although she couldn't be absolutely sure—not when he was staring at her with that penetrating look in his eyes. Macon inwardly squirmed. She had a vague notion that she should stand up, but something about Jacob Blackfort made her oddly grateful for the security of her desk. "Duly noted, Mr. Blackfort."

He extended his hand. Macon slipped her fingers into his warm grasp, shaking a little more firmly than was necessary, just to prove that she could. "Well," she said, indicating the chair across from her desk, "now that you're here, may I get you some coffee?"

He dropped into the chair so abruptly, that Macon wondered if he'd been struggling to stay on his feet. "That'd be great. I've been on an airplane for the past several hours. I could use a caffeine jump-start."

May started, apparently remembering her own presence in the room. "I'll get it. Do you take cream and sugar?"

He shook his head. "Just black. Thank you."

May mumbled something unintelligible. She shot Macon a maternal who-is-this-man-and-what-are-you-going-to-do-with-him look, before she slipped from the office, closing the door behind her.

Still feeling uncharacteristically nervous, Macon folded her hands on top of her desk. "You've come in from out of town, did you say?" she asked, seizing on his earlier explanation about the plane.

His gaze seemed to slide into focus. He looked as though he was ready to fall asleep in the burgundy leather chair across from her desk. With a brief nod, he leaned forward in the chair. "That's right."

He seemed to fade away again. It made her feel better, somehow, that she was behind the desk. Something about this m&n was intimidating, and she had never liked feeling intimidated. Sitting behind the wide cherry desk gave her a feeling of control.

Several long seconds ticked by. Macon shifted slightly in her chair. "Mr. Blackfort, I . . ."

Macon broke off the explanation when the door opened and May entered with Jacob's coffee. "Will there be anything else, Mr. Blackfort?" May asked. Macon didn't miss the fact that May's silvery hair was freshly combed, and a new layer of pink lipstick had been applied. Macon met her gaze over Jacob's head with a wry, knowing look.

"No, thank you," he said, seemingly unaware of the silent communication passing between the two women. "This is just fine."

May beamed at him, then made her way to the door, stopping to throw Macon another meaningful glance over her shoulder. Macon glared at her before turning her attention back to Jacob. "Now, Mr. Blackfort, what can I do for you?"

He closed his eyes briefly as he took a long sip of the coffee. "I knew you'd have great coffee." His eyes popped open. Some of the fatigue in them seemed to have ebbed. "Please, call me Jacob."

She narrowed her gaze at him. She decided to let the cryptic comment about her coffee slide, for the moment at least. "Very well, Jacob, you've gone to quite a lot of trouble to see me this morning. It must be fairly important."

With a brief nod, he reached inside his jacket for his wallet. He handed it to her across the desk. "I'm with the U.S. Secret Service."

Macon raised her eyebrows as she flipped open the leather wallet to examine the badge and I.D. "Did someone kill the president?" she quipped.

The joke fell flat. Jacob didn't seem to notice. He shook his head. "Not that I know of. I'm rarely involved in presidential protection. I'm with the investigations branch."

Macon closed the wallet, and handed it back to him. "The Secret service is under the Treasury Department, isn't it?"

He nodded. "I'm impressed. Our efforts protecting the president are so visible, not many folks know we do extensive investigations for Treasury."

"I went to high school with a lot of political people. Some of them were Secret Service kids. You can't grow up in Washington and not know the players."

Jacob took another sip of his coffee. "I'll spare you the tour guide's lecture, then."

Macon nodded. "So what can I do for the Secret Service?"

He set his cup on her desk. She wondered if it was her imagination, or if he shed his mantle of casual politeness with the simple act. All of a sudden, he was all business. "I'd like to talk to you about that someplace other than your office," he stated as he paused to check his watch. "It's nearly noon. Can I buy you lunch?"

"May I buy you lunch?" she said, instantly regretting the automatic reflex that had spurred the grammar prompt.

He blinked. "I asked you first."

Macon forced a small laugh to cover her embarrassment. The comment had been rude. For the life of her, she couldn't understand why this man had her so off balance. "I'm sorry. That was reflexive. I'm forever trying to train my clients to use better grammar. It was instinct." She paused. "It was also rude."

For the first time since he'd entered her office, he smiled at her. The result was devastating. "That's twice you've apologized to me in less than," he checked his watch again, "fifteen minutes. I think for that, you have to let me buy you lunch."

"Shouldn't I be the one doing the buying?"

He shook his head. "I'm the one interrupting your day. It's only fair that you let me pay for your lunch."

"Why can't we talk here?" She wasn't sure why she felt the need to persist. She just wasn't entirely comfortable with the idea of having lunch with Special Agent Blackfort.

"Because I haven't checked the office for taps," he answered bluntly.

Macon looked at him in surprise "Is this some kind of a joke?"

He shook his head. "I assure you, Ms. Stratton, there's nothing funny about it."

Macon studied him another long minute before reaching over to flip open her calendar. She glanced at her appointments for the rest of the afternoon. "I've got a one-thirty meeting with a client on The Hill. We'll have to be back by then."

"No problem."

Macon rose to her feet, feeling suddenly anxious to get out of the closed confines of her office, and the far-too-close proximity of Jacob Blackfort. "All right. We'd better get going, though. I can't be late for this meeting."

When he stood, Macon thought again how imposingly tall he was. "You won't be," he said. He motioned for her to precede him out of the office. She stepped around the desk, trying to ignore the intense look in his eyes. "Ms. Stratton?" His voice halted her progress to the door.

"Yes?" She turned back and saw him looking at the roses that had been delivered to her that morning. Nat Baldwin, a close friend, and the young publisher of *Electioneering* magazine, had sent them to congratulate her on her award.

"Are those roses from Jeff Parker?" he asked.

Macon raised an eyebrow. She wasn't sure whether to be shocked that he knew about Jeff Parker, or irate that he would ask such a personal question. "I don't think that's any of your business, Mr. Blackfort."

He leveled his gaze at her. "My office has spent three months checking your background. I just read the file. I have some concerns about Parker's reputation, and I want to know how much of an obstacle he's going to be."

His blunt statement so took her by surprise, she forgot to be angry at his audacity. "Three months?"

"It takes a while."

"I've been under investigation for three months, and no one told me?"

"That's because there are no skeletons in your closet. If there were skeletons, the bones would have been rattling loud enough for you to hear." He took two long strides so that he towered over her.

Macon frowned at him, feeling claustrophobic with him looming over her. As the spicy, clean scent of his cologne, mixed with some other equally intoxicating combination of fresh air and maleness closed in around her, her mouth went dry. "Mr. Blackfort . . ."

"Jacob," he persuaded, his voice soft, lethal.

"Mr. Blackfort, what's going on here?"

Her curt question seemed to get his attention. He shook his head with a weary sigh. The aura of power that surrounded him evaporated in the wake of the fatigued look he gave her. "My apologies, Ms, Stratton. I'm a little tired today. I'm probably not handling this with the right amount of finesse. I promise I'll explain everything over lunch."

Macon pulled open the door. "I should hope so." She heard the sting in her own voice. She shot Jacob Blackfort a quelling look, daring him to press her further.

His only response was an arched eyebrow and a slight lift of his shoulder that sent her flying out the door.

$\mathcal{T}wo$

Ten minutes later, Jacob drove along Rock Creek Parkway, thoughtfully tapping the leather covering of his steering wheel with his index finger. Macon hadn't spoken since he'd settled her into the elegant tan leather interior of his Alfa Romeo roadster. He hadn't missed the surprised look on her face when she'd seen his car, and he'd barely resisted the urge to laugh as he'd watched her mentally calculate its worth.

The lady's face was as readable as a tabloid. Every expression betrayed exactly what she was thinking. And at the moment, she was looking at his Italian leather loafers from the corner of her eye and trying to decide what business a federal employee had wearing eight-hundred-dollar shoes, two-thousand-dollar hand-tailored suits, and driving a sixty-thousand-dollar car. "I'm expected to maintain a certain appearance of affluence," he said. "It's part of my undercover work."

She looked at him. He decided he liked the guilty flush that stole into her cheeks. "I beg your pardon?"

He bit back a smile. In the few minutes he'd known her, he decided Macon Stratton would never simply say *what* like the rest of the population. She was strictly an *I beg your pardon* kind of lady. "I said, I'm expected to maintain a certain level of affluence as part of my undercover work."

Her stormy blue eyes registered a slight spark of embarrassment. "Do you feel obliged to tell that to everyone you meet?"

He didn't resist the urge to smile at her frosty tone. "Only those who inquire."

"I didn't ask," she said, just a touch too defensively.

He slanted a look at her. "You didn't have to."

Macon muttered something beneath her breath as she squirmed uncomfortably in her seat. "Where are we going?"

He allowed her abrupt change of subject. "Rock Creek Park."

"Well, I know that. I've lived in this city for twenty years. I mean where are we going to lunch?"

"Rock Creek Park," he repeated. "I understand there are several hot-dog vendors of considerable repute scattered throughout the Park."

Macon seemed to soften. He was entranced by the way her eyes went warm, and her fingers unclenched, and her lips turned into the barest hint of a smile. He'd seen those eyes flashing blue fire at him in her office. They were even more powerful when they went all soft and warm as they were now. He suspected that the full force of Macon Stratton's warmth could melt an iceberg. "If it suits you," he said, "I thought we could grab a bite and find a park bench. It's a nice afternoon."

"Big spender," she teased, her smile turning genuine, blooming slowly with all the magic of a butterfly breaking from its chrysalis.

And it had a staggering effect on him. He liked

the way it lit her eyes and made their stormy blue color more intense, deeper. The top was down on his car, and her honey-colored curls ruffled in the wind, framing her face in a cloud of sun-brightened gold. Jacob had to physically resist the urge to touch the curls and decide for himself if they were as soft as they appeared. He shook his head to clear the thought. He had to get some sleep. He had to get a grip.

He searched his mind for a minute before he found the thread of their conversation. She'd been teasing him about lunch. "It's on the government," he said. "I don't want to waste the taxpayers' money."

Macon laughed. It set off a firecracker in his head. She didn't seem to notice the way he was gripping the steering wheel. "Then you should have let me buy," she said, her voice light, conversational. She seemed to be relaxing. "That's the advantage of the private sector. We can waste all the money we want and nobody balks but our accountants."

Jacob wheeled his car into an empty parking space in the lot, then switched off the ignition. "I will not be accused of mooching lunch. My honor, you know." He took a deep breath before he looked at her. He was relieved to find that some of the impact she was having on him was beginning to fade, or maybe he was growing used to it. In any case, he felt his lungs filling with air once more. "Let's go find a hot-dog vendor."

She stepped out of the car, then paused to adjust her suit jacket with a sharp tug. "I suppose once we find a nice secluded bench, with no one lurking in the bushes, you'll tell me what this is all about?"

He managed a wry smile, something he was very proud of considering the way her jacket hugged her figure. "Something like that. I have to confess, though, I've spent the last few weeks in one of the coldest places on earth. Just the luxury of being outside is worth a fortune to me."

"Well, then, who am I to rob you of the opportunity." She looked around and spotted the vendor cart several yards away. "There it is," she said and started toward it.

Jacob followed a few paces back, studying her, recovering. Nothing in her security file had prepared him for his first encounter with her. He'd known what she looked like, of course. There had been over a dozen recent photos. But nothing had prepared him for this oh-so-proper woman— lady, he corrected—who ran a tiny political empire with the finesse of a Chicago party boss, and toyed nervously with the hem of her skirt when she was trapped in the car alone with him. And turned his stomach into knots.

He observed with open masculine pleasure the way her tailored suit—it was some shade of pink he suspected would have a complicated name if he asked her—hugged her lusciously feminine curves when she walked. The matching alligator shoes—he recognized alligator—and blue and pink scarf gave her an air of sophistication without diminishing her femininity. Macon Stratton was a lady all the way to the toenails; painted a pale shade of pink unless he missed his guess.

There was something delicate about her, about the way she moved, that disturbed him. He knew he hadn't been completely honest with her in her office, neither would he be, but despite his suspicions about the case, he wouldn't want Macon caught in the inevitable fallout. She seemed too fragile.

He had to smile at that. God, if she knew what he was thinking, she'd probably deck him. Delicate or not, instinct told him there was fire beneath that cool exterior. She walked fifty feet or so before she turned around abruptly to look at him. "Why are you doing that?"

He blinked, hoping she didn't really know he was ogling her like some randy teenager. "Doing what?"

"Walking like that." When he continued to blankly stare at her, she rushed out, "Back there. Like you don't want to be seen with me."

He laughed, relieved. He stepped up beside her, then took her elbow in his large hand. "Sorry. Force of habit."

Macon looked at him in confusion as he tugged her along toward the vendor cart. "What's that supposed to mean?"

He felt sheepish, and strangely adolescent. "I was protecting you," he explained. "I was in protective services for a few years. I was always the guy who walked behind the president. They figured if anyone took a shot at his back, I'd get the bullet before he did. It's just second-nature now."

Macon's eyes widened. "Oh."

Jacob couldn't decide whether she was impressed or distressed, so he decided not to ask. They stepped up to the vendor cart. Jacob reached for his wallet. "What'll you have?"

She looked at the menu pasted on a dirty chalkboard above the cart. "Two chili dogs with catsup, mustard, onions, relish and cheese."

He raised his eyebrows in amusement, finding

her appetite both refreshing and attractive. In his experience, high-polished ladies like Macon Stratton lived on rabbit food. Unbidden, the thought that she might indulge so dramatically in other pleasures caused a suffusion of heat to shoot through his blood. He forced his expression to remain calm. "Anything else?"

She looked back at the menu board. "A large bag of chips, a double-fudge brownie and a Diet Pepsi."

He nodded, then gave his order to the vendor. A few minutes later, they were seated on a bench under a tall oak tree. Jacob handed her her share of the food. She looked so at home, so perfectly at ease in her pricey clothes and expensive shoes seated on a park bench, holding a hot dog and watching as a young man on roller blades danced and bobbed down the sidewalk. Jacob felt an unpleasant tightening in his gut. He frowned, and bit into his hot dog.

Macon zealously peeled the foil wrapper back from one of the greasy hot dogs. She gave him an expectant look. "I'll eat. You talk."

He swallowed. He wasn't sure he wanted to watch her eat. He might explode on the spot. "When do I get to eat?"

She had taken a bite of her hot dog, and she finished chewing while he watched her lips move. "While I ask questions," she said, finally.

He settled back against the bench, thinking he'd never seen a woman look sexy while eating a hot dog. "Sounds fair enough. As you know, I'm with the Secret Service. I'm currently involved in an investigation of a highly sensitive matter, and I need your help."

Macon popped open her Diet Pepsi. She took

a long swallow. "My help?" she asked, her surprise evident.

He nodded. "I'm not free to give you a lot of the details just yet. Suffice it to say, I need a political cover. The Service has been looking into this for several months, and if you'll agree, we'd like your help."

"Why me?"

He took a swig of his Pepsi, searching for the right words, wanting to tell her enough without telling too much. "Several reasons. The most important of which is that your background check is crystal clear, and you have the right political contacts."

She narrowed her gaze at him. "I don't think I like the thought of the Secret Service digging into my background without my notice. Is that legal?"

"For us it is."

She glared at him. "Well, how much do you know?"

"All the big stuff." He sensed her irritation, so he shifted on the bench, seeking to reassure her by assuming a more casual posture. "Look, Ms. Stratton, it's no big deal. We didn't do any personal work. Just enough to ensure you weren't involved in shady political dealings."

"I'm not," she said indignantly. "I never have been."

"I know that. That's why you made the cut."

"And what political contacts are you talking about?" She paused, her hot dog in midair. He watched in fascination as she licked a speck of mustard from the corner of her generous mouth.

"I need a way to circulate in and around Washington as a newcomer to the political scene without arousing too much suspicion. I want you to introduce me as a small-time Cheyenne, Wyoming media guy that you're using to do some work on the Chapman account."

Macon shook her head. "No one's going to believe that. Everyone knows I personally handle every account. Especially Chap's."

Jacob nodded. He knew from her file that Senator Duvall "Chap" Chapman had been Macon's first employer in Washington. He'd given her a job on the Hill when nobody else would give her the time of day. She'd deliberately refused to use Senator Stratton's name in those days, wanting to make it on her own. Jacob thought it had been rather naive, but Macon had pushed her way up the ladder until she'd learned enough to start her own firm.

Her biggest accomplishment to date was the *Electioneering* article. *Electioneering* was the premier political industry magazine. Each year, the sixty-thousand-plus readership nominated and elected Washington's Most Politically Powerful Player. Prior winners had gone on to manage presidential campaigns, hold cabinet positions, and build successful consulting empires in the industry. At twenty-eight, Macon was the youngest consultant ever to make the cover, and the only woman in the award's fifteen-year history.

"I thought of that," he said. "We'll need to convincingly portray a partnership. I think it would be best if we say from the outset that we met a year ago at Taste of the West in Cheyenne. I noticed in your file that you attended the event last year. It was crowded, busy, the perfect place for us to have met."

Macon swallowed another bite of her hot dog.

"And you're going to convincingly play the role of some Western politico making his first exciting trip to Washington."

He raised an eyebrow. "You'd be surprised."

"I'd have to be."

Jacob's eyes were riveted on the frosty moisture that her soda had left on her upper lip. He was fighting the battle of his life as he resisted the urge to lick it away. Instead, he reached over to wipe it off with his thumb. He ignored the startled look she gave him. "Leave the undercover part to me. All I need you to do is make the proper introductions. And set it up with Senator Chapman, of course."

Macon lifted her napkin. She wiped furiously at her mouth. "Of course. And as part of my patriotic duty, I'm supposed to just go along with this without knowing any of the details—despite what the cost may be to my business."

He shook his head. "If you'll agree to come to the office and look at some slides for me, we'll go over everything there. I'm not prepared to discuss the details out in the open."

"What office?"

"My office on Seventeenth Street."

"What slides?"

He looked at her carefully. "I can't go into that right now."

Macon sighed in exasperation. "This is awfully strange, Mr. Blackfort. I mean, am I really supposed to believe all this?"

He shrugged. "What do I have to do to convince you?"

"I don't know. You have to admit this is . . . bizarre."

"Undoubtedly, but I promise it'll all make a lot

more sense to you if you come to the office tonight, and let us explain it to you in detail.''

She sighed. "I'll think about it.''

"You'll *think* about it?'' He was starting to feel irrationally irritated that this woman was not falling into step as easily as he'd anticipated. He was starting to feel downright aggravated that she was having such a potent effect on his sensibility.

"Well, surely you didn't expect an answer from me right away?''

He didn't answer. She polished off her second hot dog. Jacob wadded the foil from his own as he watched her concentrate on her meal.

A dog barked in the distance as the mournful wail of a siren jarred the peaceful atmosphere of the Park. Jacob pulled his attention back to Macon's question, and away from places they had no business being. "Ms. Stratton, I really need to know if I can count on you," he said while she chewed a bite of her brownie.

She looked at him in surprise. "I don't want to disappoint you, Mr. Blackfort, but I have a business to consider.''

"I know.'' He couldn't resist the urge to tease her a little. It didn't seem fair that he should be the only one suffering any discomfort in the interview. "You're Washington's Most Politically Powerful Woman.''

To his amazed delight, Macon blushed. He didn't know there were women in Washington who still knew how to blush. He suddenly forgot his irritation and winked at her. Macon looked flustered and said, "That's not what I meant. It's an election year. I have clients. They have to come first.''

"Ms. Stratton, all I want you to do is agree to

meet me at the office tonight and look at some slides. Is that too much to ask?"

She shrugged. "I'll think about it."

Jacob knew better than to argue. He checked his watch. "All right. I'll take you back to your office, and you can *think* about it." While I spend the rest of the afternoon thinking about you, he silently added.

Macon nodded and handed him her trash. "Thank you."

She started back toward his car, and he trailed slightly behind again until she stopped and waited for him to walk alongside her. He paused briefly before leading the way back to the car.

They made the fifteen-minute ride back to Macon's office in silence. Jacob tried to concentrate on the traffic despite his mind's determination to focus on the seductive scent of her perfume. He pulled up at the busy curb in front of her office, then switched off the ignition before turning to look at her. He dug into his jacket pocket and produced a business card. "Here's my card. If you decide to come tonight. Here's the address. I'll need you around seven."

Macon looked at the card and nodded, letting herself out of the car. She closed the car door and leaned on it, studying Jacob for a minute. "I'll let you know."

He nodded. "Thank you, Ms. Stratton."

Three

"So?" Maylene Porter was perched on the edge of her chair, staring at Macon.

Macon waited for the heavy glass door to glide shut behind her. "So what?" she asked, knowing full well that May was dying for a report on her lunch with Jacob.

May leaned back in her chair, arching painted eyebrows at Macon. "Don't play dumb with me, young lady. I want to know just what you and Mr. Tall, Dark and Sexy-as-Hell have been talking about for the last," she paused and checked her rhinestone watch, "forty-seven minutes."

Macon smiled. "Haven't you ever heard that curiosity killed the cat, May?"

"Honey, if curiosity was going to kill me, I'd have been dead and buried a long time ago." She jabbed a pink-tipped finger in the direction of the plush chair next to her desk. "Sit and deliver, Macon. I've been just about eaten alive while you were gone. I nearly followed you to lunch, and would have if the phone would stop ringing. I was tempted to take Jeff Parker with me. It would have done that boy a world of good to know he's not the only fish in the sea." May snorted. "Despite what he thinks, he's not even the hottest."

Macon dropped down in the chair, inwardly

squirming under May's close scrutiny. "Aren't you worried the phone will keep us from talking now?"

"Nope. I switched on the machine. There's nowhere to hide."

"All right, May. I know when I've been licked. What do you want to know?"

"Start with who the man is, and work your way around to what you're going to do with him."

"I'm not going to do anything with him."

"You're not letting Jeff Parker stand in your way, are you?"

"May, will you stop worrying so much about Jeff? I've told you. Jeff and I are just friends."

May snorted. "Jeff Parker doesn't have friendship on his mind."

"Well, I do." Macon gave her a sharp look. "That's it."

May seemed to sense her dark mood,—and abruptly shifted the subject. "I'm not interested in Jeff anyway. I know you can handle him. What I want to know is what you're planning to do with Jacob Blackfort."

"I told you, I'm not planning anything."

"You are if I have anything to say about it. Who is he?"

Macon hesitated, not really wanting to lie to May, but knowing instinctively that Jacob wouldn't have insisted on leaving the office if he hadn't wanted the information he gave her to remain confidential. "He says he's a media consultant from Cheyenne. He wants to do some work on Chap's campaign."

"I hope you didn't bite his head off."

"I did tell him that I don't normally use outside vendors."

"But you're willing to make a concession in this case, right?"

"I don't know. I'm not really comfortable with this guy." That at least was true. If anything, it was an understatement. Instinct told her that Jacob Blackfort posed a serious threat to the protective shelter of her well-ordered world.

"Why not?" May asked. "Have you ever heard of him?"

"I may have met him last year when I was in Cheyenne with Chap Chapman for the Taste of the West."

"Last year!" May looked horrified. "You met a man who looks like that last year, and you're just now bringing it up. Honey, I think you better have your pulse checked."

In spite of herself, Macon laughed. "I said I might have met him. I'm not sure."

"If I met that man, I'd be sure."

Macon toyed with the nubby fabric on the arm of her chair. "Well, anyway, I told him I'd consider it. I'm not certain what I want to do yet."

May leaned forward and placed her plump hand on Macon's knee. "Now, Macon, I want you to listen to me real hard. Honey, I've been with you a long time, and when it comes to your business, I know better than try and tell you how to run it, but I figure I have a right to meddle about some things. This is one of them."

Macon met her gaze. "It's not a big issue, May. He just wants some contract work."

"Well, then you ought to make him want something else."

"May!"

"I'm serious. A young woman like you has no business running about alone all the time. And certainly no business taking up with the likes of Jeff Parker. It's not healthy." She leaned back in her chair. "Gordon and I were discussing this the other day."

Macon's eyebrows drew together at the mention of her stepfather, Gordon Stratton. "You discussed my private life with Gordon?"

"Well, for Heaven's sake, Macon, it's not like I gave away military secrets to the Communists. The man's your father."

"Stepfather." It was a reflex answer.

"He's the only father you've ever known, honey, and Lord knows, he thinks of you like his own daughter."

"I'm just not comfortable with the idea that you've discussed my private life with Gordon. That's all I'm saying." It was no secret to Macon that Maylene and Senator Gordon Stratton were better than friends. May had been chasing Gordon since the first day she'd laid eyes on him in Macon's office, but despite their persistent meddling, Macon still managed to maintain a comfortable emotional distance from the man who had been her father since her mother's death seventeen years ago. It would be too painful to do anything else.

May studied Macon for several long seconds. "We're just concerned that's all. It's not right for you to keep running from everything and everyone just because you're afraid of getting hurt."

Macon knew she'd better head off May at the pass, or she'd get dragged into a very old argument. "You're being ridiculous, May. The last thing I need right now is another complication in my life. Things are going so well with the business, I wouldn't have time anyway. Besides, it's an election year. You know I can't afford to invest too much of my time in anything."

"It's an election year every year somewhere in this country, Macon. That's not the real reason, and you know it. As long as I've known you, you've always had some excuse for not getting involved with this man or that." May fixed Macon with a hard stare. "You do the same thing to them that you do to Gordon. He keeps hanging in there with you, but they won't. Are you still going to be telling yourself it's an election year when you're fifty years old with no one to go home to?"

"That's absurd, Maylene. I'm twenty-eight. It isn't as if there is some tremendous rush for me to get married." Macon couldn't bring herself to hold the other woman's gaze, so she picked at an invisible piece of lint on her mauve skirt, watching May from the corner of her eye.

May's lips curved, her expression knowing. "You're not fooling me, Macon, and I doubt if you're fooling yourself. Are you attracted to this man?"

"I just met him."

"So? Are you attracted to him?"

Who wouldn't be, Macon thought. "He's very nice-looking," she conceded.

May gave an unladylike snort. "That's the understatement of the year. Is he nice—the other way I mean?"

"Yes. I suppose so." Although Macon didn't really think "nice" was a word people usually applied to Jacob Blackfort.

"Is he single?"

"I think so. Yes."

"Is he straight?"

"May!" Macon gave May a censorious frown.

"Well, is he?"

Macon was absolutely certain Jacob Blackfort had a very healthy masculine appreciation for the opposite sex. "I didn't ask."

"But he is."

"I guess."

"Does he chew with his mouth open?"

"May, this is silly. The next thing you're going to ask me is whether or not he's financially stable. I just met the man."

"But your hormones are racing, aren't they?"

They were, but Macon didn't really think she wanted to confess that to May. "What makes you say that?"

"If you're breathing and you're female, a man like that has a certain effect on you. Besides, your face is flushed and your palms are sweating."

Macon stopped rubbing her hands against the chair arms. "They are not."

May smirked at her. "Uh-huh. So when are you going to see him again?"

Despite herself, Macon felt a small smile of concession begin to tug at the corner of her mouth. It was, she decided, not such a bad feeling to know she had an excuse to see Jacob Blackfort again. Besides, there was only one way to get Maylene to stop prying into her social life, and Macon knew if she didn't put a stop to the conversation, May would start pressuring her about Gordon.

Resolute, she pushed herself out of the chair and strolled to her office door. "Tonight," she said over her shoulder. May chuckled in delight. "Oh shut up, May. We have a business to run." May's knowing cackle followed Macon into her office.

* * *

"Way to go, Charlie," Jacob said. His voice dripped sarcasm as he strode into his office a few minutes later. "Why didn't you tell me you were sending me into a viper pit?"

Charlie Darrow looked up from his desk in surprise. "What the hell are you talking about?"

Jacob motioned for Charlie to follow him inside his private, cubicle-sized office, where he shut the door and sat down behind the desk. Charlie Darrow, his friend and partner for the last five years, looked at him warily as he settled his bulky frame into the chair across from the desk.

Charlie was the picture of an old-school Secret Service man. His once rangy athletic build had spread out a bit over the past few years. His hair was beginning to thin on top, but he could still perfect "The Face"—that perfect, stonewall, impenetrable look demanded of every agent before, during, and after a crisis. Charlie was nearing retirement though, and he preferred to do most of his work behind the desk, while Jacob was the action man on the team.

It had only been in the last few months that Jacob had caught himself longing for the kind of life Charlie enjoyed—a life where the world was warm and the people cared. The weeks he'd spent in Thule had been too quiet, too long, too lonely. He'd had too much time to think about past hurts and present ills. It hadn't helped any that sharing the afternoon with Macon Stratton had vaguely reminded him of sitting by a warm fire on a rainy winter afternoon. It had been entirely too comfortable and inviting for his peace of mind, and always at the back of his mind was the notion that he'd get burned if he got too close. He shook off his uncharacteristic melancholy, then forced himself to concentrate.

"It didn't go so well with Ms. Stratton, I take it?" Charlie said.

Jacob snorted as he leaned back in his chair. "She's not the most receptive individual we've ever worked with. Wary as hell."

"Well, what did you expect, Jake? You don't develop a reputation for being above reproach in this city without some healthy skepticism. Is she going to help us?"

Jacob shrugged. "Hell if I know. If she shows up tonight to go over those slides, then, yeah, I think she will."

"What's the purpose of the slides? We've gone over them a million times and there's no evidence of Gordon Stratton anywhere at the sites."

"She's a pro. She'll be able to see things we wouldn't. Maybe she'll turn up something we missed."

"Maybe. You counting on it?"

"Not really. I got to tell you, though, I don't like this bit about setting up Gordon Stratton through his stepdaughter." He shot a brief glance at the bustle of activity outside the inner window of his office. "I'm not even convinced it's legal."

"Well, hell, Jake, we can't very well march in there and tell the lady we think her stepfather is crooked as a three-dollar bill, now can we?"

"Maybe not, but it doesn't mean we ought to lie."

"We're not lying. We're just withholding classified information."

Jacob shot him an acid look. "This was Quiver's idea, wasn't it?"

Charlie shrugged. "I got you called back from Thule, didn't I? At least you're here where you can keep an eye on things."

"And answer to Peter Quiver."

"Quiver has laid this course of action. If you don't like it, I'm sure he'd be glad to send in someone else."

"Yeah. Maybe we could find somebody with even less of a conscience than me—I—me," he frowned when he caught himself correcting his own grammar. Damn Macon Stratton. "Oh, what the hell," he muttered as he dropped his head back against his chair.

Charlie narrowed his eyes. He reached for the oak cigar humidor Jacob kept on his desk. He selected a cigar and lit it. Within minutes, the office was spiced with the acid aroma. "What's got you so worked up? It wouldn't be the first time a civilian didn't want to get involved."

"I don't know. She just wasn't what I expected from reading the background file."

"Do you think we made the right choice?"

"Who's to say? Have we got a backup to get to Stratton if she doesn't play along?"

Charlie shrugged. "Not really. Quiver is locked into this. He's convinced Macon Stratton is our best bet. If you don't get her to cooperate, he'll probably just threaten her into it."

Jacob wearily rubbed a hand over his eyes. "Damn it, Charlie, we're so close." He curled his fingers on the arm of his chair. "I wish I knew why Pete was so hot to bust Stratton. I can't help feeling like we're missing something massive here. Something that ought to be so obvious that we're going to hate ourselves when this is all over.

If Stratton really is our guy, I'm not convinced that Macon will lead him to us."

"If?"

"We don't have any proof, Charlie. Just circumstantial evidence."

"Yeah. Right."

"No prints. No pictures. No case. We've got to catch him in the act or it won't stand up in court. You know that."

"The guy is guilty as hell. He's got motive, opportunity and means. Quiver is going to be on your back like a cheap suit until you bust him."

"I just don't feel right about dragging Macon Stratton into a situation she's got nothing to do with."

Charlie stamped out his cigar in the small glass ashtray. "No more than the rest of us. Look, Jake, Peter Quiver wants your butt. You know it, I know it, hell, the whole damned department knows it. He still doesn't believe that line we fed him about Kristen."

"That's because it was a line."

"It was a line that saved your ass. Don't forget that."

"I know, Charlie. The whole thing is just so damn frustrating. I can't do my job because he's so determined to force me out."

Charlie stood up and leaned across the desk, studying the dark circles under Jacob's eyes. "You're running on empty, buddy. Go home and get some sleep. We'll beat this."

Jacob reached for a stack of manila folders in his in-box. "I will, Charlie. I just want to finish these reports."

Charlie rolled his eyes, and strode to the door. He jerked it open before turning back to look at

Jacob once more. "And don't worry about the viper. I got a gut feeling on this one."

Jacob shot him a weary smile as he flipped open the door of the small refrigerator behind his desk. He pulled out a Diet Pepsi, and popped the top. "I hope you're right, Charlie." He took a long swig as he watched the door of his office click shut.

Resolutely, Jacob tried to banish thoughts of Macon Stratton from his mind. It wasn't an easy task. Despite his best efforts to concentrate on his trip report, an image of Macon walking just ahead of him at Rock Creek Park kept intruding. No one had warned him that a woman's business suit could be so damned sexy if the right woman was wearing it. That thought disturbed him more than he wanted to admit.

Since his disastrous relationship with Kristen Ager had ended two years before, he had studiously avoided emotional entanglements. Limited by both the pressing demands of his job and the scars Kristen had left in her wake, Jacob had restricted his encounters with women to passing acquaintances and mutually acceptable short-term affairs.

Macon Stratton wasn't that type of lady. She had a way of making him feel like an awkward teenager seeking a date for the prom. She made his palms sweat and his loins ache and his heart race. And despite the screaming and flashing warnings of every instinct he possessed, he couldn't resist her.

Somehow, through some miracle of concentration and fatigue, he managed to stare at the stack of reports on his desk for the better part of the afternoon without really accomplishing anything at all.

Four

"Take your hand off my knee, please." Macon peeled Jeff Parker's fingers off her knee and dropped his hand back into his lap. She'd been so absorbed in thoughts of Jacob Blackfort, she'd nearly forgotten that Jeff was in the car. And that she wanted to kill him. Nearly, but not quite.

It had been a mistake to let Jeff accompany her to her meeting that afternoon. At the bi-monthly social gathering of Washington media consultants, Jeff had all but announced that he and Macon were seriously—physically—involved. She had managed to extract herself from the situation with some modicum of dignity, but at the moment, Jeff Parker was standing perilously close to annihilation.

He paused as he downshifted his black Jaguar. He flashed her a grin that was nothing short of lascivious, then returned his fingers to her knee, brushing aside the soft mauve fabric of her suit skirt. "Come on, baby. You're driving me crazy. I've been thinking about you all day."

Macon shoved his hand aside a second time. "Look, Jeff, I don't know what you're trying to pull, but I'm not amused."

He turned down Sixth Street and headed for

her office. "We've been going out for six weeks now, and—"

"We are *not* going out."

He frowned at her and pulled to a stop in front of her office building. "What's with you today? You've been acting like a porcupine since we arrived at that meeting."

Macon grabbed her briefcase as she pushed open the car door. "When you offered to give me a ride to the Capitol Hill Club today, I didn't know you intended to imply to my colleagues, *my colleagues,* that you and I were on the way to some afternoon tryst." She slammed the door and stared at him. "The fact that I asked you to escort me to two receptions and a dinner party in the last six weeks hardly constitutes a life-changing commitment, Jeff."

He eased out of his car, pausing to check his reflection in the rear-view mirror. Macon felt her temper slip another few notches. Jeff Parker's pretty-boy looks made him one of the most sought-after bachelors in Washington. Unbidden, a memory of Jacob Blackfort's black hair and blue eyes flashed into her mind. She suddenly wondered what she'd ever seen in the soft, paunchy line of Jeff's face.

He was an Administrative Assistant to Senator Carter Blake, and Macon had first met him when the senator had signed her as his media consultant. Jeff's attentions had been flattering, perhaps even a little overwhelming, but he'd more than crossed the line that afternoon. He smiled at her across the top of the Jag. "Come on, Macon. A guy's gotta protect his reputation, you know."

She shot him what she hoped was a killing glance. 'You're disgusting." She turned on her heel and stalked toward the building. She heard Jeff slam the door of his car. She entertained a brief hope that he'd decided to leave. When she saw his hand reach around her and open the door, she quelled an inward sigh of irritation.

"Macon, you have to listen to me."

Macon put her briefcase down on the security desk, then smiled briefly at Eric Tullman, the building security guard and former linebacker for the Washington Redskins. "Good morning, Eric."

"Afternoon, Macon. You want me to sign this fella in?"

Macon shook her head. "No. He's not coming upstairs."

Jeff frowned. "For crying out loud. You're acting like a baby."

"You want me to get rid of him?" Eric asked, his frown turning menacing.

Macon thought it over. It was definitely tempting. She paused before shaking her head. "I'll handle it, Eric." She looked at Jeff. "Listen, Jeff, I don't know what that was all about this afternoon, but I'm not going to tolerate it. Whatever there might have been between the two of us is over. If you don't want to keep this strictly business I don't want to see you or hear from you again."

Eric leaned back in his chair and crossed his massive forearms over his chest. Jeff blinked, his handsome features marred by disbelief. "You've got to be kidding."

"I'm completely serious."

"She's serious," Eric said, giving Jeff a brief nod.

"Shut up," Jeff barked.

Eric sat up in his chair, and Macon stepped

forward and poked her finger into Jeff's chest. "Just who do you think you are, Jeff Parker? You've got no right to talk to him like that."

Jeff glared at her. "He's the security guard, for God's sake."

"He's my friend."

"Then maybe you should reevaluate who you spend your time with."

Macon felt a wry smile tug at her mouth. She was tempted to tell Jeff she'd take one Eric Tullman over a hundred Jeff Parkers any day. She was tempted to tell him Eric Tullman didn't resort to veiled innuendoes to protect his masculine ego. She was tempted to tell him she thought he was slicker than stewed okra in a Teflon pot, and that any iota of respect she'd ever had for him had long since evaporated, but Eric had stood up and looked as though he was seriously considering flattening Jeff to the wall. While the possibility was intriguing, Macon didn't relish the task of getting Eric out of trouble on Jeff's behalf. "You know, Jeff," she said, deliberately keeping her tone casual. "I think you're probably right."

Jeff shot Eric a smug look, then reached for Macon's arm. "Of course I'm right."

Macon knocked his hand away. "It is definitely time for me to reconsider how I invest my time, and in whom I invest it. I think I should forewarn you, however, that you are almost certainly not going to make the cut."

Jeff sighed. "Now, baby, just settle down and let me explain."

Macon walked toward the elevator. "Go away, Jeff. You're starting to annoy me."

The doors slid open. Macon stepped inside, relieved to be escaping the scene. She would have punched the fourth-floor button, but Jeff stalked forward, sneering at her. "You know what, Macon? Adrian Snell was right about you."

At the mention of Adrian's name, she jabbed her finger on the *hold* button. She'd dated Adrian Snell for almost a year before they'd ended their relationship eight months ago. Adrian had been pressuring Macon for a commitment she hadn't been ready to make. "What has Adrian got to do with this?"

Jeff tipped his sunglasses down on his nose and fixed her with a cool look in his brown eyes. "Adrian bet me a hundred bucks I couldn't get you to sleep with me. You really are an ice maiden, aren't you?"

Macon ignored the sting Jeff's words caused. She looked at Eric instead. The enormous security guard had stalked forward three more steps and was looming over Jeff's shoulder. "Go ahead and hit him, Eric," she said, taking her finger off the elevator button. "It'll make us both feel better." As the doors slid shut, she saw Eric pick up Jeff by the waistband of his trousers. She sagged against the elevator wall and closed her eyes, exhausted by the confrontation and the hurt of Adrian's betrayal. Like a bad toothache, Jacob Blackfort's memory forced its way back into her mind. What was it he'd said about Jeff? Something about having suspicions regarding his background? Macon frowned. She didn't like the thought that Jacob knew more about Jeff than she did.

It was hard to believe it had been less than three hours since Jacob had come to her office. Between his bizarre request and Jeff's outrageous behavior, it seemed an eternity. As the elevator

glided to a stop, Macon thought about the way
her day had started. It had begun with the article
in *Electioneering* magazine. It should have been an
exhilarating day. Damn the Jeff Parkers, Adrian
Snells, and Jacob Blackforts of the world for
screwing up a perfectly decent minor triumph.

Macon breezed her way through the outer door
of her office. She listened in absent relief as May
lied to a caller. "I told you, Mr. Ateon," Maylene
continued in her soft southern drawl, "Ms. Stratton won't be in until this afternoon. I'd be happy
to leave a message for her, though."

Macon listened idly to the phone conversation.
She picked up the growing stack of pink message
slips on May's desk. She flipped them, satisfied
when only one or two registered higher than a
four on her self-invented annoyance scale. May
finally got rid of the offending caller, and shot
Macon an exasperated look. "How's Jeff?"

Macon frowned at a message from a particularly annoying vendor and crumpled it, tossing it
in the trash. She wasn't prepared to give May any
of the details. "Irritating," she said. She ignored
May's speculative look. "If Tom Ateon calls back,
May, I won't be in this afternoon at all."

May frowned at her. "You sure you don't want
to tell me about Jeff?"

"Positive."

"Will you at least tell me what to do if he calls?
What's his status on the phone list?"

"History," Macon muttered. She stalked toward
her office. Maylene could launch into a predictable litany of relief and praise for Jeff Parker's
new status on Macon's list of personal cast-offs.

She stepped into the elegant atmosphere of her
room, where she absorbed the familiar feel of the

oak-paneled walls and plush mauve carpet. The place had a calming effect on her frayed nerves, and she looked around, allowing the tangible evidence of her success as a media broker to wash away some of the hurt Jeff had caused her that afternoon.

It jarred her, somehow, that the memory of Jacob Blackfort's presence in the office was still so intrusive.

She frowned when the intercom on her desk buzzed. "Yes, May?"

"It's Jacob Blackfort on line three."

Macon resented the way her stomach flip-flopped. "I'll be right with him," she said, as she dropped her briefcase into a chair. Macon shrugged out of her suit jacket before she picked up the phone. "Macon Stratton," she said.

"Macon," his voice slid over her jangled nerves with the soothing effect of warm, scented water, "I'm sorry to bother you again."

"It's no bother." She sank down in her desk chair. "I still haven't made up my mind about this evening," she lied.

"That's not why I called."

Macon studied the vase of pink roses on her desk. "No?"

She heard his raspy sigh on the other end of the phone. "No. I just realized that I forgot to ask you to keep our meeting this afternoon confidential." With a rueful laugh, he continued, "I suppose I'm more tired than I thought."

Macon remembered the lines of fatigue that had rimmed his eyes. "It's all right," she assured him. "I didn't think you would want me to discuss it. I haven't told anyone."

"Thank you." There was a long pause. Macon fingered one of the pink roses. "Macon?" he said.

"Yes?"

"How was your meeting with Jeff Parker?"

She bristled. "What do you know about that?"

"I'm sorry," he said. "I didn't mean to make you angry."

"Are you having me followed?"

"No." She heard his chair groan as he leaned back in it. "No. I called for you before and Maylene told me you were with him. I—" He paused. "—I know it's none of my business, but—"

"That's right," she snapped. "It's none of your business."

He ignored her. "But I'd watch my back around him if I were you."

Macon felt irritated that everyone, even Jacob Blackfort whom she barely knew, seemed so concerned about the status of her relationship with Jeff Parker. "Is that all, Mr. Blackfort?"

"No," he said. "You never did tell me who those flowers were from."

"I didn't want to tell you."

"But they weren't from Jeff Parker?"

She thought about telling him he could rot in hell before she'd give him any more details of her personal life, but suddenly felt the fight drain out of her. "No, the flowers aren't from Jeff Parker. You'll be relieved to know that Jeff Parker isn't an issue at all. As far as I'm concerned, Jeff Parker is a nonentity."

She wasn't sure, but she was fairly certain she heard Jacob exhale a long breath. "I'm sorry to have taken up so much of your time," he said. "I'll hope I'll see you tonight."

She set the phone down with careful deliberation before plucking the card from the roses. In Nat's scrawly type the message read—"I knew you'd make it. Bye, bye, Babe. See you at the polls."

Macon laughed out loud. She'd known Nat for nearly ten years, and every phone conversation concluded with Nat's now famous tag line. They stood on opposite sides of the political fences, but they'd managed to remain friends despite the stress of political life in Washington. As she fingered the soft petals of the pink roses, she decided a lunch date with Nat Baldwin was just what she needed to salvage her week. If nothing else, he'd make her laugh. He always did.

Unbidden, she remembered the feel of Jacob's callused thumb on her upper lip as he'd wiped away the dewy residue from her soda. She shivered, then reached for the phone. Whether it was her lingering irritation with Jeff, or simply the satisfaction of keeping a secret from Jacob Blackfort, she wasn't certain, but an elegant lunch for two, while Nat Baldwin told her she was the most brilliant woman he'd ever met, was just the prescription for her rapidly shredding nerves.

Four hours later, for the nth time that day, Jacob decided that no matter who Jeff Parker was and who he knew, he was a very stupid man. Jacob still couldn't believe he'd used the flimsy excuse of confidentiality to call Macon and grill her about those flowers. The thought of them had been nagging at him ever since he'd first seen them in her office. Still, he felt like a fool—a sensation he wasn't used to, and sure as hell didn't like. When he'd called Macon's office the first time that afternoon, Maylene had told him Macon was at a meeting with Jeff Parker. Jacob had tried to convince himself that only concern over what Macon might tell Jeff had caused his ensuing frustration. But it hadn't worked.

If he'd had any doubts that his interest in the situation went beyond his concern for the investigation, they'd been sufficiently squashed when he'd heard the suppressed anger in her voice as she'd spoken of Parker. Jacob had been elated. On a strictly elemental level, he'd been elated.

And the thought had rattled him so severely, that he'd managed to spend the rest of the afternoon dreaming up ways to get revenge on Jeff Parker. More than once, he'd contemplated calling his friend at the IRS to see if he could legally initiate an audit.

Jacob was vaguely aware that the sun was setting outside his office window when he heard his door swing open. He looked up in guilty surprise as Macon took a tentative step inside. "Macon!" His gaze pivoted to the clock on the wall. He felt off balance, unprepared to see her standing there after he'd been thinking about her all afternoon. "It's only six. I wasn't expecting you until seven." Damn, she looked good. Just as good as he remembered.

She shrugged. "That was the general idea."

Jacob raised an eyebrow. "Why didn't they buzz me to come sign you in?"

Charlie appeared in the doorway behind Macon. "Your phone's on Do Not Disturb, pal. Aren't you going to offer the lady a seat?"

Jacob shook his head to clear it as he rose to his feet. "I'm sorry. My mind's still buried in these reports. Would you like to sit down, Macon?"

She walked into the room, then settled herself in one of the battered leather chairs. "Thank you," she said, sounding more prim than ever. Jacob swallowed a smile. Her presence in his office shouldn't be having such an intense effect on him, but it was.

"Can I get you anything, Ms. Stratton?" Charlie asked. "Some coffee maybe?"

Macon looked pointedly at the Diet Pepsi on Jacob's desk. "Actually, have you got another one of those lying around?"

Jacob swung open the refrigerator door. The blast of cool air tickled his heated skin. "A woman after my own heart." He wondered if his voice sounded strange to her. "The coffee around here is poisonous. Especially when Charlie makes it." He picked up one of the frosted cans, and popped the tab for her, before handing it to her across the desk. "Do you want a cup for that?"

She shook her head. "I'm an out-of-the-can kind of woman." Jacob felt his stomach clench. Dear God, he was losing his mind. She waved the can at him. "Thank you. I'm afraid I'm unforgivably snooty where coffee is concerned. I've learned not to trust anyone else but Maylene to make it for me."

An uncomfortable silence filled the office while Jacob and Macon stared at each other. Charlie cleared his throat. "Jake, do you want me to set up the slides?"

Macon shot Charlie an apologetic look. "It's all right. I know I'm early. I can wait until seven."

"Why are you early?" Jacob asked. He fought

the urge to ask her if she'd been forced to cancel plans with Parker on his behalf. He hoped so.

She lifted one shoulder in what might have been a shrug, her expression sheepish. "Obstinacy. I thought if I took you by surprise, I might regain the upper hand, at least in part. This whole thing is a bit overwhelming for me."

Jacob sank back down into his chair. "I don't think I did the best possible job presenting things to you this afternoon. I'm sorry about that."

Macon tilted her head to study him. He had removed his suit jacket, and something about the sight of him in his starched white shirt with the sleeves rolled midway up his forearms and the black suspenders slashing across his wide chest was even more intimidating than before. The look in those startling blue eyes was somehow disquieting. She began to doubt the wisdom in the impulse that had prompted her to come. She had been driven more by curiosity than prudence, and she'd learned in the past how dangerous that could be. "Mr. Blackfort, I would like you to know my presence here is in no way a commitment. You told me you'd give me more information if I came here tonight. I'm not prepared to make any kind of a decision until I have all the facts."

He nodded. "That's fair enough. I'll tell you what we'll do. I'll let Charlie set up the slides, then you and I will talk over some of the details. How does that sound?"

"Fine."

"All right. Have you had dinner?"

She shook her head. Something in the way he was looking at her made her uncomfortably aware of the small dimensions of his office. "No. Can you afford two meals in one day?"

He laughed. The sound sent an electrical current down her spine. Jacob's face, already handsome, was nothing less than devastating when he laughed. She thought about asking him if he had a license to operate that smile.

"I don't think dinner will break the expense budget," he said. "Pizza or Chinese?"

She cocked her head thoughtfully. "If anyone ever accuses you of being a spendthrift, send them to me. Pizza, I think. I like everything but fish and pineapple on mine."

He nodded, remembering the greasy, heavily laden hot dogs she'd consumed at lunch. "Somehow, that doesn't surprise me. Charlie, send out to Joey's, will you?"

"Sure. I'll get everything set up."

"Thanks, Charlie."

Charlie pulled the door shut behind him once more. Macon fidgeted. Jacob was still watching her with that heated expression in his aquamarine eyes. "All right, Mr. Blackfort. You have the floor."

Jacob got out of his chair, then walked around the desk to sit on the edge of his desk facing her. "If I'm going to call you Macon, I insist that you call me Jacob. And don't be so nervous. We're not going to feed you to the sharks."

Macon decided honesty was definitely the best policy. "The truth is, Mr. . . . uh, Jacob . . . you intimidate me. It's not a feeling I'm used to, and I'm finding I don't like it at all."

He nodded, his gaze thoughtful. "I'm sorry. It wasn't at all my intent." He reached up to loosen the knot of his tie, years of interrogation and experience telling him Macon would feel more at ease if he appeared relaxed and less in control of the situation. "You'll have to chalk it up to years of experience. One of the first things they teach us in training is how to be intimidating." He looked down his nose at her, donning his very best "Face" for her benefit. It had the desired effect. Macon laughed.

"That's very good," she said. "I can understand why any would-be assailant with an Uzi would back down under that."

Jacob grinned at her. He worked loose the top button of his shirt. "I hope you don't mind if I relax a bit," he said, seeking to give her some control. "I'm somewhat tuckered out. And before we begin, I want to apologize for that phone call this afternoon."

Macon's eyes widened. "Apologize."

He shrugged. "That was out of line. I was nervous about Parker, and I stepped out of bounds. I want you to know that your private life is your own." He shook his head. "I'm not normally this inept, but I'm not normally this tired."

The open admission melted what was left of Macon's reserve. "It was really no trouble. In fact, I'm sorry I snapped at you. I was in a foul temper after my meeting, and I suppose I took it out on you. And if you don't mind my saying so, you look exhausted."

He rubbed his eyes with his thumb and forefinger. "I haven't had much sleep in the past few days. I'm pretty much wiped from the jet lag."

Macon noted the edge of fatigue behind the words. She wondered vaguely what she'd ever seen in him that was intimidating. He looked human, vulnerable with his dark hair mussed, and his eyes drooping slightly in weary exhaustion. She laid her hand on his knee, meeting his gaze.

"We don't have to do this tonight, you know. I could always come back another time."

At the jolt of energy that shot through him from the feel of her warm fingers resting on his knee, Jacob reached for a thick manila folder. He handed it to her with a slight yawn. "No, I'd rather go ahead now. I don't want to waste too much time."

She flipped open the folder. "Am I going to understand any of this?"

"I'll give you a basic outline. That's just some background information in case you want to check any facts."

"Isn't this supposed to be classified?"

He shook his head. "Everything in there is public record. The really good stuff is locked in my trick briefcase."

Macon glanced up in time to catch the teasing glint in his blue eyes. "All right, 007, fire away."

He groaned. "Rule number two: never call me by a number. If you want to use my code name, it's Black Arrow."

Macon blinked. He'd said that in the most non-committal way, as if he'd just walked up to her in a bar and said he was a Virgo. "I'll remember that. What's rule number one?"

His grin was wicked. "Eradicate anyone who forgets rule number two."

"Sounds like risky stuff."

"Oh, it is. We're very serious about all this code, you know."

"Liar. That's why the president's code name is printed in *Newsweek* all the time."

Jacob looked appalled. "You have to allow us some level of mystique, ma'am. You'll wound the ever-fragile masculine ego."

Macon decided there probably wasn't a thing in the world fragile about Jacob Blackfort. She diverted her gaze somewhat nervously back to the manila folder. "What's this?" she asked, holding up a complicated-looking form with varying amounts of foreign and U.S. currencies plotted on a bar graph.

"Largely the core of why you're here," he answered, allowing her to steer the conversation back to the issue at hand, not willing to admit how much he liked having her in his office. Her perfume was the same delicate scent he remembered. Jacob sniffed appreciatively, liking the way it mingled with the lingering scent of Charlie's cigar. He had a strange feeling that he would never be able to forget the scent of that perfume. It was one of those fragrances that burned into a man's memory, creating a funny tugging sensation in his gut. He barely resisted the urge to bend his head and nuzzle the spot below her ear, seeking the source of the delicious aroma. He cleared his throat instead. "One of the primary responsibilities of the Secret Service is counterfeiting control and investigation."

Macon nodded. "I knew that. That's the reason your organization was originally established, wasn't it?"

"Yeah. Lincoln set up the Service in 1865 because of the problem with counterfeit greenbacks."

"You already told me that you're rarely involved in protection activities. So I take it you're a counterfeiting investigator?"

"Of sorts. I also do a lot of work with the U.S. Customs guys, and the international and federal bank regulators."

"Sounds fascinating."

Her tone dripped sarcasm. Jacob smiled at her. "I've always been an odd guy. That must be why I like this stuff. Anyway," he continued, picking up the piece of paper she'd indicated previously, "this represents about the last two years of my life exclusively. I've spent over four years on this case all together."

"What is it?"

"Probably the biggest international money and banking fraud in the history of the world."

"I thought that was BCCI."

He tapped the folder with a long forefinger. He knew Macon was referring to the scandal over the Bank of Credit and Commerce International that had held Washington enthralled for years. "This is bigger."

Macon stared at his large hand, so tantalizingly close to her own. The memory of Jeff's pale fingers on her knee snapped into focus. She swallowed. "How can it possibly be bigger than BCCI?"

"BCCI, also known as 'Crooks R Us,' was making money and gaining power by using illegal activities to increase their profits. These guys, on the other hand, are making money the old-fashioned way: they're printing it."

"But surely you've handled lots of counterfeiting operations before. What makes this one so different?" He was fingering a piece of paper with absent precision. Macon watched as his tanned fingers flipped the page in the folder.

"The size of the operation. Before this, a large counterfeiting operation consisted of about $300,000 in American currency."

"This is larger?" she asked, much more interested in the funny things the sight of his hand was doing to her insides.

"To the tune of $750 billion worldwide."

That got her attention. Macon looked at him in shock. "$750 billion?"

"That's right. What they're seeking to do is control the global financial market by controlling the flow of currency around the world."

"Is that possible?"

"They've done a pretty damn good job so far." Jacob flipped through the folder and found another chart. He pointed to several figures and explained, "In some cases, what they've done is actually buy the entire currency worth of third-world countries."

"What do you mean?"

"A third-world nation, by definition, isn't staked with a lot of capital. These guys go in there and purchase every piece of infrastructure and every item of value in the entire country. They become the governments' creditors, and then they own the currency and net capital worth of the country. They can control the flow, production and circulation of their currency and economic growth rates."

"But what difference does it make if somebody owns the net worth of, say, Namibia?"

Jacob flashed a smile at her. "Pivotal country, Namibia. If it were just one or two, it wouldn't be such a vast problem, but in industrialized countries, it's a different ball game. They can't very well purchase the net worth and capital interests of a developed, industrialized nation. What they can do is control the strength of their currency."

"You lost me."

Jacob nodded sympathetically. "International

finance wasn't meant to be taught in a fifteen-minute lecture, and I'm too tired to be doing even a halfway decent job of it." He dug through the folder again, and finally produced an ominous-looking diagram with several bar graphs and something Macon suspected to be international conversion rates. "By controlling the production of currency in third-world debtor nations, they can control the strength of the dollar, or the pound sterling, or the franc, for example, in that country."

He looked up to see if Macon was following him. She nodded. "The strength of any nation's currency is also affected by the amount of currency in circulation."

"I've never understood that," she confessed. "I mean I have a vague idea of how this all works, but it's always baffled me. I just assume the Federal Reserve knows what it's doing."

"It baffles me, too, if it makes you feel any better. I just pretend I know what's going on, and bluff my way through the rest. At any rate, large sums of counterfeit dollars can severely affect a national currency. Complicate that with an international ring of smuggling, drug running, arms dealing, and just about every other illegal activity you can think of, and you have a very big mess."

"You've been investigating this for four years? Exactly how widespread is this?"

He studied the intent look on her face, finding, with no small amount of surprise, that he didn't give a damn about the numbers. What he gave a damn about was the way her lipstick was just slightly smudged at the corner. He coughed, then forced himself to answer her question. "To date, we have record of their activities in nearly every country in the world. Just to give you some general idea, BCCI was a client, not a vendor."

Macon let out a low whistle. She knew from the newspapers that BCCI's client list had included most of the world's dictators and drug lords. If the infamous bank had actually worked with the person that Jacob was tracking, it was a daunting prospect. "So where on earth do I fit into all of this?"

Jacob shifted his weight to accommodate a sudden tightening in his groin. He'd like nothing better than to tell her where she fit. "About six months ago, we got our first big U.S. bust. Almost on a fluke, customs intercepted a shipment of some $200 million in counterfeit U.S. currency making its way here via a Canadian cruise liner. It was the first time we've been able to get U.S. bank regulators to really sit up and take notice."

Macon scooted to the edge of her chair, hoping he wouldn't notice. When he'd leaned forward, the tantalizing scent of cologne and male had closed in on her. "You told them all this stuff about international currency markets and they didn't listen before?"

He nodded. "Unbelievably, yes. At that point, I had no choice but to begin investigating U.S. federal corruption as well. Just like we suspected all along that several big guns were taking bribes or being blackmailed by BCCI, it's no different in this case. In fact, it's probably the same guys."

Macon had read the accusations that the Federal Justice Department and banking regulators had been dragging their feet on the BCCI investigation. Many people believed it was due to some senior level corruption. She had been inclined to believe it was due to bureaucracy. "Do you think the administration is involved?"

"Nope. I think the administration is political. There may be some guys in the executive branch who are taking bribes, but nothing widespread. I have a different theory altogether."

"You think it's a Capitol Hill scandal?" Macon had been in Washington too long not to know that most Washington scandals eventually worked themselves around to Capitol Hill or the White House.

"I think it's one or two, no more than five or six, power brokers in Washington who have enough connections and enough power to make a few key people look the other way. I've never been hyped on conspiracy theories, and I don't believe there's widespread corruption aimed at destroying the U.S. economy. What I do believe is that several key political operators, elected officials notwithstanding, are making a lot of money at the world's expense. They're the guys I want. If I get them, the whole house of cards will cave in. Foreign governments are a lot more likely to look the other way than the U.S. justice system. If we find our guys here, the rest will come crashing down with them."

"And you think I can help?"

Jacob dragged his gaze from the folder in Macon's lap. When he turned his head, his mouth was just inches from hers. A long, tense silence punctuated the next several seconds. "Like I told you this afternoon," he said in what he considered a remarkably calm voice, "we picked you for two reasons. First, because your reputation and career are above reproach. You've got a face that reads like a book and you couldn't pull off a convincing cover-up if your life depended on it. Everyone trusts you, and therefore, they're going to trust me."

"Thanks. I think."

His gaze remained riveted to her lips. "It was meant to be a compliment."

She touched the tip of her tongue to the corner of her mouth. "And the second reason," she guessed, "is that I am the best person to help you set up your cover." He wondered if he imagined the breathless quality in her voice.

"That's right. I need to circulate in Washington for a while. I need access to the power and the industry. The Wyoming story is a perfect front."

Macon moved slightly away from him, breaking the charged atmosphere. "Why Senator Chapman? Why not somebody else?"

"There are two reasons for that, too. The first one is I really am from Wyoming and one of the first rules of undercover work is don't tell more lies than you have to."

"And what's the second reason?"

"You have great rapport with the senator. His record is flawless. We believe you can get his co-operation without having to reveal too much in the process."

Macon studied the sea of numbers on the chart in her lap. She wished Jacob would stop staring at her profile. "Chap trusts me as much as I trust him. I'm not going to ask him to do anything that might endanger his campaign."

"You won't be. I'd pull the plug before I'd let that happen. We're here to help people, cliché though it sounds, not the other way around. I'll make sure every bit of damage control is handled at the highest possible level. Besides, if Senator Chapman helps us with this, he'll be a hero of

American justice. It can't help but benefit his public career." Jacob leaned back in his chair and watched her expressive face as she considered what he'd told her. She flipped absently through the file, stopping occasionally to look at a document that caught her eye.

When she finally looked up at him, he felt a brief flare of satisfaction at the hesitant look in her eyes. She had been just as aware of the chemistry between them as he had. "Is there anything else you would need from me?" she asked.

Oh, yes, he thought. "I haven't told you anything today that I wouldn't tell a reporter if he came asking, although I'd hope you wouldn't invite one to check us out. Everything in that file is already public record. It's just that no one else has ever compiled it that way.

"Tonight, I need you to look at some slides we've gathered and see if you can identify any of the players for us. We've already had our reconnaissance staff do it, but you're an insider and might see something they missed. Then I'd need you to introduce me around Washington and let me follow my nose where it leads me. If it goes any farther than that, I'd have to do a more comprehensive security check. I'd need you to fill out a bunch of forms, and I'd waste about $30,000 of the taxpayers money making sure you'd never been a member of the Communist Party." He paused and smiled at her. "But for now, I don't know that it will go beyond the slides and the introduction." He shrugged. "We'll just have to play it by ear."

Macon tapped her finger thoughtfully on top of the folder. "I already arranged a meeting with Chap for tomorrow at two-thirty if that suits your schedule. I told him I'd call him in the morning and confirm it. I meant what I said about his campaign."

Jacob nodded gravely. "I meant what I said, too. And thank you."

"I also won't do anything to endanger my business or its reputation."

"I'm counting on that," he said quietly.

Macon smiled in return. "All right, let's have a look at those slides."

Five

"No, I don't see anything," Macon groaned and buried her face in her hands. They'd been in the small cramped room for over three hours, staring at the slides. They were mostly pictures taken at political fundraisers and rallies. The first time through them, Jacob had pointed out several international key players to her. She'd recognized most of the candidates, but the bulk of the gatherings were too small for her to recognize more than a few of the attendees.

The small room had poor ventilation, like most federal buildings, and had begun to grow stuffy over the last hour or so. The smoke billowing from Charlie's cigars hadn't helped matters any, and Macon's throat had begun to feel raw. Fatigue was getting the better of her, and to make matters worse, Jacob had turned into some type of drill sergeant, demanding that she stare at every slide until the light burned the back of her eyes and her head began to pound from the intense concentration.

"Are you sure, Macon?" Jacob asked in barely contained exasperation.

His condescending tone snapped what remained of her control. "Yes, I'm sure! I was sure before and I'm sure now. I don't see anyone I recognize and before you ask, NO! I don't want to go over the batch again for good measure."

Jacob's hand fisted into a tight ball and he stared at her. His frustration was tangible in the tiny room. "Damn it, Macon, I need this. There has to be a reason all these guys keep turning up in the same places! Just concentrate, for God's sake."

To Macon's horror, she could feel tears stinging the backs of her eyes. It must have been the lingering effects of the day, the strain of her afternoon with Jeff Parker, her confusion over her unwanted reaction to Jacob Blackfort. But damned if she'd cry in front of the insufferable beast. Charlie leaned forward, his smoldering cigar in one hand, the other hand braced among the half-empty pizza boxes. He looked at her closely. "Look, Ms. Stratton, we really need to find a link here. This is the whole reason we brought you in here in the first place."

They were piling on, and when she started to speak again, her voice wobbled ominously. Jacob whipped his head around so abruptly, she had the insane notion that it might snap off. "I can't help it," she said. "If I don't see anything, I don't see anything. Maybe you should get someone else to look at your damn slides and quit treating me like a criminal."

Charlie swore beneath his breath. Macon looked at him sharply. "And put that cigar out. It smells awful and it's making my throat hurt!"

Jacob reached over to flip on the light. His eyes riveted on Macon. "Are you all right?" he asked.

"Well, hell, I'm just fine. Can't you see that? I feel just great. Why shouldn't I? You bring me in here and treat me like some crook you've dragged in for an interrogation. Why shouldn't I feel just as fresh as a damned spring chicken?"

Jacob blinked twice, taken totally off guard by her outburst. It took less than five seconds for him to realize what he'd done. "Charlie, put out your cigar and get Ms. Stratton a box of Kleenex please."

Charlie shot him a grateful look before he stubbed out the cigar, as he hurried from the room. Jacob moved over to take the seat across from Macon. "God, Macon, I'm so sorry. I just got so involved."

Macon looked up at him. She was beginning to feel more than a little foolish. Why did the man have such a mind-shattering effect on her? She sniffed once, then managed a tremulous smile. "I hate cigars."

He exhaled a long breath, his relief obvious. "Come on, let's wrap it up for tonight. We'll go over the slides again another time."

Macon was about to answer when the door burst open. Charlie shuffled in, his expression awkward. He carried a roll of toilet paper. "Sorry, Jake, we didn't have any tissues."

Jacob rolled his eyes as he took the roll from him. "Geez, Charlie."

Charlie shrugged apologetically. Jacob handed Macon the roll of toilet paper. She tore off a long piece with a half-laugh, then blew her nose inelegantly. "I'm sorry," she said. "I feel like an idiot."

Jacob shook his head. "No, I'm the idiot, and I'm the one who's sorry. I shouldn't have pushed so hard."

Macon blew her nose again, feeling thoroughly foolish. "I'll make a deal with you. Give me another Diet Pepsi, and I'll go over the slides once more." She shot Charlie a dry look. "And no cigars."

Jacob frowned. "Are you sure? You don't have to."

Macon nodded, noting the beard stubble that had somehow appeared along his jaw during the last few hours. He looked like hell. "I'm sure."

Jacob's eyes reflected his appreciation. "Thanks, Macon. Charlie, bring the lady a soda and let's roll the camera."

One hour later, and several more rounds of the slides already behind them, Macon nearly came out of her chair in shocked surprise. "Oh my God! Back up one slide!"

"Back up the frame, Charlie," Jacob ordered quietly. "What do you see, Macon?"

Macon reached for the laser pointer Jacob had used earlier. "Go back one more."

Charlie pushed the button. The slide popped into focus. "Right there," Macon said, fumbling in the dark for the button on the pointer.

"Where?" Jacob asked, wrapping his strong fingers around her hand to guide her thumb to the button on the pointer.

Macon flipped it on, then narrowed the red beam on a face in the back of the crowd. "Right there! I can't believe I didn't recognize him before. It was the beard, I guess. And he's kind of out of focus."

Jacob shot her an amused glance. He decided not to point out that she was rambling. "Who is it?"

"His name is Elliot Raines. As in Raines Communications. Now go forward two slides." Charlie pushed the button until the required photo slipped into place. "There!" Macon said, focusing the red beam. "There he is without the beard, standing at the back of the crowd."

Charlie looked at Macon quizzically. "He's a political consultant. We'd already had a positive ID on him from analysis. What's the big deal?"

"The big deal is that Elliot Raines is the biggest Democrat media consultant in the business. He regularly handles the presidential races."

Jacob looked at her intently. "What's so important about his being there?"

She stared at him in open surprise. "For a guy who understands international economics, you haven't got the first clue about politics. There's no reason for Elliot to be at these events."

Charlie shrugged. "Maybe he's just a junkie."

Macon shook her head. "He's a junkie all right, you have to be to succeed in this business, but both of these are Republican events. No way would Elliot Raines himself be at a Republican event, especially not one that's only a state-level function. His only possible excuse is opposition research, and he'd send a flunky to do that."

Jacob flexed his shoulders in what Macon thought might have been a suppressed yawn. "It's worth checking out, anyway. Are you sure that's him?"

Macon nodded. "He," she said absently. Jacob stared at her. "Are you sure that's he," she said. "I asked you."

She glanced at him in surprise, just realizing what she'd done. The conversation was beginning to sound like a run-through of "Who's on First?" "Sorry. It was another rude grammar prompt." She gave him a sheepish smile. "It's an instinct, as I told you, but feel free to bite my head off and tell me to mind my own damned business."

Jacob was watching her with a quizzical smile. "Do grammar gaffes always set your teeth on edge?"

She wiped at a wrinkle in her rose skirt. "Some worse than others. I have pet peeves just like everyone else." She sighed and met his gaze once more. "Nothing grates me quite as much as misused pronouns."

He smiled at her. "I kind of feel that way about fingernails on a chalkboard."

"You think I'm ridiculous, don't you?"

He shook his head and Macon watched in fascination as his startling blue eyes grew darker. "No," he said, and she wondered if it was her imagination, or if his voice dropped an octave. "I don't think you're ridiculous."

She took a deep breath to keep herself from melting. "For future reference, I'll teach you the grammar rule. Then you don't have to worry about aggravating me."

"That's undoubtedly an excellent idea."

He sounded as though he might be teasing her, but Macon seized on the excuse of the grammar rule to regain her equilibrium. "You use the subject pronoun after the verb *to be*. So, to answer your question—yes, I'm sure that is *he*. Dead sure. I can't believe I didn't see him before."

Jacob flashed her an amused look. "Okay it's *he*. Let's roll through the entire set one more time and see if you can spot him in any of the other photos. It should be easier now that we know what we're looking for."

They went through the slides again. Macon spotted Elliot in two more photos. Jacob found him three times she missed. Finally, Charlie switched off the projector to pull out the identified photos. "I'll get these down to analysis for a closer look." He glanced at Macon. "It was nice meeting you, Ms. Stratton."

"It was nice meeting you, too."

Charlie left the room. Jacob gave Macon a grateful look. "Thank you," he said quietly.

She shrugged. "I don't know if I was much help. That is odd about Elliot, though."

"You were a tremendous help. That's why I needed an insider to look over the slides. I figured you could find something I might miss."

"I just don't understand it. Elliot is a very good friend of mine. We may represent opposite parties, but I have a huge amount of professional and personal respect for him. I've known him for years. I'm sure there's a reasonable explanation."

Jacob shrugged. "Maybe. It's definitely forth a look, though. Especially when we found him in so many places."

Jacob's success at picking Elliot out of the blurry crowd shots had been amazing. "Remind me never to play 'Where's Waldo,' with you," she said.

He laughed. "I'm miserable at other things, I assure you. I bet you could pummel me at Scrabble."

Macon yawned. "Not tonight, I couldn't. I'm beat."

He nodded. "Let me grab my jacket, and I'll walk you to your car." He stopped short when Macon drew in a quick breath, checked her watch, and groaned. "What's wrong?"

"My car! I left it in the garage at my office. I

didn't think I'd be here that long, so I took a cab over."

"No problem. I'll drop you off."

"No, you can't. They close the garage at eleven-thirty every night for security reasons. I can't get my car until tomorrow. I guess I'll have to take a cab home."

"That's not necessary. I'll drive you. It's on my way home anyway. My apartment's over in Skyline. I'll drop you off on the way."

She drew her brows together. "How did you . . ." she trailed off as she remembered the background file. "May I see a copy of this file you keep talking about?"

"Of course. I'll pull it for you, and I'll get you a complete copy tomorrow."

"I don't think I like the thought of your knowing more about me than I think you know." Macon blinked at her own cryptic comment, then laughed slightly. "I'm so tired, I'm not even making sense."

"I must be more tired. I understood you. I'll just go get my coat, okay?"

Macon sagged in the chair. Jacob stuck his head in the door scant seconds later. "Ready?"

"More than."

He held the door open for her, then settled his hand on the small of her back to show her the way out of the cramped office. Macon was surprised at how busy the office was at that late hour. She looked at Jacob for an explanation. "Security is a twenty-four-hour-a-day job," he said in answer to her unspoken question.

He guided her through the outer office and into the elevator. The stale air in the building had given way to a kind of musty quiet that felt oppressively warm. Macon was relieved when the elevator glided to a stop on the ground floor. They stopped only briefly at the security desk where Jacob signed her out of the building and procured her driver's license for her. Macon slipped it into her wallet, then followed him out onto the street. She didn't miss the way he walked several steps behind her once they were outside, and she smiled, too weary to point it out.

The night was unusually warm. The scents and sounds of the city hung in the air like a damp cloud. Macon watched as several pigeons reluctantly abandoned a discarded bag of potato chips to make room on the sidewalk as she and Jacob passed by. In the distance, the unmistakable sound of motorcade sirens punctuated the still evening. Macon turned her head to look at Jacob. "Nights like this one make Washington feel like home to me."

"What do you mean?" he asked, unlocking the door of his car for her.

"I mean, I've always been enchanted by this city. Do you have any idea how many major issues are being discussed?" She settled herself in the car, then waited until he opened the driver's side door to continue, "how many life-changing, *globally* important things are happening right under our noses, how many deals are being cut right now?" He slid into the driver's seat and looked at her a bit cynically. She laughed. "All right, so some of them are probably crooked. Allow me some innocent pleasure, will you?"

A brief thought popped into his head that he might enjoy showing her some not-so-innocent pleasure as well, and he paused in the act of starting the ignition, shutting his eyes. Macon noticed the brief action, and remembering his fatigue, leaned forward and placed her hand on his arm. "Jacob? Are you all right?"

He jumped, startled by the feel of her hand on his sleeve. "I'm fine. Just tired." And nuts. He cranked the engine with nerve-calming zeal, then pulled out of his parking space. He didn't look at her as he headed out of Washington.

Macon continued to study his profile from the corner of her eye as he drove through the city. He was such an odd man. Such an oddly imposing man. Such an oddly imposing *attractive* man, she finally admitted. She had to stifle a laugh at that thought. May would be proud.

Jacob exited onto the Parkway to head out past the airport. Macon was beyond asking why he knew the way to her house. She was somewhat mollified when he had to ask directions once they turned into her subdivision, however. "Thank you for the ride," she said, pushing open the door of the car when he rolled to a stop in her driveway.

Jacob leaned forward and wearily rubbed his eyes. "No problem. I'll call you tomorrow about the meeting with Chapman, all right?"

"All right," she said softly, looking at him in concern. He was draped across the steering wheel, his fingers rubbing at his temples. "Jacob, are you sure you're all right?"

He exhaled a deep breath. "Just fatigued. I'll be fine."

He didn't move from his exhausted pose. Macon hesitated. "Would you like to come in and at least have a cup of coffee? Maybe you shouldn't drive if you are feeling so tired."

He lifted his head. He managed a slight smile. "I've been worse off than this." He didn't bother to tell her about the weeks at a time he'd gone without sleep. The truth was, he was having trouble convincing himself right at that moment. He could feel the exhaustion all the way down to the bone. "I can make it."

Macon mumbled something he suspected was a curse against manhood. "Then one cup of coffee isn't going to hurt you, is it? Come on inside for a few minutes. It'll make me feel better."

He hesitated only briefly before he switched off the ignition. He eased himself out from behind the driver's seat. Macon walked up the front stairs and unlocked the dead bolt while he fought the urge to lean against one of the porch posts. He'd never been so tempted to go to sleep standing up before. She let them inside, then flipped on the foyer light, as she waved her hand in the direction of the living room. "The couch is in there. Make yourself at home. I'll start the coffee."

Jacob rubbed the back of his neck as he walked into the living room. It was lit only by the outdoor floods from the neighboring houses, but even in the dim light, he could make out the colonial decor. Leave it to Macon, he thought. Her house was a showplace of good taste. He shucked his jacket and draped it across the arm of a wing chair. Then he sank down on a couch that he decided was the most comfortable sofa ever made.

The house exuded a kind of homey comfort that had grown so unfamiliar to him, he was almost disconcerted by it. After years of living out of his suitcase, the welcoming warmth of Macon's home felt odd. It was the kind of house where people raised families and had parties like open houses and wedding receptions. It smelled like oil soap and cinnamon. Everywhere there were soft corners and feminine touches that conjured up images of Christmas morning, and rainy afternoons with a fire in the fireplace, and half a dozen children tracking mud through the kitchen. Jacob's lips turned in a half smile. He was more tired than he thought.

The sense of rightness, of homecoming in Macon's house tugged at his tired body and his tired mind like quicksand, pulling him deeper and deeper into a lulled sense of time and place. The sudden image of his own starkly furnished Skyline apartment grated on his sensitized nerves like sandpaper. He pushed it aside as he leaned his head back against the sofa, closing his eyes and inhaling the warm aroma of vanilla-spiced coffee that wafted from the kitchen. And he was lost in the silence of a dreamless sleep.

"Here you go," Macon said, entering the room with two mugs. "You did say you liked it black, right? I . . ." Her voice trailed off when she realized he hadn't moved. "Jacob?" she prodded, tentative. He didn't respond. "Jacob." She used a bit more force, and kicked his foot for good measure. He still didn't budge.

Macon exhaled a deep breath. She set one of the coffee mugs down on the table. She reached over and switched on the light by the couch, taking a long sip of her coffee. The warm liquid tickled her nose, and she took a deep, calming breath, inhaling the dark aroma while she studied his relaxed features. He really had seemed exhausted. She winced in sympathy at the dark circles under his eyes. "Macho idiot!" she admonished. "Any decent person would have gone home and gone to bed."

Macon set her mug down on the low table. After several more attempts to shake him awake, she gave up. She reached for Jacob's feet to slip off his black loafers. He sighed in his sleep. She looked up swiftly, gauging the sound. When he showed no more signs of life, she lifted his feet onto the couch, and watched him shift his big body as he sank gratefully into the soft cushions. Macon picked up her mug with a wry smile, then headed for the stairs.

From the linen closet, she pulled out a thick feather pillow and two blankets. She carried them back downstairs and lifted Jacob's head, settling it on the pillow. When he didn't so much as flutter his eyelids, she sat back and laughed. "Some secret agent you are. All the enemy has to do is wait until you're asleep. They could get away with hell." She tugged his tie loose, laying it carefully over his jacket. On impulse, she removed his pistol from his shoulder harness and laid it on the coffee table. While she trusted Jacob, there was no reason to take unnecessary chances. She would carry the firearm upstairs with her and return it to him in the morning. Cautiously, she spread the two blankets over him. He rubbed his cheek against the pillow like an overfed cat and sighed, sounding thoroughly content.

He certainly seemed harmless enough curled up on her couch. Macon took another sip of her coffee, picked up his pistol, and continued to watch him. What was it about him that made her so sure he was lying to her, not telling her the whole truth about his investigation or her involvement in it? Was May right? Was she more scared of Jacob Blackfort the man than she was of the challenge he'd given her?

Briefly, she contemplated the feeling of unease his presence caused her. She replayed in her mind her earlier conversation with Maylene. She admitted to herself what she had been unable to admit to May that afternoon. She wasn't just wary of Jacob Blackfort, she was scared to death of him. He wasn't the type of man who passed in and out of one's life like a gentle summer breeze. Oh no. Jacob Blackfort was definitely of the hurricane variety. Macon's world was too settled, her life too certain, her goals too sure. She didn't have room for the enormous presence of Jacob Blackfort. She argued with herself while she watched him. She even almost believed it.

Six

It was happening again. Jacob felt the water rising around his ankles and knew he was trapped in the hole.

He tried to force his eyes open and couldn't. It was so dark, so black. There was nothing but the feel of the steadily rising water and the smooth dirt walls of the deep pit. He groped blindly for something, anything, to pull himself out of the hole, but the water continued to close in around him. It reached his neck and he gasped for air. There was something different this time. It hadn't been there before. A light. At the top of the hole. He reached for it, but the water edged over his chin and started to fill his mouth. Another few seconds and . . .

Jacob opened his eyes, momentarily disoriented, gasping for breath. He looked around Macon's living room, squinting against the early morning light pouring in through the enormous windows.

It had been the dream again. He hadn't had the dream in nearly a year, but he felt the sweat on his body and knew it had been the dream that had startled him awake. He sucked in several deep breaths, waiting for his heartbeat to slow.

Then he remembered Macon, and resolutely, he forced aside the disturbing remnants of the dream. He'd had the nightmare before. He knew he'd survive. He closed his eyes with a soft groan and tried to decide how to handle what he suspected would be a confrontation with Macon Stratton when he saw her. She'd probably be mad as hell. She didn't seem like the type to appreciate having men pass out on her couch. A brief pat on his left rib cage indicated that his suspicion was correct. His .38 Magnum was missing from his shoulder holster. Macon Stratton was no fool. Only a fool would have tucked him between two blankets and left him, fully armed, asleep in her house while she was alone and unprotected. He felt strangely relieved at her common sense.

A familiar aroma captured his attention. Angry or not, she wasn't above pity if she'd made enough coffee for two. The warm, dark smell of brewing coffee, and the merry gurgle of the percolator made his stomach rumble unpleasantly. He remembered he hadn't eaten anything since that dreadful pizza the night before.

He tossed off the blankets as he swung his feet to the floor. He was still slightly disoriented, and sweaty, from the lingering effects of the nightmare. His head felt as if someone had stuffed it with cotton, and he was ready to kill for a shower, but for now, he'd have to settle for coffee. Jacob followed the scent to the kitchen. When he stuck his head cautiously in the door, Macon was seated at the table, heavily absorbed in a copy of *The Washington Times.*

She flipped down one corner of the paper to peer at him. "Good morning," she said.

He looked at her somewhat uncertainly. "Good morning."

"Help yourself to the coffee." She waved a hand absently in the direction of the coffee maker. "It's almond mocha. I hope that suits."

"It's fine."

"If you want breakfast, there's a loaf of bread in the refrigerator. You might be able to scrounge a box of raisin bran from the back of that cabinet, but I can't guarantee how fresh it is."

She didn't look up from the newspaper again. Jacob picked up the blue pottery mug sitting on the counter. His pistol was lying beside it. Without comment, he slipped the Magnum back into its holster before pouring himself a cup of coffee. He noticed that his hands were still unsteady from the effects of the nightmare. "Toast is fine," he said.

Macon grunted something noncommittal, clearly absorbed in the article she was reading. Jacob tugged open the refrigerator, pulling out the loaf of wheat bread. He slid two pieces in the toaster and turned around, leaning against the counter to study her profile. She was already dressed for work. Only the jacket of her green suit was missing. He didn't miss the way her skirt had ridden up her thigh when she sat down. His eyes traveled the length of her leg, settling appreciatively on the graceful turn of her ankle. He mumbled something beneath his breath about having been in Greenland too long if a glimpse of ankle was making him hot. He looked up to find Macon studying him intently.

"Are you all right?" she asked.

He wondered if he looked as guilty as he felt. "Of course."

"Do you want butter?"

"What?"

"Butter. For your toast," she added helpfully when he didn't answer.

He jerked around as he realized he hadn't

heard the toast pop up. He reached for it, bouncing the hot bread lightly in his fingers. Macon looked at him, a curious smile on her lips, and pointed to the cabinets above his head. "The plates are in there. Silverware's in the top drawer on the left. If you decide you want the butter, it's in the refrigerator."

Jacob dropped the toast on the counter. He reached for a plate, mentally berating himself for acting like an idiot. He buttered the toast and cleaned up the crumbs, managing to turn over his coffee and clean that up too, before he finally settled himself across from her at the table with a fresh mug of coffee, feeling as though some of his equilibrium had been restored. "Macon, I think I should apologize."

She flipped down the corner of the newspaper again. She wondered if the world was ever going to snap back into focus. He looked damned appealing sitting there with his hair mussed and his shirt wrinkled. "It's just coffee. You cleaned it up."

"No, I mean, for last night. Not the coffee. I mean, I'm sorry about the coffee, too, but mainly for falling asleep and all. Well, you know."

Macon folded the paper and set it on the table. She looked directly at him for the first time that morning. She'd avoided it since he'd entered the kitchen, not entirely comfortable with her reaction to his full day's beard growth and open-collared rumpled shirt. She was willing to bet he was one of those men who had a sexy-as-hell-the-morning-after look. "How long has it been since you last slept?" she asked.

He groaned and swallowed a long drink of his coffee. "What day is it?"

"Tuesday."

"Then it was Friday. I think. Maybe Thursday."

Macon raised her eyebrows and leaned back in her chair, wishing somewhat hysterically that she had a photograph of how terribly normal they appeared having breakfast together. "You don't know?"

"I've been on a lot of airplanes lately. I lost track."

She shrugged. "Then I suppose it's understandable that you'd collapse like that."

"To you, maybe. I'm not normally prone to act like such a fool."

Macon shifted in her chair. "It's no big deal, Jacob. We all get tired."

He finished off his toast and chased it down with an enormous swallow of coffee. "Still, I hadn't intended to put you out. I've been nothing but an inconvenience since I walked into your office yesterday."

She studied him for a long moment. "Are you sure you're all right? You don't seem to be quite yourself."

"How do you know what myself is?" he asked, his lips curving into a shadow of a smile.

"I'm not even going to touch the grammatical problems in that question. I would just like to believe that someone who is responsible for American security isn't normally so . . ." She paused, looking for the right word, ". . . susceptible to human impulses. You seem out of sorts."

"I'll confess this is a first for me. I'm not in the habit of making strange women put me up for the night. I assume you tried to wake me up."

She nodded. "You wouldn't budge."

"I was afraid of that."

"You don't remember stretching out on the sofa?"

He shook his head. "No way. The last thing I remember is taking off my suit coat. Thanks," he met her gaze, "for the pillow, I mean."

Macon focused her gaze on the spoon in her coffee. "Southern hospitality and all that. It was really no big deal."

"I must be getting old. When we start out with the Service, they train us for this sort of thing. We're supposed to function on no sleep for up to a week at a time. Lack of food comes with the territory."

"What do you do after a week?"

"You take your cyanide capsule."

His expression was so serious, Macon was startled for a moment before she caught the teasing glint in his eyes. She watched him polish off his coffee. He breathed a sigh of pleasure and set the mug down on the table. "You have excellent taste in coffee, Ms. Stratton, just as I knew you would."

"That's the same thing you said yesterday. What do you mean?"

"You can learn a lot from a simple background file. You have a few open accounts at gourmet coffee shops around town. It stands to reason you'd like good coffee."

Macon frowned at the observation. "I really want to see that file."

He nodded. "I'll get it for you today. If our meeting with Senator Chapman is still on, I'll bring it to you when I meet you on the Hill."

Macon couldn't help noticing that his eyes seemed extraordinarily blue that morning. Before she could stop herself, she blurted out the question that had been bothering her since the day before. "Do you wear contacts?"

He blinked at the rapid change of subject. "What?"

"Contact lenses. Do you wear them?"

"No. Why do you ask?"

Because I'm fascinated by the color of your eyes, she thought. "I was going to offer you something to clean them with. It's uncomfortable if you sleep in them."

"Oh. No, I don't wear them, but I'd like to take a shower if the offer for the bathroom extends that far. My suitcase is in the trunk of my car, and I'd like to change clothes. Is that all right?"

Of course it's all right. Why on earth should I mind that you'll be naked in my shower and I'll never look at the grout the same way again, Macon thought, wondering wildly when she'd last cleaned the bathroom. "Of course. Do you have anything that needs to be ironed?"

"I'll need to press my suit if you'll show me where the iron is."

"I'll do it while you shower. It will save time."

"Am I supposed to be in a hurry?"

Macon stifled the urge to tell him she was in a hurry to have him out of her house. He was wreaking havoc with her concentration. "Well, no, but, I thought if you don't mind, you could drive me to work. It will save me cab fare."

"Oh! Oh, hell, yes. I should have thought about it. It completely slipped my mind that you didn't have your car. Do you have a meeting this morning?"

"Well, no. I just don't like to get in past nine or so."

"I can take you right now if you're in a hurry."

She shook her head. "I normally don't leave for another thirty minutes. You have time for a shower if you're fast about it."

He stood abruptly from the table and carried his dishes to the sink, rinsing them briskly before he placed them in the dishwasher. "Let me just go outside and get my suitcase. I'll be ready in twenty minutes." He shot her a wicked look. "Fifteen if you press my suit."

"The clock's running."

He headed for the living room, where he collected his keys and the rest of his clothes. Stepping into his shoes, he let himself out the front door and walked down to his car. Several of Macon's neighbors were standing at the end of one of the driveways, evidently waiting to put their kids on the school bus. He groaned inwardly when the four mothers and one harried-looking father looked at him in open speculation. He wasn't sure she was going to like being gossiped about by her neighbors.

Jacob grabbed his small travel bag out of the trunk, and dropped his coat and tie inside before shutting it again and heading for the house. Inside, he found Macon busily folding the blankets he'd used the night before. He smiled at her. "Your neighbors were curious about me. I'm afraid you might have a few questions to answer about the strange man who spent the night at your house."

Macon laughed, uneasy with the suggestive look he gave her. "Good for them! They'll be delighted to finally have something to gossip about."

He unzipped his bag and pulled out a fresh black suit from the front compartment. He added a pale gray shirt and a black and white tie to the pile along with socks, a T-shirt, and a pair of jade green briefs Macon tried not to notice. But she did.

She was so disconcerted by the notion of Jacob wearing those green briefs, that she dropped the pillow on the floor. With a muttered exclamation, she bent to retrieve it, as did he, and their fingers collided. Jacob's head snapped up, his gaze locking with hers, and she froze, clutching the pillow where the warmth from his hand seared the sensitive skin of her palm.

Something hot flared in his eyes as he looked at her. She wasn't quite sure she could identify the emotion, but she felt an answering jolt of electricity shoot through her. She swallowed hard at the sudden burst of tension that crackled through her nervous system and caused goose bumps on her arms. Jacob's eyes held her gaze a moment longer, and just when she thought her knees might buckle, he dropped his clothes onto the chair and took a step toward her. A startled gasp escaped her lips.

Her world had been off kilter since he'd walked into her office the preceding day, and she was certain she felt it tip on its axis as he reached for her. He locked one hand on her nape and prodded her forward the necessary few inches, crushing the bundle of blankets and pillow between them. She just caught the heated look in his eyes before he tipped his head and captured her lips in a cool, tender kiss. Macon sucked in a surprised gasp before she relaxed under the unexpectedly tender seduction of his kiss.

It was over in the barest of seconds, long before she was ready for it to end, and when Jacob lifted his head she sighed, waiting several heartbeats before she opened her eyes. Jacob ran the pad of his thumb over her lower lip. "I was afraid you might be embarrassed," he said, his voice a low rumble. She stared at him. "About the neighbors, I mean," he clarified.

Macon stepped back abruptly. She felt the heat suffuse her face and she fought the urge to press her hands to her warmed skin. "Heavens, no!" she said, even as she admitted to herself that her embarrassment didn't have a damn thing to do with her neighbors. Scooping up the pillow, she averted her gaze and sought to brush over the charged situation. "Ever since I moved in here, they've been wanting something to gossip about. Now they have it." She made a great show of re-adjusting the blankets and pillow while studiously ignoring his amused gaze before she looked at him again. "The bathroom's upstairs at the end of the hall. There's a hotel bathrobe on the back of the door and the towels are clean. If you leave your suit and shirt here, I'll press them while you shower." *And the whole time, I'll try and ignore the visual picture of you and my grout alone together in my shower.*

Jacob settled a hand on her shoulder. His ex-pression made him look predatory and amused all at the same time. "This isn't over, Macon. What's between us, I mean."

"Maybe not, but I don't want to be late for work." She shrugged off his hand and stalked to-ward the stairs.

Seven

When Jacob strolled into Duvall Chapman's office at two-thirty that afternoon, he couldn't believe he'd spent the better part of the day racking his brains for a good reason why he'd kissed Macon Stratton. One look at her perched on the edge of a leather chair, her brows drawn together in a censorious frown, and he knew exactly why he'd done it. And wanted to do it again. So much so that he felt the heat surge in his groin. He smiled at her before extending his hand to the senator. "I'm Jacob Blackfort, Senator. It's nice to meet you."

Chap Chapman stood up, gave Jacob a once-over, then gave his hand a hearty shake that hinted at his former career as a pro-football line-backer. The man's size and strength hadn't become any less intimidating with his advancing years. "And you," the senator said, his gaze turning speculative. "Macon says you're an associate of hers?"

Jacob slid into the seat next to Macon. He laid the manila folder with her file in it on her lap. "Here are the materials I promised you," he said quietly before returning his attention back to Senator Chapman. "That's right, sir. Macon has graciously agreed to show me around Washington for' a few weeks."

Macon glared at Jacob as she dropped the folder in her briefcase. He was still wearing the black suit she'd ironed for him that morning, but the Italian leather loafers were gone. He had replaced them with a pair of black cowboy boots. The expensive-looking black Stetson he carried in his hand completed the ensemble. She privately thought the outfit should have looked ridiculous, and was considerably peeved that it didn't. It looked sexy as hell.

She brushed a piece of lint from the skirt of her teal suit and said, "I was just telling Chap how eager you are to get started, Mr. Blackfort."

He flashed his million-dollar smile at her. "Were you?"

The senator drummed his fingers on his desk. "She was, at that. I don't believe I've heard the name, though, Blackfort. Macon says you're from Cheyenne."

Jacob looked back at Senator Chapman and shifted in his chair, propping one booted ankle on his knee. "My folks are actually from White Hawk, but I live in Cheyenne proper."

Macon started to fidget. Things weren't going well. The senator knew her very well and he'd been intrigued, if not suspicious, before Jacob had arrived. Now, he was virtually grilling the man on a spit. "It's like I told you, Chap," she said, "this is a new venture for Jacob, er, Mr. Blackfort."

"Blackfort," the senator stroked his chin, thoughtful. "On second thought, I think I do know the name. Does your daddy own one of

those large ranches in the hills near White
Hawk?''

Jacob nodded. "That's the one."

The information seemed to satisfy the Senator,
and with the necessary credentials verified, the
two men talked for several minutes about the
state of affairs in Wyoming. If Macon hadn't been
so surprised, she might have laughed. The Secret
Service agent in the hand-tailored suit she'd met
the day before didn't even resemble the man in
Chap Chapman's office. Instead, Jacob Blackfort
had transformed himself into a hard-working
rancher's son trying to make his way in the world
of politics. She could tell, however, that Chap was
still wary. "Chap," she said, as soon as there was
a lull in the conversation, "I just wanted you to
meet Jacob so you would know his name when I
use him for some media buys next month."

The senator looked at her closely. "If that's
what you think is best, Macon, then you know I
don't have a problem with it. But, why the change
in strategy?"

"What do you mean?" she asked.

"We've never used outside guys before. Why
start now?"

"I don't want you to think you're not a top
priority for me, Chap, it's just that—"

He waved a hand to interrupt her. "I know better." His gaze slipped back to Jacob. "I was just
wondering why you picked Blackfort here."

Macon swallowed. She didn't want to lie to
Chap when he'd been such a good friend to her.
"I think he's the best man for the job," she said.

"How'd you two meet?" Chap asked, his eyes
not leaving Jacob's face. Macon winced at the
look she saw in Chap's eyes. He had slipped out

of his role as her client, and was assessing Jacob with a definable parental glint.

From the corner of her eye, she saw Jacob lean back in his chair with a slight smile. He reached over and took Macon's hand, lacing his fingers through hers.

She barely prevented her mouth from falling open. "Well, Senator," Jacob drawled, "the last time Macon was in Wyoming, I had the pleasure of meeting her at the Taste of the West." He flashed Macon a brilliant smile before returning his attention to Senator Chapman. "I believe you hosted the event last year."

Chap met Jacob's gaze. "That's right. I did. I'd forgotten that Macon flew out for the event. From the looks of things, I'm glad she did."

Macon pulled on her hand, trying to regain possession, but Jacob held fast. "So am I, Senator," he drawled. She glared at him when he flashed her an adoring smile.

Chap seemed oblivious to the undercurrent. "Well, well, I must say this is a pleasant turn of events." He smiled at Macon. "You know it's fine with me, of course. You should have been up front from the beginning, Macon."

She felt a blush creep up her face, so she sat up straighter, hoping to bluff her way through the rest of the interview. She gave her hand another yank. Jacob held on. "Chap," she said, "I think you should understand—"

"Macon's not comfortable with gossip," Jacob cut in smoothly.

The senator nodded. "Never has been." He beamed at Macon. "But, damn, Macon, you could have trusted me."

She gritted her teeth. "I do, Chap. You know I do."

He seemed appeased. "By all means, feel free to use Mr. Blackfort for whatever purposes you can dream up, Mac."

Macon groaned at the suggestive comment, but didn't dare say anything about it. She was sure Jacob would embarrass her if she did. "Thanks, Chap. I don't think we need to take up any more of your time."

"No trouble at all," he said. "I'm glad you came by. Real glad."

Macon stood up, jerking her hand from Jacob's grasp. The senator rose to his feet to round the desk in two quick strides. He took both her shoulders in his big hands. "Now you take care of yourself, Mac. I keep telling you there's more to life than politics. Don't forget that."

Her laugh was short, mirthless. She wanted more than anything to escape Chap Chapman's office and give Jacob Blackfort a solid chunk of her mind. "Give Doris my love will you, Chap?" She started toward the door.

The senator slipped his hand under her elbow. "I'll do that. I'm sure she'd like to have you out for dinner soon." He extended a hand to Jacob. "That goes for you, too, Blackfort."

Ignoring Macon's frosty gaze, Jacob shook the senator's hand. "Thank you. My schedule is clearer than Macon's since I just got to town, but we'll check the calendar." He picked up her briefcase and handed it to her with an amused smile. "Ready to go, Mac?" he said, his smile warm.

"Ready," she snapped, walking past him to the door, barely containing the urge to kick him in the shin.

She managed to keep her temper in check until they were in the corridor, where she turned on him with an angry glare. "What the hell was that?"

"Now, Macon, calm down."

"Do not tell me to calm down. I will not calm down. I want an explanation for this . . . this charade. Just who the hell do you think you are?"

Jacob stifled the urge to laugh. Her eyes were glittering, and he had a nearly overwhelming temptation to tell her she was beautiful when she was angry—just to see how far he could push her. He had no doubt she'd exact revenge if he did, so he slipped a hand beneath her elbow and started walking with her. When she tried to jerk her arm loose, he tightened his grip. "You're overreacting."

"I am not." She pulled at her arm again. "Where are you taking me?"

"I assume you're ready to leave. If you're going to yell, you might as well do it outside where you won't cause such a disturbance." He flashed a smile as they walked past an older couple clad in vacation attire. He continued to move toward the door.

"I am not yelling."

"Yes, you are." He gave her elbow a tight squeeze. "I'll give you a ride back to your office and you can yell to your heart's content."

Macon glared at him. "I don't want a ride."

"Well, you're getting one. So shut up."

Macon looked appalled at his abrupt command. He had the satisfaction of seeing her momentarily speechless. He steered her into the large atrium where he punched the elevator button.

She tapped her foot on the marble floor. The

sound echoed off the marble walls in an angry tattoo. "I don't know why you think you have a right to be mad, Jacob Blackfort. I'm the one you dragged into this."

"It's no big deal, Macon."

"It is a big deal." She gave the elevator button a savage push. "Why is this damned thing so slow?"

Jacob decided against suggesting they walk down the single flight of stairs to the ground level. He watched her instead. She was in a real stew, a first-class tantrum, and he was more than a little intrigued by the effect it was having on him.

When he thought of her, his mind conjured up a woman who was always in control, always proper, always flawlessly dressed and exquisitely poised, always afraid someone might disapprove if she failed to meet their standards. What he saw now was a rare combination of velvet and steel, silk and fire that probably had a lot to do with how she'd reached the top of her profession. Not to mention being an enormous turn on.

He sauntered over to the marble steps where he sat down, leaning back on his elbow. He couldn't resist the temptation to goad her a little. "I don't know why you're taking this so hard, Mac."

Abruptly pivoting on her toe, she impaled him with her stormy blue gaze. "Do *not* call me that."

He shrugged. "Whatever. I just don't understand why you're in such a snit over this."

She thrust her briefcase into his lap, and planted her hands on her hips. "Are you insane? Don't answer that. You are, aren't you? You're nuts. Of all the agents in the world, I got one that's bananas."

Jacob cast a quick look around, relieved to find they were alone. When she calmed down, he'd have to give Macon a gentle reminder about the rules of undercover work, but for now, he couldn't resist a quick gibe. Riling her temper made him feel ten feet tall. "Is that anything like, 'Of all the gin joints in the world, why did she—' "

"Oh, shut up, you big jerk." Macon waved her hands in agitation. "You have no principles at all. Why the hell do you think you have the right to take over my life?" She gave the elevator button another quick jab, then started pacing, shaking her hands at her sides.

Two female congressional pages—Jacob recognized their telltale blue trousers and white blouses and set their ages at about sixteen— walked through the stairwell shooting Macon a curious glance. The glance they shot him was even more curious, in an adolescent female sort of way. On reflex, he winked at them, eliciting a peal of giggles as they hurried up the stairs. Macon's glare could have frozen Niagara Falls. "*Must* you do that?" she bit out.

"Do what?"

"Flirt with every woman you see." She jabbed at the elevator again, exhaling a sigh of relief when the door slid open.

Jacob decided it didn't matter that the elevator was headed up instead of down. He levered off the stairs. Grabbing her elbow, he hurried her into the mahogany-paneled elevator. No sooner did the heavy brass-plated doors slide shut, than he jammed his finger on the emergency-stop button. "Now," he drawled, "if you want to have this conversation, let's have it right."

"What are you doing?"

Ignoring her, he pried her briefcase out of her fingers. It dropped to the floor with a dull "thud." Somewhere in the background, Macon heard the distinct, insistent sound of clock buzzers announcing a vote on the Senate floor. Like warning bells, she thought. There was something in Jacob's aquamarine gaze that had shifted. She saw a sudden predatory glint in his eyes that reminded her of a wolf scenting the air before fixing on his prey.

Jacob took both her hands. He raised them above her head, plastering them against the cool dark walls of the elevator, then leaned forward, bringing his face inches from hers. "What's the matter, Macon? You stopped yelling."

She wriggled her fingers, trying to free them from his grasp. Why couldn't she breathe properly? "I—let go of me."

Jacob shook his head. "Un-uh. You wanted to talk, so talk. We're alone now. You can say anything you want."

Macon drew in a deep breath, wishing she didn't like the clean, soapy scent of him quite as much as she did. "You're insufferable."

"Undoubtedly." He leaned closer to her so she was completely pinned between his big body and the wall of the elevator.

"Incorrigible." She was having trouble concentrating.

Jacob ran his tongue over the firm curve of his mouth. "That, too."

"Pig . . . Pig-headed." She swallowed when he exhaled, and his breath fanned her eyelashes.

"Definitely." He tipped his head and brushed

his lips over hers in the barest whisper of a caress. "But you still haven't told me why you're so mad."

"Because—" Macon tried to draw a deep breath and found she couldn't. The weight of Jacob's body pressing her against the elevator wall had constricted her lungs. That must be the reason. "Because you lied to Chap."

"Only about how we met, Macon. The rest was true," he said, and slid his lips over her cheekbone.

She shook her head, thinking it was a mistake when his lips settled on the curve of her ear. "About—about us. You let him think we're—"

Jacob nipped at her earlobe. "We're what?"

Macon turned her head, locking her gaze with his. "You let him think we're romantically involved." Great way to explain herself, she thought. She could feel herself blushing.

A warm smile curved his lips. "Are you always so proper?" When she didn't answer he slid his lips over the arch of her eyebrow. "I let him know I'm hot for you, Macon Stratton. What's so bad about that?"

"Because you're not," she wailed.

Jacob's smile turned lascivious. "Wanna bet?"

Macon stared at him. "Jacob, you can't mean you—"

"Shut up, Macon," he said, and bent his head to capture her lips in a longs hot kiss that didn't even vaguely resemble the softer version he'd given her that morning. This one was carnal.

And Macon was on fire. She'd tried to deny it all morning, but the memory of Jacob's firm mouth on hers had plagued her since their heated exchange in her living room. Uncertainty warred with want for the barest of seconds before she gave up the fight, admitting that this was what she wanted all along. My, oh my, but he tasted nice.

Jacob seemed to sense her surrender. He wasted no time in taking full advantage by sweeping his tongue into her mouth. When she tipped her head back against the wall, he released her hands, muttering a satisfied grunt when she immediately knocked his hat off and threaded her fingers through his hair. He slipped his hands inside her suit jacket to caress her through the soft silk of her blouse.

Macon leaned into him with a soft sigh, enjoying the feel of his warm hands, his firm mouth. One of his hands held her firmly against his hard length, the other swept up her rib cage to settle on the rounded swell of her breast.

And the earth moved. Well, actually, she thought, it was the elevator. The elevator! She tugged at his hair. "Jacob."

He kissed her again. "Jacob," she insisted against the pressure of his mouth. "The elevator." He ignored her. "It's moving."

"Ignore it," he said, rubbing his thumb over her taut nipple through the thin silk of her blouse.

Macon shuddered. "The door's going to open," she said, wondering when the elevator had started to spin as well as travel up its cable.

Jacob didn't seem to notice anything until it glided to a stop, and the sudden pull of gravity arrested his attention. He turned his head just as the door slid open.

Macon stared in horror at the older tourist couple they'd seen earlier in the corridor. They were standing just outside the elevator doors, gaping at the sight of Macon and Jacob, passionately entwined. Jacob shot them a brief smile, then pushed the button, closing the door in their faces. When the elevator started to move again, he stepped back, then reached to straighten her clothes. "Do you still doubt what I said, Ms. Stratton?"

She stared at him. "What?"

"You said you didn't think I was really interested in you. Do you want another demonstration, or was that one good enough? Didn't you hear bells? I did."

The world snapped back into focus the moment she heard the Senate buzzers start ringing. She pushed his hands away and gave her jacket a sharp tug. "They weren't bells. They were Senate buzzers, and yes, I heard them. I think your demonstration was fine, thank you very much."

Jacob grinned at her as he stooped to retrieve his hat and her briefcase. "It was a whole hell of a lot better than fine."

She grabbed the briefcase out of his hand, then pushed the proper button for the ground floor. "Just what precisely is your point, Jacob?"

He dropped his hat back on his head. "Don't get bristly on me again, Macon. You know exactly what my point is."

The elevator sank to a stop. When the doors opened and Senator Lane Carland and his Administrative Assistant, Edward Mucklin, stepped on, Macon felt a surge of relief. Jacob would be forced to abandon his pursuit of the topic. She smiled at the two men. "Hello, Senator. Edward."

Edward Mucklin shot her a curious glance.

"Macon," he acknowledged. "I saw that piece on you in *Electioneering*. Congratulations."

"Thank you, Edward. It was a great honor."

Without warning, Jacob reached up and rubbed his thumb over her top lip. She swung her startled gaze to his. "Your lipstick is smeared," he said, wiping away the smudge with his thumb.

Macon wanted to sink into the floor. Edward was staring at her as if she'd just grown a second head. Lane Carland shot her an amused look and said, "I'll be seeing your stepfather at a Judiciary Committee meeting this afternoon, Macon. Anything you want me to tell him?"

Macon swallowed. There was no hope now. Lane Carland and Gordon Stratton were two of the biggest gossips on Capitol Hill. Hill employees counted on the Carland and Stratton staffs to know everything, but everything, that was happening in Washington. Macon had nearly twenty clients in Congress, and another ten in the Senate. In addition, she was exceedingly well-known to the support staff on the Hill, and she knew that by late afternoon, rumors of her liaison with some dark man in an elevator of the Russell building would be flying over fax machines and burning up the phone lines. She mustered what little dignity she could, ignoring Jacob's arrogant look of amusement, and met the senator's inquiring gaze head-on. "Tell him, I said hello," she said weakly.

Eight

"What time do you want me to pick you up?" Jacob's voice slid through the phone line and across Macon's nerves like a heated glass of orange liqueur on a rainy winter afternoon.

Not liking the sudden poetic turn of her thoughts, she frowned at the receiver. She still hadn't fully recovered from their earlier meeting with Chap, or the disastrous encounter in the elevator. Worse, she had been forced to field at least half a dozen phone calls on what she now privately referred to as Jakegate, and to handle what amounted to a third-degree interrogation from Maylene. Jacob Blackfort might be a good agent, but he didn't have a thing on Maylene Porter.

What had positively capped the whole thing off had been Gordon Stratton's call. Macon knew her stepfather meant well, even knew he wanted to heighten their relationship to a more personal level than Macon had ever allowed. Gordon had been very good to her, even adopting Macon after her mother's death, but Macon had always kept him at an emotional distance. He tried. He tried very hard, but even as a child, Macon had been afraid to get too close to Gordon. He was another adult who could leave her alone.

When he'd called that afternoon to invite her

to dinner the following week, he'd insisted that she bring Jacob along. Despite his efforts to sound casual, Macon had heard the stung note in his voice. Gordon had been hurt that he'd heard about Jakegate from someone other than his stepdaughter. Macon still hadn't thought of a way to convince Gordon that she wasn't on the verge of marrying a man he'd never met. She'd felt guilty that Gordon had been hurt, and irritated that Jacob had caused it. The fact that she couldn't prevent her stomach from fluttering every time she thought of Jacob's kiss had capped off her day.

By the time he called, she was fighting a pounding headache. The last thing she wanted to do was spend an evening cooped up with him. Belatedly, she realized she hadn't answered his question. "I still don't see why I can't meet you somewhere," she said.

"We went over this before, Macon. If Washington is going to believe you and I have a thing going, we'd better have a history that starts before yesterday afternoon. I need to talk to you, and we can talk while we drive."

"I have an invitation on my desk to a fundraiser for Governor David Rauley. It would be an excellent place for me to begin introducing you to the political circle."

"We're not ready for that yet. What are you going to do if somebody asks you where I went to college, or what size shirt I wear, or what color my eyes are? These things take time. Lots of time."

Macon resisted the urge to tell him she knew exactly what color his eyes were. They were aquamarine with just a hint of silver, and they turned slate blue when he kissed her. Instead, she concentrated on the rough edge in his voice. He sounded tired, and frustrated, and angry, and she suddenly regretted her slightly shrewish attitude. There was no reason to make him suffer for the effect he had on her. "I'm sorry I irritate you so much, Jacob," she said softly. "I'm just off balance by this whole thing."

She heard him smile. "You don't irritate me, Macon. You're a little harder to read than most, and I'll admit your mood swings occasionally catch me off guard but—"

"I do *not* have mood swings."

"Yeah, whatever. Anyway, you definitely do not irritate me."

Macon toyed with the pen in her desk set, sliding it in and out of the pen holder. "Yeah well, you could have fooled me."

"Why?"

She dropped the pen back in its holder. "I don't know. You just seem like you're aggravated. I'm not trying to be a pain, you know. I just didn't expect this to be so complicated."

"It shouldn't have been. I hadn't planned on this aspect of things."

"Well, I'm still sorry I irritate you."

"Maybe we'll have to try a few things and see if I can lighten up a little," he said. Macon heard his chair squeak in protest when he leaned back in it. She pictured him with his feet propped on his desk. "For starters, I'd be a lot less aggravated if you told me when I can pick you up."

"You *may* pick me up at six o'clock."

He ignored her grammar prompt. "Six is perfect. I'll meet you at your office."

"Do you want me to wait outside?"

"Isn't that a little like blowing the horn in your driveway?"

"It's easier to find a parking space in my driveway than it is in downtown D.C."

"I'll manage," he said. "I'll be by around six."

"All right. Good-bye, Jacob."

"Bye Macon." Jacob hung up the phone, then tipped his head back against his chair. He twirled a pencil in his fingers. Macon Stratton was one hell of a woman. She'd berated him all the way back to her building about what he'd done in Senator Chapman's office. Even after he'd explained his reasons to her, she still hadn't wanted to concede.

Macon seemed determined to keep their relationship strictly on an impersonal basis. If he had half a brain, he'd be relieved as hell. He wasn't even telling her the truth, for God's sake. When she found out he was using her to bust Gordon Stratton, she'd probably hate his guts.

But try as he might, he couldn't put her out of his mind. There was something about her that tugged at a hidden part of him. It wasn't just passion, although there was certainly a healthy amount of that. No, there was something about Macon Stratton that twisted his insides into a hard, unrelenting knot. Something that went well beyond the physical attraction. Not that there wasn't plenty of physical attraction to keep his mind occupied, of course, and he knew Macon wasn't exactly immune to him. Hell, she'd practically come unglued in the elevator, which had wreaked havoc with his libido for the better part of the afternoon.

Jacob smiled at the memory. Damnation, he wanted that woman. If all else failed, he could always just maneuver her into another elevator. He was in the process of thinking through his best possible strategy when Charlie came hustling through his door. "Jake! I'm glad you're in."

Jacob dropped his feet to the floor. "Wham's up, Charlie?"

Charlie waved a fat manila folder. "I've got the report from downstairs on this Raines guy."

"Elliot Raines?"

"Yeah, the one Macon picked out of the photos."

Jacob held out his hand. "Let me see."

Charlie handed him the folder and sat down. "There's some pretty good stuff in there. Seems Raines' business is doing well. I mean really, really well."

Jacob flipped through the folder, pausing to study several sheets of paper. "Large cash deposits?"

"To the tune of five digits a pop."

Jacob examined a photo before replacing it in the folder. "They could be consulting fees."

"They could also be payoffs. Check that last chart."

Jacob pulled out the paper and looked at the list of names. "There are some pretty shady characters on here."

"That's right. And all of them have been seen with Elliot Raines in the last four months."

"Any connection to Stratton?"

"Page five."

Jacob nodded and closed the folder, handing it back to Charlie. "Let's check it out. We'll need all the usual stuff, including the phone logs, bank records, and tax returns. Get me the best information you can on the expense records, too."

"I'll get on it first thing in the morning." Charlie took the folder and stood up. "By the way, Mary Jean wanted me to invite you to dinner."

Jacob stood up and stretched, checking the time on his watch. "Can't tonight, Charlie. Tell Mary Jean I'll take a rain check, will you?" He had about a half hour before he had to leave to meet Macon.

"You're not working late again, are you? Because—"

"Relax, Charlie. I'm leaving on time tonight."

"Whatcha doin'"

Jacob flashed him a wry smile. "As it happens, I have a date."

Charlie's breath came out on a low whistle. "Well, damn. A date date. Like a real man-woman thing?"

Jacob nodded. "A real man-woman thing. Jeez, Charlie, I am still breathing you know."

"I was beginning to wonder. You haven't gotten out much since that thing with Kristen."

Jacob gave his ex-fiancée, Kristen Ager a passing thought, then dismissed it before the memory spoiled his good mood. "Well, I'm getting out now. So you can quit worrying."

"So who is it? Anyone I know? Some knockout blonde I hope."

"It's Macon Stratton."

Charlie raised his bushy eyebrows and watched as Jacob rolled down the cuffs of his white shirt. "You said you weren't working late tonight."

"I'm not." Jacob buttoned one cuff, then went to work on the other.

Charlie blinked twice before his weathered face split into a broad grin. "So what the hell are you doing hanging around here? Damn, Blackfort, aren't you going to go home and change first, throw on a little cologne or something?"

Jacob shook his head. "No."

Charlie snorted. "That one's a real looker, Jake. Smart as a whip too. I thought so last night, but you'd better treat her right, or you'll screw it up."

Jacob laughed. "I know that. I'm not a complete idiot."

"No, but you definitely have your moments."

"Tell Mary Jean I said hello, Charlie."

Charlie didn't take the hint. "Maybe you should take her a bottle of wine. Or some flowers. Flowers are good. She'll think you're sensitive."

"Good-bye, Charlie," Jacob said, glancing meaningfully at the door.

"So where are you gonna take her?"

"Why? Do you want to spy on us?"

"The thought did occur to me. Mary Jean and I could make sure you didn't louse it up with her. Mary Jean says it's criminal for a good-looking man like you not to have children. Continuation of the species and all."

"Thanks. I think I can handle this one solo."

Charlie tucked the folder under his arm. With his hand on the doorknob, he glanced back. "You know that Italian restaurant in Adams Morgan is real nice, maybe you could—"

"Good-bye, Charlie." Jacob rounded the desk and shoved Charlie through the door.

"Oh! Yeah. Bye, Jake. Have a good time. We'll talk it over in the morning."

Jacob shut the door after Charlie and leaned back against it. "We will most definitely not talk it over in the morning," he mumbled as he reached for his jacket. If things went according to plan, his gentlemanly instincts would prevent him from discussing the outcome of the evening. He was beginning to suspect that the only way he was going to cool the fire in his belly, a flame that was rapidly soaring out of control, was to find out just how much heat lay beneath the surface of Macon Stratton's cool exterior facade. If she burned as hot as he suspected, he wasn't even sure he'd live to tell about it.

Nine

When Jacob walked into the elegant interior of Macon's reception area a half hour later, he was relieved to find that Maylene Porter had left for the evening. He was not in the mood for yet another well-intentioned inquisition. "Macon!" he called. "Are you here?"

"In here."

He found her in her office, leaned back in her chair, talking on the phone. He mouthed the word hello and sat down.

"Listen Preston," she said, obviously irritated. "I'm not going over this with you again. You promised me at least thirty-percent saturation on those ads and I got fifteen. Either you rerun them or I take this up with the FCC."

Jacob processed the threat about the Federal Communications Commission and knew Macon didn't make it lightly. This was no lightweight she was haggling with. She rubbed her eyes with her thumb and forefinger while she listened to the mysterious Preston's answer. "No," she said. "That's just not acceptable. I don't want a refund on the deposit. I want the ads run."

She rolled her eyes at Jacob and held the phone away from her ear. He could hear the man yelling on the other end. Jacob had a sudden ir-rational urge to hit him. Macon looked tired.

"That's it, Preston. I'm not going to negotiate on this. I'll expect your media calendar over my fax machine by Friday morning." She slammed the receiver down in the cradle and groaned, dropping her head into her hands.

"Tough day?" Jacob drawled.

She didn't look up. "The worst. That was Pre-ston Newman. He's one of my media suppliers in the Midwest, and I got an independent audit to-day that says Joe Carson is trailing the incumbent by two to one in his district in Illinois. Consider-ing that Preston has been running my ads during the late-night movies instead of the evening news, it's no wonder."

"What are you going to do?"

Macon rubbed her fingers at her temples. "I think he's going to toe the line. He knows he's a dead duck if I trump him in front of the FCC. I hope he'll come through."

"Can you pull the race out?"

"I think so. Our persuasion mail program is very strong." She shrugged. "It was a gamble anyway. Congressman Hullman is going to be a tough one to beat." She tipped her head back against her chair and raised tired eyes to his. "In the mean-time, it's jerks like Preston Newman that put the hell in election years. I'm exhausted."

Jacob smiled at her. "I have just the cure for that, Ms. Stratton."

She hedged. "Do you think we could—"

"Don't even think about ditching me. I have the most relaxing evening of all time planned for you. You'll feel like Jell-O when I'm done with you."

I've got news for you, Macon thought, remembering the elevator. All it took was one kiss and her insides turned to goo. A whole evening with him, and she'd probably evaporate. "Where are we going?"

He shook his head. "It's a surprise. Are you ready?"

She shot him a wary look. "I've never liked surprises."

Jacob narrowed his eyes at the strange remark, but didn't comment. "This one you'll like." He stood up. "We'd better get going."

Macon stood up and reached for her suit jacket where it lay draped over the back of her chair. Jacob rounded her desk in three quick strides. He grabbed the jacket to hold it out for her. Pausing only briefly, she slid her arms into the sleeves, waiting while he settled it on her shoulders. She could feel the heat of him against her back, felt it draining the tension out of her neck and shoulders. When he leaned down and planted a soft kiss at her nape she shivered. "What are you doing?"

Jacob smiled against her skin and lifted his head. "You smell good," he said.

Macon stepped away. "Jacob, I—"

He held up his hand. "Don't get defensive, Macon. I'm not going to attack you. Just try to enjoy yourself. Okay?"

She hesitated. "I don't know about this. I think maybe we should, well, maybe you should just take me home."

"Look, Macon. We don't have a choice. We're committed to this course of action now. Chap Chapman expects us to be close. The only way we'll pull this off is if you decide to cooperate."

"You promised this wouldn't affect my business."

"And it won't."

"Jacob, I don't think a personal relationship is in our best interest."

"Since when do best interests have anything to do with personal relationships?"

"That's not funny."

"It wasn't meant to be."

"I simply mean that you and I aren't compatible enough to pursue this beyond our professional involvement."

Jacob fought a smile at her prim tone. "And just what makes you think that?" He reached up and traced a finger on the full curve of her lower lip. "I can think of a few areas where we're very compatible."

Macon batted his hand away, but not before he saw the flush steal into her cheeks. "Is that all you can think about?"

"What?" he asked.

She frowned at him. "You know very well. I'd like you to stop teasing me."

"I'm not teasing. Believe me, honey. I'm not teasing."

Suddenly feeling exposed by the knowing look in his eyes, Macon pulled the lapels of her jacket closer together. "I just don't think it would work between us, Jacob, and I don't see the sense in pursuing a relationship where we'd both get hurt in the end."

"Why are you so sure of that?"

"Because you and I come from different worlds. You live in a world where things are fast-paced and dangerous and exhilarating. I sit behind a desk all day, and I like it. I like the security.

I like the sameness. I like knowing that the most dangerous thing that could happen to me is getting hit by some bozo on the Shirley Highway. I couldn't become seriously involved with a man who chased bad guys and brandished his weapon for a living."

Jacob's breath came out in a prolonged hiss. "You're pretty damned sure about what I want, aren't you? Is that why you and Jeff Parker are no longer an item? Did you have him all figured out too?"

She was startled by his sudden irritation. "That was really low, Blackfort. My relationship with Jeff Parker, and I use the word *relationship* very loosely here, is none of your business."

"I think it's very much my business. You're trying to nail me into some preconceived notion you have of who I am and what I am. If you did that to Jeff Parker, it's no wonder he tucked tail and ran."

Macon gasped. "That's not true. I threw Jeff out, not the other way around. He was a snake and a cheat and a liar and I got rid of him, and I still say it's none of your business."

"Oh yeah? Then you tell me. Are you really trying to hold me at arm's length because you think we're incompatible, or are you doing it because you're still upset about Parker?"

"Neither is the issue. I'm in the middle of an election year. I have twenty-seven clients with tough races to service. I'm not going to devote a passel of my energy toward playing cops and robbers with you. Jeff Parker is not even at issue here."

When she finished the brief tirade, she was breathing hard. Jacob studied her for a minute through half-closed eyes. Macon Stratton was a tough lady. A tough lady who was, at the moment at least, scared to death at the thought of an intimate relationship with him.

Forcibly, Jacob reined in his temper. "Macon," he said, deciding persuasion was a better choice than intimidation. "I'm sorry. That was out of bounds."

"Yes. It was."

"It's just that I need you."

"Surely you can find someone else to help you with this case."

Jacob shook his head. "I'm not talking about the case." When he saw her surprised look, he ran his hands up her arms to settle them on her shoulders. "All right, it's true that I need your help to make this case, but that's not what I meant."

"It's not?"

He shook his head. "No. I meant I need you, somehow, in my life. I don't know what it is about this situation that makes you so nervous, but if it helps, I'm not exactly thrilled about it myself."

"I—I don't know what to say."

"Look, Macon, I'm not asking for a lifetime commitment here. I'm just telling you that this thing between us exists. If you can't handle it, I've got to know now."

She stared at him for several seconds. "I don't know. I don't know if I can handle it or not."

Jacob wove his fingers into the soft hair at the nape of her neck. "I'm attracted to you. You've got to know that, but it doesn't mean I'm prepared to jeopardize this case."

"Jacob, I—"

He held up his hand. "I've been honest about

that from the start. If you're uncomfortable with the way things are proceeding, I apologize, but if you're going to back out on me, now's the time to do it while I can still contain the damage." He crossed his arms over his chest. "I don't want to fight with you every step of the way, but I don't want to have to establish a new cover either."

He paused, sure he'd later regret what he was about to say. But there was something in her eyes, a tiny spark of fear that made him forge ahead. "So I'll make a deal with you. I promise to try and keep my hands to myself, and to shut up about Jeff Parker, although I'm not sure I can make that promise in good faith, and in exchange, you promise to help me."

"What do I get out of this?"

"Satisfaction in a job well done."

"Oh, please."

"Damn, Macon. What do you want from me?"

"Why are you pushing me so hard?"

"Because we have a lot of ground to cover. I'm very close to closing the book on this case, and I don't want to blow it. If I'm going to pull this off, I need your help. We started something today in Chap's office, and I need a decision right now whether or not you want to finish it."

"It's not that I want to back out, you know?"

"No? Then what is it, exactly?"

"This makes me nervous."

"No joke."

Macon stared at him. How could she explain it? How could she tell him what he did to her? No one had ever affected her the way Jacob Blackfort did. She had a feeling he could disarm every defense she had in a matter of seconds. After she'd worked so hard to build the life she now had, she wasn't ready to let him destroy it. She sure as hell wasn't ready to walk out on an emotional limb with him. Emotional limbs inevitably broke. And Macon didn't want to hit the ground.

Uncomfortable with the train of the conversation, she steered it back to business. "I don't know what to do. What if I screw up? What if something goes wrong and I'm responsible? What if something happens?" Silently she added, *What if you're lying to me like I think you are? What if I fall for you and you turn out to be another Adrian Snell who is using me to get what he wants?*

"You're letting your imagination run wild with you, honey. This is a simple procedure on your part. All I need you to do is convincingly play the role of a woman who has been captivated by my considerable charms."

He wagged his eyebrows at her. Macon swallowed. "I don't know, Jacob. I'm just not sure."

"I don't have time for you not to be sure. I've got to make a decision in a hurry. I got the report in on Raines today, and it looks very promising."

"Elliot Raines?"

"Yeah. You should see the list of goons he's been keeping company with."

"He's not guilty, you know."

"Who's not."

"Elliot. He's not your man."

"You're the one who pointed him out to me."

"I said it was highly unusual for him to attend small-time Republican events. I didn't say he was guilty."

Jacob rubbed a hand over his face. "Look. Raines or not, we're closer than we've ever been. I don't want to lose this opportunity, but I need a commitment from you. Now. So what's it going to be?"

"I don't know. I haven't had enough time to think about it."

"Well, you'd better think of something. I'm running out of patience and time."

Macon took several deep breaths, forcing herself to hold his gaze while she turned over the problem in her head. The truth was, Jacob Blackfort didn't just make her nervous. He scared her to death. And it had nothing to do with his investigation. No, Jacob made her nervous because he affected a much more primitive part of her. Something about Jacob Blackfort made her life up to this point seem very ordinary, unsettled. Jacob threatened her contented existence with a wild, reckless yearning for something more. Something she'd long ago decided she didn't want. The same yearning had possessed her mother. And her mother had died because of it.

Macon stared at the determined set of his jaw, the fire in his blue gaze. A restless urge stirred in her, and she knew, in that moment, that no power on earth could prevent her from accepting Jacob's challenge. Recklessness and caution had warred for her attention. Recklessness won. Hands down. The blood started to roar in her ears. "Do I have to decide right now?"

"Right now."

"If you push me, I might back out."

"Maybe. I don't think so. You're a born risk-taker, Macon, no matter how much you want to deny it. I think you're curious as hell. You just want me to force you into this so that I'll have to take the blame if anything goes wrong."

Macon's breath came out in a whoosh. "No one

should be allowed to read people as well as you do. It gives me the creeps."

"I'm not trying to manipulate you. I'm just frustrated."

He was. She saw it in his eyes. He was frustrated and tired and somehow, that reassured her. Jacob was many things, but she knew instinctively that he wouldn't knowingly allow her to get hurt, and in some dark corner of her mind, she was forced to admit that he was right. All at once, her life seemed too planned, to predictable, too lonely. She did want the adventure of a few weeks with Jacob Blackfort, even if it meant she bore the scars of it forever.

The realization shocked her. She had never been willing to open herself up to the kind of hurt she knew Jacob could inflict. Nevertheless, she couldn't deny that she wanted to take that risk. She wanted it badly enough to look beyond what seemed like limitless obstacles and concentrate on the warm feeling in her heart. Reassured, she took a deep breath as she reached out to straighten his tie. "I live in a small world, Jacob."

He narrowed his gaze. "What do you mean?"

"I mean my world is consistent. It's filled with consistent things. Things that are familiar to me. It's comfortable there."

"What are you saying, Macon?"

She lifted her eyes from the perfect knot of his tie and met his intense gaze. "When I was a little girl," she said, "I had an imaginary friend. He was always chiding me about living in a small world. He didn't believe in comfort. That's why I let him do all the daring."

"Comfort isn't always a bad thing, you know." His voice was soft and deep and seductive, and

Macon imagined herself swaying toward him slightly. Maybe she did. "My friend was a handsome prince who lived in the forest."

"Did he ride a white horse?"

She shook her head. "A palomino. He rode a palomino."

Jacob's lips twitched. "Did he give good advice at least?"

"And just what is wrong with a palomino?"

"Any self-respecting handsome prince rides a white charger. Everybody knows that."

"Well, mine didn't. He rode a palomino." She paused and trailed her fingers down the front of his shirt. When she encountered a loose thread, she twirled it around a button. "He taunted me a lot. I think I invented him as a symbol of what I wanted to be." She dropped her hands back to her sides. "I spent a lot of my time being afraid when I was a little girl. Afraid of dying. Afraid of the dark. Afraid of losing another parent. Afraid of risks."

Jacob tipped his head. "So where did you consult with this sage?"

"I'd stand out on my balcony, which was really the roof outside the dormer in my bedroom, and he would ride up on his palomino and climb the wall. I would tell him I was afraid and he would goad me out of it."

"Are you afraid now, Macon?"

She met his gaze. "Yes."

With gentle fingers, Jacob brushed her hair away from her forehead. "Of what?"

"Of you."

His eyes registered his surprise. "Of me?"

She nodded. "You're threatening to make my world bigger, Jacob. I think I like it small."

"But your imaginary friend is taunting you again?"

Macon drew a deep breath. "He would always use the same argument to persuade me. Personally, I think it was a cop-out on his part. He probably couldn't think of anything better to say."

"Go for the glory?"

Sure now of her decision, she shook her head. "Are you kidding? My prince would never say anything so mundane. That sounds like a line out of a bad football movie."

Jacob's smile was genuine. "I should have known. No half-baked clichés for you."

"That's right. Only the gourmet kind."

"So what's your imaginary friend telling you now?"

" 'Jump,' he says, 'or you'll never know what lies beyond your bedroom window'."

"Did you ever jump?"

She shook her head. "I was too scared."

"Are you scared now?"

"Deathly."

Slowly, Jacob twined his fingers in her hair. "Did it ever occur to you that what was beyond the window might be worth conquering the fear?"

"Only a few times. I was such a coward, though. I could never make myself take a risk like that."

Jacob's fingers drew lazy, soothing patterns on her scalp. "What about now?" he asked, his voice a silken, heated caress.

Macon smiled at him. "Do you promise to catch me?"

He returned her smile and pressed a soft kiss to her forehead. "I guarantee it."

Ten

Three hours later, Jacob tossed her a fortune cookie. "Okay, Macon, let's go over this one more time."

With a groan, she flopped back on the couch in her office. The light outside had faded to a dusky twilight glow, and the office was dark except for the halogen lamp on her desk. "I don't want to."

He broke open his fortune cookie, studying her in the shadowy light from the street lamps. "Come on, sport. If any one's going to believe you and me are involved—" Her groan interrupted him. "What?" he said.

"You and *I*. You and *I* are involved." Her voice was pained.

He grinned at her, enormously proud of the way he'd trapped her. "Thanks. I didn't know you felt that way."

"Oh, shut up."

Jacob laughed. "If any one's going to believe the two of us have a thing going, you're going to have to know some stuff about my life. I mean, it's not like I just dropped into your office one day and *poof*, instant relationship."

"But that's what happened."

"Not as far as everyone else is concerned.

We've been conducting a covert relationship for a year, remember?"

"This is ridiculous. No one's going to believe I've had a secret relationship with you since last year. Why wouldn't I just tell them the truth?"

"This is Washington, D.C. It's the most paranoid city on earth. People don't even tell each other what time of day it is, much less details of their personal lives. Everyone's going to believe it, as long as you're convincingly enamored of me."

"If I'd wanted to be an actress, I'd have majored in theater in college."

"Is it that much of a burden?"

She leaned her head back against the arm of the sofa, closing her eyes. "It is when I'm this tired, and you're acting like Attila the Interrogator."

"It's all part of the world outside your bedroom window, Macon," he teased.

She picked up one of the tweed pillows and buried her face in it. "I can't believe I told you that. Are you ever going to let me out of this office, or am I stuck here for the rest of my life?"

Jacob smiled. Once Macon had capitulated, he hadn't wanted to risk spoiling her good mood. Rather than going out for dinner, he'd suggested they order Chinese take-out and stay at her office. During the ensuing three hours, he'd grilled her for information about her family and background, supplying her with similar details about his own. He pulled the pillow away from her face, and waved his fortune at her. "It says right here, 'Lengthy preparation is the key to success.' "

She glared at him as she snatched the fortune

out of his hand. "Let me see that." She read it before tossing it on the floor. "It does not. It says, 'You are honest and kind.' Hah! Shows what they know."

"Don't you want to know what yours says?"

"No. I want to go home."

Jacob leaned back against the arm of the sofa and watched her. She looked damned appealing. Her hair was mussed and rumpled, giving it a slept-in look that was wreaking havoc with his libido. He'd found during the course of the long evening, that Macon had a tendency to play with her hair when she was agitated. Every time she ran her fingers through the cropped honey-gold curls, Jacob's body tightened at the sight of the soft tendrils twining around her hand.

She had shed her jacket early in the evening, and unbuttoned the top two buttons of her white silk blouse. Whenever she leaned forward, he was afforded a tantalizing glimpse of something lacy, and he was having a hell of a time keeping his mind out of her blouse and on her family history. "I'll make a deal with you," he said. "We go over this, one more time, and if you get more details right than I do, we'll call it quits."

"That's not fair."

"Of course it's fair."

She struggled to a sitting position. Her blouse stretched across the rounded swell of her breasts. Jacob shifted his position to alleviate his ensuing discomfort. She didn't seem to notice. "It is not," she said. "You have practice at this. You're the one that memorized my background file in one reading."

"You're the one who carries around entire reports on opposition research in your head. Tell me you can't reel off half-a-dozen facts about any of your clients, and any of your clients' opponents, off the top of your head."

"That's different."

"It is not."

She frowned at him. "Besides, you have an unfair advantage."

"Such as?"

"Such as you haven't been wearing stockings for eighteen hours, and your feet don't hurt."

He was tempted to tell her he'd been thinking about her stockings for the better part of the evening, along with a few other things that would probably earn him a swift kick in the butt, and that plenty of other things hurt. Deciding that discretion was definitely the better part of valor, he reached for her foot. "So I'll even the score."

"What are you doing?"

He lifted first one foot, then the other into his lap. Slipping off her pumps, he dropped them to the carpet. "Relax. I'll have your mind off your stockings in no time." He began rotating his thumb in slow circles on the ball of her foot.

"I thought you were supposed to keep your hands to yourself."

He stopped the soothing stroke of his fingers. "Do you want me to stop?"

Macon hesitated. He could see the indecision on her face. "No," she said.

He rewarded her by running his thumb along the arch of her foot. She groaned as she dropped her head back against the couch. "Do you want to start, or do you want me to?" he asked.

"Ask me questions."

"Okay." He kept up the stroking rhythm of his

fingers, working his way over each foot with precise care. "Read your fortune first."

"I don't want to."

"I'll quit," he said, stopping the rhythmic
movements of his fingers.

She reached for the cookies. "You're a beast.
Do you know that?"

"We can't all be handsome princes on palomi-
nos."

Glaring at him, she broke open the cookie to
pull out the white slip of paper. She stared at it
for several seconds.

"What does it say?" he prompted.

She met his gaze. "You planned this, didn't
you?"

"I did not. What does it say?"

Macon rolled her eyes as she handed him the
fortune. "You read it."

Jacob took the paper and held it to the dim
light. He started to laugh. "Lengthy preparation
is the key to success."

Macon groaned. "Who gave you permission to
stop rubbing my foot?"

He smiled at her and resumed the gentle mas-
sage. "Convinced now?"

"I still think you set me up."

"No way. It's an omen."

"Omen my eye." Shifting, she closed her eyes
as she leaned her head back against the arm of
the sofa. "All right. Start asking me questions."

"Where am I from?" he asked, rubbing his
thumb with increased pressure along the ball of
her foot.

"From a place where they end sentences with
prepositions."

He pinched her foot. "Don't be cute. I want a real answer."

"Cheyenne," she replied. "Your father raises cattle." She pushed herself up on an elbow to look at him. "At least, that's what you told Chap. You told me you don't have any family."

"I don't," he said, more abrupt than he'd intended to be.

"But Chap said he recognized your father's name."

"There is a Blackfort ranch in Cheyenne. Let's move on, okay?"

"Why don't you want to talk about your family?"

"I just don't." She looked like she might protest, so he said, "Look. There's nothing to tell. What family I do have, I haven't spoken to in a long time. And I'm not going to."

"But why?"

"Because I'm not, and it's none of your business."

"You know everything about me."

"That's right. I do."

"So why can't I know this?"

Jacob resisted the urge to shake her. "Because I said so." He took heed of her mutinous expression. "Just suffice it to say that the conversation isn't one I'm real comfortable with."

"With which I'm comfortable," she prompted.

He knew she was teasing him. "Macon," he said, his voice a low growl.

"I was only teasing."

"I don't like to be teased."

She tipped her head to one side as she studied him. "But don't you want to have a family, a wife, children, something?" she asked, turning the conversation back to exactly where he didn't want it.

"No."

She blinked. "No? But why—"

"Macon, enough. I don't want to talk about it."

She looked like she wanted to argue, but after a short pause, she dropped back against the couch and shut her eyes again. "All right."

Jacob took a deep breath, then continued with his earlier questions. "All right. So what kind of cattle are they? On the ranch, I mean."

She opened one eye and affixed him with a nasty glare. "The one your father, who is not your father, owns?"

"Yeah. That one."

"Black Angus."

"And?"

"And antelope."

"Not bad," he said, moving his fingers to the top of her foot, "although, I think I should tell you, they aren't really antelope, they're pronghorned deer."

"Fascinating."

He pinched her toe. "In fact, we don't raise them, we just try to control them. The herds are so large, they cause a major hazard to the ranchers. The joke is that Wyoming issues reverse hunting licenses. Everyone who fails to bag a pronghorn has to pay a fine."

"You know," she said, studying him through half-closed lids, "I want to really thank you for telling me that. Next time I have the 'livestock' category in Trivial Pursuit, I'll clean up."

Jacob laughed and tickled the bottom of her foot. "Smart aleck. Are you ready for more questions?"

She rolled her eyes at him. "Do I have to?"

"Yes."

"Lead on, Attila," she mumbled.

Jacob continued stroking her foot. "What's my full name?"

"Jacob Blackfort. No middle name. Like Harry Truman."

Pausing, he worked at the back of her heel with his thumb. Her eyes had drifted shut, and she lay back against the arm of the sofa, so eminently touchable. He dragged his thoughts back to where they belonged. "How old am I?"

"Thirty-two."

"When's my birthday?"

"Christmas Day." She opened her eyes again. "You know, it's no wonder you're such a pain. I'll bet your whole family clucked over you every Christmas and you thought all the hoopla was for you."

"I'll ignore that. My family did not cluck." He finished working on her ankles, then moved his hands to her calves. "What about my youth?"

"It was lurid, I assume."

He flicked a finger against her knee. "Be nice. Where did I go to school?"

"University of Wyoming, Cheyenne."

"Major?"

"International Economics."

"Current profession?"

"Official answer?"

He nodded as he trailed a finger along her shin bone. "Yeah."

"International investor who is thinking about buying a media firm in Cheyenne and wants my help to break into the field."

"Not bad. One thing you got wrong. I'm not

really buying out Dom Petrie's firm. Dom is a close friend of mine from Wyoming, and he's agreed to let me use this as a cover. As far as everyone, including the Service, is concerned, I bought him out."

"The Secret Service doesn't know the truth?"

Jacob shook his head. "My director wanted me to muscle Dom out of his business. I didn't think it was necessary when I knew I could trust Dom. There was no reason to ruin his business by letting it go down the tubes in an election yea. He's feigning ill health until after the new year. When this is all over and he has a miraculous recovery, he'll return as full owner of the company. In the meantime, his assistant, Karen Wilkerson, is running the place with his help. All off the record, of course."

"Of course."

"I only told you that because I didn't want you to think I'd do that to a friend. No one else knows."

"Not even Charlie."

"Not even Charlie."

"That's a big risk you're taking."

"Some things are worth it." He shrugged. "Now, let's see, I believe I counted thirteen facts, and I'll throw in the last one about Dom as a gimme. That makes fourteen."

"Is that all?"

He rubbed one finger against the back of her knee. He was satisfied when he saw her lips clench slightly. "Yeah. That's all. Is it my turn?"

She nodded. Jacob rubbed his thumbs on the sides of her right knee, keeping his gaze on her face. "I've learned that your father died when you were an infant and it was several years before your mother remarried."

"That's two."

He spread his fingers on the back of her knee, grazing the flesh of her inner thigh. "You lived in Raleigh with your mother until after her death. That's when Gordon Stratton brought you to live permanently in Washington."

"Four."

Jacob lightened the pressure of his hands, caressing her legs through the whisper-soft silk of her stockings. "You like moo goo gai pan, sweet-and-sour chicken, and irises are your favorite flower."

"How do you know that?"

"That's what you ordered for dinner tonight. I assumed you either like moo goo gai pan and sweet-and-sour chicken, or you're a glutton for punishment." He tapped his temple. "I've got a mind like a steel trap."

Macon glared at him. "No. I mean the irises. How do you know that?"

"There was something in your file about a flower shop where you do regular business. I called the florist this afternoon and asked if you'd expressed a preference. I was afraid I might have to come up with a peace offering."

"That's cheating."

He pinched her calf. "Yeah? Well, I've also learned that you blush when you get embarrassed."

Macon's eyes flew open. "What?"

"That you like to play with your hair." He shifted his hands slightly, moving them to a position above her knee that hinted broadly at a deeper intimacy. She appeared to stop breathing.

"I've found that your perfume is the most seductive scent on earth, and that even after I've left you, I find myself remembering its fragrance."

"Jacob—" Macon felt the goose flesh on her legs. She started to tremble. The heat in his gaze was so captivating that her breathing went shallow, and her heartbeat accelerated.

He used his other hand to trail a finger along the lace edge of her camisole where it was visible beneath her white silk blouse. "I've discovered that you like lacy underwear, and I go nuts wondering just precisely how much lace there is under the veneer of these business suits." He shifted, keeping one hand locked on her thigh as he moved his body over hers on the couch.

Capturing her gaze, he moved his thumb in a slow, mesmerizing circle on the sensitive flesh just above her knee. "I know that your mouth tempts me nearly beyond belief, and I don't have anywhere near the willpower I thought I did."

"Jacob, I—" She should tell him to stop. The words formed on her lips, but nothing but a tiny burst of air rushed past, and even that sounded more like a sigh.

He pressed a hard kiss to her lips, more to prove his point than to interrupt her. "And," he said, moving his hand higher up her thigh, "I've learned that I want you so bad, my whole body hurts." He moved against her. "Feel it?"

"Badly," she said, her voice a breathy whisper, her skin acutely attuned to the feel of his warm hands. "You want me badly."

"You're telling me," he groaned, and covered her lips with his.

Jacob felt himself drowning in the sensation of the kiss at the same moment he realized that he couldn't get enough of her. She was warm, and soft, and the tiny mewling sound she made in the back of her throat when he kissed her, seized hold of him with the force of a hurricane wind. He shifted slightly, tightening his grip on her thigh as he deepened the kiss, driven as much by a need to absorb her into his body as by the throbbing sensation in his groin.

Macon's hands drifted over his chest and across the taut breadth of his shoulders in an absent caress that left a trail of tingling hot sensations on his skin. When she plunged her fingers into the hair at his nape, his resolve shattered. He plumbed the dark, moist recesses of her mouth with his tongue.

He had the vague, fleeting idea that he mig)c ignite when she arched closer to him, bringing her soft, full breasts into heated contact with his chest. A pulse of white-hot liquid rushed through him, searing his insides, making him impossibly hard, impossibly ready. He responded to the now-urgent need by pushing her deeper into the sofa, and sliding one leg between her thighs. He swallowed a groan of pure, masculine delight when she squirmed beneath him, and her pelvis shifted into tantalizing contact with his own hardness.

He laced the fingers of his free hand into her hair, finding it as soft and as welcoming as he knew it would be. "You're so soft," he whispered against her lips. "So incredibly soft." He slid his hand from beneath the hem of her skirt and reached for the buttons of her blouse. More than he wanted to breathe, he wanted to inhale great breaths of her bewitching scent and find its source.

At the feel of his fingers on her flesh, Macon gasped. She had never experienced such a rush, such an uncontrollable surge of need. Clenching her fingers on his scalp, she pulled his head closer, demanding another kiss. The spicy, clean scent of him filled her senses and overruled the tiny thread of sanity that kept beckoning her to exercise more caution. Jacob groaned in approval when her fingers tangled in his hair, and he slanted his lips over hers, sliding his tongue along the curve of her lower lip.

It wasn't enough. Macon arched into him with a small shudder. She slid her tongue into his mouth where she found his taste as inflaming as his scent. Jacob's fingers trailed over the curve of her breast as he unbuttoned two more buttons on her blouse. The warm feel of his callused fingertips caused the tight knot in her belly to spread down her legs and curl her toes into the sofa.

Macon moaned against his mouth. Jacob swallowed the intoxicating sound and dragged his mouth away. Her blouse was open to her waist, and he inhaled a deep, drugging breath. Her heated sigh caused a warm burst of her delicate, seductive scent to drift into his dazed mind. When he slipped his hand inside her blouse, he wasn't surprised that his fingers trembled. He was splintering into a million pieces. The smell and sight and taste and feel of her were waging war on his self-control.

Brushing his fingers over the swell of her breast, he found the tip with unerring accuracy. It instantly tightened into a hard knot. At the cry that wrung from her throat, Jacob's insides quaked, his stomach screwed into a fist.

"Jacob . . ." Macon's voice was a breathless pant.

He kissed her again, rubbing his thumb over her hardened nipple. "I'm not going to hurt you," he whispered against her mouth. "I'd never hurt you. I just want to touch you." He kissed her again, harder, and dipped his hand beneath the lacy cup of her camisole. "God, you're so warm. Like hot satin." He rubbed his fingers against one of her taut nipples as he trailed a series of kisses down her throat. "Are you this warm inside?"

Vaguely, she wondered if his words should have shocked her. Instead, they set off tiny explosions of pleasure in her bloodstream. Wanting more, she sucked his lower lip into her mouth.

Jacob felt his body tighten, clench, twist with a wanting so acute, so intense, that a raging flame sang through his blood with the force of an inferno. Her nipple had peaked against his palm, and he tugged the tails of her blouse free from the waistband of her skirt. He spread it wide so he could feast on the sight of her flushed skin. His breathing was ragged and harsh when he bent his head to take one soft nipple into his mouth, laving it through the thin silk of her camisole. He simultaneously reached for the hem of her skirt with his other hand.

His warm hand slid up her thigh, and all at once, as if a warning had been sounded, it was too much for her. She was drowning, suffocating with the feel of his weight, and his heat, and the cascade of desire and emotion he'd set off inside of her. She drew a sharp breath when his fingers grazed the ultrasensitive flesh at the top of her thigh. Panic flooded through her, damping the fire as effectively as a tidal wave of Arctic seawater. She pushed at his shoulders, shivering when he lightly nipped the swollen bud of her nipple with his teeth. "Jacob . . ." Macon pulled at his head. "Jacob, wait. Please wait."

The plea in her voice seemed to break through his sensual haze. He stilled his hand on her thigh and met her gaze. His eyes were cloudy, not quite focused. "What's wrong, Macon?" His voice sounded slightly hoarse.

She sucked in a ragged breath. "This is too much. It's too fast. I—" She looked away, feeling foolish.

Even in the dim light, Jacob could see the blush on her cheeks and the panic in her eyes. He took a shuddering breath as he closed his eyes. He began mentally counting backwards from one hundred until he felt his body begin to settle and his heartbeat slow. He reached seventy-two before he felt certain he would live if he didn't have her.

His thigh was still wedged between hers, and the feel of her moist, heated core nestled in tantalizing proximity against his aching groin threatened to send him back over the edge. He shifted enough to remove the temptation. Still not daring to look at her. "Do you want me to stop?"

She nodded. "I'm sorry."

He heard the hint of tears in her voice, and his eyes flew open. Her face was flushed, her hair mussed from being touched by his hands. Her swollen lips, still warm and wet from his kisses urged him to kiss them again, to quell whatever reservations she had with a strategic seduction, but it was her eyes that undid him. The bright shine of unshed tears made the stormy blue color of her eyes even more intense, more startling, more vulnerable. "Don't cry," he whispered, hoping he sounded tender despite the rough edge that still peppered his voice. He reached up to cradle her face in his hands. "Dear God, don't cry. I'll stop. I'd never hurt you."

Macon shook her head, and a tear slid free. She wiped at it with the back of her hand. "I can't do this. I'm sorry. I'm so sorry."

Jacob was beginning to feel like the lowest form of life on earth. Just a few hours before, he'd glibly promised that he'd keep his hands off her. As soon as her defenses had been lowered, he'd pounced on her like some overheated teenager.

He began buttoning her blouse with slow, deliberate precision. He buttoned it all the way to the throat before he dropped a chaste kiss on the curve of her cheekbone and rolled off the couch. She apologized again. At the miserable tone in her voice, something hot and tight twisted into a knot in his stomach as he landed with a thud on the carpet. He buried both hands in his hair. "Stop saying that. You have nothing to be sorry for, honey."

"Yes, I do. I shouldn't have . . . I should have told you first. I shouldn't have let things go so far."

"I meant what I said. I'm not going to hurt you."

She sat up. "I know."

Jacob groaned and closed his eyes. "You might just kill me, though."

"I'm sorry."

He smiled a wan, ironic smile, and kept his eyes shut. "Stop saying that," he said again. "It was my fault. I was supposed to keep my hands to myself, remember?" Macon didn't answer him, so he levered up on one elbow to fix her with a searching stare. "Macon?" Her lips trembled. "It was supposed to be a joke, honey."

"No one's laughing," she whispered.

He nodded. "No one's laughing." Carefully, he brushed a lock of her hair off her forehead. "Do you want to tell me what's wrong?"

She looked at him with stricken eyes. "Are you angry at me?"

He arched a brow. "Because you said no?"

"Because I said no after . . ." she trailed off.

Jacob felt a funny stirring in his gut. Something that oddly bordered on rage. Not because Macon had asked him to stop, but because she was afraid of his reaction. Something, more likely someone, had given her that fear. He wanted to know who. He wanted to beat "who" to a bloody pulp.

He shifted to sit on the sofa next to her. "No, I'm not mad. I'm disappointed, I'll admit, but I'm not mad. You had every right to say no, Macon." He shot her a wry grin. "For that matter, so did I."

She shivered and started toying with the hem of her skirt. "I should have told you first. I shouldn't have let things go so far. It's my fault."

Jacob took her hand, bringing it to his lips. He kissed the palm before flattening it against his chest where his heart still thrummed at heavy cadence. "It takes two to tango, you know. Last time I looked, you weren't the only one going at it on the couch."

She blushed. "It's different. You had every intention of this culminating in, I mean, you wanted to . . . you would have . . ."

"Made love to you?" She nodded. He smiled at her. "Yes, I would have."

She finally met his gaze. He still held her hand

against his chest, and he felt it tremble under his fingers. "I should have told you before things got out of hand that things aren't going to go that far between us. I don't want them to."

He watched some of the vulnerability fade, and saw the familiar signs of her cool facade begin to slip back into place. He decided he'd better divert it before he lost her. He tightened his fingers on her hand and leaned down to place a soft kiss on her still-swollen mouth. "What are the adds I can get you to change your mind?"

Her ghosted smile was fleeting. "Not good."

"Should I take this personally?"

"No. It doesn't have anything to do with you."

"That's reassuring," he drawled.

She drew a deep breath as she slid her hand free of his grasp. "I'm making a mess of this. I didn't mean to insult you."

"Are you going to tell me what this is about?"

She studied him for a minute. "It's very important to me. If you scoff at me, it's going to hurt my feelings."

Her admission cost him a heartbeat. He stared at her for several seconds. "Do you think I'd do that?"

She hesitated. "Sometimes. Sometimes I'm not sure that you think I'm capable of feeling anything real. You seem to think I'm indestructible."

He did. Indestructible like glass was indestructible. Indestructible to evenly distributed pressure, but easily shattered if not handled properly. Jacob frowned and spread his hands on his thighs. "I think you're very complicated, and that people misunderstand you because you want them to."

She shrank back against the arm of the sofa

and tucked her bare feet under legs. "That hurts, Jacob."

"But it's true?"

She thought it over before slowly nodding. "Yes. I suppose it's partially true."

"Why is that?"

"Off the record?"

He sighed in irritation. "You should know anything like this is off the record. Exactly how much of a jerk do you think I am?"

She sighed. "I don't think you're a jerk."

"What do you think?"

"I think you're very complicated," she replied, repeating his earlier words. "And I think people misunderstand you because that's what you want."

It took Jacob a few seconds to realize she'd repeated his earlier assessment of her own character. He exhaled a long breath and smiled at her. "We're some pair, you and me."

"You and I," she said. "You and I are a pair."

Jacob's smile broadened at her grammar prompt. "I'm glad to see you're back to your old self."

She met his gaze. "Well," she said, still toying with the hem of her skirt. Jacob watched in fascination as she unraveled a long thread. "I suppose you'd like some sort of explanation."

He remembered her fear, the genuine panic he'd seen in her eyes. He wasn't quite ready to let the matter drop. "You said no. You had a right to say no. You don't have to explain anything."

She shook her head. "I don't think you understand."

"I understand more than you think, Macon. Somewhere along the line, somebody's convinced you that you're supposed to give men whatever they want, and if you don't, you've committed some heinous crime against humankind."

"That's not true."

"Then why did you apologize five times for calling it quits?" He paused. "And why did you look like you were terrified of me when you did it?"

She wet her lips with the tip of her tongue. "I feel like I led you on," she said, her voice barely above a whisper.

"Did you?"

She shook her head. "I didn't mean to let things go so far. It's just that I tend to lose my ability to concentrate when you're touching me."

He grinned at her. "Thank you."

"Don't sound so impressed with yourself," she grumbled.

"I can't help it. It's that masculine ego thing. There's something about knowing I can make the prim and proper little lady turn into a firecracker that speaks to the more primitive side of my nature."

She sighed and twined the thread from her hem between her fingers. "Jacob, I think you should know that I have no intention of letting this happen again. I'm not going to sleep with you. Not now. Not ever."

"I can understand why you wouldn't want to mix business with—"

She held up her hand. "It doesn't have anything to do with that."

Jacob studied her through narrowed lids, taking in the delicate pink flush that slowly found its way back into her face. He was beginning to suspect that Macon was going to tell him something about Jeff Parker that was going to make his hair stand on end. "Are you going to tell me the real reason?"

She looked away. "It's just that in today's climate, in the world we live in, it just seems smart to distance oneself from physical entanglements."

At her prim tone, he felt a smile begin to form at the corner of his mouth. Had he not known how sensitive, how vulnerable she was feeling, he might have yielded to the temptation to tell her he was envisioning something a lot hotter, a lot more erotic, and a lot more serious than anything that might be called a physical entanglement, but a second, more sobering thought occurred to him, and he tipped his head. "Are you," he paused, "all right?"

Macon frowned at him. "Do I have any diseases, you mean? No. No, I don't."

Jacob exhaled a long breath. "I'm glad."

Macon stared at him for several long seconds. "Do you want to know what happened between Jeff Parker and me?" she said abruptly.

Jacob hesitated. He wasn't sure he did. "Do I?"

She ignored his question. "Jeff called me about six weeks ago and asked me out. He's the administrative assistant to one of my clients. That's how we met. I didn't learn until later that Jeff is a good friend of Adrian Snell."

Jacob recognized Adrian's name. "You were fairly seriously involved with Snell about a year or so ago, weren't you."

She nodded. "We ended the relationship nine months ago today."

"What about Jeff Parker?"

"He wanted me to go to a dinner party with him, and I was lonely. Adrian and I dated for so long, it was hard for me to adjust to being alone again. So I went. Jeff was nice, polite, not really my type, but available. I went out with him a few more times, and then he started pushing, really hard, to make our relationship more physical. I kept saying no, and he kept pressuring me."

"Nice guy," Jacob drawled.

Macon nodded. "A regular saint. Anyway, that afternoon after I first met you, Jeff and I attended a meeting together at the Capitol Hill Club. I left my car here, and he came by and picked me up. We were late because Jeff didn't get here on time. When we got to the meeting, about twenty or thirty of my colleagues were already seated. Jeff made some off-the-cuff remark about being late because we'd lost track of time. It wasn't what he said, it was what he insinuated. Anybody who didn't catch the idea that we'd just come from an afternoon tryst wasn't paying attention. If that wasn't bad enough, he told Adrian we'd have been on time if I hadn't spent so much time trying to fix my hair." Macon looked at Jacob. "He practically told them we'd slept together."

"What did Snell do?"

"He laughed. He looked right at me, and he laughed. I was furious and embarrassed and hurt and upset and by the time Jeff brought me back to the office, I was ready to kill him."

"You should have. You would have done the world a favor."

She managed a slight smile. "I tossed him out on his ear instead. Actually Eric did the tossing."

"The security guard downstairs?"

"That's the one."

Jacob wiped a hand over his face. "All right, so we're mutually agreed that Jeff Parker is a first-class slimeball. You didn't seem to be very serious about him."

"I wasn't. It was what he said before Eric took over that did all the damage."

Jacob clenched his teeth. Instinct told him this was the part where he had to forcibly restrain himself from hunting down Jeff Parker. "What did he say, Macon?" he asked quietly.

She raised stricken eyes to his. "You know, just because I'm not an overly emotional person doesn't mean I don't have feelings like everyone else."

"I know."

"And just because I more or less keep to myself doesn't mean my feelings aren't every bit as sensitive as the rest of the world's."

He nodded. "I know."

Macon took a deep breath. "Jeff said that he and Adrian had made a bet for a hundred bucks that Jeff couldn't get me to go to bed with him."

Jacob made a mental note to break Jeff Parker's teeth at the first available opportunity. His breath came out on a long hiss. "Son of a bitch."

A half-smile tugged at Macon's lips. "I thought of that one. I thought of a few others, too."

"Did you at least get Eric to hit him a couple of times?"

She nodded. "I told Eric he could. I had to call and explain to the security company that Jeff had threatened me, and that's why Eric had to throw him out of the building."

Jacob studied her for a few seconds. "That's not the whole story, though, is it, Macon?"

She shook her head. "No. There's a good reason why Adrian made that bet."

"There's no good reason for something like that."

"I mean, he knew he'd win it. That's why he set Jeff up. Adrian knew I'd never sleep with Jeff."

"Are you still getting over your relationship with Snell?"

"No. Adrian wanted things from me I couldn't give him. The same thing Jeff wanted." She paused. "The same thing you want."

Jacob tensed. "That's not fair, Macon. You've got no right to compare me to those two."

"I didn't mean to imply that. It's just that I've never . . . it's just that—" she broke off and buried her face in her hands. "Oh, hell."

Jacob felt something begin unfolding in his stomach. "Macon?" he prompted.

"What?" she mumbled into her hands.

"Macon, look at me."

Slowly, she raised her head. "Yes," she said. "Before you ask, the answer is yes."

Jacob smiled at her. He was starting to feel light-headed. "How do you know what I'm going to ask?"

"I'm being logical."

"What if I was going to ask you the time?"

"You weren't."

"What was I going to say then?"

"You wanted to know if I'm a virgin." She met his gaze squarely. "The answer is yes."

Jacob was almost ashamed at the rush of pure, undiluted masculine pleasure that roared through his blood. His ears started ringing, and he just barely resisted the urge to flop back on the carpet and howl at the moon. There was something so primitively arrogant about knowing Macon had never belonged to another man, he was almost intoxicated by the knowledge. He fought for several long seconds for control, knowing she would be offended, and with good reason, if he told her so.

"Are you upset?" she sounded worried.

He couldn't fight the broad smile that curved his lips. "Hell no." She looked startled. He cautioned himself as he reached for her hand. "There's no shame in being a virgin, Macon."

"I'm not ashamed."

He squeezed her fingers. "I'm glad." She didn't know how glad.

"It's just that, well, I'm not very—" She raised stricken eyes to his. "I have it on fairly good authority that I'm very likely to be one for a long time."

His heart skipped a beat. She was acutely embarrassed. The heightened flush in her cheeks gave her away. "What do you mean?"

"A long time ago, I stopped letting people get close to me. It hurt too much when I lost them. Ever since . . ." She trailed off and pushed a curl behind her ear. "I protect myself that way."

Jacob regarded her for a long minute. "Tell me the truth, Macon," he prompted.

Staring at the hem of her skirt, she took a deep breath. "My fear of emotional commitment prevents me from sexually satisfying a man."

He stared at her. Not only did the ludicrous statement sound like a verbatim quote out of some psycho-babble manual, but it had to be the most ridiculously misguided thing he'd ever heard. "Did you read that in a book?"

Macon didn't look at him. "It happens to be true."

Gently, he took her chin in his thumb and forefinger, then turned her head so he could see her eyes. "Honey, I want you to listen to me. First of all, it does not happen to be true."

She opened her mouth to protest, but he pressed a finger to her lips. "Believe me, you can sexually satisfy any man with a pulse. I should know." Her eyes widened. Jacob gave her a rueful grin. "I'll prove it if you want me to."

Before she could answer, he rubbed his finger over the curve of her mouth. "And secondly, I don't know who told you that, or where you got that idea, but he was a damned fool."

Macon's lips were trembling against his fingers. Reaching up, she wrapped both her hands around his to pull it away from her face. She was shocked at how desperately she wanted to tell him about her mother, about what it had been like to see her slow descent into degradation, about how she'd been a victim of her own passions and her own lack of self-control. She wanted to tell him how hard she'd worked to overcome the memories, the pain that had been her mother's legacy.

But she didn't. She couldn't. Instead, she held his large hand in hers and met his gaze. "There are things," she said, her voice just above a whisper, "things you don't understand. It's very complicated. I don't want to get hurt. I can't get hurt."

He wanted to pull her into his arms and promise he'd never hurt her. He wanted to soothe away every pain, every disappointment, every lingering ache, and swear to her she'd never suffer again. He wanted it so much and so intensely that it scared the daylights out of him. He took a deep breath and slipped his hand from her grasp to clench it on his knee.

The effects of their heated embrace were beginning to ebb and he was thinking more clearly now. He was stunned to realize he was actually relieved that Macon had stopped him when she had. There was something deeply satisfying in Macon's assertion, in the knowledge that she didn't take the physical attraction between them lightly, that it had a deeper meaning for her. Something that made his heart turn over and his palms start to sweat. Something that made him start to think maybe he was falling for her a lot harder than he thought he was. "I know you've been hurt," he said quietly. "I'm going to try very hard not to hurt you again, but I'm not going to deny that I want you."

"It's not that I'm not attracted to you, Jacob. You know that don't you?"

Oh, he knew all right. "Yes."

"That's why I'm sorry I let things go so far."

"You don't have to apologize."

"My mother told me that a lady never lets a man believe he's going to get things that he's not."

Jacob raised an eyebrow. "What's that supposed to mean?"

"I think to her it meant that women were supposed to give men what they wanted."

There was a world of pain behind those words. One thing he knew from Macon's background check was that her mother's activities had been, at the very best, morally questionable. "I'm glad you didn't buy it."

She looked at him in surprise. "You're not upset?"

No, he admitted to himself, he wasn't upset. Intrigued. Infatuated. Bewitched. But not upset. He took her face in his hands. "I don't think I've ever had more respect for a person than I do for you."

Her eyes registered a brief flash of amazement. "Really?"

"Really." He kissed her softly. "I won't push you, Macon." He narrowed his gaze at her, a sudden thought occurring to him. "I'm not Jeff Parker."

"I believe you."

Unable to resist, he kissed her again, a soft, nonthreatening kind of kiss. "Can we just agree to take this one step at a time as long as I promise to stop when you ask."

Her eyes widened. "You mean you want—"

He covered her mouth with his hand again. "I'll decide what I want, and you decide what you want. Deal?" She stared at him. He gave her a gentle shake. "Macon? Do we have a deal?"

She nodded.

Jacob dropped his hand. "Well, on that note, I think maybe we should turn on some lights and get back to business. I'd still like to go over a few more things with you before we go home." He paused. "Unless you think you can't be here alone with me."

A fiery blush flooded her face and buried itself in the roots of her hair. "I'm perfectly capable of controlling myself, Jacob."

"Well, darn."

She punched him in the ribs. "You're a cad."

He touched her hair, loving the way the honey blond curls clung to his fingers. "Are we all right then?" There was a strange intimacy between them. Stronger, more free, he decided, than he had ever experienced. It was the kind of bond he'd always expected after the first time he made love to a woman, and had always been disappointed when he found it didn't exist.

"Yes. I guess so."

"You don't sound sure."

"I'm sure. It's just . . ."

"Just what?" he prompted.

"I don't want to sound like I'm being unreasonable."

He recognized her lingering fear that she would somehow offend him if she established her own ground rules. He hastened to assure her, "You won't. Go ahead and tell me what's on your mind."

"I think we should try as much as possible to keep our personal lives separate from our professional lives. I don't want things to get tangled up."

He thought briefly of Gordon Stratton, and what Macon's reaction would likely be when she discovered the truth. He felt a surge of relief. He could put off telling her until she was more comfortable around him. Perhaps he'd get her to forgive him for the deception. "I'll try, but I have to make a confession."

"What?"

"I get turned on when I see you in business suits."

Shock registered in the depths of her eyes. "Are you serious?"

"As a heart attack."

Macon laughed. A light made its way back into her eyes. "Can I make a confession of my own?"

"Sure."

He could tell she was uncomfortable, but she held his gaze. "I get turned on when I think of what's under yours. The suits that is."

He leaned back on his heels and laughed. "You are a delight, Ms. Stratton."

Macon fidgeted on the sofa. "Would you like me to wear something else to the office?"

He shook his head. "God, no! If your business suits affect me like this, I can just image what would happen if I saw you in jeans and a T-shirt. I'd probably ravish you."

Jacob watched, entranced as the delicate pink in her face deepened to a heated flush. "No more of that, Jacob. I think you'd better turn the lights on."

He saluted her. "Yes, Kemosabe."

Macon slipped off the couch and was halfway to the door before she glanced back at him. "I'll make some more coffee while you cool off. The balcony's over there if you need a gust of fresh air."

Eleven

Macon drummed her fingers on top of the file cabinet next to Maylene's desk as she waited for the coffee to brew. She was still trying to regain her equilibrium in the wake of Jacob's heated kiss, and his unexpected reaction to their conversation. There was no doubt that their relationship had taken an irrevocable turn. She'd undoubtedly feel better if she knew where they were headed. She had a sneaking suspicion they were about to fall off a cliff neither of them had anticipated. She was so deep in thought, she barely noticed the shrill ring of the telephone.

She snatched up the receiver on the fifth ring. She had contemplated surrendering the call to the answering machine's domain, but knew a call at this late hour must be important. "Hello."

"Macon, thank God I caught you."

She recognized Nathaniel Baldwin's gravelly voice right away. He sounded frantic. "Nat! What on earth is wrong?"

"Is it true about Jacob Blackfort?"

Macon felt the hairs on her neck stand up. The scene in Chap Chapman's office had caused considerable gossip, and she'd fielded a solid number of phone calls as a result, but Nat didn't sound curious, he sounded worried. "Yes, it's true."

Nat's muttered curse was vivid. "What the hell are you thinking, Macon? Do you have any idea who this character is?"

"I think you're overreacting."

"Overreacting! Hell, Macon, what did he tell you?"

"What do you mean what did he tell me?"

"I don't know what this guy said to dupe you into a relationship with him, but you're playing with fire. Believe me, the important thing is that you get rid of that guy. Fast."

Macon felt her temper start to heat. "I don't really think this is any of your business, Nat."

"The hell it isn't. I've been trying to call you all damned afternoon and couldn't get you. Did you actually make it with him in the Senate elevator?"

Macon gasped. "That is completely out of line, Nat Baldwin."

"There are rumors all over town. Are you out of your mind?"

"Calm down," she snapped, rapidly growing irritated with the waspish tone in Nat's voice and what constituted a serious invasion of her privacy. Friend or not, Nat Baldwin had no right to question her private or professional life. "Why are you so upset?"

"Do you know who this guy is?"

Macon hesitated, unsure of how much Nat knew. "Do you?"

"Hell, yeah, I know. He just bought out Dom Petrie's operation in Cheyenne. He's using it as a cover to extend his influence in Washington."

Macon darted a glance toward the door of her office. She could see Jacob silhouetted against the frosted glass. He hadn't budged from the couch.

She turned her back to the office door and cradled the phone against her ear. "You think so?"

"I know so. I talked to Dom myself. He said this guy is ruthless, dangerous, and serious trouble. Do you know he's got international holdings and accounts in half-a-dozen third-world mud holes?"

Macon frowned at the anxious edge in Nat's voice. "Yes. I knew that. What does that have to do with me, Nat?"

"Hell. You don't want anything to do with this guy. Not anything. The only reason he's crashing on you is to milk you for your contacts in Washington."

"That's why most people crash on me. I seem to recall you didn't have any trouble with it when you needed a job in Washington after you graduated."

"Cut it out. This isn't funny. This guy is bad news. I'm your friend, and I'm worried."

She shifted the phone to her other shoulder, casting a second worried glance at the door to her office. Jacob had evidently opened the balcony door. She heard the distinct sounds of Washington traffic drifting in on a cool current of air. At the sound of a horn blast in the distance, Macon shivered, clutching the phone more tightly in her hand. "Look, Nat. I appreciate the call, but I'm perfectly capable of taking care of myself. I've been doing it for a long time. I—"

"This isn't a joke. This is serious stuff. If you're smart, you won't believe a word he tells you. Not one."

She leaned her head back against the wall. "I'm very tired, and I don't want to argue with you. You ought to know me well enough to know I'm not going to just swallow anything Blackfort tells me—without a good reason. I know him, Nat Don't worry."

"He's slick. He's been known to trump up all kinds of stories to get what he wants."

"For heaven's sakes. I just—" She stopped short of telling Nat she'd just met Jacob. "—I'm just dating him. I'm not going to sign my life over to him."

"Yeah, well, just be careful. I mean really, really careful. Don't trust him, Macon. I'm serious."

"I can tell." There was a long pause. Macon wasn't even sure he was still on the other end of the phone. "Nat?"

"Yeah?"

"You still haven't answered my question. Where did you hear about the incident at the Russell building?"

"I'm a reporter. I have sources."

"Nat, I don't think—"

"Look. I have a folder of stuff I want you to look at. Can you meet me Thursday night."

"Sure. I'll come by your office."

"No!" He sounded panicky at the suggestion.

"Why not?"

"Just because. We should meet somewhere neutral."

"This is silly."

"It isn't, Macon. Just say you'll meet me Thursday after work."

"All right," she grumbled. "Where?"

"Lincoln Memorial."

"Should I wear a trench coat and dark glasses?"

"Cut it out. I'm not kidding around."

Macon was too tired, and too irritated, to argue. "All right, Nat. I'll meet you Thursday. How about six-thirty?"

"That's fine. And Macon?"

"Yes?"

"Don't tell anyone I called, okay?"

"I won't. Good-bye."

"Yeah. Bye."

Macon waited until she heard the dial tone before she hung up the receiver and frowned at it. Nat hadn't even closed with his usual glib "Bye-bye, Babe. See you at the polls." She had always been close to Nat, considered him one of her closest friends in Washington, but even so, the call was strange. He had sounded genuinely upset by her association with Jacob, and she was more than a little distressed that he already knew so much about Jacob's supposed background. The Secret Service had gone to extraordinary lengths, it seemed, to give Jacob an ironclad cover.

Still, it bothered her that Nat had been so disturbed. It only served to reinforce her suspicion that Jacob wasn't telling her the whole story about her involvement in the case. Briefly, she contemplated marching into her office and demanding a few answers, but she doubted he'd give them to her.

The gurgling coffee pot hauled her thoughts back to the present. She jerked away from the wall, reaching for two mugs. She would have plenty of time to contemplate Nat's phone call before Thursday evening. She filled both mugs with the steaming coffee, then turned back toward her office with one in each hand. She nearly dropped them when she found Jacob lounging in her doorway, watching her through half-lidded eyes.

"Who was on the phone?" he asked.

She searched her mind for an appropriate answer. Had she said Nat's name during the conversation? Had Jacob heard her? "Nat Baldwin," she said.

He strolled across the office to take one of the mugs from her. To her relief, he seemed satisfied with the simple answer. He studied her over the rim of the mug as he took a long sip of the coffee. "Are you sure you're all right?" he asked. "You look a little upset."

Macon sat on the edge of May's desk. "No, no. I'm fine. Really."

His gaze was speculative, but he didn't comment. "You'd tell me if something was wrong?"

"Yes."

He paused for long seconds, still studying her, before he put his mug down on the desk. "You look tired. I think maybe we should call it quits for tonight."

Macon sighed in relief. The anxiety of the last half-hour had all but used up whatever reserves of energy she had, and after the unsettling experience of Nat's phone call, she was sure she'd never survive another of Jacob's interrogations. "I think that's an excellent idea. I'm exhausted all of a sudden."

"The next couple of days are really hectic for me. I won't be able to see you outside of business hours."

She couldn't have been more relieved. She needed time to think through the startling attraction she felt for this man and determine how best to deal with it. "I understand."

"Saturday's okay, though. How about if I pick

you up at your place around ten and we go to lunch somewhere."

Macon mentally flipped through her calendar. "No," she said slowly. "I can't on Saturday. I have plans."

A frown flickered over Jacob's face. "What kind of plans?"

A brief recollection of Nat's anxious tone tripped through her thoughts. She found herself resenting Jacob's demanding tone. "Just plans," she said.

He stared at her a minute. "Aren't you going to tell me?"

She shook her head, her frayed nerve endings quickly drawing taut at his adversarial tone. "No. No, I'm not. I don't see that it's any of your business." He uttered a vivid curse. She frowned at him. "There's no need to be crude."

Jacob glared back at her. "After what just happened," he jabbed a finger in the direction of her office door, "you're telling me you have plans that are none of my business? Damn, Macon, the air you breathe is my business."

She shifted uncomfortably on the desk. "You don't own me."

"Would it surprise you to find out that I want to?"

She stared at him. "What?"

"I want to own you," he said, placing a warm hand on either side of her waist, nudging her knees apart so he could stand between her thighs. He bent his head to brush a soft kiss over her still-swollen mouth. "I want to own your scent." He tightened his hands on her waist. "The way you feel. I want to know when I see you every morning that I have the right to touch your hair, to kiss you." He kissed her again, more thoroughly. "I want to know that I'm the only one who has the right to look at your legs and think they're the sexiest pair I've ever seen."

"Jacob." His name was a feeble protest at best, and Macon's head fell back, yielding to the gentle persuasion of his mouth on her jaw line.

He trailed his lips along her jaw and settled on the curve of her ear. His voice was hot and wet, a silken web of seduction. "I want to know that I own your thoughts just like you own mine."

Macon shuddered. "You do," she whispered. "I think—" She shivered when he nipped at her earlobe. "I think about you all the time."

"Even Saturday?" he prompted.

She sagged into him, the fight draining out of her. "Would you like—" She paused when his tongue traced the whorl of her ear. "—would you like to come along?" The instant she said the words, she quivered at the thought of how easily Jacob could manipulate her, how easily he'd won the small contest of wills. She was sinking too deep, too fast. The thought made her summon the strength to push him away. And she would have, too, if he hadn't settled his mouth on hers.

Jacob kissed her, a leisurely, exploratory, thorough kiss. He finally lifted his head and traced a finger on the wet curve of her lower lip. "What time should I pick you up?"

Twelve

Jacob turned into Macon's driveway on Saturday morning at eight-thirty. He switched off the ignition, then idly tapped his fingers on the steering wheel. Except for the one meeting she'd taken him to on the Hill, he hadn't seen her since that night in her office. On the phone, her tone had been brisk, professional, giving no hint of the intimacy they'd shared. She showed none of the turmoil that had become almost second nature to him in the three days since he'd last seen her. He had been almost shocked when she'd phoned his office to remind him about their date.

Macon still had not told him where they were going, or what mysterious plans she had made for that morning, and he had not been able to shake the suspicion that she was deliberately holding out on him, seeking, in some way, to test him. Resolutely, he levered himself out of the car. If Macon Stratton thought she could scare him off with whatever game she was playing, then she hadn't counted on one thing. Deep in the night, when he was lying in bed, unable to sleep when his mind was filled with erotic fantasies of what she would feel like beneath him, on top of him, around him, he had admitted that he was obsessed with her. There wasn't a thing in the world she could do to change that.

He vaulted up the stairs, then knocked on her door. The sooner she got that into her head, the better off they'd be.

Macon opened the door a few seconds later. The sight of her in well-worn blue jeans and a faded blue sweatshirt was in startling contrast to his mental picture of her in silk and lace and the prim tailored lines of her business suits. He felt his stomach lurch, as an unexpected surge of desire shot through his system. By the time his hungry gaze reached her face, he realized that she looked surprised to see him. "Hello," she said. "I wasn't sure you'd come."

Jacob didn't even bother to push his way into the house before he pulled her into his arms and covered her mouth with a deep, ravenous kiss. He plundered her lips until she melted into him and kissed him back. He edged a hand under the hem of her sweatshirt to press her tightly against him with a hand at the small of her back. When he finally lifted his head, he was absurdly pleased at the flushed look on her face. "What made you think I wouldn't come?" he asked.

Macon pulled away from him, slowly, pausing to adjust her sweatshirt, before she met his gaze again. She cleared her throat. "I . . . you just didn't seem very thrilled about it yesterday on the phone."

He leaned against the door frame. "What I wasn't thrilled about was the idea that I'd had to wait so long to see you again."

She stared at him. "Oh."

"Yeah." He smiled a slow, sultry smile. "Oh."

"Well, then," she said, with what he suspected was forced brightness. "I'd guess we'd better go."

She grabbed her coat from the hall tree, then dashed past him. She pulled the jacket on as she unlocked her car. As he sauntered down the stairs, Jacob's gaze roamed over the curve of her legs, outlined in the slim-fitting blue jeans. He smiled appreciatively. She was jittery, nervous, as anxious as the sea in the first whispers of a rising storm. And damnation, he wanted her. Jacob gave her a knowing look before sliding into the passenger seat of her car. He noted, with no small amount of satisfaction, that her fingers shook when she started the ignition.

Twenty minutes later, when Macon turned onto the Beltway and headed for the Old Town Alexandria public library, she finally allowed herself a surreptitious glance at Jacob's hard profile. He hadn't spoken since he'd settled his large frame into the passenger seat of her car. He seemed content to simply watch the passing scenery, unconcerned with Macon's destination or agenda.

The effects of three days' worth of separation had done nothing, she'd discovered, to abate the growing attraction she felt for Jacob Blackfort. Clad now in low-slung, loose-fitting white jeans, a black turtleneck and faded gray denim jacket, he looked no less intimidating, no less powerful, no less devastating than he had in his well-tailored business suits. Even now, she had to fight the urge to reach out and lay a hand on his knee.

From the minute he'd kissed her that morning, she'd known she'd lost the battle to simply force him out of her mind, to set aside the memory of his hands, his mouth, his presence, where they couldn't threaten her ordered existence. The realization had put her on edge. She caught herself gripping the steering wheel with a tight, white-knuckled grasp. Finger by finger, she willed her hands to relax, waiting until she was certain she could speak calmly before she tried to talk to him. "Were you able to find out anything more since we last spoke?" she asked, wincing at the frosty tone in her own voice.

Jacob shot her a wry smile. "About the case you mean?" Macon nodded. He shrugged. "After you agreed to help, there were several loose ends to tie up. I wanted to ensure that my cover was iron-clad, that no suspicions would be raised about you as a result of your relationship with me."

She wondered if she had imagined the slight change in inflection in his deep voice when he said "relationship." She ran her tongue over the curve of her lips to moisten them. "I see. I wasn't aware it was so complicated."

Jacob laid his hand on hers where it rested on the steering wheel. She jumped at the feel of his warm fingers as he pulled her hand away from the steering wheel and into his lap. "I don't want to talk about work today. Tell me what you've been doing."

Macon swallowed. Her hand rested on the corded strength of his thigh, held fast in the warm grasp of his fingers. She felt her palm start to sweat. "The usual," she said, struggling to keep her voice calm. "I mapped out two media campaigns, fought with six different vendors, and tried to spin a potentially volatile situation for one of my congressional clients in California." She flashed him a brief smile. "I'd say it was a pretty typical week." *Except for the fact that every*

*second was consumed by thoughts of you and what
you're doing to me.*

Jacob rubbed his thumb over her hand. "Do
you want to know what my week was like?"

"I thought you didn't want to talk about work."

"I don't," he said. "I want to talk about how I
thought about you all the time. How I lay in bed
and remembered what your skin felt like under
my hands."

Her mouth went dry. "Jacob!"

He ignored her. "How I sat in my office and
stared at the walls and pictured you everywhere,
on my desk, in my chair, on my lap." He fixed
her with a hard stare, made more acute by the
startling blue color of his eyes, visible even in her
peripheral vision. "I thought about kissing you,
about touching you, about the way you're starting
to bewitch me."

"Jacob, I—"

"And I admitted to myself that I can't pretend
I'm not involved in this relationship." He
squeezed her hand. "I'm very involved, Macon.
Seriously involved."

"You promised you wouldn't push me." She
pulled her hand away and gripped the steering
wheel, guiding the car along the exit ramp.

"I promised I wouldn't push you to go to bed
with me," he said, "and I intend to keep that
promise."

"Then what do you call this."

"I didn't say I wouldn't try to get you to change
your mind."

Macon jerked her car into the parking lot of
the library, and came to an abrupt stop in a parking space. "We're here," she said, her voice
sounding breathless, agitated.

Jacob leaned over and kissed her, a hard, brief kiss. "Yeah, we're here."

She hurried out of the car, then didn't even wait to see if he was following her as she fled toward the crowded safety of the library.

Jacob shut the car door with a deliberate *click*. A brief smile tugged at the corner of his mouth as he watched her hurry up the brick steps. Sometime, deep in the night, he'd decided that his only chance lay in keeping her off balance. Macon Stratton liked being in control. She liked being more sedate, and more proper, and more disciplined than everyone around her. Jacob knew he wouldn't make any progress with her unless he could keep her scrambling for her equilibrium.

As he watched her fumble with the enormous brass and walnut door, he knew that whatever she was, she was most definitely off balance.

By the time he was seated with his back against the wall, watching Macon read to a group of twenty-five Down's Syndrome children, she wasn't the only one off balance. Jacob had been completely, utterly, unprepared for what awaited him inside the library. Nothing in her background file, nothing in his experience with her, had readied him for the sight of Macon Stratton seated cross-legged on the floor, surrounded by a sea of small faces and eager questions. It was obvious, even from his vantage point by the door, that the children adored her.

From the moment they had stepped into the tiny, well-lit, room, little squirming bodies had flocked around her. Jacob had not been afforded more than a passing glance by the teeming throng of Macon's young admirers.

For the next two hours, he had watched as she read stories and played games designed to help the children's motor skills and encourage their participation. The oldest in the group could not have been more than seven or eight years old. Jacob's stomach had been slowly tightening into a hard, cold lump as he sat on the edge of the room and watched the children laughing with Macon.

He had known from the instant they'd walked "to the room that his instincts had been correct. Macon had been testing him, indeed, hoping to judge his reaction to the children and find him wanting. She was still determined to prove that he was too much of a risk for her. He had quickly brushed aside the cold knot of resentment that realization had caused, in light of the more pressing urgency of his reaction to a room full of kids.

She could have asked almost anything of him, anything at all, and he would not have been fazed. But the sight, the sound of her enjoying the group of children was tying him into knots. Macon should have children, probably a half-dozen or so. At the thought, his breathing became shallow. The blood pounded in his ears. Macon was the kind of woman who deserved, needed, a family with a house full of kids and a husband who came home every night. No amount of wanting her, no amount of desire and longing and need, was going to change the fact that he couldn't give her that.

With the demands of his career as an excuse, he'd decided long ago that he could not, would not, have a family. It wouldn't be fair. His wife, his children would have to go days, perhaps weeks on end with no idea of his whereabouts. But there, in the little room with the sun shining through the windows and the bunnies and blocks and puzzles and pictures of childhood scattered about in delightful chaos, Jacob Blackfort took a long look inside the black, empty cavern of his soul.

And he saw the images of his own family, the one he still denied having, the one he'd tried to push from his mind, from his heart. He saw the pained look on his father's face the last time they'd argued, he heard the hurt in his mother's voice as she asked him to come home, to try again. He felt the anguished tears his sisters had cried when he'd walked out the door for the last time. It was dark in that cavern. Dark and frightening and unbearable. Resolutely, he slammed the door shut, unwilling to look any longer. Afraid he'd crumble if he did.

He was on the verge of stalking from the room when he felt a tug on the leg of his jeans. A glance down confirmed his worst suspicion. A little girl, no more than two years old, was clutching a worn yellow blanket. She stared at him with the largest eyes he'd ever seen. She smiled at him as she lifted her arms and said, "Up peas."

Jacob had to search his mind for a minute, vaguely thinking that he'd heard of English peas and black-eyed peas, but never up peas, before he remembered that two-year-olds tended to speak a language of dropped consonants and slurred vowels. He stared at the tiny, golden-haired child with something akin to panic. "You want up?"

She nodded. "Up peas."

Jacob pointed to Macon. "Don't you want to hear the story?"

She shook her head. "Up."

Women really were all the same, he thought. Cajolery hadn't worked, so she'd switched to a demand. He thought about telling her no, but at that instant, he caught Macon's glance above the heads of her devoted crowd. She was watching him, with an indecipherable question in the depths of her blue eyes. Jacob picked up the little girl, then settled her on his lap. She rewarded him with a bright smile before she dropped her head against his chest and popped her fat little thumb into her mouth. Macon looked away.

The greedy sucking sounds his little charge was making with her thumb soon faded. Jacob glanced down to find the child asleep on his lap. The knot in his stomach grew tighter. Another hour passed, an hour that felt like a lifetime, before reading group ended and parents started to arrive. In a bustle of coats and mittens and waves good-bye, with promises to see them in two weeks, and sloppy, loving kisses, Macon saw each child out the door. She waited until the last one had pressed a half-eaten sucker into her hand with an adoring smile as she raced out the door, before she turned to look at Jacob.

The little girl in his arms continued to sleep. He met Macon's gaze as she crossed the room and lifted the child from his lap. "Thank you," she said, her voice quiet, her expression unreadable, "for taking care of Natalie." Macon shifted the child to her shoulder. "Her mother works in the library. Natalie is really too young to be in the reading group, but I didn't have the heart to turn her away when I know her mother needs the money she saves on day care."

Jacob felt a sudden chill at the loss of the child's

heat against his chest. He resisted the urge to shiver. He stood up instead. "No problem," he said.

Macon wrapped Natalie's blanket around her tiny shoulders. "I hope you weren't terribly bored over here by yourself, but you did insist on coming and I—"

"Macon," he said, linking his fingers beneath her elbow. "You're jabbering."

She looked offended. "I am not. I never jabber."

"You are." He started walking with her toward the door. "Are you through here?"

She nodded. "Yes. Natalie's mother straightens up the room in exchange for Natalie's participation in reading group."

He opened the door. "Good. I'm ready to leave."

She shot him a startled glance. "Jacob, are you angry?"

"No."

"You sound angry."

"I'm not."

She hesitated. "You're the one who insisted on coming."

He clenched his jaw. "I'm not angry."

"Well, I think—"

"Macon," he said, cutting off her protest. "I'm going to wait for you by the car."

She studied him for a minute before she nodded. "All right. Let me just find Natalie's mother."

When she finally joined him at the car ten minutes later, he was beginning to feel, at least in part, that his equilibrium had been restored. The distance from the children had done wonders to put the world back into perspective, to unwind some of the cold tension in his belly. Macon met his gaze over the top of her blue Honda as she unlocked the automatic doors. "Are you sure you're all right?" she asked.

He pulled open his door, then sank gratefully into the bucket seat. "Fine. I'm fine."

Macon turned to look at him as she fastened her seat belt. "You're sure you're not angry?"

"I told you. I'm not mad."

She hesitated a few seconds longer before she shrugged, then started the car before backing out of her space. They were halfway to her house before he felt like he could speak again. "I don't have much experience with children," he said, wondering if she had any idea of the magnitude of the statement.

She looked at him abruptly. "The way you handled Natalie, I would have thought you were a natural."

He shook his head. "My sisters have kids, but I've never seen them."

Macon's fingers tightened on the steering wheel. She listened to the sound of Jacob's breathing. She remembered his abrupt change of conversation when they'd discussed his family that night in her office. She waited until it became obvious he wasn't going to speak again. "Do you want to talk about it?"

He met her gaze then. The look in his eyes was so vulnerable, so intense, she nearly started to cry. He shook his head. "Not now. When we get home. Okay?"

Macon reached over to cover his hand with hers. It was a purely reflexive action, meant to comfort, to soothe. She was unprepared for the crushing, bruising force of his fingers clamping onto hers. She didn't pull her hand away, though, merely shifted it to lace her fingers through his. They drove the rest of the way to her house in silence.

They turned into the driveway, and she shut off the engine, turning to look at him. She was not surprised, but in fact relieved, when Jacob pulled her across the seat and buried his mouth on hers.

Thirteen

Jacob kissed her with a slow, savage hunger that begged for warmth and solace. He nearly groaned in relief when Macon kissed him back as she reached up to cup the plane of his face with her soft, warm hand. She ran her thumb over the curve of his cheekbone before she tentatively ended the kiss and pulled away. He let out a ragged gasp.

"I put some soup on before we left," she said. "Do you want to come inside?"

What he wanted was to flee the memories that were plaguing him with the merciless power of a hurricane-force gale. What he wanted was to get into his car, drive away, and never again see this woman who was tossing him into such heated, chaotic turmoil. What he wanted was to ravish her there, in the car, burying himself inside of her until he didn't have to think about what it meant to care for people, for people to matter. He nodded. "All right."

Macon slipped from the car. She worked her way up the walk, pausing twice to see if he was following her. She opened the door and flipped on the hall light, motioning Jacob toward the living room. "We can eat in there. I'll bring you your soup."

He walked into the living room and dropped down on the couch, feeling like he'd just trudged a hundred miles across a desert in search of water. He couldn't remember the last time such a simple experience, something so insignificant as seeing Macon in a room full of children, had affected him like this. He felt the sweat on his forehead and seriously contemplated the notion that he might be going insane.

Macon came into the living room carrying a tray and set it on the coffee table. She regarded him with a worried look before she pressed a warm bowl into his hands and took the seat opposite him. "It's lentil. I hope that's all right," she said.

He nodded. It could be hemlock, and he wouldn't care. He took several fortifying swallows of the hearty broth before he met her gaze again. "You think I'm nuts, don't you?"

She shook her head and put her bowl down on the table. "I think you're very upset about something. That doesn't make you nuts."

The breath drained out of him. Jacob dropped his head back, against the sofa. "It was seeing you with those kids that undid me."

She swallowed another spoonful of soup. "I should have warned you that they were Down's Syndrome children. That can be a little over-whelming for a person to take in all at once."

He shook his head. "It wasn't that. It had nothing to do with that."

Macon looked at him in surprise. "But I thought—"

"You thought it would disturb me to be with those kids and that's why you took me in the first place. Isn't it?"

Her face colored. "No, I—"

He fixed her with an impaling glare. "At least tell me the truth."

Macon hesitated only briefly before she nodded. "All right. Yes, I suppose it's true. You were so insistent on going. So demanding that I share my plans with you. I guess in the back of my mind, I expected you to have a problem with the children."

He reached for the glass of Diet Pepsi she'd placed on a coaster by his knee and took a long swallow, waiting until the bubbles disappeared on his tongue. "It could have been any group of kids, and I probably would have still gone into a tailspin."

"Don't you like children?"

He shrugged. "I never thought about it before. It's the fact that you like children that got to me."

She frowned. "What on earth are you talking about?"

Leaning forward on the sofa, he propped his elbows on his knees. "In the last two days, I had made a decision that I was going to do whatever it took to have you."

Her eyes widened. "What?"

He nodded. "It's true. But then I saw you with those kids. You should have at least a half-dozen, do you know that?"

Macon stared at him. "I do love children, and I do want to have some one day, but I can't understand why you—"

"Because I'm not going to have any. Not ever."

"You sound very sure about that."

He studied her, exhaling a long breath. "I lied to you about my family, you know?"

She nodded. "So I gathered. Today was the first time I'd ever heard you talk about them."

"They live in Wyoming. All except my sister Blu who lives in Colorado with her husband and three kids."

"Why did you tell me you don't have a family?"

"Because I don't. Not in the sense that I have one that claims me."

Macon rubbed her palms on her thighs and watched him. "Did something happen?"

He snorted, the cold knot in his stomach had finally given way to a hot lump of coal that seared his insides and tore at his gut. "Yeah. Something happened."

"Jacob?"

He shook his head. "It's nothing I need to repeat. It's all very sordid and ugly, and if I told you, you'd probably be as appalled with me as they are."

Macon got up and walked around the coffee table, taking the seat next to him. She reached over and took his hand. "I'm sure it couldn't have been that bad."

He looked away. "It was that bad. Suffice it to say, I'd never planned on having a family. As badly as I screwed up the first one, I'm sure I'd screw up the second one too."

"I think you're being very hard on yourself."

He met her gaze again and pulled her into his arms. "One day," he said, "one day, I'll explain it to you. I just can't right now."

"You don't have to explain anything," she said quietly.

He thought briefly of the look of disgust he'd last seen on his father's face. Tried to picture the same look on Macon's delicate features and felt the twisting begin in his stomach all over again. "Macon?"

She tipped her head and looked at him. "Yes?"

"Will it be all right if we just sit here a while. Like this?" He felt like an idiot for asking. Even to himself he sounded like a child seeking comfort.

Macon reached up and pushed a lock of his hair off his forehead with a brief smile. "I'd like that," she whispered.

Fourteen

Macon gritted her teeth at eleven-thirty Monday morning when the sound of drilling came from the extra office and intruded on her phone conversation. She and Jacob had remained on the sofa in her living room for the better part of Saturday afternoon. He had seemed in need of her comfort, and she had given it, feeling even closer to him than she had before. She had felt a few brief moments of panic when she realized how deeply he affected her, but nothing could have prevented her from offering him the solace he seemed to find in her nearness.

By late Saturday afternoon, he had appeared to regain some of his composure. They had not spoken again of his family, and bit by bit, Macon had seen him rebuild the careful control he always maintained. She had not, however, been able to dismiss images of the boyish vulnerability despite her best efforts. When he'd finally left on Saturday, she had felt almost wounded by the emotional stress of the afternoon, and that was why his Sunday afternoon phone call had come as such a surprise.

In a few terse sentences, Jacob had explained that he'd decided to move into the extra office in her suite, and would do so on Monday morn-

ing. No amount of arguing on her part had dis-
suaded him. There had been no traces of the sensitive man she'd seen the afternoon before. He
was a hard negotiator on Sunday afternoon.

He'd argued, persuasively, that it was the most
logical place for him to be. That it would certainly
give their fictitious relationship added credibility
in the eyes of the Washington insiders. Macon
had grudgingly obliged only after he'd promised
not to disrupt her work day when he moved in.
Worse, she'd had to spend the morning accepting
knowing looks from Maylene and watching as the
older woman preened beneath Jacob's solicitous
attentions.

Macon turned and contemplated the view out
her window. She'd be lying to herself if she didn't
allow that the new personal closeness she felt to
Jacob was even more upsetting than his proximity.
She was used to men losing interest when she
told them she had no intention of taking a physical relationship past a certain point. That had, in
fact, been the primary wedge that had ended her
relationship with Adrian Snell. He'd wanted sex,
and she hadn't. It was as simple as that.

But nothing was simple with Jacob Blackfort.
He had been right when he'd accused her of trying to push him away by taking him to the library
on Saturday. She had been sure he would react
poorly to the children. Instead, his rare attack of
vulnerability had served only to bind her closer
to him in a deep emotional sense that she almost
resented. He was sucking her into something she
wasn't certain she'd survive. It was disconcerting.
It was unsettling. It was scary as hell.

She had known when he called her on Sunday
that having him in her office could very well

prove to be too much for her. With him constantly under foot, and serving as her escort all over Washington, she wasn't sure she could handle the emotional pressure of holding him at arm's length. She was sure, however, that arm's length was the only safe place for him to be.

The drill sounded again, breaking into her brooding reverie, and Macon felt a growing surge of irritation. She concluded her conversation, slammed her pen down on her legal pad and pushed her chair back, intent on giving Jacob Blackfort a solid piece of her mind.

He was leaning against the door of her office, watching her. He looked incredibly, criminally, sexy in his black jeans and baggy gray sweatshirt. He flashed her a broad grin. "Sorry about the noise."

She frowned at him. "You weren't supposed to disrupt my day. Remember?"

"I'm hanging pictures."

"Pictures! Don't you think that's going a bit far. It isn't as if you're going to be here long."

"Pictures give the impression of longevity, even when there's nothing in the drawers." He pushed away from the door and strolled across the office to her desk. He placed his hands on her upper arms and rubbed in a slow caress. "Quit frowning like that. I'm through with the drilling. Everything's in."

Macon sighed. He smelled spicy and clean and decadently fresh all at the same time, and she forcibly pushed aside the memories the mere scent of him stirred up in her insides. "I'm sorry I'm such a grouch. I'm not having the best day." She hoped he didn't notice the catch in her voice. She looked at him through narrow eyes. "How are you feeling?"

He shrugged, effectively slamming the door on the subject of his Saturday behavior. "Fine. Want to break for lunch?"

"I don't think I have time."

Jacob sat on the edge of her desk and pulled her into the wedge of his thighs. He bent his head to nuzzle her throat. "Want to stay here and neck instead?"

She pushed at his shoulders. "Jacob! Stop that." Even to her, the protest sounded half-hearted.

"Damn but you taste good."

She pushed harder, knowing she'd succumb to his gentle persuasion if she didn't put some distance between them. "I told you, Jacob. I don't want to pursue this aspect of our relationship during business hours. Especially not when you're right here in my office." She looked anxiously at the door. "Someone might come in."

Jacob leered at her. "Does that mean you're willing to talk about pursuing it after business hours? I do know the way to your house, you know."

She ignored him and reached for a piece of paper on her desk. "I made this list for you." She pressed it against his chest, shooting him a warning look.

His fingers curled into the paper, but he never took his eyes off her. "What is it?"

"People I think you should look into. I have an invitation on my desk from the American Association of Political Consultants for their annual meeting and reception two weeks from Saturday. I think we should go."

"Why, Ms. Stratton," he said, a twinkle in his blue eyes. "Are you asking me for a date?"

She thought about reminding him what had happened the last time he'd accompanied her on a 'date,' but something in the inflexible look in his eyes had warned her from broaching the subject. She frowned at him instead. "Most, if not all, of the people on that list will be in attendance. It will give you an excellent opportunity to observe them in a non-working environment."

He shrugged. "All right. What's the attire?"

"Black tie. The color scheme is right up your alley. Do you own a tuxedo?"

"Yeah, no problem."

She nodded. "Fine. You can meet me there. It's at the Capitol Hilton." Now if you don't mind, I'd like to get back to work."

"Sure I can't talk you into lunch?"

"Positive." She paused and gave him a weak smile. "I told you I was a grouch today."

He grinned at her. "So you did. I suppose I should feel good and duly warned."

"I'm sorry. I'm just really under the pile."

"Anything I can help with?"

She shook her head. "Not unless you want to shake down a couple of clients for the money they owe us. I can't front media buys for two races because we're short on cash. I'm trying to piece together the funds, and I've got to get this jerk over at Chisholm Marketing to get on the stick and make Chap's video. Other than that I—"

"I'll do that."

"What?"

"The video. I'll take care of it. Do you have the guy's number?"

"Jacob, you can't—"

"Sure I can. Is there more involved to this than calling the guy and threatening to pull the contract if he doesn't deliver by a certain date?"

"You have to coordinate his schedule with Chap's."

He shrugged. "The senator expects to be hearing from me. It will give me credibility, and it will take a burden off your desk." He held his hand out. "Fork over the file, Kemosabe."

Macon shook her head. "I don't know, Jacob."

"Don't you think I can handle it?"

"It isn't that. It's just—"

"Just that you're used to doing everything yourself and would rather kill yourself working than turn over some mundane task to a novice."

She sighed and picked up a thick blue folder. "His name is Fred Chisholm." She handed the folder to him. "Happy reading."

He bent his head and kissed her briefly. "I'll buzz you if I run into trouble."

It wasn't until late that afternoon that Macon learned what trouble really was. She was on her way to a meeting, and decided to stick her head in Jacob's door and tell him she was going out. Maylene shot her a wry look as she walked across the reception area.

"Going somewhere?" May prodded.

Macon paused by May's desk and scooped up a stack of phone messages, idly leafing through them. "I have a meeting with Phil Henson. I was going to let Mr. Blackfort know I'll be out of the office for a while."

May tapped a red nail on her desk. "Mr. Blackfort is certainly fitting in quite nicely around here, don't you think?"

Macon met her gaze. "Are you suggesting something?"

"Only that this extra office has been empty a long time. It's nice to have someone rattling around in there." She paused and reached for a folder. "He handled the problem with Fred Chisholm. Chap's shooting his video on Tuesday."

Macon accepted the folder. "Very efficient."

"It would have taken you two days to get results with Chisholm."

"Fred Chisholm thinks I don't know anything because I'm a woman. Jacob is quite good at threatening people. I'm certain Fred took him seriously."

May nodded. "Who wouldn't?" she drawled.

In spite of herself, Macon smiled. "Are you meddling, May?"

"Of course I'm meddling. You've got the hottest man that ever crossed the Potomac inside your office, and you're treating him like an errand boy."

"I am not."

"I've seen the way that man looks at you, Macon. I keep looking for scorch marks on the carpet."

There might just be some, Macon thought. "Jacob and I are testing the waters. It might work out, and it might not. It's nothing to get overly excited about."

"The best way to test the waters is to jump right in."

"Then I'd be over my head."

"That's the point. I don't think you're ever going to let yourself go until you don't have a choice." May leaned back in her chair and looked at Macon with an expression of motherly concern. "Take a risk, Macon. Just this one time, take a risk. You might regret it for the rest of your life if you don't."

A brief vision of a prince standing on her balcony citing words of wisdom popped into Macon's head, and she muttered, "There's a whole different world outside the bedroom window."

"What?"

"Oh." She looked at May. "Nothing. I was just talking to myself." Macon put the phone messages down. "Who knows? Maybe you're right."

May's eyes widened. "Are you saying what I think you're saying?"

"I'm saying that maybe you're right. That's all." She set her briefcase on the edge of May's desk. "I'm going to tell Jacob I'll be out of the office for a while." Feeling reckless, she added. "Hold all calls will you, May?"

Macon almost laughed at the startled look on her assistant's face as she sailed into Jacob's office. At the sight of him, standing behind his desk, the phone to his ear, his big body silhouetted against the window, she froze. His face was a mask of tense irritation, and she watched as his eyes registered a flash of cold anger. Macon hesitated.

He looked up and motioned her into the office. "Look, Peter," he told the receiver. "I'm not going to discuss this with you again. Don't screw with me." Macon heard the muffled sound of shouting on the other end of the line. Jacob's fingers tightened visibly on the receiver. "No," he bit out. "Absolutely not. This conversation is over."

He slammed the phone down in its cradle so

hard, Macon flinched. "Did I catch you at a bad time?" she asked.

Jacob groaned and flopped down in his chair. "No. It wasn't anything I wasn't prepared for."

"Who were you talking to? If you don't mind my asking."

"I don't mind. It was my boss."

That seemed odd to Macon. She didn't picture Jacob responding well to authority. Of course, based on what she'd just seen, he didn't appear to respond well at all. "Is there anything I can do?"

He shook his head. "No. I'll handle it." He indicated her overcoat with a brief nod. "Are you going out?"

"Yes. I wanted to let you know I have a meeting with Phil Henson. He's a vendor I use. I'd have asked you to come along, but I didn't really think it was very pertinent."

Jacob picked up a pencil and twirled it between his fingers. "Probably not," he said, "I did want to ask you about something, though."

"Sure."

He opened the folder on his desk and pointed to a row of figures. "I noticed this while I was reviewing the Chisholm file, and I just wanted to know if this is fairly regular bookkeeping. Charlie's going to be pulling some financial records, and I would like to know what we're looking at."

Macon rounded the desk. "What do you mean?" she said, laying her hand on his shoulder and looking at the report. His muscles flexed beneath her fingers, and she barely resisted the urge to snatch her hand away.

He indicated a column with his fingers. "Why do you bill in irregular intervals?"

"You mean sometimes thirty, sometimes sixty, and sometimes ninety days?" Macon inhaled a deep breath of his cologne. It had to be criminal for a man to smell that sexy.

"Yeah."

"That is fairly standard in the industry. It has to do with when Federal Election Commission, or FEC, reports are due, and how much of the campaign costs the client wants showing up on the report. If his fundraising-to-cost ratio is odd, it could raise questions. Most of the time, the ratios only look inflated because the fundraising income hasn't caught up with the bills. Each contract is negotiated on a separate billing basis."

"How so?"

"Every time I bid a job, I negotiate payment terms separately. That way, we can keep the reports looking right."

He nodded. "Does everybody do this?"

"For the most part." She turned and sat on the edge of his desk. "FEC reports are public record. It's a favorite media pastime to go down to the FEC and pull a candidate's report. They usually don't know what they're looking at, so they tend to read things the wrong way. Delayed billing is one of the best, and only, defenses we have against the media's determination to stir up trouble. That's what makes Nat Baldwin so valuable to all of us. He knows politics, and he knows journalism. *Electioneering* is a huge boon to the industry."

Jacob leaned back in his chair and studied her. Macon forcibly restrained herself from smoothing a lock of his ink black hair off his forehead. Jacob exhaled a slow breath. "Wouldn't this make it fairly easy to move large sums of money through your books with little or no trail?"

Macon shrugged. "I guess. Some people probably do. I've never doubted that there are a lot of crooked people in this business."

At that, Jacob's brow furrowed, and Macon traced along the creases with her forefinger. "Are you upset about something?"

He captured her hand and placed a brief kiss on her fingertips. "Macon, has it never occurred to you that some of the people around you, some people you trust, might not be what they seem?"

"Are you talking about Elliot Raines again?"

He shrugged. "In a sense."

Macon shook her head. "I can't explain about Elliot. I just know—I know he's not doing what you think he is. It's an instinct thing. Like breathing."

Jacob reached for her. The next thing she knew, she was in his lap, and he was nuzzling her neck above the black velvet collar of her coat. "Ah, Macon," he whispered. "How does a person get to be Washington's Most Politically Powerful Woman without turning cynical?"

She smiled. "She decides not to. Life's no fun if you don't trust anyone."

He closed his eyes before he dropped his head onto the curve of her shoulders. "Are you going to hate me if I have to shatter a few of your illusions?"

Macon tugged on his hair until he looked at her. "Jacob, you're really upset, aren't you?"

He nodded. "I don't want to do this to you."

"Do what?"

"That's the worst of it. I don't have clearance to tell you. That's what I was arguing with Peter Quiver about."

She traced a finger along the grim curve of his

lips. "You ended that sentence with a preposition."

She saw a reluctant smile tug at his mouth. "Aren't you even a little curious about all this?"

"I'm very curious, but it won't do me any good. Will it?"

"What won't?"

"Being curious. Asking questions?"

He sighed. "No. It won't."

"So why should I dwell on it?"

His hands tightened around her waist. "I don't want to hurt you."

"I believe you."

"What if I do?"

For a moment she had a glimpse of the softer, more sensitive side of Jacob Blackfort—the side that rarely appeared and that had a devastating effect on her when it did. "You're starting to frighten me."

His breath came out in a ragged rush. "I'm sorry. Hell, I'm sorry for this whole thing." He stared at her for a moment before he bent his head and captured her lips in a long, tender kiss. When he finally lifted his head, Macon's breathing was irregular. "Just promise you'll listen to me when the time comes. Okay?"

She studied him for long seconds before she nodded. "All right," she said, but she couldn't stop the sliver of foreboding that tripped along her spine and warned her that he was about to learn a whole new meaning for "trouble."

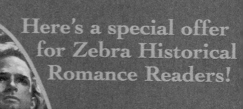

HERE'S A SPECIAL INVITATION TO ENJOY TODAY'S FINEST HISTORICAL ROMANCES— ABSOLUTELY FREE! *(a $19.96 value)*

Now you can enjoy the latest Zebra Lovegram Historical Romances without even leaving your home with our convenient Zebra Home Subscription Service. Zebra Home Subscription Service offers you the following benefits that you don't want to miss:

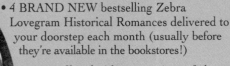

- 4 BRAND NEW bestselling Zebra Lovegram Historical Romances delivered to your doorstep each month (usually before they're available in the bookstores!)

- 20% off each title or a savings of almost $4.00 each month

- FREE home delivery

- A FREE monthly newsletter, *Zebra/Pinnacle Romance News* that features author profiles, contests, special member benefits, book previews and more

- No risks or obligations...in other words you can cancel whenever you wish with no questions asked

So join hundreds of thousands of readers who already belong to Zebra Home Subscription Service and enjoy the very best Historical Romances That Burn With The Fire of History!

And remember....there is no minimum purchase required. After you've enjoyed your initial FREE package of 4 books, you'll begin to receive monthly shipments of new Zebra titles. Each shipment will be yours to examine for 10 days and then if you decide to keep the books, you'll pay the preferred subscriber's price of just $4.00 per title. That's $16 for all 4 books with FREE home delivery! And if you want us to stop sending books, just say the word....it's that simple.

It's a no-lose proposition, so send for your 4 FREE books today!

4 FREE BOOKS

These books worth almost $20, are yours without cost or obligation when you fill out and mail this certificate.
(If the certificate is missing below, write to: Zebra Home Subscription Service, Inc., 120 Brighton Road, P.O. Box 5214, Clifton, New Jersey 07015-5214)

Complete and mail this card to receive 4 Free books!

YES! Please send me 4 Zebra Lovegram Historical Romances without cost or obligation. I understand that each month thereafter I will be able to preview 4 new Zebra Lovegram Historical Romances FREE for 10 days. Then if I decide to keep them, I will pay the money-saving preferred publisher's price of just $4.00 each...a total of $16. That's almost $4 less than the regular publisher's price, and there is never any additional charge for shipping and handling. I may return any shipment within 10 days and owe nothing, and I may cancel this subscription at any time. The 4 FREE books will be mine to keep in any case.

Name _____

Address _____ Apt. _____

City _____ State _____ Zip _____

Telephone ( ) _____

Signature _____
(If under 18, parent or guardian must sign.)

LF0596

Terms, offer and prices subject to change without notice. Subscription subject to acceptance by Zebra Home Subscription Service, Inc. Zebra Home Subscription Service, Inc. reserves the right to reject any order or cancel any subscription.

A $19.96 value... absolutely FREE with no obligation to buy anything, ever!

ZEBRA HOME SUBSCRIPTION SERVICE, INC.

120 BRIGHTON ROAD

P.O. BOX 5214

CLIFTON, NEW JERSEY 07015-5214

Fifteen

The footsteps drew closer. Macon clenched the lapels of her coat together and walked on, fighting the urge to glance back as she hurried toward her rendezvous with Nat Baldwin. It was ridiculous to think someone was following her. No one knew about the meeting unless Jacob had overheard more of her conversation than he'd let on.

She scolded her overactive imagination and hastened across the Lincoln Memorial grounds, wishing Nat had not been so secretive and alarming when he'd called.

The sun was sinking quickly, and the dim light cast long, eerie shadows on the monument grounds. The footsteps drew closer still. Macon took a deep breath and increased her pace, searching the cold, unforgiving marble pillars for a glimpse of Nat. A glimpse of anyone.

"Out for a walk, Ms. Stratton?"

She sucked in a startled breath and spun around. The dark, shadowy figure loomed behind her, his face obscured by the brim of his hat and the back lighting of a street lamp. A plume of smoke curled around his head, and he plucked the cigar from between his lips before he stepped into the light. Macon sagged against a pillar in relief. "Charlie. You scared me."

"I'm sorry." He stopped in front of her and regarded her through half-lidded eyes. "I didn't mean to frighten you."

Macon glanced around, wondering where Nat was. "What—what are you doing here?"

Charlie rolled his cigar between his fingers. "Just out for a walk," he said, his gaze intense. "You?"

She swallowed. "I'm meeting a friend here."

He took a long draw of the cigar and puffed the smoke into tiny rings. "That so?"

Macon drew herself up against the pillar, beginning to feel suspicious. "Yes. That is so. I wasn't aware my personal activities were under scrutiny, Mr. Darrow."

"Who said anything about scrutiny, Ms. Stratton? I told you. I was out for a walk. You seem a little uptight."

She squeezed the lapels of her coat, curling" her fingers into the soft wool. "You startled me is all. I thought someone was following me. Silly, wasn't it?"

Charlie shrugged. "I reckon so. There's no reason anyone would want to follow you, is there?"

"Of course not."

He pulled off his hat and spun it between his large fingers. "Well, then. I guess I'll be going. I'll tell Jacob you said hello."

Macon suppressed a shiver and watched Charlie until he disappeared between the trees. She was certain he'd been warning her with his cryptic message, and even more certain he had been following her. Her head started to throb and she realized the stress of the situation was rapidly getting the better of her.

"Macon."

Already on edge, she jumped at the sound of Nat's voice. She turned and fixed him with a hard glare. "What's this all about, Nat?"

He held up his hands. "Take it easy. Is he gone?"

"Charlie?" she asked. Nat nodded. "Yes," she said. "He's gone."

"Who was he?"

She stopped just short of telling him. There was something about the haggard look in Nat's eyes that bothered her. "Just a friend. It was a coincidence is all."

Stepping out of the shadow of the monument, Nat stooped to kiss her cheek. "How are you?"

"All this sneaking about is starting to get to me." She pulled her coat closer when a cold gust of wind whipped around the monument walls. "Are you going to tell me what this is all about?"

Nat produced a manila folder from beneath his coat. "I just want you to read this. It's information on Jacob Blackfort."

Macon accepted the folder with a slight frown. "Nat, I don't think you understand about Jacob. He's—"

"He's dangerous is what he is. Look. I don't know what he's told you. Did he give you the FBI story? Secret Service maybe?"

Macon fought hard to maintain a neutral expression. A mournful boat whistle sounded in the distance, and her eyes strayed to the darkened waters of the Potomac where the lights of the city were reflected on the rippled surface. A breeze ruffled the leaves of the towering oaks that surrounded the Memorial grounds, and she shivered at the eerie sound of the wind. "What are you talking about, Nat? I told you before that Jacob is merely here because he's helping me with some consulting work on Chap's campaign. It's that simple."

Nat snorted. "Yeah, right. Knock it off, Macon. I know you better than almost anyone. I don't know what's going on between you and Blackfort, but I do know the guy is poison. There's stuff in that file that will make your hair stand on end."

"Where did you get this?"

"That's not important. Just trust me on this. That guy is big trouble, and you could get hurt. Real bad."

Macon slipped the file inside her coat and studied Nat's expression. He looked terrible, worn out. There were dark circles under his eyes, and he looked like he hadn't shaved in nearly a week. The collar of his shirt was half in and half out and she reached up on impulse to straighten it for him. "I appreciate your concern, Nat, but I know what I'm doing." She smiled at him. "You've known me a long time. Don't you know by now that I don't just rush into things?"

He shifted from one foot to the other, studying her in the dim light. "Just don't let your heart run away with your head. Okay?"

She nodded. "Scout's honor."

Nat's breath came out in a half laugh, and he rolled his eyes heavenward. "I know you think I'm nuts with all this secrecy and all, but I just wanted you to know what you were getting yourself into. The guy's been out of the country for the last few months. I didn't find out until a couple of weeks ago that he wasn't even where he was supposed to be. I was following his activities in Europe when he disappeared. I didn't catch up with him again until he showed up in your office. Listen, I—Damn, just go home and read the file. Call me if you have any questions."

"Aren't you afraid the phones might be bugged," she quipped.

He frowned at her. "That's not funny, Macon."

"All right, all right. I was just teasing you. Why are you so edgy?"

"I just have a lot on my mind." He kissed her cheek once more. "Just call me tomorrow. Okay?"

"All right. Bye, Nat," she called to his retreating back. He lifted a ha"nd in acknowledgment, but didn't t &rn around. Macon clutched the folder beneath her coat and shivered from a chill that had nothing to do with the night air.

The short trip to her home took less than twenty minutes in the non-rush hour traffic. For the better part of the ride she thought about Nat's odd behavior. When he'd asked her if Jacob had claimed to work for the Secret Service, she'd nearly lost her composure. How much did Nat know and why? And why was he so worried that Jacob posed a threat to her? For that matter, why had Charlie been following her? How had he known she was meeting Nat at the Memorial? She was certain he'd meant to imply a warning with his words, but a warning against or about what?

The slight throbbing in her temples increased, and she cast a quick glance at the manila folder on her passenger seat. The sun had long since disappeared, and only the eerie shadows, reflected from the headlights of passing vehicles cast any light inside her car. She turned on the radio, welcoming the warm, green glow from its dial. and the familiar sounds of her favorite contemporary station.

As the music filled the car, she thought about the contents of the folder. She hoped it would contain at least a few answers to the mystery of Jacob Blackfort. She'd spend a few hours going over the contents, she decided, and if things still didn't make sense, she'd demand some answers from Jacob in the morning. Despite what Nat thought, she was sure that at least part of what Jacob had told her was true. She had been to his office. She had met several of his associates. No matter what Nat had been led to believe, by no matter whom, Jacob Blackfort was with the Secret Service. That didn't mean, however, that be didn't have plenty of explaining to do.

Feeling suddenly exhausted, she turned her car onto her street. If need be, she'd go by his office in the morning and ask him face to face. Together, they could figure out a way to reassure Nat. She didn't think they could just ignore his concerns, and she was certain she wouldn't be able to put him off much longer. He'd expect some sort of reasonable explanation from her after she'd read the folder, no matter what it contained.

Her blood turned suddenly cold a few seconds later when she turned into her driveway. Jacob's car was parked in front of her house.

Sixteen

Jacob watched from the dining room window as Macon picked her way up the walk. She stopped and looked at his car for several long seconds before she continued on toward the front door. With a heavy sigh, he released the curtain before he stalked back toward the living room to wait for her. He'd lit a fire earlier, and the room was dark except for the amber glow of the flames. Jacob sank down in one of the comfortable wing chairs and picked up his scotch and soda. A long swallow helped bank some of his anger.

He had scarcely believed it when Charlie had called him and told him Macon was meeting Nat Baldwin at the Lincoln Memorial after work. He knew that the clandestine meeting had nothing to do with her long-standing relationship with the reporter. Nat Baldwin had been a thorn in Jacob's flesh for a long time. Jacob was prepared to bet the farm that Macon would have a nice fat folder full of news clippings and memoranda. He'd have to spend the better part of the evening explaining them to her. He'd had nearly two hours to contemplate the rage that had settled in his gut when he'd spoken with Charlie.

He took a long drink of his scotch. Damn Nat Baldwin, he thought, staring into the fire.

"Jacob?" Macon switched on the light in the hallway. "Jacob, are you here?"

He took another drink. "In here."

She walked into the living room. With a sweep of her gaze, she quickly assessed the fire, his casual pose in the chair, and the drink in his hand. "I see you've made yourself at home."

"Yeah. I didn't know how long I'd have to wait."

Macon dropped her keys and her briefcase on the hall table. "How did you get in?"

Something in her frosty tone irritated him, and he lounged back in the chair, assessing her with a cool gaze. "I knew anyone as predictable as you are would leave a key outside. I found it on top of the door frame."

Her only response to the barbed comment was a slight squaring of her shoulders. "Congratulations. I'd like you to leave now."

He shook his head. "No way. How was your meeting with Baldwin?"

Macon started unbuttoning her coat. "What meeting?"

"Don't play games with me, Macon," he snarled. "Charlie told me about your little tryst at the Lincoln Memorial tonight. That's why Baldwin called you the other night, wasn't it?"

Her fingers stilled. "I'd hardly call it a tryst, Jacob. Nat is a good friend of mine. I talk to him often."

"After dark in the middle of nowhere?"

She shrugged and continued unbuttoning her coat. "If I choose to. Would you care to tell me why Charlie was following me?"

"Care to tell me why he needed to?"

"You go first."

Jacob clenched his fingers on his glass. "Damn it, this is not some game we're playing here. Do you have any idea what you're dealing with?"

She draped her coat over the back of a chair and reached for her briefcase. The locks snapped open, sounding like gunfire in the charged atmosphere of the room. She removed the manila folder and shut her briefcase once more before she turned to look at him. "I think I'm beginning to understand." She tossed the folder onto the coffee table in front of him. "Perhaps you'd better look that over while I make myself some coffee."

Jacob narrowed his gaze at her. "You don't believe him do you?"

"I'm not sure what I believe. I know I don't like the idea that Charlie Darrow was following me all over town. I don't like the idea that you broke into my home and are sitting here like some predator waiting to swoop down on me. And I especially don't like the idea that I'm suddenly under attack in all this. I'm helping you, Jacob. Not the other way around. Or had you forgotten that?"

He held her gaze a minute longer before he reached for the light switch. When he snapped it on, the harsh light stung his eyes. "I think we should talk."

Macon nodded. "I'm going upstairs to change. Do you want a cup of coffee?"

"No." He picked up the manila folder. "I'll take a look at this while I wait."

She disappeared down the hall without a word, and Jacob flipped open the folder and took another drink of his scotch. "Damn you, Baldwin," he muttered, thumbing through the articles and papers. He'd seen most of it before.

There were newspaper articles about his various investments and financial dealings, a few mentions of his name in connection with international banking scandals, and several memos and briefings that had been released to the press a few years before as part of Jacob's cover with the Secret Service. There were several old pictures of him in various locations. Strasbourg, Paris, Istanbul. Several of the snapshots showed Kristen Ager hanging prettily on his arm. He came across one where he was seated in a Paris cafe.

Jacob recalled the incident with a bitter smile. It had been Christmas Eve, and Kristen was supposed to meet him for dinner. She had been two hours late, and Jacob had never shaken the notion that she'd been with another man. He'd spent the next day, Christmas day, his birthday, brooding over it. If he hadn't been so obsessed with her, he would have known then that she would be trouble. Jacob laid the picture aside before scanning the rest of the articles in the folder.

Macon came back into the room, clad in jeans and a baggy sweatshirt, carrying a mug of coffee. "So," she said, "what's in there?"

Jacob reshuffled the papers back into the folder and waited until she took a seat on the couch. He handed it to her. "The usual. Where would you like me start?"

She flipped open the folder and glanced at several articles. "Why does Nat have this?"

"Because he thinks he's going to be the next Woodward and Bernstein."

Macon frowned at him. "Is this the next Watergate?"

Jacob sighed. "Sorry, I was trying to make a joke."

"You failed."

"Dismally, it seems. Nat Baldwin has been suspicious of my comings and goings for a long time, Macon. He's a journalist whose full-time job is watching the political arena. I roll around with some pretty heavy hitters. It's only natural that Nat would find me intriguing."

She studied an article. "Why was Charlie following me?"

"We have a tap on the office phone." He held up his hand when Macon glared at him. "We just activated it the other night. I was going to tell you today in the office, but you were having a bad day. I figured it could wait."

"You should have told me before you turned it on, or did you just figure you could seduce me into not caring."

"That was out of line."

"Was it?"

"Yes. You're the one who wanted to keep the personal separate from the professional. I'm trying to do that."

"By tapping my phone? By sending Charlie to follow me?"

"I didn't send him. He went on his own."

"Oh, sorry. I fail to see the distinction."

He sighed in exasperation. "Look. It just didn't occur to me to tell you. It wasn't like I thought you'd be doing anything you'd care if we heard. It's primarily there because I'm there, not because it has anything to do with you. We turned it on after business hours so you wouldn't have an interruption in your phone service, and it didn't occur to me it would be a problem. I didn't even know Charlie had listened to your conversation with Baldwin until after you left the office tonight."

"So Charlie was monitoring my calls, and when he heard me make the appointment with Nat, he decided to follow me."

Jacob studied her a minute. He could see the tense lines around her eyes and knew Macon was wary, if not acutely agitated. He reached up and loosened the knot of his gray silk tie. It was going to be a long night. "We make our living being suspicious, Macon. Charlie was concerned, not just about you, but about me, too. He had no idea what you might discuss with Nat Baldwin. He just wanted you to know he was aware you were having the meeting."

"Why didn't he just hide in the bushes with a microphone and record the whole thing?"

Jacob flashed her a brief smile. "He wanted to. When he called and talked to me about it I told him he couldn't."

"He tried to intimidate me, Jacob. I felt like I was dealing with the Mafia."

"Charlie's a little rough around the edges, but I don't think he meant to frighten you. He was concerned that you might not understand the gravity of the situation. He wanted to put you on edge so you wouldn't slip and reveal something to Nat Baldwin."

She shut the folder and dropped it back on the coffee table. "Reveal something? You mean like who you claim you really are and what you're doing here?"

He narrowed his gaze on her. "What do you mean, 'who I claim I am?' "

"Nat asked me which story you were using. He

wanted to know if you'd told me you were with the FBI, or the Secret Service."

Jacob swore under his breath. "What did you tell him?"

Macon glared at him. "I didn't tell him anything. That's not the point, and stop yelling at me."

"I'm not yelling."

"Close enough. I'm the one who's been violated here, Jacob. Don't forget that. I don't think you're telling me the truth." She picked up a pillow and held it in her lap, twisting her fingers into the ruffled edge.

"What the hell is that supposed to mean? You can't possibly believe I haven't been up front with you all along."

"Can't I? I've known Nat Baldwin a lot longer than I've known you, Jacob. Why shouldn't I believe him?"

"Damn, Macon. I can't even believe we're having this conversation. That you'd actually contemplate that I'd lie to you about something this important."

"Wouldn't you?"

"No," he said, feeling bitter. She didn't begin to know the struggle he was having in not telling her about Gordon Stratton. In light of that, the suggestion that he'd set her up was almost too much to swallow. "No, I wouldn't. Especially not given the relationship that you and I have."

"What relationship is that?" she asked.

He swore. "This is not some casual acquaintance between you and me. Do you really think that whole episode in your office the other night just happened because I can't keep my pants zipped?" A car passed by her house, the wide arc of its headlights throwing the curves of Macon's face into stark prominence for a fleeting second.

She frowned at him. "You don't have to be crude, you know."

"This is not a damned Sunday-afternoon picnic."

"And you are yelling."

Jacob closed his eyes momentarily, struggling for a rein on his temper. When he opened them again, Macon was watching him, her gaze wary, tense. He released his breath on a long sigh. "I'm sorry. I'm sorry."

"What's going on, Jacob?"

"I told you the truth. I don't know what else you want me to do."

"But you didn't tell me the truth, did you? Not the whole truth I mean."

"What are you talking about?"

"Why me, Jacob?"

He looked at her closely. "I told you."

Macon shook her head. "I don't believe you picked me for this case simply because I know Chap, and I have a clean business record. I didn't get this far by being naive. What do you want from me? Exactly."

"You're overreacting, Macon. It's been a long day, and you're upset."

"Don't lie to me, Jacob. You're using me, and I want to know why. You can't expect me not to be curious after that cryptic conversation we had this afternoon. You were visibly shaken by your phone call with Peter Quiver, and I want to know why."

"I already told you I can't tell you anything."

"I don't expect you to reveal anything to me. Just don't lie to me."

"I'm not lying."

"But you're not telling the truth either."

"Why do you think that?"

"Because I make my living reading people. You're not being honest with me, and if you don't give me some answers, I'm ending this entire charade."

"You can't do that."

"I can. I'm a private citizen. No one's paying me to be your stooge."

"You are not a stooge. Don't be melodramatic."

"Well, excuse the hell out of me, but all these late-night rendezvous and phone taps and secret agents following me around have caused my imagination to run wild."

He took a deep calming breath and reached for her hand. "Your hands are cold," he said, absently rubbing her fingers between both his hands.

"I've had a difficult evening. I have a headache."

Jacob met her gaze. "Macon, listen to me. You are right that there is more than one level to this investigation. Many of the things I've withheld from you, I've withheld for your own protection."

"Do you think encounters like the one I had tonight with Nat Baldwin are in my best interest?"

"I think the less you know, the better off you'll be in the long run."

"How can you do this to me?"

"I'm just doing my job."

She shook her head and jerked her hand away. "That's not what I mean. You're lying to me when we, when you—oh forget it."

"In spite of the fact that you and I have a personal relationship. Is that what you mean?"

When a log cracked in the fireplace, Macon

jumped at the slight hissing sound. "We don't have a personal relationship," she said, her voice quiet.

"Come on, honey. We're both too old to play games. I've been all over you since the day we met, and you're not exactly immune to me. We may not have one now, but we're sure as hell headed that way."

"And what am I supposed to do? Let you waltz me down some primrose path and pray that I don't get hurt when it's all over?"

"I've never made you any promises."

"No you haven't, have you?"

"But that doesn't mean I don't want to."

Her eyes registered a brief, flaring emotion he couldn't quite identify. She looked away. "Is this where you give me another confession about your shady past?"

He would have resented the barb, but couldn't quite bring himself to feel he didn't deserve it. "This is business, Macon. Don't get the two mixed up."

"I think you should leave, Jacob. I have a lot to think about."

"I'm not leaving until this is settled."

"What is there to settle?"

"I have to know that you trust me."

Her gaze collided with his once more. "Why should I trust you?"

Jacob moved out of his chair and eased himself down on the couch next to her. "Macon, you have to listen to me."

"I don't want to. I just want to go to bed and forget this whole thing ever happened." She started picking a thread on the pillow. "Do you think I could wake up in the morning and pretend this was all a bad dream?"

Jacob smiled at her. She really did sound miserable. He reached over and covered her hands with his. "Honey, listen to me. Nat Baldwin has a right to be concerned about you. If anything, you should be flattered he was worried enough to take what he probably considered an enormous risk, but you're blowing this completely out of proportion."

"Oh, really?"

"It's not that significant. Baldwin has a collection of clippings on me that are all part of my cover. The Service has spent years building me up as an international tycoon. I'm supposed to look shady to the outside world. It's how I work my way into undercover situations."

Macon shivered. "If Nat's concerns are so insignificant, then why did Charlie feel like he had to follow me tonight?"

"We're very close on this case, Macon. You've given us some great leads. I believe we only need a few more weeks. Maybe even days."

She raised her eyes to his, and he saw the worry hidden deep in her stormy blue gaze. "I don't want to do this anymore, Jacob."

He brushed a tendril of her honey blond curls off her forehead. "I know this has been a lot of stress for you. Maybe I've pushed harder than I should, but—"

She shook her head. "Not that. I" made a commitment to you that I would help you see this case through to the end, and I will. You've admitted that there's more at stake here than you've told me, and I believe I have a right to those answers." He started to interrupt, but she held up her hand. "Let me finish, please."

"All right."

"I don't know what you want from me, Jacob, but I'm tired and I'm frustrated, and I can't fight you anymore. You keep pulling at me, personally, and I'm not strong enough to deal with it. I have a business to run. I have clients who need my attention, and you're turning my world upside down. I can't take this anymore."

He grabbed one of her hands and pressed it against his heart, holding" it in place with his warm palm. "I need you, Macon. Personally and professionally." He caught her suspicious look, and he smiled at her. "No kidding. I've never tried to deny that, and I'm not going to start now, but this is the biggest case of my career. There's a lot riding on this, and I need your help. If we can just hang on for a few more weeks, it will all be over."

"What's going to happen to me?"

"I swear to you I will do whatever's necessary to protect you. You're not in any danger, no matter what Baldwin told you." He brushed a tendril of her hair off her forehead. "I'd take a bullet for the President of the United States, and I don't even like the guy. Don't you think I'd lay a lot more on the line for you?"

She smiled weakly in response to his quip. "That's very gallant of you, Mr. Blackfort."

"It's also very true. Nothing's going to happen to you, Macon. All you have to do is trust me. Just a little while longer." Even as he said the words, Jacob felt something unpleasant tighten in the vicinity of his heart. What would she do when she found out he was using her to set up Gordon Stratton? Could he live with it if she turned on him?

She hesitated. "I feel like I'm in way over my head."

He couldn't stand not telling her at least part of the truth. Damn Peter Quiver and his twisted strategy to nail Gordon. Macon didn't deserve what they were doing to her. "There are a lot of details you don't know. You're better off not knowing them. When this is all said and done, a lot of your long-time acquaintances are going to go down. I don't want you caught in the middle of that."

Her forehead creased, and Jacob felt her fingers tremble against his hand. "What do you mean?"

"Just suffice it to say that I want you to feel good about saying you didn't have anything to do with it. I don't want you to get a reputation for turning on your colleagues, even if they are crooks."

"You're scaring me."

"I'm protecting you."

"How much can you really protect me, Jacob? Aren't you asking me to lay a lot more on the line than just my professional reputation?"

"No. And even that will be completely safe-guarded. I promised you from the first day that I wouldn't let anything happen to you or your business. I'll keep that promise. I swear."

"How far are you prepared to go?"

"To any length necessary."

Seventeen

By noon the next day, Macon was ready to tell him to go to any lengths necessary to get out of her hair. She strolled into her office for the fourth time that day, and for the fourth time, she was distracted by the sight of him in slim-fitting black trousers and a snowy white shirt. She fixed him with a hard stare. "What?"

He raised an eyebrow. "Testy, testy. Having a rough day?" There was a look in his eyes that said he desperately wanted a truce declared.

She wanted it too, enough to forget the tensions of the previous evening and accede to his gentle persuasion. "It would be a hell of a lot less rough if you weren't so bent on distracting me."

He waved a folder at her. "I wanted to ask you about this report you did on Chap's campaign, but it can wait until later. Why don't you let me take you to lunch?"

"Another spending spree at Rock Creek Park?"

He grinned at her. "Something like that." Jacob dropped the folder on her desk and reached for her hand. "Come on. You'll have fun."

"Fun?" She gave him an incredulous look. He was standing so close that she could smell the spicy scent of his aftershave. "There's no such thing as 'fun' in an election year."

"Trust me, Kemosabe."

She frowned at him. "You know, usually when Tonto calls the Lone Ranger, Kemosabe, it's because he's about to get them both into a lot of trouble."

Jacob shook his head. "No trouble. I promise. I'm tired, and I want to get out of the office for a while. It will give us a chance to talk."

"Is talking all you had in mind?' "'

His grin was wicked. "Unless you'd like to lead me astray."

Macon abruptly stood up so that he was no longer looming over her. When she'd left for work that morning, the weather was already shaping into one of those rare Washington days where it seemed almost criminal to stay indoors. "Do you promise to have me back in forty-five minutes?"

He nodded. "Scout's honor."

"You don't look like any boy scout I've ever known," she said, as she reached for her jacket.

By the time Jacob turned his car onto the interstate, Macon was starting to feel duped. "Where are we going?" she said, suspicious.

He slanted her a sideways glance. "It's a surprise."

"You're not going to have me back in forty-five minutes, are you?"

Jacob shook his head and reached for her hand, lacing his fingers through hers. He'd put the top down on his car, and the sun was just warm enough to make the air feel crisp without being chilly. "So we might be a little late," he said. "Just relax and enjoy the ride."

Macon grumbled beneath her breath and tipped her head back against the seat rest. "Never trust a man who wears snakeskin boots," she said, casting a disparaging look at his footwear. "It's not a good sign."

Jacob laughed and squeezed her hand. "I'll see if I can find my other pair."

Macon turned her head so she could look at him. The wind made it very difficult to talk, so she took several deep breaths of the fresh air and closed her eyes. She had to fight down a feeling of guilt, almost as though she expected a detention slip from May when she returned from the office. Jacob was right, she told herself, it was ridiculous for her to remain chained behind her desk on a day like this.

Jacob guided his car onto the beltway, and Macon knew with a sudden flash of clarity that they were headed all the way to Baltimore. She opened her eyes just long enough to let him know she was on to his game, and then settled back in her seat. It really was a nice day.

They passed the rest of the fifty-minute trip in silence, and by the time Jacob turned into the parking garage at the Inner Harbor, Macon was feeling almost drowsy, she was so relaxed. He grinned at her. "Come on, sleepyhead. No trip to Baltimore would be complete without fish and chips."

She yawned. "Too much grease."

He helped her out of the car before he locked the doors and activated the alarm. "You have to learn to live life on the edge more, Ms. Stratton. One overdose of cholesterol isn't going to kill you."

"Tell that to my waistline," she mumbled.

Jacob placed a hand on either side of her waist so his fingers fanned out on her hips. "I think

your waistline is just about the right size," he
whispered, and kissed her once for emphasis.

What remained of Macon's bad mood completely evaporated. She followed Jacob through
the extensive food pavilion at the Inner Harbor
and waited while he bought two paper cones of
fish and chips. The harbor pavilions were very
popular with the business crowd, and Macon
watched as young executives hurried through the
enormous food court, jostling for tables and chairs
that faced the enormous windows. The scent of
fish and fried food hung heavily, but not unpleasantly, in the air, and she inhaled a deep breath of
a scent that was unmistakably fresh crab.

Jacob smiled at her from his spot by the fish
and chips vendor as he doused each paper cone
with a liberal portion of malt vinegar. Then he
returned to her side and guided her over to the
outside terrace.

"Okay," he said, "to get this absolutely right,
you have to take your shoes off and swing your
legs over the side."

"What?"

"That's how you eat fish and chips. I learned
it in Felixtowe, England, where they invented fish
and chips. Have you ever been to Felixtowe."

"No," she said, not quite capable of keeping
the smile off her face.

"Well, I have. Twice. And you have to eat them
this way. They don't taste right if you don't."

Macon gamely stepped out of her shoes and sat
down on the edge of the terrace so she could swing
her feet over the side. Jacob handed her both
cones. "Hold mine while I take my boots off."

He sat down beside her and pulled off both
boots. He stripped off his socks and stuffed them

down inside. Then he accepted his paper cone from her. "Ah," he said. "I can close my eyes and feel like I'm back in Felixtowe."

Macon took a bite of her fish. "What were you doing there?"

He looked at her and shrugged. "Nothing fun. Except for eating fish and chips that is."

"Were you working on this case?"

He nodded. "Yeah. I told you this has consumed most of my life for the last four years."

She swallowed a French fry. "Isn't it hard? Being gone all the time, I mean."

She watched as his expression softened momentarily, only to see the shutters drop back in place. "I guess."

Macon frowned. "Do you realize that every time we try to talk personally about you, you brush it off, but you're always pushing me for personal details?"

He took a bite of his fish. "Do you think so?"

She nodded. "I know so. Why do you do that, Jacob? What are you hiding?"

"Would you believe me if I told you it was part of my training, part of being an agent?"

Macon shook her head. "I don't think so."

Jacob bit into a French fry. "It's hard to explain. I've already told you how things are with my family, and there are things that happened in my life that are," he paused, "difficult. Things I'm not proud of."

"Things of which I'm not proud," she said with a soft smile.

He rewarded her with a soft laugh. "Can you hold this conversation while I go get us something to drink? I forgot."

Macon nodded and took his cone from him

once more. "I'm not going to let you change the subject, you know?"

He groaned. "I was afraid of that. Hold on."

She watched him stride over to a vendor. He looked ridiculously powerful with his trouser cuffs rolled up and his shirtsleeves turned back. Like a banking tycoon on vacation in Bermuda. Macon smiled at the thought. Jacob didn't seem like the man who took vacations. He played hooky, yes, but he didn't take vacations.

There was an intensity about him that bothered her. Like he deliberately kept himself busy, deliberately stayed occupied, in order to avoid thinking too much or being alone, or doing anything that involved personal risk.

He returned to her side and handed her a Diet Pepsi. "Okay?"

She nodded. "Fine." She handed him his cone. "So there are things you aren't proud that you did. What's that got to do with the way you live your life now?"

He took a long drink of his soda. "A lot." Jacob leveled his gaze at her, his eyes serious. "I like to imagine my life started four years ago. This case has consumed that period of my life, and I want to keep it that way."

"That's sad, Jacob."

"It's realistic," he said, and his voice had a new harshness she hadn't heard before.

Macon decided to let the subject drop, and consequently, they spent the rest of the afternoon in companionable conversation. Jacob showed her around the Inner Harbor. Except for the brief phone call he allowed her to make to Maylene, they resolutely put business aside. Macon found herself enjoying his company more than she had enjoyed anything in a long time.

Only occasionally did something come up that threatened to intrude on the unreality of the day, and each time, she deliberately thrust it aside, determined to allow herself the small pleasure of a day with Jacob Blackfort's undivided attention.

She was beginning to feel an unpleasant tingle on her nose that suggested too much time in the late-afternoon sun, when Jacob took her hand and grinned at her. "I guess my forty-five minutes are up?"

She nodded. "Long gone. I should make you stay after work and write 'I will not delay Macon' at least a hundred times on the blackboard."

Stopping in front of a relatively secluded bench, where they were partially shielded from the crowd by the corner of a bank building, he pulled her into his arms. "I needed this today, Macon. It might be the last real time we have together for a while."

She looked at him in surprise. "You sound awfully grim all of a sudden. What's wrong?"

Jacob shook his head. "Nothing's wrong, really, it's just that things are going to start to be very busy. I'm going to have to demand a lot from you in the next couple of weeks, and I wanted you to have this to remember."

"You're being very pessimistic."

"I'm just being cautious. I want you to promise me something, Macon."

She studied him for a minute. "If I can."

"I told you that I would try and keep our professional relationship and our personal relationship separate."

"I know."

"And I'm going to do my best to keep that promise."

"I'm sure you will."

"But if you start to have doubts, if things go wrong, promise me you'll give me the benefit of a doubt."

"What's wrong with you, Jacob?"

He sighed. "I'm not very good at this. There are just some things I'm worried about. Maybe I'm jumping the gun, I don't know, but I want you to promise you'll try and listen to me before you jump to any conclusions. All right?"

She hesitated, searching his eyes for answers to questions she didn't know how to ask. "All right."

Jacob kissed her briefly. "Thank you," he said.

He sounded like he'd just been given a reprieve from a firing squad.

Eighteen

The next two weeks did indeed prove to be an enormous challenge, and Macon began to seriously doubt that her life would ever return to normal. Jacob seemed to have taken over. They had spent nearly every night making the circuit from political fundraisers to private receptions. He had been attentive, solicitous even, but except for the torrid kiss he gave her each night on the doorstep of her house, he remained detached.

On the few occasions when he ventured out of his office, he seemed preoccupied. He remained, for the most part, buried in his work. She was disturbed to realize that she was beginning to worry more and more about the nature of their relationship. She tried to think back to their conversation in Baltimore and make sense of Jacob's cryptic words, but the more she thought about it, the more frustrated she became. He was impossible to read. She was starting to think that Jacob was having second thoughts about pursuing their relationship at all. He had been solicitous the afternoon they'd gone to Inner Harbor, but there seemed to be none of the passion they'd shared before. A dozen times, she'd chastised herself for being so foolish, and tried to convince herself she felt better with him at arm's length, but by the time she reached the thirteenth war with her self-esteem, she'd run out of arguments.

It was late on a Friday afternoon when she summoned up enough courage to ask him. Resolutely, she marched across the reception area, doing her best to ignore May's knowing look. She knocked on his door.

"Come in," he barked.

Macon slipped inside and shut the door behind her. She waited for him to look up from the file he was studying. He looked alarmingly handsome. Dressed, as usual, in shades of black and white. Jacob had the whitest shirts she'd ever seen. They lay against his sun-darkened skin as bright as mountain snow. Even with the cuffs turned back, lessening the severity of his pressed and starched appearance, he looked powerful, intimidating, dangerous. She contemplated fleeing the office. He met her gaze and smiled the same polite, detached smile that had been driving her crazy all week. "Hi there," he said.

"Hi. Are you busy?"

Jacob shrugged and pushed aside the folder. "A little. Something on your mind?"

Macon swallowed a nervous giggle. Something was on her mind all right. She crossed his office and rounded his desk, sitting on the corner so she could face him. "I wanted to remind you about the reception tomorrow."

He glanced briefly at his calendar. "American Association of Political Consultants. Capitol Hilton. Eight o'clock. I won't forget."

She nodded, picking up a paperclip and twirling it between her fingers. "Good. I, uh, also wanted to let you know that I'm on my way to that Renaissance Women fundraiser I told you about."

"I remember. Sure you don't want me to go?"

She shook her head. The gathering would be small, and Macon only intended to put in a token appearance. "There's no need. You said you had plans for tonight."

"I'm meeting Charlie," he said.

There was a long uncomfortable silence, and Macon again entertained the notion of bolting for the door. When she looked at him again, the tiny lines of fatigue around his eyes proved to be her undoing. "You look tired."

He shrugged. "I haven't been sleeping well."

"Have I been keeping you up too late at night?" she teased, referring to their hectic social schedule.

Jacob leaned back in his chair and fixed her with a stare that made her stockings turn to water inside her shoes. "Yeah," he drawled. "You've been keeping me up nights."

Macon's eyes widened. She could not possibly have misunderstood his innuendo. "Jacob, I—"

"Look, Macon, I don't want to be short with you, but if you have something to say, I wish you'd say it instead of sitting there perched on my desk like a damned siren, waiting for me to ravish you."

She felt a current, hot as liquid fire, start spreading through her blood. "Jacob, I just came in here to—"

He rubbed a hand over his face. "I mean, what the hell do you want from me? You said you wanted me to keep my hands off you, and I'm trying. God knows I'm trying. But then you stroll in here all warm and smiling and stare at me with the sultriest damn look I have ever seen. I'm not made of steel you know."

Macon smiled, feeling suddenly sexy and feminine and in control all at once. His burst of irritation was ridiculously pleasing to her. Somehow, knowing that he had been as affected as she by the stress of the last two weeks made her feel powerful.

She realized, with something of a start, that Jacob did that to her. With one look, he told her he knew exactly what she was thinking, and that he was thinking the same thing. She was almost lightheaded with the heady realization. She glanced meaningfully down at his groin. "Parts of you seem to be."

Jacob's mouth dropped open. "What?" His voice sounded strangled.

Bracing one hand on the desk, she leaned forward and wrapped the other around his nape. "The reason I came in here," she whispered, brushing a butterfly soft kiss across his lips, "is to find out if you taste as good in daylight as you do—"

She wasn't allowed to finish the statement. Jacob hauled her off the desk and tumbled her into his lap. "You are a siren, aren't you?" he groaned, seconds before his lips crushed hers and he plunged his tongue into her waiting mouth.

Macon leaned into him, running her hands across the width of his chest. Jacob took full advantage of her willingness and plunged his tongue into her mouth. Her head started to spin with the heady taste of him. He ran the tip of his tongue along the curve of her teeth before delving deeper, and Macon threaded one hand through the dark hair at his nape, holding his mouth firmly to hers.

When he finally tore his lips from hers, she whimpered in dismay. The sound was followed by a gasp of delight when she felt his mouth, hot and damp against her ear. He stabbed the tip of his tongue inside, and Macon shuddered. "Jacob." His name came out on a moan.

He moved his mouth along her jaw. "You taste so good. Feel so good. I ache for you, honey."

Macon clenched her fingers in his hair and brought his lips back to hers. His hand moved up her rib cage and teased the full curve of her breast. The feel of her lace camisole scraping against the sensitized nub of her nipple was almost unbearably erotic, and Macon finally ended the kiss and buried her face against his neck.

She felt the hammering pulse at the base of his throat and pressed a brief kiss to it before she looked at him. His head was tipped back against his chair, his eyes closed tight. She traced a finger over the silky black arch of one of his eyebrows. He sighed, and opened his eyes.

"I guess you do," she said, only after she drew several deep breaths and felt her heartbeat begin to slow.

His aquamarine eyes, still cloudy with passion, registered confusion. "I do what?"

"Taste as good in daylight."

A smile tilted the corner of his mouth and he gently set her away from him. "Honey, you're enough to drive a man to drink. Do you know that?"

Macon stood up and straightened her suit jacket. "Are you upset with me?"

He shook his head. "Lord, no."

"Then why—" she trailed off, embarrassed.

"Why have I been acting like a stranger these past two weeks?"

Macon nodded.

Jacob met her gaze and reached up to trail a finger over the full curve of her lips. "I'm busy." He indicated the stack of reports on his desk. "I've been poring over files and reports until the numbers are starting to swim in my head."

Macon looked at him, skeptical. "A man who can understand international finance but can't read a Federal Election Commission report?"

Jacob shook his head. "I have been very busy. So have you."

"Is that the real reason?" she asked.

He hesitated. Before she could react, he abruptly leaned forward and pinned her to the desk with a hand on either side of her hips. "No." He stood so that he towered over her. "The real reason is that every time I kiss you, touch you, *look* at you, I go a little insane. I'm trying to keep my promise, Macon."

She reached up to trace the curve of his lips. "You're a good man, Jacob Blackfort."

"I'm a tortured man is what I am."

"Maybe, maybe tomorrow after the reception we could . . ." She was about to tell him they could go to her house and pursue the non-business end of their relationship when May's voice broke in on the intercom. "Macon?"

She frowned at Jacob's phone. "Yes, May?"

"There's a call for you on line one. She said it was very important."

"Who is it?"

"She wouldn't say. Just said she had to talk to you right away."

Macon sighed and straightened Jacob's tie. "All right, May. Ask her to hold. I'll take it in my office." She looked back at Jacob. "I'm sorry if I shocked you today."

He shook his head. "Pleasantly surprised was more like it. Feel free to slip in my office anytime you need reassurance."

She smiled at him. "I just might do that." Macon left his office without a backward glance and hurried past May's desk. May was shooting her black looks that said she knew exactly what had been going on in the privacy of Jacob's office. Macon studiously ignored them.

She shut the door of her own office behind her and leaned against it briefly, replaying the scene with Jacob in her mind. He was beginning to seriously disturb her concentration. He was beginning to seriously disturb her life. Forcibly, she turned her attention to the phone and snatched up the receiver. "This is Macon," she said.

"Ms. Stratton?" The voice on the other end was soft, feminine, well-modulated.

"Yes."

"Ms. Stratton, I'm Little Dove Blackfort."

Macon's fingers tightened on the receiver. "Yes?"

"I believe you know my son Jacob?"

Nineteen

When Jacob stepped into the ballroom of the Capitol Hilton the following evening, his temper was as black and foreboding as his codename, the Black Arrow. He'd had an enormous argument with Peter Quiver the previous afternoon. Quiver was getting anxious. He wanted results, and he didn't give a damn what they had to do to Macon Stratton to get them. Jacob had come within a nose of threatening the director if he didn't back off the case. Quiver had threatened back.

After the heated scene in his office, Jacob had been on the verge of telling Macon he wanted to stay home with her the following evening so they could talk, but just after she'd gone into her office to take the mysterious phone call, Charlie had phoned him to report that Gordon Stratton had just deposited half a million dollars in an overseas account. Jacob knew only a transaction of counterfeit bills would require that much currency. Quiver knew about the deposit, and he was too unpredictable for Jacob to feel comfortable letting Macon out of his sight.

When he'd gone in search of her, however, Maylene had glibly informed him that she had left for the day and was expecting to see him at the reception the following evening. He hadn't been able to reach her by phone all day, and by the time he arrived at the Hilton, he was in a foul mood.

He paused inside the door of the ballroom, sweeping the black-tie crowd with his eyes. He found Macon almost immediately. She was standing a few feet from the dance floor talking to Elliot Raines.

Jacob leaned against the door frame and watched her. Some of his irritation was melting at the sight of her, safe and sound. A warm, masculine appreciation of her appearance began to stir his blood. She was wearing a red silk dress that clung in all the right places and emphasized all the right curves. Her honey-colored hair was swept up off her nape and held in place with a glittering comb. Several unruly tendrils whispered against the soft skin of her neck, teasing him. He'd been in such close proximity to her for the last two weeks, that everything about her teased him. He felt his body grow heavy at the thought. Jacob's smile turned to a dark scowl when he saw the way Elliot Raines was looking down the draped neckline of her dress. Jacob's temper slammed back into full force.

He pushed away from the door and started across the crowded ballroom. As he closed the distance, Jacob saw Raines shift and gaze down Macon's dress once more. He accelerated his pace, barely avoiding a collision with a tray-laden waiter. "Sorry," Jacob mumbled under his breath, focusing in on Macon again.

He dodged two more encounters with prospective obstacles and glided to a stop next to Macon, where he slipped his arm around her waist, and gave her a possessive squeeze. "I'm sorry I'm late," he said. He liked the way she fit against him. She seemed made for just that purpose. An erotic thought of how she'd fit against him if they were both naked flashed in his mind, and he felt his palms go damp. He forcibly dismissed it. "I got tied up."

Macon flashed him a look that spoke volumes. He ignored it. He wasn't about to let her extricate herself from his possessive grip. Not when Elliot Raines was testing the waters. She finally gave up the small struggle and patted his arm. "It's all right. I was worried you might have gotten lost." She smiled at Elliot. "Jacob doesn't have the best sense of direction, and it has been so hard for him to accustom himself to Washington's layout."

Jacob almost laughed at her attempt to goad him. He probably would have if Elliot Raines hadn't been watching her with such rapt adoration. Jacob studied the other man. He was handsome, Jacob supposed, in a pretty sort of way. His wavy blond hair was swept away from his tanned face, and his tailored tuxedo gave him an air of sophistication Jacob imagined some women found attractive, but it did little to disguise the slouch of his chin and the slight paunch in his frame that suggested too many late nights and too much booze. Jacob stuck out his free hand. "I'm Jacob Blackfort."

Macon started. "Oh, I'm sorry. Jacob, this is Elliot Raines, a longtime friend of mine and one of the other side's best consultants." She flashed Elliot a radiant smile that curled Jacob's toes. "This is my colleague, Jacob Blackfort."

Elliot shook Jacob's hand and gave him a wry smile. "Nice to meet you, Blackfort. I understand

you'll be doing some work with Macon on the
Chapman race."

"That's right. My operation is based in Cheyenne."

Elliot took a long drink of his scotch. "Do a
lot of political business in Cheyenne?"

At the condescending comment, Jacob felt Macon stiffen beside him. He clamped his fingers
tighter into her waist. "You'd be surprised. I got
the contract with Macon didn't I?"

Elliot's gaze slid to where Jacob's hand was still
settled at Macon's waist. "Evidently," he drawled.

Jacob smiled at him. "You'll have to excuse us,
I'm afraid, Raines. I spotted a friend of mine
when I came in, and I wanted to introduce him
to Macon. Elliot nodded and bent down to kiss
Macon's cheek. "Of course. Promise me a dance,
darling?"

She smiled at him. "Certainly, Elliot."

Jacob wasted no time in guiding her toward the
opposite end of the room. "What a prick," he
muttered.

"Jacob, really."

"Yes. Really. The guy is a pompous jackass. How
can you tolerate him?"

"Elliot is a very good friend of mine."

"Elliot was looking down your dress."

Her mouth dropped open, and she stopped
walking. "He was not."

Jacob slanted a knowing look at her. "Yes he
was." He paused and grabbed two glasses of
champagne from a passing waiter, pressing one
into Macon's hand. "Not that I'm totally without
sympathy, you understand. You look like a million
bucks in that dress."

Macon feigned disgust, but Jacob saw the tidy

smile that hovered at the corner of her mouth. He wondered what she'd do if he kissed her. "You don't look so bad yourself, Blackfort. You clean up pretty good."

Jacob laughed and waved one of his black ostrich-skin boots at her. "I thought the boots were a good yokel touch."

She nodded. "Very nice with the tuxedo. I'm glad you did away with the snakeskin."

He took a long drink of his champagne and reached up with his free hand to brush a tendril of her hair behind her ear. "I'm glad you approve." With no small amount of appreciation, he noticed the slight flush in her face seconds before he shifted his gaze to the room. "So what do you think? Am I going to find my man here?"

Macon followed his gaze. "It's a very good turnout. I'd say there are at least twenty-five honest-to-goodness sleaze balls."

"Including Elliot Raines?" Jacob met her gaze once again.

"We've had this conversation before. You know what I think about that."

"Yeah. I know."

Macon frowned at him. "You promised you'd keep an open mind about this, Jacob."

He nodded, feeling more than a little guilty. She looked beautiful, vulnerable. She was going to hate his guts when she found out he'd used her. "So I did. You know what we're looking for right?"

"Right." She sighed and placed her glass on a nearby table. "Come on. I'll introduce you around."

"Macon?"

"Yes."

"Aren't you going to kiss me hello?" In the wake of Charlie's news about Gordon, Jacob needed to know that at least his personal relationship with Macon was on sure footing. If she cared about him, even a little, she might forgive him when everything was over. The notion that he was simply manipulating her in a different manner made him slightly sick with guilt, but he wanted her more than he wanted a clean conscience.

She frowned. "Do you think that's necessary?"

He blinked. He was sure he wasn't imagining the edge in her voice. "Necessary?"

"Yes. Don't you think everyone here already has heard we're a couple? A public display of affection hardly seems necessary."

He was thinking more along the lines of a public ravishment. "I don't want you to kiss me because of what people think. I want you to kiss me because I want to kiss you back."

"We're in public," she snapped.

Jacob's eyes narrowed. Macon was definitely not herself. He indicated a couple to their left. "It's not stopping anyone else."

She frowned at him. "That's Jeff Parker, you know."

Jacob froze. "Where?"

She pointed to the embracing couple. "The gentleman in that twosome of which you're so enamored. Still want to act like them?"

"Would you be terribly offended if I left your side long enough to hit that guy?"

Macon shook her head. "You're incorrigible."

"Yeah, but can I hit him?"

"Jacob, this is neither the time nor the place

for . . ." She let the sentence trail off when he stepped closer to her and pulled her against him.

He slid a hand down her back and rested it on her hip. He liked the way her color heightened and her lips parted. He felt himself growing hard. "Then what if I just kiss you instead? Please, Macon. I ache." He moved against her meaningfully.

She looked around, obviously embarrassed. "This is outrageous."

"Come on, honey. No one's paying attention. Just one kiss."

"Oh, all right," she mumbled and stretched up on tiptoe to place a chaste kiss on his mouth.

He wrapped a hand around her nape and deepened the kiss. When he lifted his head, she blushed. He grinned at her. "Much better."

Macon pushed at his chest with a slight frown that didn't quite reach her eyes. He felt ridiculously pleased. They spent the next two hours circulating in the crowd. The room was packed, and the hot, stuffy atmosphere was making him uncomfortable. To make matters worse, the band was too loud. It was difficult to concentrate as Macon quietly briefed him on the contacts and clients of several key players before she made introductions. He had to pause occasionally and inhale a deep breath of her perfume to keep his mood from completely disintegrating.

Macon's contacts were extensive, something he'd learned in the past two weeks, and with her help, Jacob made a mental note to check on five different consultants and their international connections. What should have been an extremely fruitful experience, however, was severely hindered by the soft feel of Macon tucked against his side, and the nagging worry that something was seriously bothering her. Something had changed drastically since she'd strolled into his office the day before. Finally, he could no longer resist the urge to have her alone and he grabbed her hand.

"Jacob!" she looked at him sharply. "Where are we going? I want to introduce you to Maria Shrone."

He shook his head. "I want to dance with you first."

"Dance. We didn't come here to dance, Jacob."

He reached the dance floor and turned her into his arms, almost sighing in contentment when her soft curves molded against him. He wrapped his arms around her and started to move to the music. "I couldn't take any more of this proximity, Macon. Your perfume and this dress are driving me nuts."

He slid one large hand down her spine and fitted her more intimately against him. Macon held herself stiff for several long seconds before the persuasive sway of his hips and the leisurely stroking of his hand seemed to melt her reserve. She flowed against him and laced her hands behind his dark head with a deep sigh. "You're the most stubborn man I've ever known, Jacob Blackfort."

He grinned at her. "Yeah, but I got my way. It should be against the law for a woman to feel this good plastered up against a man's body."

Macon cast a furtive glance around. "Don't say things like that. People will get ideas."

"I'm getting a few of my own."

Her eyes were reproving. "I'll bet."

Jacob gave her a quick squeeze. "Want to tell me what's wrong now?"

She didn't look at him. She picked at his lapel instead. "Nothing's wrong."

"Come on, honey. You sailed out of the office yesterday without even saying good-bye, and tonight, you're barely speaking to me." He paused as a sudden thought struck him. "You're not embarrassed are you? About yesterday I mean?"

Her gaze collided with his. "Of course I'm not embarrassed," she snapped.

Jacob frowned. "What's with you tonight?"

Macon leaned her head against his chest. He suspected she was trying to hide her gaze from his. "I don't want to talk about it right now, all right? Can we just drop it?"

He hesitated. He didn't want to drop it, but he had a niggling suspicion that Macon would just grow angry if he pressed her. "All right."

They danced in silence for a few minutes before Macon spoke again. "So what did you think of Scott Tallow?"

I think I haven't the vaguest interest in talking about him. "Never trust a man who's named after lard and looks like it to boot."

She poked his ribs. He wanted to kiss her again. "I'm serious," she said.

Jacob shrugged and spun her around. "He seems harmless enough." He didn't have any connections that Jacob knew of to Macon's stepfather.

"One of his clients is the Chairman of the House Banking Committee."

He nodded. "I remember. I'll have Charlie check it out."

"And how about Lynton Carlisle."

"The tall guy with the handlebar mustache?"

"That's the one."

"Seems shady. You were right." Jacob cast a quick glance over his shoulder. "Look, Macon, this is not the best time, okay."

"What do you mean?"

He bent his head so his lips were next to her ear. "I mean we shouldn't be discussing this in public. Now smile and act like I'm saying something sinful in your ear."

She drew in a sharp breath. "I'm sorry."

"No problem. It takes a while to get used to. Do you want me to say something sinful?"

She gave his hair a sharp tug. "Behave yourself."

"What for?"

"Because I said so." She tipped her head back and studied him. "You're a very good dancer."

He rubbed his hips against hers suggestively. "You're not so bad yourself. It kind of makes me wonder if you'd be this good at other things." When Macon blushed, he laughed. "Sorry, honey, I can't resist the urge to make you blush like that."

"Stop calling me that." She paused. "And I do not blush."

"No. Of course not."

When the song ended, Macon extricated herself from his arms. "I think we should circulate some more. I don't——"

Jacob froze at the sight of the tall, dark-haired woman waiting for them as they stepped off the dance floor. He didn't miss the wary look in Macon's eyes.

"Hello, Jacob," the woman said.

Jacob stared at her for several seconds. He felt, rather than saw, Macon grow tense beside him.

"Mother," he said. "What are you doing here?" He looked at Macon. "What's she doing here?"

Little Dove Blackfort laid a hand on Jacob's sleeve. "It's not Macon's fault. I came of my own accord. I need to talk to you, Jacob."

Macon tugged her hand free of Jacob's grasp and stepped away. "I'll leave you two to talk. I see a colleague I haven't spoken with in awhile."

Jacob reached for her arm but she eluded his grasp. Feeling unaccountably abandoned, he looked back at his mother. "This is a . . . surprise."

Little Dove nodded, her eyes sad. "I suppose it is. Can I convince you to dance with me? We haven't danced in a long time. Your sister's wedding I think."

Jacob nodded and cast a fleeting glance at Macon's disappearing form. He escorted his mother onto the floor, fighting down a sense of acute irritation as he watched Elliot Raines swoop down on Macon. The information Charlie had gathered about Elliot seemed to suggest a connection to Gordon Stratton's activities, and Jacob didn't like the fact that Raines showed such a keen interest in Macon. Especially not when he'd just finished reviewing a list of Elliot's clients and contacts that included so many terrorists and international criminals, it made Ivan Boesky look like a saint.

With no small amount of difficulty, he turned his attention back to his mother and the sad look in her eyes. "It's good to see you," he said, feeling odd, strained, like his tuxedo jacket might burst at any moment under the tension in his shoulders and neck.

She smiled softly. "I'm glad. I'm glad it's good, Jacob."

He watched her for several seconds. "Why are you here?"

Little Dove rubbed her fingers along his shoulder. "I found out you were in Washington just last week. Senator Chap Chapman called to talk to your father."

Jacob looked at her warily. "Was Dad upset?"

She shook her head. "Your father isn't upset anymore. None of us are."

He swallowed a thick knot of guilt that had lodged firmly in his throat. "Mother . . ."

"No, Jacob. I want you to listen to me. I knew this was the only way. You have been carrying this burden too long, and I knew I wouldn't get you to put it down unless I came to see you like this."

He shook his head, feeling sick to his stomach. He hadn't told Macon the truth about his family. He hadn't told anyone. Not even Charlie knew what had happened, and why Jacob had left Wyoming. "After what happened, after what I said to you, to Dad, he said he didn't want to see me again. He had the right to say that."

She smiled a mother's smile. He felt it scorch a path into his heart. Something enormous and cold and black started to melt. "You and your father are too much alike, Jacob. You were frightened." He would have denied it, but she squeezed his shoulder. "It's true. You were just a child when your father lost the ranch. I know how hard it was for you growing up in Wyoming as my child. I know what it's like to be the outcast, Jacob. You were a half-breed. My people didn't want you and neither did your father's. It shouldn't be that way now, not anymore, but it is."

He shuddered. "It was the same for Blu, and Jillian, and Dancy, and Megan," he said, thinking of his older sisters. "It was worse for them. The boys called them whores, Mother, but they didn't turn on you like I did." He felt the ballroom start to spin. This was all too much, too soon, too fast.

Little Dove cupped his cheek. "You were twenty-three and you were angry. So was your father. Can't you forgive him for that?"

Jacob stopped dancing. His head was pounding. "There was nothing for me to forgive. Dad was right. I was self-absorbed. I was ashamed of who I was. I stayed ashamed. I've been ashamed, Mother. It's only recently that I—" He trailed off and watched her, anguished. "It's only recently that I've begun to realize how much I've lost."

"You can have it back. You can have it all back."

He stared at her. "Why are you here? Really?"

"I've been trying to find you since you left. You've never stayed in one place long enough. The only information I could find was in various newspaper articles." Her eyes darkened, and Jacob knew she was thinking of the various reports of his supposed illegal activities. The same ones Nat Baldwin had given Macon.

"Mother—"

She shook her head. "No. We have a lot to talk about, Jacob. I wanted to see you, and I did this," she indicated the ballroom, "because I'm a coward. There was less chance that you would reject me here."

"I'll never reject you again," he said quietly.

Tears sprang into her eyes, and she kissed his cheek. "The call from Senator Chapman was an answer to prayer. I got him to give me Ms. Stratton's phone number. I called her yesterday afternoon and begged her to pick me up at the airport and take me to you."

He scanned the crowded ballroom once more and finally located Macon. She was standing in a corner talking to Nat Baldwin. Jacob reached down and took his mother's hand. "Will you come home with me? Now? I want us to talk."

She nodded. "Yes."

Jacob kissed her cheek. "Do you have a coat?"

"No. It's not nearly as cold here as it is at home."

He nodded. "I've never gotten used to the warmer weather, or the humidity. I miss the mountains."

"Maybe you'll see them again soon."

He swallowed. "Maybe." Jacob looked at his mother, at the tiny worry lines around her still-beautiful eyes, at the flawless perfection of her skin. She was still the beautiful woman he remembered—still the tall, graceful symbol of what he'd once hated so much in himself. He was filled with a self-loathing so strong, he felt it clawing at him. He had trouble breathing for a minute. His mother was watching him, and he knew by the wisdom in her eyes that she knew what he was thinking, and that she'd forgiven him already. He had only to forgive himself. "I'll go and tell Macon we're leaving. I'll bring the car around front for you."

"All right," she said quietly.

Jacob gave her hand a final squeeze before he pivoted on his heel and started working his way back through the crowd. When he reached Macon's side, he exhaled a long breath. "Hello."

She looked at him, gaze apprehensive. "Is everything all right?"

He slipped his arm around her waist, needing her warmth. "I hope it will be soon. I'll explain everything." He met Nat's calculating gaze and extended his hand. "Hello. I'm Jacob Blackfort."

The young man shifted nervously and extended his hand. "Hello, Mr. Blackfort. I'm Nathaniel Baldwin."

Jacob shook his hand. "So you're the one stirring up all the trouble in Macon's life these days."

"Trouble?" Nat gave Macon a cautious glance.

Jacob nodded, looking at Macon, amazed that his voice sounded so calm when his insides were in turmoil. "Ever since that article ran in *Electioneering*, I haven't been able to steal a moment alone with her." Macon coughed. Jacob flashed her a bright smile, then returned his gaze to Nat. "I hold you responsible."

Nat glared at him. "She deserved it. Macon really earned that award. Sometimes those things get handed out for the wrong reasons, but not this year."

Macon smiled at Nat, turning her back on Jacob once more. "So are we still on for lunch next week, Nat?"

He nodded, pausing to shoot Jacob a hostile look. "I'm counting on it. I'm sorry I ditched out on you last week. I've got a killer deadline."

"It's no trouble. Would you still like me to meet you at your office?"

"Sure. Fine."

Jacob settled his hand on Macon's shoulder. "I don't want to be rude, Nat, but I was just hoping I could persuade Macon to leave. I'm beat. Jet lag, you know."

Nat mumbled something beneath his breath before he leaned down and kissed Macon's cheek. "Well, bye-bye, babe," he said, using his familiar glib line. "I'll see you at the polls."

"Good-bye, Nat." She waited until he walked away before she turned anxious eyes to Jacob. "Are you angry?"

He shook his head. "No. Are you?"

Her eyes widened. "Why would you think that?"

"This couldn't have been easy on you."

Macon shrugged. "I wouldn't say it was hard, either. Where's your mother?"

"I told her I'd bring the car around. Macon," he paused, "how much did she tell you?"

"Nothing really. I picked her up yesterday and settled her in a hotel. She said the two of you had a lot to talk about."

He sighed. "I told you it was complicated, and it is. Thank you for picking her up at the airport."

Macon studied him for a minute. "I'm starting to see that side of you again."

"What side?"

"The one that doesn't put in an appearance very often and is always devastating to me when it does."

His smile was rueful. "Just let me walk you out to your car and I'll give you the more essential details. Tomorrow, we'll talk. I'll tell you everything."

She stepped away from him. "I think you should just go on home with your mother. The two of you obviously have a lot to talk about. I don't want to be in the way."

He shook his head. "You're not in the way. I need to be close to you, Macon. Even if it's just a few minutes."

He watched the play of emotions across her

face before she reached out and grabbed his hand. "Fine. We're leaving."

Seconds later, she stepped into the Hilton elevator and pushed the button for the parking garage. It had been the vulnerable look in his eyes that had proved to be her undoing. She'd been on edge all evening worrying about the confrontation with his mother. Jacob had been visibly shaken when he'd seen Little Dove for the first time. He still didn't seem to be fully recovered.

She watched him from the corner of her eye as he leaned back against the elevator wall. His eyes had a haunted expression that bothered her, made her ache to comfort him. She remembered the way his big body had trembled the last time they'd discussed his family. She knew that his inner turmoil was threatening to surge out of control. In the poorly lit elevator, the haggard lines of his face looked even more stark than they had in the ballroom. It took every ounce of will she possessed not to throw herself at him and encourage him to cry on her shoulder. Lord knew, he looked like he needed it.

Jacob took a deep breath. "Thank you. For coming with me, I mean."

Macon met his gaze. "Is everything going to be all right, Jacob?"

"My mother," he said, pausing to wipe a hand over his forehead, "I haven't seen her in almost ten years. I haven't been home since I left Wyoming and went to work for the Secret Service."

She watched the flash of pain that streaked across his face. The elevator hissed along its cable, and Macon steadied herself by leaning on the handrail. "She said at the airport that she didn't even know where you were until Chap called your parents' house."

He nodded. "That's right."

"Why, Jacob?"

He looked at her, his eyes filled with self-recrimination and guilt. "When I was twenty-three years old I told my father that he'd lost his ranch and thrown all of us into poverty ten years earlier because he'd been so hot to marry an Indian whore, he'd given up everything."

Macon gasped. "Oh, Jacob!"

"Dad lost the ranch when I was twelve. A couple of bankers did him in. It was nearly impossible for him to rebuild because there was so much hate and prejudice in Cheyenne. No one would lend him the money to rebuild.

"My sisters and I grew up as poverty-stricken half-breeds. We were the kids nobody wanted, and I hated my father for that. When I was sixteen, Dad threw me out of the house because of my attitude. I wouldn't talk to any of them, even though my sisters tried to get me to go home. I finally made it through college, and when I did, I turned up on my father's doorstep dead drunk and half out of my mind. I said some of the vilest things I think it's possible for one man to say to another, and Dad said he never wanted to see me again. I left Wyoming at a dead run and never looked back."

"Until now," she said, softly and stepped across the elevator to wrap her arms around his waist.

"Until now," he said. She heard the hint of tears in his voice.

The elevator stopped and Jacob walked with her into the garage. Her heels clicked on the cold concrete as they walked toward her car. The garage smelled damp and musty. Macon shivered, sidestepping a large puddle of water. "Why is your mother here, then?"

"She says she wants to put it behind us. I think she means it."

Macon looked at him. "Don't you want to put it behind you?"

"I'm not "sure I can. How am I supposed to forgive myself for that?"

"If your mother can forgive you, don't you think you can?" She paused by her car and started digging in her small evening bag for her keys. The air in the garage was heavy and cold, and she felt a telltale pressure at her temples. She'd been on edge since Jacob's mother had called her the day before, and now that the confrontation was finally passed, she was starting to suffer the effects.

In the background, she heard the squeal of tires in the parking garage and wondered if someone else was feeling as agitated as she. She forced her hand deeper into the small evening bag. "I think you need to go home and talk this through, Jacob. I can see how upset you are."

He sighed. "I'm sorry if I'm taking this out on you. You can't know what it did to me to see her tonight."

"I can see what it did to you. You're falling apart inside."

"Ah, Macon," he said, as he reached out to touch her face, "I need you so much."

She found the keys and pulled them out, turning toward the car door. "I'll be at home if you want to talk. I hope you can work this out." She pulled the door open and turned back to look at him. "You've got to let it go. It's hurting you more than anyone."

Jacob stared at her. "What am I going to say? How can I even start to take back what I said about her?"

"Start by telling her you love her. The rest will probably fall in place after that." She paused, then leaned up on her tiptoes to kiss him softly. "I recommend you keep a box of tissues handy."

He rested one hand on the roof of her car. "I can never thank you enough for what you did tonight, Macon."

The squealing tires had grown closer, and Macon looked over her shoulder. She saw the reflected headlights on the concrete wall of the upper level. "I'm glad you weren't angry. You've been so tense lately, I knew this wasn't a good time for a major upheaval in your life."

Jacob laid his hand against her face. His fingers felt extraordinarily warm against her cool flesh. He rubbed his thumb along the curve of her jaw. "Thank you for caring enough to risk this. I'm sorry if I made you think I'd be angry at you for trying to help me."

"Except for that one time when you were so upset, you never wanted to talk about your family. I didn't want to pressure you."

He managed a brief smile. "Sometimes a little pressure is not such a bad thing."

"Sometimes," she agreed. The tires squealed again as the other driver rounded a curve in the large parking deck. She wished she could say something to make the dark, haggard lines of Jacob's face fade away. She leaned up and softly kissed his chin instead. "Have a good evening, Jacob."

He bent his head and kissed her on the lips, a gentle, tender kind of kiss. "Go home and get some sleep. We'll talk—" Jacob snapped his head around when the roar of the other car's engine drew closer. Macon felt the tension emanating from him. He narrowed his gaze on the white sedan speeding through the parking garage.

"Jacob?" Macon cast a quick glance at the vehicle. "Is something wrong?"

"Get in the car, Macon." He was already shoving her into the driver's seat.

"Why?"

"Just get in. Start the car."

She fumbled with the keys even as Jacob slammed the door shut. "Jacob, you don't think—" The white sedan raced around the last corner. It was headed directly for them.

"Start the car, Macon. Drive!"

"Jacob!" She cast a frantic glance at the white sedan bearing down on them.

"Do it!" He backed away from her car, never taking his eyes off the other vehicle.

Macon twisted the key in the ignition and the engine roared to life. In the rearview mirror, she saw the white sedan racing between the concrete pillars directly toward Jacob. In seconds, it would hit him. Instinctively, she slammed her car into reverse and backed into the path of the other vehicle.

The impact was so forceful, her car was crushed against one of the concrete pillars and her head slammed against the driver-side window. The last thing she remembered was the sound of Jacob yelling at her. She made a mental note to correct his grammar when she could open her eyes again.

Twenty

"Honey. Macon, can you hear me?" Jacob clutched at her hand and smoothed the hair back from the angry knot on her temple. "I need you to try and open your eyes, okay?"

Her face was as white and colorless as an icicle. Jacob frowned and glanced up at the paramedic. "Are you sure she's going to be all right? Why isn't she awake yet?"

"We didn't find any signs of internal damage, Mr. Blackfort," the young man said. "She'll have a concussion for sure, but nothing more serious than that."

Jacob frowned and looked back at Macon. She'd scared him to death, and if she ever woke up, he was going to kill her himself for backing her car into the path of that oncoming vehicle. They'd arrested the driver, of course, but despite Charlie's rather blistering interrogation, they hadn't been able to get anything out of him. To make matters worse, Macon was still unconscious, and Jacob was beginning to feel frantic. "Come on, Macon," he pleaded, squeezing her hand, "it's time to wake up, baby."

He thought maybe her fingers tightened on his, but he wasn't sure, so he leaned in closer. "Macon? Did you say something?" Her lips parted.

The barest whisper floated over his cheek. "You're going to have try harder," he pleaded. "I can't hear you."

Macon cleared her throat and pulled on his hand. He bent his head so his ear was next to her lips. "What?" His voice sounded strangled.

Her voice croaked when she finally got the words out. "Not asleep. Unconscious. Can't wake up, have to regain . . . consciousness."

Jacob stared at her for a moment, not certain he'd heard her right. Then the breath he'd been holding came out in a rush and he dropped his forehead onto hers with a soft smile. "Thanks, Macon. God, I'm glad you're all right. You scared me to death."

Her eyelids fluttered shut on a soft sigh, and Jacob looked at the paramedic. "Do you need to admit her, or can I take her home?"

The young man hedged. "Well, we really should take her in, Mr. Blackfort."

"But?"

"But, if you'll promise to check her eyes every two hours and make sure her pupils aren't dilated, well, then I guess it's all right. I think it's a mild concussion at best."

Jacob nodded, relieved. "Fine. Anything."

"Hey, Jake!" Charlie Darrow motioned to him from the site of the collision.

Jacob gave Macon's hand a final squeeze. "Be right back, honey. Don't go anywhere." He stood up and strode quickly to where Charlie was crouched down examining something on the pavement. "Yeah, Charlie?"

"Look at this," Charlie said, scooping up a cuff link in his gloved hand. "It probably fell off when we hauled that ass hole out of the car." He pointed to the two vehicles still crunched together. "Henderson's guys must have missed it because it rolled clear of the site."

Jacob slipped on a latex glove and took the cuff link, holding it to the light. "Twenty-four karat gold," he said. "And unless I miss my guess, this is a genuine pearl. Not the sort of thing you'd expect a character like that to be wearing. Someone could have dropped it earlier. It might have just been lying here."

Charlie shook his head and pointed at the clasp. Several white threads and a tiny clump of fabric clung to it. "Nope. See that. It was torn free. Someone would have known and picked it up. I think you should dust it and see if it's got our guys prints on it."

Jacob nodded. "I'll have Connie look at it first thing in the morning. What are you thinking?"

"I'm thinking our guy probably got into a scuffle with someone who was wearing that and wrenched it off of him. When he realized how much it was worth, he pocketed it to sell later." Charlie paused and took a long draw of his cigar. "Make sure you have Connie check for a second set of prints. It's going to be tough on something that small, but it's worth a look."

Jacob nodded and dropped the cuff link in a tiny plastic sealable bag. He put the bag in his pocket and peeled off the latex glove. "Thanks, Charlie. Maybe we'll get something out of this guy yet."

Charlie grinned at him. "Don't give up on me just now, Jake. I'm not even halfway done grilling him."

"I know. It's just, this shouldn't have happened. It's way too early for this kind of action unless

Gordon Stratton is on to us, and he wants to scare me away from Macon."

Charlie shrugged. "You've been pushing a lot of random buttons. You must have hit one without knowing it."

Jacob looked back over his shoulder to where Macon lay still and unconscious on the gurney. "We're going to have to talk about our strategy tomorrow. I won't have a repeat of this."

Charlie followed Jacob's gaze, his expression grim. "I'm with you on this Jake. If you want to discuss it with Quiver and see if he'll let us back off, I'm in favor of it. We can't risk injury to a civilian."

Jacob met Charlie's gaze, his lips set in a grim line. "Especially not this civilian."

Charlie's expression registered his surprise, but he masked it quickly. "Take her home, Jake. We'll talk about it in the morning. I'll handle the report."

"Thanks." Jacob exhaled a long breath and headed back to Macon. It took fifteen minutes to get her settled in his car and ensure that a tow truck was coming to take care of her own. By the time they were headed out of the city, he felt like he'd been hit by the car instead of Macon. He cast a furtive glance at her, reposed in sleep, in the passenger seat of his car.

Like a bad movie, the events in the parking garage skidded through his memory, always crashing to a halt when the white sedan slammed into Macon's car and crushed it like a tin can against one of the concrete pillars. He reached out a shaking hand and enfolded her cold fingers in his grip. "Everything's going to be just fine, honey. You'll see." If he had to, he'd let Gordon

Stratton walk away a free man in order to protect
Macon. He wasn't going to let Peter Quiver play
God with her life anymore.

The drive to his apartment in Skyline took less
than fifteen minutes. When he hadn't driven
around to pick up Little Dove, she'd come down
to the parking garage to find him. She'd arrived
just in time to see him pounding on the side of
Macon's car, trying to get her to talk to him. He
wasn't sure what he would have done if his
mother hadn't been there. She'd been the one
to call the police. And she called Charlie when
Jacob had given her the number. She'd been the
one who'd kept him calm by letting him talk to
Macon while they waited for the ambulance to
arrive.

When Charlie had come roaring into the parking garage in his sedan, Little Dove had briefed
him on the situation, and then informed Jacob
that she would take a cab to her hotel, collect
her things, and meet him at his apartment. He
didn't even remember when she'd taken the keys
out of his jacket pocket. He'd been too busy
watching the paramedics pull Macon out of her
car.

He cast Macon a furtive glance as he turned
into the parking garage of his building. His fingers tightened on hers as he took in her ashen
face and the darkening bruise at her temple.
Cold fury raced through his blood as the thought
of Elliot Raines popped into his mind. Elliot
Raines wearing a distinctive pair of gold and pearl
cuff links. Jacob had remembered the moment
Charlie had found one of the pair on the parking
garage floor. It seemed Elliot and Gordon had
more in common than he'd originally thought.

Macon's fevered arguments on Raines's behalf popped into his mind, and he groaned inwardly. He was going to have to hurt her not once, but twice. He wasn't sure she'd ever forgive him, but she'd be alive. That's what mattered.

He pulled into his reserved space and switched off the engine. He wasn't sure yet why he hadn't told Charlie about the cuff link, but he knew as sure as he knew his own name it belonged to Elliot Raines. And if Jacob proved that Elliot had hired the driver of that white sedan, he was going to take personal pleasure in beating him to a pulp.

With a heavy sigh, he rounded the vehicle and lifted Macon out of the passenger seat. The red silk of her dress poured over his arms and fell in a waterfall nearly to the ground. He shifted her weight, careful not to jostle her. He smiled slightly when she sighed and turned against his chest. Jacob kicked the door of his car shut and headed for the elevator.

When the door opened scant seconds later, Tommy Winkle, the eighty-year-old elevator operator peered at Jacob in stunned surprise. Tufts of white, wiry hair stuck out from the brim of his red cap. His red uniform and shiny gold buttons looked strangely out of place amid the shiny chrome and black concrete building, but the tiny man had been guiding passengers up and down the elevator shaft of Skyline South for nearly fifty years. Jacob grinned at him. "It's all right, Tommy. The lady's had an accident and I'm responsible for her this evening."

Tommy Winkle, Jacob imagined, had seen just about everything in the five decades he'd worked in the building. He swept a knowing glance over

Macon and flashed a broad smile at Jacob. "Eighteenth floor then, Mr. Blackfort? The other lady is already upstairs waiting for you."

Jacob nodded. "Thanks, Tommy." He leaned back against the elevator wall while it glided silently up the cable.

At the eighteenth floor, Tommy hit the emergency-stop button and preceded Jacob out the elevator. "I'll get the door for you, Mr. Blackfort," he said, jangling the enormous key ring on his belt.

Jacob shifted Macon's weight and trailed after him down the hall. "Thanks, Tommy. If you could alert security that I'm not expecting anyone tonight and to keep a close eye on things, I'd appreciate it."

Tommy swung open the door of Jacob's apartment and stepped back into the corridor. "Of course, Mr. Blackfort. I'll be on the elevators all night. No one will be coming up without your permission."

Jacob smiled at him, a weary, worn-out little smile. "I don't doubt it, Tommy." He gave the old man a brief nod, then pushed the door shut with his foot. His first priority was to get Macon settled into bed and check her eyes, just to be safe. Then he'd call Charlie. His mother was waiting for him in the living room. "How is she?" Little Dove asked.

Jacob shook his head. "They think it's nothing more than a concussion. We're supposed to check her eyes every two hours until morning."

"Shouldn't they have admitted her to the hospital?"

"I wouldn't let them." He ignored his mother's

knowing glance and strode down the hall toward his bedroom.

"Do you have anything she can wear?" Little Dove asked, trailing after him. "I'll get her out of her clothes."

He shot Little Dove a wry glance. "I don't suppose there's any chance you'd let me do it."

Little Dove poked him in the back. "Not while I'm in this apartment, young man."

At her words, Jacob shifted Macon's weight in his arms, and kicked open the door to his room, taking care to hide his expression from his mother. What should have been a simple gibe cut across old wounds and bridged years of lost opportunities. He felt a wave of sadness wash through him. It was followed by the same sick, guilty feeling he'd first experienced when he'd seen his mother in the ballroom of the Capitol Hilton. He stopped by the bed and met Little Dove's gaze. "Mother—"

She shook her head. "Let's get Macon comfortable first. I don't imagine you'll be getting much sleep tonight. We might as well fill up the empty hours talking things over."

Jacob nodded, trying to ignore the hard knot in his throat, and carefully laid Macon on his large bed. In the dim lighting, supplied only by the outside lamps and passing vehicles, her red silk dress spread across his black comforter like an island of flame-colored silk in the midst of a midnight sea. Jacob's eyes widened at the thought. His poetical side had died, or so he thought, with the passing of his youth. He looked at Macon again. Perhaps not.

He crossed the room to rummage through a drawer until he found a pair of black silk pajamas.

"Will these do?" he asked. Little Dove nodded, and he tossed them to her.

At Little Dove's insistent frown, Jacob turned his back while she undressed Macon. In truth, he was almost relieved he hadn't been forced to see to the task. His fantasies were bad enough without adding any first-hand knowledge to them. God knew, he hadn't slept for days, the last thing he needed was a vivid memory of the feel and scent and look of Macon Stratton naked in his bed.

"All right, Jacob," Little Dove said. "She's dressed."

Jacob turned around and stared. The loose-fitting silk didn't help matters any. If anything, the way Macon's curves filled out his pajamas was enough to tempt a saint. Jacob muttered an oath and crossed the room to tuck her beneath the gray sheets. He spread the black comforter over her before he sat down on the side of the bed and switched on the light.

Little Dove laid a hand on his arm. "I'll wait for you in the kitchen."

Jacob nodded without looking away from Macon's pale face. When he heard Little Dove shut the door to his room, he exhaled a long, shuddering breath. He squeezed Macon's shoulder and shook gently. "Honey. Macon, wake up. I need to look at your eyes. Wake up, baby."

She whimpered in her sleep and snuggled deeper into the pillows. Jacob sighed. "Come on, honey. Just open your eyes for me. Just a little bit."

She drew in a long shaky breath and her eyelids fluttered open slowly. "Ouch," she whispered.

He nodded. "I know." Gently, he pried open

her right eyelid with his thumb and forefinger and looked closely at the pupil. "This one's okay." He repeated the procedure with the left. "This one too." He smoothed her hair off her forehead. "Go back to sleep, Macon. Everything's fine."

She slipped deeper into the bed. "Cold," she muttered.

Jacob reached for the white comforter at the bottom of the bed and spread it over her. "Better?"

"Um-hmm." She was asleep before she finished her answer.

He leaned down to place a gentle kiss at her bruised temple, switched out the light, then slipped from the bedroom.

Twenty-one

Jacob walked into his kitchen to find Little Dove stirring a mug of cocoa with a cinnamon stick. She smiled at him. "Do you still like cinnamon in yours?" she asked.

Jacob nodded and dropped down on one of the hard kitchen chairs. Little Dove handed him his mug before she took the seat across from him, cradling a mug of her own in her elegant hands. Jacob stared for several long seconds at her hands. Fleeting memories of those hands—laid against his forehead, ruffling his hair, applying bandages to scraped knees and offering soothing encouragement to bruised egos—flashed in his mind like frames of a silent movie. He raised anguished eyes to hers. "What am I going to say?"

Little Dove shook her head and reached across the table to squeeze his hand. "Why don't you let me talk first? That might make it easier."

Jacob was awash with self-loathing. "There's no reason why you should make it easier for me. Do you know, did Dad even tell you what I said about you that night? My God! How can you even stand to be in the same room with me?"

"Jacob—"

He shook his head. "I called you a whore, Mother, and that was just the beginning. I told

Dad that we'd lost everything because he'd been so hot for your Indian body, he hadn't been able to control himself." Jacob paused and took a long swig of his cocoa. He wished it was a scotch and soda. "Did he tell you that?"

Little Dove nodded. "Yes. He told me the rest, too."

Jacob swallowed. "Like I said, how can you stand to be in the same room with me?"

She smiled a mother's smile. "Jacob, did you mean those things?"

He paused. "At the time I did."

"I mean, really really mean them. Were you speaking with your heart?"

He shook his head. "No."

"There's your answer."

"Mother—"

"Be quiet a minute. You always did have a tendency to rush into things head first. When we lost the ranch, you were twelve years old. You couldn't possibly have understood what was happening. All of a sudden, your friends wouldn't speak to you. We had to move to that hovel we lived in, and even the Sioux children wouldn't have anything to do with you. You watched while your sisters got tormented. You had to listen to all kinds of abuse that shouldn't exist in this world." She tipped her head to look at him. "You came home three days out of five with a black eye or a bruised rib or bloodied knuckles you hoped I wouldn't notice."

He exhaled a deep breath. "You always knew."

"I was your mother. It was my job to know."

"It still doesn't excuse what I did."

"No. It doesn't. You and your father were too much alike. It's the reason you fought so much.

You both had different dreams for your future. He wanted you to work the ranch with him. You wanted to see the world."

"I wanted away from Wyoming. I wanted to forget who I was."

"Maybe. Given the circumstances, that was probably understandable. At the time you left, there was no ranch. I believe that's what started the argument."

Jacob nodded. "It was the night I graduated from college. It had taken me almost six years because I was working full time as a ranch hand for Carter Kale." He smiled bitterly. "Dad was enraged when he found out I'd gone to work for Carter. Leaving home had been bad enough, but when he learned I was working for the man that took his ranch, it was the final blow. I think that's probably why I did it in the first place. I hated Carter. I just used him to get back at Dad."

Little Dove traced a circle on the table with her finger. "I remember."

Jacob drew a deep breath. "I had just gotten my diploma, and all I wanted to do was throw it in Dad's face. When I showed up at the house, he was sitting on the porch, like he was waiting for me, like he knew I was coming."

"Did you know your father went to your graduation ceremony?"

"What?" Jacob stared at her.

Little Dove nodded. "He was there that afternoon. He was so proud of you, Jacob."

Jacob groaned and dropped his head back against the wall. "Oh God."

"I didn't know he hadn't told you."

"He didn't." His voice sounded hoarse. "Of"

course, I was so damned drunk, he might have told me, and I don't remember."

"You remember the rest of the conversation don't you?"

"Too well."

"Then you would have remembered that. I told you the two of you were too much alike."

Jacob shuddered and swallowed another drink of his cocoa. "It started because Dad asked me when I was going to quit working for Carter and come home to work for him. If I hadn't been so plowed, I probably would have recognized it as a peace offering."

"That was hard for your father."

Jacob nodded. "I know. I know it was hard. And I threw it right back at him. I told him there was nothing to come home to. There was no ranch, and there never would be." He looked at her expressive face. "It was downhill from there."

Little Dove placed her mug on the table and folded her hands together. "You said what you said in anger, Jacob. Didn't it occur to you that your father did too?"

"He had a right to be angry. God! He would have had a right to beat the hell out of me."

Little Dove shook her head. "Are you ever going to forgive yourself for this, or are you going to keep running?"

"I don't know." He dropped his head down into his hands. "It's only been recently, the last three, four months maybe, that I couldn't forget. I ran so hard, so fast, I didn't think it would ever catch up with me."

"Didn't it occur to you when you gave Senator Chapman your father's name that we might find out where you were?"

"I think I wanted you to," he said into his hands.

"Oh, Jacob."

He heard the tears in her voice and lifted his head. "You never used to call me Jacob. Not ever."

Her smile was sad. "I didn't know how you'd feel about your Sioux name. I told you I was a coward."

He shook his head. "You're probably the most courageous woman I've ever met."

"Not so courageous. I had to beg Macon to take me to the party so I wouldn't have to face you on my own."

"Mother, there are things—things you don't know about what I do." He reached across the table to cover her clenched hands with one of his own.

"I have never believed the papers."

He sighed. "You must have thought . . . something."

She shrugged. "There were times when it was very hard not to doubt you, Jacob. There have been stories in the papers, well, we couldn't find you, and the evidence was so strong."

He held up his hand. "You were supposed to believe them, Mother. That was the point."

"You don't have to say anything else."

"I want to. I'm not supposed to, but I'm beyond the point where I care."

"I don't want you to do anything you're not comfortable with. I don't need to know any more."

"I need to tell you, though. It was true that I was running from you and from Dad and from

home, but not the way you think. I'm not involved in anything illegal. I just look like I am."

"Are you working for the government?"

"Yes."

"Macon is helping you, isn't she?"

"Yes."

"What happened tonight. It wasn't an accident."

He shook his head. "I wish it had been. I've
been working on the same case for almost four
years now. We're getting so close to cracking it,
some people are starting to get nervous."

Little Dove leaned back in her chair and fixed
him with a hard stare. "She's falling in love with
you, Jacob. You know that don't you?"

He spread his hands on the table and studied
his fingernails. "I'm afraid the feeling might be
mutual."

"It's hardly a disaster, you know?"

Jacob's fingers clenched into a fist. "What kind
of family life could I possibly have? I've done such
a fine job with my first one, there's no reason to
believe things will be any better the second time
around."

"You have to let this go, Son. It isn't going to
heal overnight, but it will heal. You've been running for a long time. Perhaps it's time you
stopped."

He met her gaze. "I'm not sure I know how."

"It's in your heart, Jacob. Trust it."

"Do you remember what you said earlier tonight about my Sioux name?"

"About your not wanting to use it?"

"Yeah." He sighed. "No matter how hard, how
far I ran, you were still a part of me."

"I'm glad."

"I wanted to forget. I tried to forget, but I couldn't." He met her gaze squarely. "My code name is Black Arrow."

He watched as tears brimmed in Little Dove's dark brown eyes. "Jacob Swift Arrow Blackfort. Welcome home."

"That's not good enough, Charlie."

Macon leaned against the doorjamb and watched Jacob's taut profile as he stared at the window and barked orders into the phone. He looked even more intimidating than usual in a pair of baggy black sweat pants and a loose white shirt. The sun was setting, and the room was lit only by the weakening rays of pink light and the glow of street lamps. Silhouetted against the window, Jacob appeared to be simultaneously fatigued and tense.

She had no idea how long she'd been asleep, or even how she'd managed to get into Jacob's apartment and what she assumed were his pajamas. Her head was pounding, and except for a few brief flashes, her memory ended with the sight of the white sedan slamming into her car. "Jacob." Her voice croaked.

He spun around and stared at her. She immediately noticed his shadowy beard growth and the weary look in his eyes. "I have to go, Charlie," he told the receiver. "I'll call you back." He slammed the receiver down in the cradle and dropped the phone on his desk with a loud clang. "Macon. Are you all right? What are you doing out of bed?" He hurried toward her.

She nodded. The movement made her head hurt so much, she thought her eyes might pop out. "I—I wanted some water."

Jacob reached her side and wrapped a supporting arm around her waist. "Here." He guided her toward the gray couch. "Sit down. I'll get it for you." He hurried away, and Macon leaned back against the cushions, suddenly exhausted. "How's your head?" he called from the kitchen.

She was glad he hadn't turned any lights on. She tipped her head back against the couch. "Hurts."

"I'll bet." He returned and pressed the glass of water and two pills into her hand. "Here. I had the doctor phone in a prescription for you. This should help with the pain."

She took the two pills with a long swallow of the water. "Fine. I'm fine. Who was it?"

"Charlie. He called to—"

"Un-uh. The accident."

"Who was driving the car?" he asked. She managed a brief nod. "We don't know yet," he said. "Charlie's working him over right now."

"How long?"

"He's been at the office since the accident."

Macon shook her head. "Here. How long have I been here?"

"Oh." He checked his watch. "About eighteen hours."

She forced her eyes open. "Eighteen? May. Have to call May."

She tried to push off the couch but Jacob restrained her. "No way. You're not going anywhere. I called Maylene. She knows where you are and that you're all right. Don't worry." He paused. "I called Gordon Stratton, too. I thought he should know."

She looked at him in the fading light. "Have to go in to the office. Election year."

Jacob smiled at her. "Honey, there is no way I'm letting you out of this apartment until you start using good grammar again. I know you're sick when you aren't even talking right."

She would have rolled her eyes at him if she hadn't been afraid they'd burst from the sockets if she tried it. "I'm fine."

"Yeah, sure." He shifted on the couch so his back rested against one of the arms. Gently turning Macon, he settled her into the wedge of his thighs with her back to his chest.

"Where's your mother," she whispered, sagging into him. With his arms wrapped around her from behind, she was cocooned by his warmth.

"Go back to sleep, Macon. We'll talk about work in the morning." He started rubbing one of her shoulders with his hand, and she was asleep within seconds.

Jacob lay on the couch for a long time, holding her against him, staring out the window. Every time he thought about the cuff link, he felt a cold, pounding fury. Charlie had come by and retrieved it early that morning when Jacob had realized he wouldn't be able to leave Macon and drive into the office.

So far, the forensics lab had only turned up one clear print, and it belonged to the driver of the white sedan. There were traces of a second print, however, and Jacob had pushed for a partial match with Elliot Raines's prints. When he'd called Gordon Stratton, the senator had sounded genuinely shocked, distressed. He was either a very good actor, or he had no idea what had happened. If Elliot had taken it on himself to hurt Macon, Gordon might actually be persuaded to turn on him. Jacob could only hope. Things weren't moving nearly fast enough to suit him, however, and his mood was slowly deteriorating from bad to downright ugly.

Macon sighed in her sleep and shifted against his chest. He hugged her closer. He wondered how she would react when he told her he was going to scrap her involvement in the case. It wouldn't be overly difficult to write himself out of the picture. Macon would merely have to say that their partnership hadn't worked out, and he'd returned to Wyoming. He had more or less decided to do that anyway. He would take a leave of absence and go home for a few weeks.

At the thought, Jacob smiled bitterly. A few weeks. How could he possibly hope to solve ten years' worth of problems in a few weeks. His stomach started to churn again, and he hugged Macon closer to him.

He hated like hell to back off when he felt closer than he had in months to a major breakthrough, but as far as he was concerned, the decision was made. He had been given a rare and miraculous second chance to put things right in his life. He wasn't going to screw it up. Most importantly, he wasn't going to risk Macon's safety for any purpose, especially not Peter Quiver's.

If he'd had any doubts about where his relationship with her was headed, they'd quickly evaporated when he had seen her back her car into the path of the white sedan. When he'd seen her car slammed against the concrete pillar, the universe had momentarily stopped spinning. His body still trembled when he thought about it. Jacob couldn't remember being more terrified in his life.

* * *

Macon awoke slowly, fighting her way through a cotton haze, to find herself momentarily disoriented, and in a strange bed. Her back, she realized, was extraordinarily warm, but something had startled her. The noise. It had been that guttural noise. She heard it again over her shoulder. Shifting onto her back, she saw Jacob stretched out beside her. His face was a mask of tension. His fingers clawed at the black comforter, and his breathing was heavy and harsh.

He made that noise again, and this time, his eyes flicked open momentarily. Macon realized he was in the throes of some terrible nightmare. She reached for his arm just as he flung it out on top of the comforter. Her fingers curled around his wrist. "Jacob. Jacob, wake up."

He was back in the hole. The water was sucking at his feet, pulling him deeper. Jacob reached out, searching blindly in the obsidian darkness for a way out. The earth walls of the pit crumbled beneath his fingers. The water rose to his knees. His heart began to pound as he felt along the walls for something, anything, that would help him out of the hole. The light.

He remembered the light and looked up. It was still shining at the top of the hole, but this time, it was brighter, closer. He reached out again, and suddenly, there it was. His fingers closed on the rungs of a ladder. The water was near his waist and he slogged through it, straining to reach the ladder and pull himself out. Water surged around his shoulders as his foot found the first rung. He started to climb. The water closed in faster.

Jacob was running up the ladder, hoisting himself from rung to rung as the water sucked at him, pulled on him. He felt his clothes shred and give way. He felt his fingers slipping on the cold rungs. The light drew closer. When it seemed the water would drown him after all, a hand closed around his wrist and pulled him from the pit. He emerged into the Light, shaking from the cold, from the fear. Naked. Vulnerable. And found Macon still holding his wrist.

Jacob awoke with a start. Macon's fingers were curled around his forearm. He stared at her for several long seconds, gasping for breath.

"Jacob," she said. "Jacob, are you all right? You were having a dream."

He nodded. "A dream."

"Are you all right?"

He closed his fingers over hers, crushing her small hand. His heart was still thundering in his chest, and it took several more seconds for him to regain his equilibrium. He'd slipped into bed with Macon shortly after dawn when he and his mother had finally worn themselves out. The emotional and physical stress of the last twenty-four hours had evidently caused the nightmare to resurface. But this time, this time, it had been different. Macon had pulled him out of the pit. Macon had shown him the light. Macon had given him hope.

His hand trembled when he reached out to lay his palm against her cheek. "I'm all right." He heard the breathless tone in his voice and swallowed. "How are you feeling?"

She shrugged. "Better than last night. Are you sure you're all right?"

He leaned back against the pillows and tugged her along with him so she was cradled against his chest. "I will be in a minute. I've had the nightmare before. Let's just talk about something else for a little while. At least until my heart stops pounding."

Macon nodded against his chest. "Is your mother still here?"

"She's asleep as far as I know."

"Does she know you're in this bed with me?"

Jacob felt his coiled tension begin to ebb. He ran a hand down her spine. "She might have been bossy enough to keep me from taking your clothes off, but all the powers of heaven and earth weren't going to keep me out of this bed where I could keep an eye on you."

Macon saw lingering shadows in the startling blue of his eyes as she watched him, anxious. "Did you and your mother . . . ? I mean, I hope I wasn't in the way or anything."

Jacob shook his head. "We talked. We still have a lot to talk about, but we made a lot of progress."

She hesitated. "Jacob?"

He smoothed his hand through her hair, ruffling the curls between his fingers. "Hmm?"

"Why did you lie to me about your family?"

Surprise registered on his chiseled face. "Mother didn't tell you what happened?"

Macon shook her head. "She said that you should tell me, and only that I shouldn't blame you for not telling me you had a family. That I would understand when I heard the whole story."

He slid one large hand up her silk-covered leg until it rested at the curve of her hip. "You will, I hope."

She could feel his heart beneath her palm and realized the heavy beat was beginning to calm.

"I'm sorry you had to take care of me. You should have spent the time with her."

He reached up and touched the bruise at her temple. "Don't apologize. How's this?"

"Fine." She shivered when he trailed his fingers down her face and rested his warm hand against her throat.

"I think I had the nightmare because you scared me."

Her eyes widened in surprise. "What?"

"You scared me. When I saw you back into the path of that car—" He shook his head. "I've never been that scared in my life."

"He was going to run you over, Jacob. I knew I had a much better chance of surviving the collision than you did if he plowed you down."

She wondered if it was her imagination when Jacob's fingers seemed to tremble and his blue eyes darkened to a smoky gray. "You scared me," he repeated.

Macon squirmed, uncomfortable with the way he was looking at her, and even more uncomfortable with the way he was pressing her back against the pillows of the bed. "I'd like to get up now, Jacob. Maybe we could talk about this after I have a shower."

"I've had this fantasy about waking up with you in my bed since the day I met you. Why are you so intent on spoiling it for me?"

She felt the heated blush that stained her face. "Stop teasing me, Jacob."

"Believe me, honey, I'm not teasing you." He held up his hand, and she saw the way his fingers were trembling. "I'm in no shape to be teasing anyone. I'm still a basket case from the nightmare."

"Jacob, I . . ."

He brushed her hair off her forehead. His eyes were a glistening aquamarine in the early morning light. His firm lips curved into the barest hint of a smile. "That's not the way the fantasy goes, Macon, I should know. It's my fantasy."

"What are you talking about?"

"You're not supposed to argue with me. You just look at me with those smoke blue eyes of yours, and then I get to do this." He bent his head.

"Jacob—" Her protest was smothered by his kiss.

At the first hard contact of his lips, Macon sucked in a deep breath. His body was closely aligned with hers, and suddenly, all traces of her headache, along with her sanity, fled. He felt warm and heavy and alive, and she arched her neck to kiss him back. "Oh, Jacob," she breathed against his lips.

If he was surprised by her ardent response, he didn't seem to mind. She felt his lips curve into a broad smile, and he slowly, thoroughly ravished her mouth with his lips and teeth. When he pulled her full lower lip into his mouth and sucked on it, she whimpered and wound her arms around his broad shoulders.

"Just like that, baby. I need to feel all of you." Jacob slid one arm beneath her and pulled her into the hard length of his body.

Why hadn't she noticed before that he wore nothing but his briefs? His back was still damp with lingering sweat from his nightmare and she could feel the heat of him through the silk pajamas she wore. Her pajama top had worked its way up, exposing her midriff, and she felt the steely strength of his hardness pressing into her belly. Jacob massaged the muscles of her back with one hand, while the other trailed a line over the curve of her breast to the elastic waistband of her pajama bottoms.

When his fingers plunged beneath the fabric and cupped the rounded curve of her buttocks, Macon gasped. He took full advantage of her startled surprise and drove his tongue into her mouth. At the feel of his hardness pressing urgently against the juncture of her thighs, Macon knew a moment of panic. Jacob seemed to sense her hesitation. He dragged his mouth from hers. "Don't be afraid," he whispered, his voice a husky rasp against her skin. He pressed his lips to her cheek. "Please don't be afraid of me."

"I don't . . ." She trailed off when she felt him nip her earlobe with his teeth.

"I just want to show you how much you mean to me. I'm not going to hurt you."

"Jacob —"

His lips returned to hers. "Honey," he said against her mouth, his voice gruff and ragged, like dried leaves on shingles. "Honey, trust me. Please."

Macon tore her mouth from his and met his smoldering gaze. She was having an extraordinarily difficult time breathing. "I—I can't do this. I can't."

He shook his head and freed his hand from her pajama bottoms. He captured one of her hands from around his neck and guided it with unerring accuracy to the hard, swollen ridge beneath his briefs. "See what you do to me?" Macon's eyes widened and she tried to pull her hand away. Jacob held it fast. "Let me show you how beautiful you are, Macon."

"Jacob, I—"

He slid his lips over hers once more. "You're in control. I'll stop whenever you want me to. All right?"

She stared into his eyes. She was hypnotized by the sensual promise she saw in their depths. Slowly, she nodded her head. With a satisfied exclamation, Jacob pressed his mouth to hers in a hot, open kiss as his hands moved to the buttons of her pajama top.

Macon was drowning. Her hand was still wedged between them, and she felt the pulsing heat of him against her fingers. The feel of his warm hands, his hot breath, the pressure of his body against hers, all combined to wash over her in a sea of passion that left her floating on a forbidden cloud. Only Jacob seemed to be sure, solid, so she clung to him as he caressed her with hot, open-mouthed kisses.

When his hands parted the folds of the black silk pajama top, he raised his head to look at her breasts. Embarrassed, Macon jerked her hands up to cover herself. "No, don't," he whispered. "Please don't." His gaze met hers. "You're so beautiful. Soft." He traced the tip of his index finger around one sensitive nipple. "I just want to touch you."

Macon shivered, then wove her fingers into his crisp black hair to pull his mouth down to hers. With a low groan, Jacob covered her lips with his own and took her breasts into his palms. For long, passion-drenched moments, he caressed her mouth with his tongue and lips as his fingers rubbed and plucked and massaged her trembling breasts.

When he finally lifted his head, she whimpered in protest. The tiny bristles on his beard-roughened jaw tickled her skin as he trailed a line of kisses down the curve of her neck. He lingered at the swell of her breast, before finally taking one hardened nipple in his mouth.

"Jacob—" Macon felt her stomach tense from the exquisite sensation as he suckled her breast. "Oh, Jacob."

He licked and sucked and teased the sensitive nipple until Macon thought she'd explode, and finally, when she was sure she couldn't bear it any longer, he worked his way to her other breast. Her fingers were still threaded in his hair, and she held him close to her as unfamiliar currents of desire coursed through her blood. "Macon," he whispered her name against her breast. "I'm on fire for you."

Macon shivered when his hand came up to hold her breast, to apply just enough pressure to take her fully into his mouth. He wedged one strong thigh between both of hers until she straddled the corded length of his leg. She could feel the wet heat of her desire seeping through the pajamas. He seemed to know just how much pressure, just how much friction, she needed to plunge over the edge of sanity. Her hips jerked in reflex when he pressed his thigh more tightly against her. "Jacob, I can't—"

He tore his lips from her breast. His breathing was harsh, irregular. Macon couldn't tell if it was his heart or her own that was thundering so loudly. "Yes, you can," he said. He raised a hand to caress her lips. "Look in the mirror, Macon," he said. "I want you to see what I see." Gently, he turned her head until she saw their reflection in the mirror over his dresser.

Her eyes widened at the sight of her flushed features, the way her breasts rose and fell with her strained breathing. Jacob's fingers were buried in her hair, his other hand cupped her breast. Her knees were bent to accommodate the length of his thigh pressed against her feminine core. Swollen and red, her lips trembled. "Don't you see it?" he asked.

Macon met his gaze in the mirror. "Jacob?"

With a soft groan, he lowered his head to her breast once more. "Just watch, sweetheart. Just watch. I want you to know."

There was something decadent and wanton about watching her reflection in the mirror as Jacob moved against her body. He had taken her nipple between his teeth, and was teasing it with his lips and tongue. Macon watched, wide-eyed, as he trailed a hand across the flat plane of her stomach to the waistband of her pajama bottoms. His fingers traced along the elastic, caressing the sensitized flesh, before he settled his hand on the curve of her bottom, and pulled her firmly up against him.

The slight movement caused his thigh to wedge more tightly between hers, and Macon felt an unexpected surge of raw pleasure. "Jacob," she gasped. "What's happening?"

"Can you see it?" he asked, licking her nipple, then raising his head to blow on the wet peak.

Her body convulsed. A tight, coiling knot had formed in the pit of her stomach. Jacob brought her hand to his lips, and took each finger into his mouth to lave it with his tongue. Her gaze remained riveted on the mirror. "Can you see it?" he asked again.

The knot in her belly spread and heated as she watched the erotic sight of him nipping at her fingers. "Yes," she whispered, not sure if she was answering his question or merely surrendering to the powerful currents of heat that threatened to engulf her.

Finally, he lowered her wet hand to her breast, rubbing her fingers over the swollen, hardened nipple. He flexed his thigh between hers, and at the slight increase in pressure, the sight, the feel, the heat proved to be her undoing. Macon shattered.

Jacob held her to him until her trembling stopped. His body was slick with sweat, as was hers, and he pulled the white comforter over them for warmth as the cool morning air chilled their recently heated flesh. Macon's arms were wrapped securely around his waist. She clung to him, her face buried in the curve of his neck.

He feared that she might be embarrassed, so carefully, he set her away from him. As he suspected, her gaze was nervous, unsure when she met his. He sought to reassure her with a soft non-threatening kiss. When he lifted his head, he whispered, "Good morning."

Macon's face flooded with color. "Good morning."

He brushed her sweat-dampened hair away from her forehead. "You're not embarrassed, are you?"

Her eyes widened, as if she couldn't believe he'd asked the question. "You didn't . . . I mean . . . I'm sorry you—"

Jacob pressed his hand over her mouth. "Never

apologize to me for showing me that I can pleasure you. Do you understand?"

"But—" she mumbled against his hand.

He shook his head to interrupt her. "Never. Understand?"

Macon hesitated only briefly before she nodded. He lifted his hand away. "Besides," he admitted, his grin rueful. "I did, too."

She gave him a blank stare before her eyes grew wide with understanding. "You mean, you . . . without—"

"Yeah," he said, enchanted by her embarrassment. "I came in my briefs. I haven't done that since I was sixteen years old." He dropped a kiss on her forehead. "But then, I don't think I've ever watched a woman go up in flames for me before."

Macon looked stricken. "I don't know what to say."

Jacob rubbed his thumb over her swollen mouth. "You don't have to say anything. I wanted you to know, Macon. I wanted you to see what I see when I look at you. And I sure as hell don't want you to be embarrassed about it."

She watched him for several long seconds. He could see the indecision in her eyes. "I'm not," she said. "I'm not embarrassed." She sounded so amazed that he kissed her again.

He could feel his loins growing heavy once more, and knew it was time to put some distance between them. No matter how much he wanted her, he wouldn't take her now, not when she was vulnerable.

He ended the kiss, then rolled to his back, freeing her from his weight. "Do you think you'll feel better if you take a shower?" he asked.

Macon traced a finger over his bare chest. "I don't think I've ever felt better in my life."

He turned his head to grin at her. "God, you're tempting."

"Jacob—"

He raised her palm to his lips. "We have a lot to talk about, Macon. I don't want to rush you right now."

She nodded, knowing he was right. "I would like to take a shower," she said.

He pointed to the bathroom. "Shower's in there, but be careful in the bathroom, okay? I don't know if your concussion has upset your equilibrium, and I don't want you to fall."

She nodded. "I'll be careful."

"My bathrobe's hanging behind the door, and Maylene brought you over some fresh clothes." He pointed at the dresser. "They're over there."

Macon glanced at the clothes in mild surprise. Jacob, it seemed, had thought of everything. She gathered the pajama top together in the front before she slipped from the bed and stood up, trying to ignore the woozy feeling in her stomach. He was right about her equilibrium. She picked up the stack of clothes and headed for the bathroom, trying to act unperturbed by his intense scrutiny from his position on the bed.

By the time she emerged from the shower, Macon felt almost human again. She spent a long time in front of the mirror, staring at her reflection, shivering at the memories of Jacob's touch. During her shower, her skin had seemed unnaturally sensitive, as if he'd branded her with his lips and hands.

She combed the tangles out of her hair in an age-old ritual of nerve-calming repetitive strokes.

All the while, she marveled at the solid white interior of Jacob's bathroom. The only break in the color scheme was the black tub. She gave her reflection a wry smile. This man definitely needed some color in his life. She pulled on the red fleecy sweatshirt and blue jeans Maylene had brought her and resolutely opened the bathroom door.

She found him in the kitchen wearing the same baggy black pants she remembered from the night before, and a gray sweatshirt, nursing a cup of coffee. He smiled at her. "How do you feel?" he asked.

"Better." It was so odd, so intimate to be in his kitchen, watching him. Uncomfortable with the strange sensation, she nodded at his coffee cup. "Is there more of that?"

Jacob swung off his chair and padded across the kitchen in his bare feet. "I'll get you a cup. Sit down."

She sank into one of the white lacquer chairs and watched him pour the coffee. "Is your mother here?"

"Yes. She's still asleep. We were up pretty late."

Macon watched while he mopped up a coffee spill from the counter. She decided he probably wasn't any more ready to broach the subject of his nightmare than she was ready to broach the subject of their heated encounter. She was slightly gratified to see that his hands still shook a bit, and perspiration still clung to his damp, dark bangs. "What have you found out about the guy who hit me?"

Jacob strolled back to the table and handed her the black mug. "Here. It's probably not as good as yours, but it's all I have."

She nodded and accepted the cup, taking a tentative sip. "Not bad. I'd hire you."

"That's high praise coming from you." He sat down. "So far, Charlie doesn't have a lot. We've got a few good leads, though."

"Why do you think he came after you?"

Jacob stroked his whiskers. "Charlie has been doing some pretty significant leg work while I've been trailing these guys around the world. We have some new information that could wrap this up in a matter of weeks."

"You don't think they were trying to kill you, do you?"

"No way. When these guys set out to kill you, you're dead before you find out they're on to you. No. I was supposed to get the message that they know I'm after them, and they know I'm not who I say I am. I wasn't supposed to get killed. Not yet anyway."

Macon frowned. "So what are we going to do now?"

"*We* aren't going to do anything. I have a meeting with the head of investigations this afternoon at three. I'm going to recommend that Charlie take over the Washington investigation. Then I'm going to take myself off the case."

"But you can't do that. You're so close. You must be, after what happened last night."

He shrugged. "That's true, but it's gotten too dangerous. Especially after what happened this morning."

Macon ignored the loaded comment. "Because they know you're Secret Service?"

He shook his head. "I doubt if they know that. They would have killed me by now if they knew I was with the Service."

"I don't understand."

"So far as anyone in the investment and banking industry knows, Jacob Blackfort is an investment broker who specializes in under-the-table deals for foreign investors with lots of money. I didn't anticipate they'd start digging so quickly, and I have several suspicions as to why they did, but now that they know I'm not a political consultant from Wyoming, I'm sure they have some suspicions of their own."

Macon studied him from across the table. He looked tired and tense all at the same time. "What kind of suspicions?"

"Suspicions like I'm trying to hone in on the Washington market. Suspicions that I'm tied in with some foreign currency suppliers who might be trying to break the monopoly our guys have on funny money."

Macon took another sip of coffee. "Are these counterfeit bills so well done that they pose this large a risk?"

Jacob nodded and stood up. "Wait here. I'll show you." He returned a few seconds later with three twenty-dollar bills in his hand which he placed on the table in front of her. "One is real. Two are fake. Can you tell the difference?"

The first counterfeit bill was easy enough to find. The ink was not a perfect match, and the detailing wasn't as precise as the genuine article. She handed it to him. "This one is counterfeit."

He nodded. "This is a fairly decent quality bill. We see a lot of these. Now look at the other two."

Macon frowned and studied the two bills. "They're identical."

Jacob shook his head. He picked up one of the bills and held it to the light. "Nearly. This is the real one. We have several safeguards we use now to make counterfeiting as difficult as possible." He pointed to a band that ran through the left third of the bill. "See this?" Macon nodded. "It's a special fiberglass filament that is nearly impossible to emulate."

He held up the remaining bill and pointed to the line. "They've matched it here, though."

"That's amazing."

He nodded and pointed to the detailing on the bill. "The ink, the paper, the engraving, everything is perfect."

"How can you tell them apart?"

Jacob reached in his pocket and pulled out a penlight. He flicked it on. "This is an infrared indicator. We print U.S. currency in seven passes through the press. That means the latent heat in the ink registers differently under infrared light." He shined the light on the genuine bill. Macon identified seven distinct color patterns. "See them?" Jacob asked.

She nodded. "Yes."

He picked up the counterfeit bill and shined the light on it. "Now how many do you see?"

"Five."

He flicked the light off. "That's right. U.S. currency is so complicated and detailed, you have to have special equipment and plates to print it in seven passes. The reason these guys are able to do such a credible job is that they use currency presses in foreign countries to print U.S. notes, but the machines aren't sophisticated enough to print ire seven passes. If they ever figure out how to do that, the bills will be basically undetectable."

Macon leaned back in her chair. "And you think they're close to accomplishing that goal?"

"Very close. Last week, we got a bill in from Canada that had been printed in six passes. These bills are already undetectable to the naked eye, and they've managed to slip nearly three hundred thousand into the money supply. If they get any better, they might as well own the damn Bureau of Printing and Engraving."

"Then you can't back off now. Not when you're so close."

He laid the bills on the table and took her hand in his. "I can't not back off, Macon."

"That's a double negative, you know?" she said, unnerved by the gravity in his voice and hoping to inject a little levity.

The joke fell flat. He blinked. "What?"

"Never mind. It was a bad attempt at humor. What do you mean?"

"I mean I'm not going to risk your safety any longer. I can't."

"You're not doing this because of the accident, are you?"

"Of course I am. Your involvement in this case is over. For good. I'm not going through that again. You scared the hell out of me."

She shook her head. "Jacob, I think you're overreacting."

"Overreacting? Damn it, Macon, you could have been killed. It took ten years off my life when I saw that car slam you into that concrete pillar. I still haven't fully recovered."

"You said yourself you didn't believe they were out to kill anyone."

He sighed. "Don't play verbal games with me, Macon. It's over. That's all there is to it."

"But, Jacob, you're so close."

"To hell with close. Charlie is perfectly capable

of doing the leg work here in Washington. The safest place for you to be is as far away from me as possible."

"If that were true," she argued, "then Charlie would already know who we're after. He's been here in Washington while you've been chasing around all over the world. Hasn't he?"

"Charlie is very capable."

"Of course he is, but he doesn't have your intimate knowledge of this case. It would be ridiculous to back off now. You could set yourself back by weeks."

Months was more like it, Jacob thought, but didn't press the point with Macon. "That's irrelevant."

"It is not. Obviously we're on the right track or what happened last night wouldn't have happened at all. It doesn't make the least bit of sense to turn tail now."

"It makes a hell of a lot of sense when you think about the fact that you almost got killed. I'm not going to risk that."

"Jacob, I don't think I should be your primary concern here."

"Too late for that." Didn't she know? Didn't she know he'd aged ten years watching the paramedics pull her out of the car? Didn't she know he'd nearly beat the driver of the white sedan to a pulp before Charlie had managed to restrain him? "You don't seem to understand exactly what's going on, Macon. This isn't a game of cops and robbers. Someone tried to seriously injure, if not kill me last night."

She leaned back in her chair and studied him. "I do understand. I understand perfectly. You're having trouble separating what's between us from your work."

"Hell, yes I am."

She blinked. She hadn't expected him to agree so readily. "Well, you shouldn't. The one has nothing to do with the other. We agreed on that."

Jacob sighed and dragged his hand over his face. "I told you we needed to talk, Macon, and we do."

"We are talking."

He shook his head. "Not about the investigation. About you and me."

She swallowed. "What about you and me?"

Jacob met her gaze and trapped it. "I think maybe I'm ready to tell you about the nightmare."

Twenty-two

He took a sip of his coffee and studied Macon across the table. "It started about five years ago when I first got engaged to Kristen."

Macon stared at him. "I didn't know you were engaged."

He leaned back in his chair. "It's been two years," he said. "Kristen and I separated three weeks before the wedding."

"What happened?"

"She almost got me killed." His lips twisted into a wry smile. "I can see I've taken you by surprise."

"Well, yes, I . . ." She sighed. She could see the tiny lines of tension that edged his eyes, and she had the sudden urge to comfort him by brushing the lock of dark hair that lay across his forehead back off his face. "I had no idea. You don't have to tell me this if you don't want to."

He nodded. "I think I do." He took a sip of his coffee and placed the mug back on the table with a decisive thump. Macon wondered when the kitchen had grown so cold, and she rubbed her hands together in her lap. Jacob tipped his head against the ladder back of his chair and stared out the kitchen window. "Kristen was a beautiful woman. Beautiful like statues are beautiful. Perfect, cold, and lifeless. She was a fashion model, and we met while I was in Paris looking into the early stages of this investigation."

"Did she know who you were?"

Jacob shook his head. "As far as Kristen was concerned, I was an international investment broker. I didn't tell her the truth until after we returned to the States and started seeing each other exclusively."

"Was she upset?"

"Hardly. Kristen was attracted, seduced, by the nature of my job. The more dangerous things were, the more it turned her on. I'd come home after a particularly grueling episode and she'd get hot just listening to me talk about it."

Macon traced a pattern on the white table with her fingertip. "Sounds like a perfect situation for you."

He snorted. "Yeah, perfect. I'd kill five people in a week and know Kristen would find me irresistible in bed for it. It did wonders for my ego."

Macon met his gaze. "I didn't mean that. I just meant it must have been nice to have someone who was so supportive of your career."

"Normally, it would have been. But Kristen was obsessed, and I was too damn obsessed with her to see it."

"What happened?"

"The thrills had to keep getting bigger and better for her to get high on them. I kept trying to distract her. I let her redo my apartment, hoping it would help her concentrate on something other than my job. One day I took a bulletin the shoulder, and she nearly went wild in the hospital. I guess she decided if a bullet in the shoulder was such a good thing, one in the gut must be that much better."

"Oh my God!"

"She sold me out to one of our snitches. Told him who I was and he, in turn, told his boss. They put four bullets in my stomach in a dark alley."

"Oh, Jacob."

"I didn't know at first that Kristen was behind it. Charlie told me later that she showed up at the hospital while I was in surgery. He overheard her gloating over the entire thing to one of the nurses, and he was all over her like white on rice. It took less than two hours for Charlie to get the whole story out of her, and when he did, he put the fear of God into her.

"He relocated her within thirty-six hours to the West Coast and told her he'd personally see her in hell if she ever leaked a word of it. He plugged her into the Service computer and made sure the guys in our L.A. office kept an eye on her. By the time I woke up in the recovery room, Kristen was gone."

"Jacob, that's terrible."

"So now maybe you know why I got so frustrated the other night in your office when you tried to convince me I need a woman who would appreciate the dangerous side of my job. I tried one of those on for size, thanks. I don't think I want to risk another one."

Macon stared at him. His eyes had darkened, and his face registered a certain haggard look she'd never seen before. "Were you in love with her?"

He shrugged. "Not really. I thought I was, but I wasn't. I was enthralled by her. It's not the same thing."

"What do you mean by enthralled?"

"You already know about my family, Macon. My

mother is a full-blooded Sioux Indian. I'm a half-breed. While that doesn't carry nearly the stigma it did fifty or sixty years ago, it's still pretty rough on a kid to grow up in that environment. Especially in a state like Wyoming where tension between the Native Americans and the whites is still fairly high."

"It must have been hard on you."

He shrugged. "Maybe. It doesn't forgive what I did to my family, though." Briefly, he gave her the details of his last encounter with his father, and took another sip of his coffee. "By the time I met Kristen, I was at a full run from who I was. I didn't want to think about home, or family, or what I'd come from. She was glamorous and beautiful and sophisticated, and I wanted to be what she was. I wanted to forget myself so damn much, I nearly got killed over it."

"It's no wonder you have nightmares."

His laugh was mirthless. "Yeah. I should have known then it was an omen for the future."

She waited for him to continue. When he didn't, she squeezed his hand. "Just tell me how it starts."

Jacob shuddered and closed his eyes, tipping his head back against the wall. "When it starts, I'm in a pit. It's very deep, almost like a well. I can't see anything. Everything is black."

She watched as his lips pressed together in a grim line. She ached to reach across the table and smooth them away. "You were probably having nightmares about what Kristen was doing to this apartment," she said softly.

He looked around the stark kitchen with a grim smile. "It is kind of—"

"Monochromatic?" she asked.

"Yeah."

"Haven't you ever heard of Sherwin Williams? A little paint and wallpaper would do wonders for this place."

He exhaled a long breath. "At the time, I wanted Kristen to do the apartment. I remember thinking maybe it would take her mind off my job and focus it on our life together. I didn't really care what she did. After, well, after it was over, I didn't have the energy to change it. I'm never here anyway. I've been home more nights in the last four weeks than I have in the last four years."

Macon tucked her bare feet under her thighs and crossed her arms on the table, then decided to ask more about the dream. "So in the dream, you're in a pit. Everything is black."

"Oh, yeah. There's no way out, and the water keeps rising. My feet are stuck to the bottom, and I can't get loose. I keep looking around for a rope, or a ladder, or a foothold to pull myself out, but there's nothing. Eventually, the water rises so high, I start to choke on it. That's when I wake up. At least that's always the way it was before."

"You said this morning you think you might not have this dream again."

He nodded. "It was different today. Actually, it's been different the last two times I've had it. The first was at your house, the night I collapsed on your couch."

Macon recalled the incident and remembered how disoriented Jacob had seemed that morning. At the time, she'd chalked it up to his lingering fatigue. "I didn't know you'd had a nightmare."

He shrugged. "I've never discussed it with anyone before."

"How was it different?"

"There was a light. I could see a light at the top of the hole. It had never been there before. When I woke up, I realized the light was shining through your windows. At the time, I assumed that had caused the change in the nightmare. My brain was reacting to what my senses were experiencing."

She nodded. "That's reasonable."

He smiled at her—a slight, warm smile. "It didn't have anything to do with the windows, Macon."

"It didn't?" The look in his eyes made her nervous. She tucked her hands beneath her legs to keep her fingers warm.

"No. It didn't."

"Why don't you think so?"

"Because I saw the light again this morning."

"It was morning when you had the dream. There was light in your bedroom."

"Something else happened this time. The dream ended. It's never ended before."

"What do you mean it ended?"

"This time I found the way out of the hole. There was a ladder leaning against the wall. The water kept rising and I kept climbing toward the light. The higher I climbed, the faster the water rose. I thought I was going to drown after all, but then someone reached in and pulled me out of the pit."

She swallowed. "Someone?"

"Yeah." Jacob reached across the table and tucked a strand of her hair behind her ear. Softly, he trailed his fingers over the line of her jaw, pausing to trace the outline of her mouth. "The light wasn't from the windows, Macon." He ran his thumb over her lower lip. "It was from you."

Macon stared at him. "What are you saying, Jacob?"

"I'd be completely dismissing my Sioux heritage and everything I've ever learned from my mother, if I told you I didn't believe in prophetic dreams. Dreams and dream interpretation are very important to the Sioux, just like they are to most Native Americans. I can't discount that somewhere in my psyche, I know my dreams mean more than just random neural firings in my brain."

"Maybe you interpreted it incorrectly."

He shook his head. "I don't think so. I think I started having the nightmare in the first place because I'd lost hope for the future. I was trying to be something I wasn't, and I was drowning in it. I'd gotten in so deep I couldn't find my way out. If I hadn't been so intent on impressing Kristen by being someone other than myself, I'd have seen the signs. They were everywhere."

"You couldn't have known, Jacob."

"I should have known. I shouldn't have let it happen, but I did. It could have destroyed my career, and worse, it could have cost me my life and the trust of my family. Fortunately, I survived the attack, and Charlie never told anyone what had happened. To this day, my superiors believe it was a fluke thing, but I've never been able to get rid of the nightmares, even though no one else knows I sold my soul to Kristen Ager but me, and Charlie and you."

Macon propped her elbows on the table and buried her face in her hands. She realized, belatedly, that she hadn't even noticed his misplaced pronoun for a full ten seconds. She must be even more rattled than she thought. "I'm not sure what to say."

"Don't say anything. I just want you to know that I care about you, Macon. It took me two years before I found a woman I could trust as much as I trust you, and I care very much about what happens to you. If I didn't know it before, I knew it for certain when I saw that car slam into you, and I don't care what it costs, I'm not going to let anything hurt you. There's a sense of rightness with you I've never felt before, and it feels exactly like climbing out of a dark pit." He gave her a sheepish smile. "I sound like an idiot."

She had to stifle a sob. She was beginning to feel panicked "Oh, Jacob. You shouldn't be saying these things to me. You probably had that dream because of the conversation you had with your mother."

He watched her through narrowed eyes. "You're the one who pulled me out of the pit, Macon."

"It's just a dream. Why are you taking it so literally?"

"Because I'm falling in love with you."

She shook her head. He couldn't. He just couldn't. "Don't you understand? You can't care about me. The very worst thing you could do would be to care about me."

He had expected the opposition. He knew she was scared to death of becoming emotionally involved with him, but there was simply no denying the fact that he was already in too deep to turn back to shore. "Tell me why, Macon. Just tell me why. Whatever you're afraid of, we'll face it together."

His voice was soft, lethal to her resolve. Sometime during the night when she'd awakened to find herself being carried to his bed, her mind had accepted what her heart already knew. She was falling in love with Jacob Blackfort. And that was a disaster. "Because it makes you vulnerable." Her voice broke on the last.

"Don't you mean it makes *you* vulnerable?"

She lifted her head and looked at him. "You're the one thinking about throwing away the biggest case of your career just because of what you think you feel for me," she said, miserable.

"I already explained that to you, Macon. There are a lot of things more important than my career. You're just one of them."

She shook her head. "You don't understand. I don't want you to sacrifice anything for me. I never asked you to do that."

"Why don't you try it and see what happens?"

"Because I don't want to."

"Because you don't think I will."

She sighed. "Look, Jacob, no matter what, no matter what you decide about this case, you said yourself we can't ever have a normal relationship. Your job, your life is built around the danger and intrigue of your job. It's what you do. I can't care about a person like that."

"Why not?"

"I just can't."

"Come on, Macon. I showed you my skeleton. I want to see yours."

"Isn't it enough to know that I'm not going to allow myself to care about you."

"It's too late for that. I think you already do."

"I don't."

He grinned at her and before she knew it, he'd captured her head between his hands and was kissing her with a thoroughness that made her lungs feel like they were shutting down. His lips glided over hers in a sensual promise of raw sexual power. Macon didn't even pretend to resist. She leaned into the kiss. Jacob grunted his approval and deepened the kiss, exploring the warm recesses of her mouth with his tongue.

She hardly noticed when he dropped one of his hands and started working at the bottom of her sweatshirt. When his warm hand settled on the cool, taut flesh of her midriff, she gasped. He leaned over, pushing her back in her chair, and plundered her, rubbing his fingers in a butter-soft caress on the sensitive underside of her breast. Even through he lacy film of her bra, she felt the heat of his rough fingertips scalding her flesh. When she moaned and arched her back, pressing her breast more fully into his hand, he lifted his head and rubbed his other thumb over the curve of her mouth, simultaneously removing his hand from beneath her sweatshirt. "Now tell me again how you don't care about me."

She pushed his hands away. "Just because I'm attracted to you, doesn't—"

"Just because you turn to goo every time I kiss you."

"Your ego is amazing."

"It's your fault."

"What is?"

"If you didn't explode when I touch you, I wouldn't be so damned arrogant about it."

"I do not explode."

"Do you want another demonstration?"

"Stop it, Jacob. I'm serious."

He nodded. "So am I."

"What I mean to say is, just because I find you

physically attractive does not mean I am willing or prepared to risk a relationship with you."

Jacob leaned closer so his nose was almost touching hers. "Why not, Macon? Come on. You owe me this."

She swallowed. "Because if I—" she stopped herself just short of saying 'fall in love.' "You're just not what I'm looking for."

"Then tell me what you are looking for?"

She shook her head. "It's not that easy to define. It isn't as if I have a list."

"Then let me see if I can guess."

"Jacob—"

He ignored her. "You want a foolproof relationship, guaranteed not to hurt you. Isn't that right?"

"No, I—"

"And I don't fit the bill."

She sighed and leaned forward. "Jacob, please try to understand. When I was a little girl, I used to believe in the kind of fast-paced, whirlwind romance you have in mind. I thought one day my imaginary prince would come riding along on his palomino, wearing a cape, and climb my balcony with flowers in his hand. Then he'd give me the world, just like he'd promised. But one day I grew up, and I stopped believing in the fantasy."

"So what do you believe now?"

"I believe that if I let myself care for you, you'd hurt me. I don't like to be hurt, and I don't see any decent reason to put myself in the line of fire. Is that so bad?"

Jacob studied her for several tense seconds. "What are you afraid of, Macon?"

And suddenly, she wanted to tell him. It was just as clear in her mind as the window in Jacob's kitchen. She'd never wanted to tell anyone before, but she wanted desperately to tell Jacob. "Everyone I ever loved left me. My father, my mother, my stepbrother Tommy, all of them. They all left. A long time ago, I made the decision not to love anyone ever again because it hurt too much to lose them." She blurted out the words before she could stop herself.

He blinked. "You're afraid of losing me? That's why?"

"You'll leave me. '

"I'm not going to go anywhere, honey."

"You can't promise me that. No one can promise that."

Jacob took both her hands and clasped them together between his. "Honey, you're letting your imagination run away with you."

"How much do you know about my childhood?"

"Quite a bit. I read—"

"I know. You read my file."

Jacob nodded. "That's right."

"Then you know that my father died when I was three years old."

"Yes. It was a fluke automobile accident."

"That's right. He was killed when a tree fell across the road on top of his car, but you probably don't know what happened afterward. He didn't have any insurance, and my mother and I were left with nothing. She had to get a job for the first time in her life just to support us."

"She went to work for Gordon Stratton."

Macon pulled her knees up under her chin and leaned back in the chair. "As a secretary in his office. We lived in virtual poverty for six years, always just making the rent or just paying the water bill on time. Gordon tried almost from the beginning to get Mama to marry him, but she wouldn't. She never stopped loving my father. She never would have, either, if I hadn't gotten so ill."

Jacob shifted in his chair. "You needed surgery on a growth in your abdomen. I remember reading that."

"Yes. We couldn't afford the doctor's bills. I had to have the surgery and Mama couldn't afford it, so she did the only thing she could do. She married Gordon Stratton."

"Was she really unhappy with him?"

"It had nothing to do with Gordon. I don't think she ever stopped believing that she'd betrayed my father by remarrying. At some level, I don't think she ever forgave him for dying and leaving us alone."

"We have to go on living, Macon."

She shrugged. "Mama didn't think so. I guess that's why she died two years later."

Jacob sighed. Macon's mother had committed suicide two years after her marriage to Gordon Stratton. He had no doubt it had been very difficult on Macon, then just eleven years old. The surgery had been frightening enough, but he knew from the personal profile he'd read on her that her mother's suicide had turned a relatively well-adjusted child into a solemn miniature adult. And as far as he was concerned, it had been damned selfish of Cornelia Stratton to take her own life.

He watched the expression of quiet anguish on Macon's face and bit off an angry curse. Mentally flipping through her background file, he found the next tragedy in her young life. "And then two years later, your stepbrother Tommy drove his car off the road and died."

Macon nodded. "That's right. Tommy was Gordon's son by his first marriage. He was twelve years older than I. After Tommy's death, Gordon was all I had left. I suppose it was a good thing my mother talked him into adopting me before she died. Otherwise, I might have been turned over to state custody after Mama's death. Gordon wouldn't have been obligated to keep me.

Jacob frowned. "Hasn't it occurred to you that maybe Gordon adopted you because he was worried about Cornelia's stability?"

She looked at him, startled. "No. No, I'm sure that's not true. Gordon was devastated when Mama died."

Jacob reached out and ran his fingers over the curve of her cheek. "So were you, honey."

She shivered and shook her head. "You don't understand. Gordon and I have never been close. I assumed he wanted it that way."

Jacob shook his head. "That's not what his actions say." He covered her lips with his fingers when she would have protested. "Did you know he wrote the chancellor of your college every weekend to make sure you were doing all right?"

Her eyes widened. "He did?"

Jacob nodded. "There are copies of the letters in your file. I guess you never got around to reading it."

"No. I didn't. But why would he do that? I did very well in college."

"He wasn't checking up on you, Macon. He was worried. From what I could tell, you retreated so far into your shell after Tommy's death, Gordon considered taking you for counseling."

"I was fine. He should have known that."

"You weren't fine. You aren't fine. Honey, no matter who Gordon is, I believe he desperately wants a real relationship with you. I talked to him on the phone after your accident and he was worried sick."

"He was?"

"Of course he was. What father wouldn't be?"

"But Gordon's not my—"

"I think he wants to be."

Macon stared at him. "Did he tell you that?"

"He didn't have to. He almost came unglued when I told him you'd been injured." Jacob cupped her face in his large hand. "You're doing the same thing to him you're doing to me."

Macon felt a suspicious, unwelcome knot start working at the back of her throat. She swallowed hard. It didn't help. "I'm not, Jacob. I swear I'm not. Gordon just never—I mean we didn't—well, it just didn't seem like he wanted to be that close to me."

"Why don't you ask him?"

"I can't ask him."

"Why not?"

"Well, what's he supposed to say?"

"I think he'll answer you so quick, he'll blow your socks off. That's what I think."

She frowned at him. "This is ridiculous. I genuinely care for Gordon. I'm sure he knows that."

"But you're not close to him?"

"I don't know. I guess not." Macon looked closely at Jacob. "It's like I said. I never really thought about it."

"I think you thought about it a lot. You were just scared of what would happen if you let him inside that tough reserve of yours."

"For heaven's sake, Jacob, I'm not a fortress of stability, you know."

"Maybe not, but when you're determined to keep someone away, you're damned good at it."

She rubbed her hands on the sleeves of her sweatshirt. "Why are you doing this to me?"

"You really don't know?"

She shook her head. "No. I really don't know."

He leaned forward and kissed her softly, finally resting his forehead against hers and holding her gaze. "Because after you ask Gordon just how close he wants to be to you, I'm hoping I can get you to ask me the same question."

Twenty-three

"Do you have a match on those prints yet, Charlie?" Jacob asked when he strolled into his office several hours later. He had dropped Macon at her house, only after making her swear to him she wouldn't try to go into her office. Just to be sure, he'd called Maylene and asked her to send Macon home in a cab if she showed up at the office.

He'd spent all morning agonizing over their conversation, over Macon's fears, over what he was going to do about them. He was on the verge of sending Gordon Stratton to prison even while he was pushing Macon closer to him. After she'd confessed to him that she feared losing the people she'd loved, God, he'd felt like the lowest form of life on earth. It had been the way Gordon had responded when he'd heard about the accident that had begun to unravel some of Jacob's unshakable confidence.

Charlie looked up from his desk and frowned. "Nope. It's a partial print all right, but I don't think it belongs to Elliot Raines."

Jacob dropped down into the chair next to Charlie's desk and frowned. "Damn it."

"Look, Jake, I know you want this guy, but what makes you so sure it's him?"

"He," Jacob said before he even realized he was correcting Charlie's grammar. Charlie swore at him rather colorfully. Jacob responded with a sheepish grin. "Sorry. It just is. It has to be Raines. I'm sure of it."

"You wouldn't be operating under any preconceived suspicions would you? It could have been Stratton you know. He's the one throwing around half a mil in hard cash." Charlie leaned back in his chair and took a long draw on his cigar.

"It is not Gordon Stratton."

"What makes you so sure?"

"Because the man got hysterical when I called him and told him about Macon's accident."

The front legs of Charlie's chair hit the floor with a bang. "You did what?"

"He's the only family she has, Charlie. He had a right to know. Besides, if Raines tried to hurt Macon, I think Stratton will turn on him. Partner or not."

"What if Raines is innocent?"

Jacob shook his head. "Raines is our guy."

"Then he's working with somebody besides Gordon Stratton."

"What do you mean?"

Charlie pulled a manila folder out of his desk. "Take a look at this." He dropped it on the desk, nearly upsetting a polystyrene cup of cold coffee, and sending half a dozen yellow message slips sailing to the floor. "The fax came in two nights ago while you were at the party."

Jacob scanned the documents in the folder, frowning over the report. Edward Gilani, a Secret Service agent posing as a foreign investor, had been circulating about Washington for some time making it known, by dropping a lot of money in

the right places, that he was looking for a piece
of some very big action, and that he had a defi-
nite interest in counterfeit bills. The fax in the
folder was an anonymous message instructing Gilani to meet one Kali Ahdesh at an address on K
street thirty minutes from the time of the fax.
"Did Eddie go?"

Charlie nodded. "Yep." He pulled a briefcase
out from under his desk. "Want to see the sam-
ples?"

Jacob flipped open the case and removed a
stack of bills. Using the infrared sensor on Charlie's desk, he examined them closely. "Six
passes," he said.

"The best yet. They're clearer than the Cana-
dian bust from last week."

Jacob tossed the bills back into the briefcase.
"So why are you convinced it's not Raines?"

"Because this fax came in while you were at
that party. The same one where you claim Elliot
Raines was hanging all over our Ms. Stratton."

Jacob shrugged. "So he hired somebody."

"Maybe. Probably, but the point is, Raines can't
be handling this big of a cargo on his own. And
I don't think he'd be hobnobbing at a political
party while his flunky was making arrangements
for a three-million-dollar deal."

"Unless he wanted an alibi."

Charlie frowned. "It's possible, but I doubt it.
Anyway, Raines still hasn't got the capital to pull
this off. He needs somebody with a lot of money,
or a lot of access to cash flow to buy the materials,
make the print run, deliver the goods, and re-
place the cash before anyone catches on. Stratton's five-hundred grand definitely places him
toward the top of the suspect list, but they'd need

at least another million to make this work. Stratton doesn't have those kind of resources. Neither does Raines. We need a third player.

"Raines could be transferring money from consulting fees."

Charlie looked skeptical. "In September of an election year? Do you really think there are any candidates out there who are paying bills this side of the election and not sinking every last cent into their campaigns?"

Jacob drummed his fingers on his knee. "Maybe. I think we should look into it anyway."

"I will. I just want to stay open to other possibilities."

"Fair enough. In the meantime, I want the cuff link."

Charlie looked at him suspiciously. "Why?"

"Because I want to pay Elliot Raines a visit."

"Do you think that's smart?"

"Look, Charlie, somebody knows something. If they didn't, our friend in the white sedan wouldn't have been sailing through the parking deck on Saturday night."

"So what are you going do? Try and shame Raines into a confession?"

"Not really. I just want to gauge his reaction. I figured I'd tell him I found the cuff link in the parking lot and recognized it from the set he was wearing on Saturday." At Charlie's scowl, Jacob laughed. "Don't worry, Charlie. I have everything under control."

Charlie pulled the cuff link out of his drawer and handed it to Jacob. "There's just one more thing, Jake."

"Yeah?"

"Have you considered that maybe somebody

leaked the truth about you to whoever tried to run you over on Saturday?"

Jacob felt his blood run cold. "Somebody like Macon, you mean?"

Charlie nodded. "Yeah. Maybe."

"It's not. She wouldn't."

"Jake, I—"

"Just drop it, Charlie. Do me a favor and drop it."

Macon looked out the window of her dining room and sighed, cradling a mug of cocoa between her hands. The misting rain did little to relieve the growing anxiety she felt at being trapped in the house, or the unsettled feeling that still lingered after her conversation with Jacob that morning.

After he'd calmly told her he wanted her to ask him just what he wanted from their relationship, he'd blissfully removed the burden from her by refusing to discuss the issue until she'd spoken with Gordon Stratton—a task she still hadn't carried out and wasn't sure she wanted to. A phone call to May had quickly revealed that she wouldn't be gaining any support from that quarter, so Macon had set about brooding for most of the afternoon.

She took a long sip of her cocoa, rolling the frothy chocolate on her tongue, and tipped her forehead against the window. The more she thought about Jacob's intent to back away from his investigation, the more it angered her. She knew for certain that he was very close to culminating what had taken four years of his life to build. She suspected he'd never forgive her if she allowed him to do that.

The jangle of the telephone interrupted her concentration, and she contemplated ignoring it. The thought that it might be Jacob, and the certain knowledge that he'd overreact if she didn't answer the phone, changed her mind. She snatched up the receiver in the kitchen just before the fourth ring. "Hello."

There was nothing but silence and the unmistakable presence of someone on the other end. Macon frowned. "Hello."

"Jacob Blackfort's lying to you." The voice was low and scratchy and indistinguishable.

Macon instinctively recoiled. "Who is this?"

"A friend. Stay away from Jacob Blackfort. He isn't what he seems."

"What do you want?"

"Blackfort's going to die. You might too. If you're smart, you'll stay away from him. Look for the package in your mailbox."

Macon shivered and slammed the phone down. It rang again almost instantly. She stared at it, willing it to stop. But the ringing persisted, and she grabbed the receiver. "Listen," she said, thinking the tremor in her voice and her uncharacteristic unease must be attributable to her accident and not to any real worry about Jacob Blackfort. "I don't know who the hell you are, but—"

"Macon?" It was Gordon Stratton's voice.

At the familiar sound of his voice, she sank down into a chair, cradling her forehead in her hand, and tried to dismiss her lingering reaction to the odd phone call. "Oh, Gordon. Hello."

"Are you all right? You sound upset."

"I'm fine, Gordon. I had just gotten off the phone with a crank caller." Macon leaned back in the chair and let the rest of the tension drain out of her. She made a mental note to discuss the phone call with Jacob. "I was just a little rattled."

"I called to see how you're feeling."

Macon rubbed the back of her neck with her hand. "I've been better. My head still hurts a little, and I feel like one giant bruise."

She heard Gordon smile. "Sort of like the time you rode your bike down that hill in the backyard after I told you not to."

Macon laughed at the memory. "The worst part of that whole thing was that you knew I'd fallen and didn't want to get me in trouble by telling Mama. I'll never forget having to sit through dinner that night, pretending I wasn't in the worst pain of my life."

Gordon chuckled, and Macon felt strangely warmed and reassured by the sound. "You were always getting in over your head, Macon. It's a wonder you've lived this long, as accident-prone as you were."

"Right now I almost wish I hadn't. I hurt all over and it's hard to get comfortable."

"Can I bring you anything?" he asked.

Macon frowned, taken aback. "I—well no, I guess not. I think I have everything I need right here. Besides, it's the end of the session. I know how busy you are."

Gordon sighed. "I'm not that busy, Macon. Maybe I'll come by and see you this afternoon. Will that be all right?"

"You don't have to do that. I told you, I'm really fine. No structural damage."

"I know I don't have to come. I want to. How about three o'clock?"

Macon shot a quick glance at the digital clock on her microwave. It was just before noon. "All right. But don't push yourself on my behalf."

"You're my family, Macon. What did I ever do to give you the impression you wouldn't fit in my schedule?"

Macon felt suddenly guilty at the lingering sadness in her stepfather's voice that hadn't been there before. Or perhaps she'd never noticed. "I'm just a little rattled is all. I'm sorry."

"No problem, punkin. Are you sure I can't bring you anything?"

Macon smiled at the endearment. Gordon hadn't used it in years. She opened the bottle of painkillers Jacob had left for her on the table and shook out two into her palm. "Maybe some of that chocolate truffle stuff from Cheryl's Bakery if you have time."

"You got it. I'll see you at three. Get some rest, all right?"

"I will. Thanks." She swallowed the two pills along with the last of her cocoa.

"Bye-bye."

"Bye." Macon hung up the phone with a soft *click*. She was still shaking from the ominous phone call, then she suddenly remembered the mailbox. Jacob had brought her mail in for her that afternoon when he'd dropped her off. Her eyes strayed to the small package sitting on top of the stack. She didn't want to open it.

She stared at it for several minutes before she resolutely walked across the kitchen and picked up the box. It was small, but heavy. It was hand addressed, with no return address in the corner.

She shook it once. It didn't make any noise. Her hand shook when she reached for a pair of scissors.

Macon peeled back the paper and swallowed, looking at the small white box. She was afraid to look inside, but even more afraid not to. Warily, she slid the top off the box and parted the tissue paper. She almost screamed at the sight of the dead, black rat inside. It was impaled on a small black arrow that entered through its mouth and emerged at its tail.

Jacob's code name was Black Arrow. There was no mistaking the implied message. She dropped the box on the counter and covered her mouth with her hands—feeling suddenly sick. And she admitted, despite everything she'd told him that morning, despite the fears and the worries, and the reasons against it, she admitted what her heart had known all along. She was in love with Jacob Blackfort, and even if she lost him right then, right that very minute, the notion that she had loved him, that he had loved her in return was worth any risk. It was worth everything. She fought down a wave of panic and reached for the phone. She had to talk to Jacob.

"Macon. Honey, wake up."

Macon's lashes drifted open and with no small amount of effort, she managed to focus on Jacob. He was hunched down beside her chair. When she'd called, she sounded hysterical. He'd burnt up the highway getting to her house. "Are you all right?" he asked.

Macon lifted her head off her crossed arms with a weak smile. "Fell asleep."

He nodded. "Evidently."

"What time is it?"

"A little before two o'clock." He glanced at the pill bottle on the table. "How many of those did you take?"

"Two."

"Are you sure?"

She tried to glare at him, but wasn't sure she pulled it off. "Of course I'm sure."

Jacob smiled at her and stood up. "Okay, honey, I'm putting you to bed." He grabbed her hand and pulled her to a standing position. "Can you walk upstairs, or do you want me to carry you?"

"Walk," she said.

"Yeah, sure." He swept her up against his chest. "I don't think I want to risk it."

She sighed and dropped her head against his shoulder. "Thanks," she mumbled.

Jacob shook his head and headed for the stairs. "This is becoming a habit, you know."

"I know." She rubbed her cheek against the snowy white fabric of his shirt, belatedly remembering the phone call. "Jacob?"

"Hmmm." He started up the stairs.

"The phone."

"What about it, honey?" He reached the top of the stairs and stopped. "Which room?"

She waved her hand in the general direction of her bedroom. Jacob walked down the hall. "He called," Macon mumbled.

"Who called?" He nudged the door open with his foot and smiled at the inviting interior. Macon's four-poster bed dominated the small, elegantly appointed room. After the first time he'd seen the homey collection of quilts and plaids and ruffles, he'd not been able to stop picturing her sprawled on the flannel sheets. He crossed to it and laid her down gently on the antique quilt. He started to remove her slippers.

"The stranger. Said you lied."

Jacob dropped a slipper on the thick carpet and froze. "Who did, sweetheart?"

"So tired," she said.

He squeezed her foot. "Come on, don't fade out on me now. I need to know who called."

"Didn't say." She turned onto her side and cuddled into the pillow.

"Did anyone else call, Macon?" She didn't answer. "Come on, honey, this is important. Stay with me."

"Gordon," she said, and rubbed her cheek against the pillow. "He's coming over."

"Gordon. Your stepfather."

"Ummm."

"Did he call before or after this stranger?"

There was a long pause before Macon said, "After. Sent package. With the mail." Her fingers tightened momentarily on his hand. "Said he'd kill you," she whispered and sank into oblivion.

Jacob watched her for several long seconds. His palms had started to sweat. He pulled off her remaining slipper and tucked the quilt around her shoulders. Damn.

Jacob prowled around Macon's bedroom, feeling caged and tense. Who had called? What had they said? What had her reaction been? And what the hell did she mean about the package? He took in her sleeping form on the bed and released a pent-up breath. Bending down, he pressed a kiss to her temple. "Nothing's going to happen to you, honey,'' he promised, and reached for the phone.

"Darrow," Charlie barked into the receiver.

"Your mood's gone from bad to worse I see," Jacob drawled, combing his fingers through Macon's hair as he sat on the side of the bed.

"Damn it, Jake, where the hell are you?"

"I'm at Macon's house. Why?"

"Quiver's pissed as hell. The tantrum he pitched when you told him you were taking yourself off this case is nothing compared to what happened after you left."

"Why?" Jacob asked, alert to the rough tone in Charlie's voice. He had known Charlie Darrow too long not to know his moods. Something was drastically wrong.

"Gilani's dead."

"What?"

"You heard me. When Eddie didn't report in this afternoon, Quiver sent Deliss and Ryan looking for him. They found him floating in the reflecting pool."

"Damn it."

"Yeah. Damn it. Things are out of control, Jake. We got to lower the net on Stratton right here and now or it's going to get messy. Quiver wants a sting for tomorrow night."

Jacob's hand tightened on Macon's scalp before he realized it. He released a long breath and resumed a more gentle stroke. "I didn't get anything out of Raines this afternoon."

"Yeah, well, Connie's got something off that cuff link."

Jacob's heart started racing. "A positive ID on Raines' print?"

"Bingo. It looks like you were right. That cuff

link did belong to Elliot Raines. The D.C. police are waiting on a warrant so we can go check his apartment for the torn shirt."

"I knew it."

"It still doesn't prove anything, Jake."

"Yeah, but it narrows things down a hell of a lot."

"Maybe so, but you'd better know that Quiver's more determined than ever to keep you on this case with Macon as your cover. You'd better get to Stratton fast if you think you can get him to turn on Raines."

"Not a chance, Charlie. I'm not risking her safety."

"Quiver's not going to let you throw what could be our last chance away because you're hot for this woman."

"I'm warning you, Charlie."

"Damn it, Jake, quit thinking with your crotch. You saw those bills this morning. This is our best chance. Maybe our last."

"I'm not going to put Macon in the middle."

"We'll watch her. You know we will. I mean, hell, Jake, if anybody can protect somebody it ought to be us."

Charlie's attempt at humor fell flat. Jacob frowned into the receiver. "There's nothing funny about this. I'm dead serious."

"If you're not careful, you'll just be dead. Period."

"Yeah, but Macon's not. That's what matters."

"We need her, Jake. You're going to have to face that."

"This was never part of the deal."

"She made it part of the deal when she let that guy slam into her car. They already know she's involved. If you drop her now, things could get worse."

Jacob looked down at Macon's face, reposed in sleep. The bruise at her temple had turned a nasty purplish blue. He could feel a cold knot of anger churning in his stomach. "What does Quiver want?"

"Bait."

"No. No way in hell."

"Now hold on a minute."

"I said no. We're not using Macon to draw out Raines."

"Quiver's going to ask her if she'll do it whether you want him to or not."

"Over my dead body."

"That's a distinct possibility."

"Damn it, Charlie, she's already been threatened once. I want this to end right now."

"What do you mean she's already been threatened."

Jacob let out a harsh sigh, already regretting the small admission. He'd changed his mind about telling Charlie about the mysterious phone call. "I'm not sure," he confessed. "It could be nothing."

"What are you holding out on me?"

"Off the record until I know for sure. Okay, Charlie?"

"Sure. Sure. What's going on?"

"When I got here, Macon was pretty much out of it. The painkillers really knock her out."

"But?"

"But she mentioned something about a phone call from a stranger and a package. Something about telling her I lied to her. It could be nothing."

"Yeah, but it could be something. You want me to check it out?"

Jacob looked down at Macon again. "Yeah. Call the phone company. Get a trace on the last two incoming calls on her phone. One of them should be Gordon Stratton. It's the other guy I want."

"Sure thing, Jake. How is she anyway?"

"Okay I think. I'm going to be staying here for the next couple of days. Call me as soon as you have anything."

"You bet. What about the package?"

"What package?"

"You said the caller mentioned something about a package. What was in it?"

"Oh. I don't know. It's downstairs. I brought it in with her mail. I'll go down and check. Hold on, all right?"

"Sure."

Jacob laid the receiver down on the nightstand, then hurried downstairs. He found the white box in the kitchen and picked it up, parting the white tissue paper to look inside. At the sight of the dead rat, he let out a low whistle and picked up the phone. "Charlie?"

"Did you find it?"

"Yeah."

"What's in it?"

"A dead black rat. It's got a black arrow stuck through it."

Twenty-four

"Jacob?" Macon sat up in her bed.

She felt a movement beside her. "I'm here, Macon. Go back to sleep."

She was momentarily disoriented by the fuzzy feeling in her head and the weak light fighting its way through the curtains in her room. "What time is it?"

"After six. You've been asleep all afternoon. Gordon came by."

"He was supposed to come at three," she mumbled, rubbing her eyes with her fist.

"He did. Left you a box of something downstairs."

"You should have awakened me."

"You were sleeping like the dead, honey. He didn't want me to disturb you."

Her eyes finally focused on Jacob's form, reclined on top of her blue down comforter. And she remembered. "Oh my God, Jacob." She clutched at his arm. "The rat. Did you see the rat?"

With her question came the realization that she would not go back to sleep. He sat up. "I saw the rat. I suppose there's no chance of your going back to sleep?"

Macon shook her head. "I can't sleep at a time

like this. How can you be so calm? Don't you know what that rat means?"

Jacob reached over to flick on the light. Macon's face contorted into a wry grimace. "Sorry," he muttered. "Are you hungry?" He swung his feet to the floor and started to pull on his socks.

"No I'm not hungry. Somebody wants to kill you. I want to know what you're doing about the rat."

He didn't look at her. "Charlie has it. He's checking the box for prints."

"Prints!" She scrambled to her knees, and laid a hand on his back. "Are you crazy? You're not going to find any prints. He would have worn gloves. These people always wear gloves. Everyone knows that. Don't you people watch television?"

She was starting to sound hysterical. Jacob had to stifle a grin. He reached over and squeezed her shoulder, bending his head to drop a brief, hard kiss on her lips. "Relax, Macon. We have everything under control."

"Under control? Under control? You don't have anything under control. There are strange men calling my house and threatening me. I'm receiving packages that fully imply someone wants to kill you. You don't have the first idea who it is, or where they are, and you expect me to believe you have this under control?"

With a laugh, he tumbled her back on the bed. "Take it easy, Kemosabe. You're going to blow a gasket. For your information, we happen to have a very good idea who it is, we do know where he is, and we're just a few days from busting the guy. Give me some credit, will you?"

She blinked. Jacob was moving his hand up her

rib cage in a leisurely caress and she was fast losing her concentration. "Oh."

"Yeah. Oh."

His hand settled on the curve of her breast and she sucked in a deep breath. She hadn't realized until then that she was wearing one of her silk nightgowns. The feel of his warm hand through the slippery silk made her heart miss a beat. "Jacob . . ."

He rubbed his lips over hers in the barest caress. "Yeah?"

"What—what are you doing?"

"What do you think I'm doing?" His lips settled on her earlobe.

"This is not the time for this."

"Relax, honey. I'm not going to take things too far. I promised you I wouldn't. I just want to be close to you. This," he paused and clasped her head in his warm hands, "all of this has been so hard. It's like I told you this morning. I'm falling in love with you, Macon."

She stared at him. His eyes had turned a smoky gray, and the intense heat she saw in their depths turned her insides to melted butter. She felt something explode inside her heart, and she just barely resisted the urge to throw her arms around his neck and whoop. Despite her lingering fears, despite the uneasy, almost desperate need she had to cling to him, to never let him go, she had known the instant she'd opened that package that she couldn't deny her feelings for him any longer. "Jacob . . ."

He shook his head. "Don't say anything. Please don't say anything. I know it's too soon for you."

Macon reached up and toyed with the wrinkled

collar of his white shirt. "Jacob, I think you should know—"

"I didn't mean to tell you, not like this, not here, but I'm falling apart inside."

She shifted beneath him and moved her fingers to his chin. "Jacob, listen to me."

He shook his head and pressed a hand against her mouth. "I shouldn't have rushed you. Not when you're ill."

"I'm not ill," she mumbled against his hand, thinking she sounded suspiciously like a transistor radio gone bad.

He smiled at her. "I couldn't help it. It just happened. I needed to say it, but I want you to know I don't expect you to say anything in return."

She pushed his hand away from her mouth. "Not even if I want to say I love you too?"

"Not even—what?"

"I love you too."

Jacob stared at her. "You do?"

She nodded. "I was pretty sure when I saw you about to get flattened in the parking garage. I was still feeling panicky this morning when we talked, and I wasn't making very much sense, I know, but I knew for certain that I love you when I saw that rat." She paused and rubbed her fingers over hi, mouth. "That doesn't mean I'm not afraid. I'd die if anything happened to you, but I can't deny what I feel. I love you."

He swallowed. "Macon, I—I don't know what to say."

"There's nothing to say. We shouldn't have done it. I told you this morning that I didn't want to do it, but it's done now. I don't suppose there's any way out of it."

"Not for me there isn't."

"Me either."

He wiped her hair off her forehead and ran the pad of his thumb over the curve of her cheekbone. "You aren't upset?"

"Why should I be upset?"

"All those things you said earlier, about my work, about your fears, about risking too much, they're still all true."

"Yes."

"I've still got this enormous mess to clean up with my family. I can't promise you it will ever be resolved."

"I know."

"So why are you taking this so calmly?"

"I'm not calm about it at all. I'm just resigned to it." She rubbed the frown off of his forehead with her thumb. "I love you, Jacob. There's a lot of freedom in saying that. I don't even begin to know how we're going to settle all the problems. Do I have to have those answers right now?"

He shook his head. "We can cross those bridges when we get to them."

She smiled at him. "The first thing we're going to have to work on is your overuse of clichés."

"We'll take one day at a time," he said, lowering himself completely on top of her.

"It's really quite trying on my patience, you know?"

"We'll count our chickens when they're hatched."

She threaded her fingers into his hair when his lips settled on her earlobe. "When we've conquered that, we'll work on your grammar."

"Throw caution to the wind," he muttered, just before he blew into her ear.

"I think you might be hopeless."

He slid his lips along her jaw and kissed the corner of her mouth. When he raised his head, all traces of teasing were gone from his expression. "I'll never be hopeless again, Macon. Not as long as I have you."

And then he kissed her. And nothing else seemed to really matter. Jacob was hard and solid and strong above her, and with his weight pressing her into the bed and his lips moving over hers in a soft, giving caress, she felt the last shards of her resistance melt away like snow in a spring thaw.

He cradled her head in one hand while his other moved along the silk of her nightgown to cup her breast. He ended the kiss as suddenly as it had started and smiled at her. "I love you," he said. "I don't think I'll ever get tired of saying it."

She squeezed him tight. "I hope not." She watched him for several more seconds before she shifted beneath him and laid her palm against his face. "So what are we going to do?"

He grinned. "I want it all. I want everything from you. Babies, a vacation home—"

Macon covered his mouth before he could continue. 'I think we should agree to discuss that later. There are too many things we have to worry about."

He kissed her hand before pulling it away. "Nothing is more important."

"Maybe not, but there are certainly things that are more urgent. I want to know what you're going to do about this rat business. Someone wants to kill you, and you'd better not even think about letting it happen."

Jacob sighed and rolled off her. "Then we'd better find another place to talk. I spend far too much time rolling around in bed with you—for my peace of mind."

"Whose fault is that?"

He grinned at her and stood up. "I'll go downstairs and fix us something to eat while you dress. Charlie should—"

"Speaking of dressing," she said, interrupting him, "is your mother here?"

He blinked. "No. She's still at my apartment. Why?"

Macon plucked one of the red straps of her nightgown. "What happened to my sweats, and how did I end up wearing this?"

He leered at her. "I was always very good at sneaking around behind my mother's back."

Macon tossed a pillow at him. "You're a beast."

He grinned and picked the pillow up. "I confess I couldn't quite resist the urge. I think you look sexier in my silk pajamas, though."

She smiled a half-smile at him. "Maybe I'll put them back on for you one day."

Jacob's mouth dropped open, and Macon watched the heated look in his aquamarine eyes with no small amount of pleasure. "You have got to quit saying things like that, Macon. If I take one more cold shower, I'll turn into a prune."

She sighed and leaned back against the pillows. "All right. I'll let you off the hook. What were you saying about Charlie?"

"Charlie?"

"You remember. Tall guy. Smokes a cigar."

Jacob's smile was rueful. "You do incredible things to my concentration. I was saying, before you tried to lead me down the path of temptation—"

"As if you needed any leading."

"As if," he conceded, "that Charlie should be calling any minute now about the prints on the box. If he says what I think he will, we have a lot to talk about."

Macon sobered. "Jacob?"

"Yes, love?"

"Is this the part where I get hurt?"

He nodded. "Could be."

"Can you tell me you love me just one more time, so I won't forget."

He smiled at her. "I'll tell you all you want, Macon. I love you. No matter what happens. I love you."

An hour later, when Macon opened the door to find a grim-faced Charlie Darrow on her front stoop, she kept trying to replay Jacob's words in her head. He couldn't be lying to her. He just couldn't. "Hi, Charlie."

"Hi, Macon. How are you feeling?"

She shrugged and motioned him inside. "All right. Can I take your coat?"

He shucked it off. "About the other night, that thing at the memorial."

Macon took his coat and hung it in the hall closet. "Don't worry about it, Charlie. You were looking out for Jacob. I understand that."

Charlie nodded and tucked a thick brown envelope under his arm. "Jake said he wanted us to go over everything with you."

"That's what he says."

Charlie frowned. "Where is he?"

"Upstairs shaving."

"Did you know he could get into serious trouble for this?"

"I suspected that might be the case."

"Are you going to let him do it anyway?"

"I don't see that I have much choice."

Charlie frowned. "He could lose his job, Macon."

"I think maybe he wants to."

Charlie sighed and handed her the envelope. "You might as well start reading. Mind if I help myself to coffee?"

"No." She paused, laying a hand on his arm before he could head for the kitchen. "Charlie?"

"Yeah?"

"Could you get in trouble, too?"

He looked sheepish. "Yeah."

She rose up on tiptoes and kissed his weathered cheek. "Thanks, Charlie."

He mumbled something beneath his breath and stalked toward the kitchen. Macon went into the living room and sat down on the couch, gingerly tearing open the envelope.

By the time Jacob entered the living room, toweling his thick hair, Charlie was seated across from her, and Macon was just finishing the contents of the file. Jacob looked at her and frowned. Her mouth was compressed in a tight line, and she looked pale. He couldn't decide if it was the effect of her accident, or the content of the file. He thought briefly of his conversation that afternoon with Gordon Stratton—and grimaced. The man was visibly shaken by Macon's accident, and Jacob was beginning to have a sick feeling that there was something drastically wrong with the case he'd been building against Macon's stepfather. That, more than anything, had been the impetus behind his decision to tell Macon the entire story and damn the consequences.

"Macon," he said softly.

She looked up, her eyes a stormy blue. "Hello."

He walked over to the couch, sparing Charlie a passing glance before he bent down and dropped a brief kiss on Macon's lips. He sat down next to her and took the contents of the file from her fingers. "How are you doing?" he asked.

She stared at him. "Have you suspected Gordon all along?"

"Yes."

"And that's the real reason you wanted my help? So you could observe Gordon from a closer proximity?"

"Yes."

"And you used your time in my office to investigate his files and look over the records of his campaign I keep there?"

"Yes."

She looked hurt. "I don't believe any of this."

Charlie sighed and leaned back in his chair. "It's true, Macon. Everything in that file is a piece of evidence."

Jacob reached for her hand, she pulled it away. "You should have told me," she said.

"Would you have believed me?" Jacob asked.

"He's not guilty."

Jacob sighed. "What was on the box, Charlie?"

"Gordon Stratton's prints," Charlie said, his voice grim.

"No!" Macon looked at Charlie. "I don't believe you."

Charlie produced another piece of paper from his inside jacket pocket. "Here's the report."

She didn't take it. "There's a mistake then."

Jacob sighed and grabbed her hand before she could resist him. "Macon, listen to me. We're building a case against Gordon, it's true. But all of this is circumstantial evidence. You could be right."

Charlie sat bolt upright in his chair. "What?"

Jacob shot him a withering look. "Come on, Charlie. You know it, and I know it. Quiver's too hot to bust this guy and I want to know why."

"Jake, I don't think . . ."

Jacob held up his hand and looked back at Macon. "Until I talked to Gordon on the phone after your accident, I think I believed he was guilty. Afterwards, well, I wasn't so sure. I knew for certain he didn't have anything to do with your accident."

Macon swallowed. "What are you saying?"

"When he came by the house to see you today, we talked for a while. I want to believe he's innocent, Macon. I want that so damned badly for you that it makes me hurt inside."

"But you don't believe it, do you?"

"There's a lot of damning evidence in that file."

"Damn straight there is," Charlie mumbled.

Jacob ignored him. "I have to have answers."

"Answers to what?" Macon asked.

"Where is all that money going, and coming from? At the very least, he's guilty of misusing campaign funds."

"You don't know that," she persisted. "The FEC reports balance. I've completed them myself."

"You told me yourself it would be easy to play fast and loose with the accounts."

"But Gordon doesn't."

"No?"

"No."

Charlie plunked his mug down on the coffee table. "Then how the hell do you explain the half million dollars he just dumped into a Swiss account."

"I don't know," Macon said. "But there is a reasonable explanation. There has to be."

"Honey, listen to me." Jacob shifted so he was facing her on the couch. "The night of your accident, Charlie found a pearl and gold cuff link in the parking garage. I recognized it as one of the pair Elliot Raines was wearing at the party."

"What's Elliot got to do with this?"

"There were two prints on the cuff link," Charlie said. "One belonged to the guy in the white sedan, the other one belonged to Elliot Raines. We searched his penthouse and found the tuxedo shirt he'd been wearing at the party. There was a hole where the cuff link had been torn off."

Macon shivered. Jacob had to fight the urge to pull her onto his lap, knowing she'd be mad as hell if he did. She looked at Charlie. "You think—you think Elliot had something to do with the accident?"

Jacob squeezed her hand tighter. "The same night, one of our undercover agents set up what should have been a sting on the counterfeiting thing. If Eddie had made the bust, all we would have needed were their ties to U.S. Government officials to bring down the whole thing."

"Do I want to know what happened?"

"Eddie turned up dead the next day," Charlie said.

Macon turned her gaze to Jacob. "It couldn't

have been Elliot then, he was at the party all night."

"What if he was working with someone?" Jacob prompted.

"Someone like Gordon?" she said.

Jacob nodded. "Yeah. For instance."

"It's not true, Jacob. It's not."

"Macon, listen. I know, in fact I'm surer of this than I have been of anything in a long time—"

"More sure," she said, sounding miserable.

Jacob squeezed her hand. "More sure. Gordon had nothing to do with what happened in that parking garage."

Charlie shifted in his chair. "Damn, Jake."

"It's true, Charlie. There is no way that man could have been as shaken as he was if he'd known what was going to happen."

"There was every way," Charlie argued. "If Stratton thought he and Raines were taking you out and later found out Macon had been injured, it would go a long way toward explaining his reaction."

Jacob shook his head. "No way. No way would Gordon have taken a hit at me when Macon was around. Not after what I saw today. That man is falling apart."

"Do you think Raines double-crossed him?" Charlie asked.

Jacob shrugged. "Maybe, but I'm beginning to think maybe Gordon's not guilty at all."

"Neither is Elliot," Macon insisted.

"Honey," Jacob reached up and touched her face, "you've got to be objective about this. Elliot's fingerprints were on the cuff link. That placed him at, or near, the scene of the attempt. You can't ignore that."

"There's a reasonable explanation, Jacob. Did you ask him for one?"

"Of course I didn't ask him. He would have lied."

"How do you know?"

"I hardly expected him to tell me he'd set us up."

"It's just not true, Jacob. You have to believe me."

Charlie rubbed his big hands on his thighs and fixed Macon with a hard stare. "Then how do you explain the enormous sums of money we've found going through his accounts. Mark my words, the guy's on the take."

"No. There are things—things you don't know," she said.

Jacob stared at her. Macon was starting to lose some of her paleness and he saw a certain spark in her eyes he wasn't sure he liked. "What are you talking about?"

"Just things. I can't tell you, but I think you should go to Elliot and tell him what you suspect. He'll be honest with you. I know he will."

"You aren't making any sense," Charlie said.

Macon shrugged. "Just talk to Elliot. You owe him that. You owe it to yourselves."

"And what about Gordon," Jacob prompted.

"There's a reasonable explanation for that, too. You said yourself that Peter, Peter—"

"Quiver," Charlie supplied.

"Quiver is pressing too hard. Haven't you thought to look there." She turned to Jacob. "You told me right from the start that you expected high-level government corruption. Why couldn't it be coming from within your own department?"

"Shit." Charlie stared at Macon.

Jacob winced. He had hoped she wouldn't draw that conclusion. "I have considered that. I'm looking into it."

"Well, hell, Jake, when were you going to tell me?" Charlie asked.

"Soon. I didn't want to risk getting you in trouble."

"We're both up to our eyeballs now."

"I know." Jacob looked at Charlie. "If you walked out right now, I'd deny that you know anything about this."

Charlie shook his head. "No way. Even if they fire me, I've still got twenty years of retirement coming. I hate that slimy little bastard as much as you do, and I want to be there when you hang him out to dry."

Jacob turned back to Macon. "I have to have answers to these questions, Macon. I can't stop looking no matter what my suspicions."

"Only now," she whispered, "you're trying to prove Gordon is innocent instead of trying to prove he's guilty."

"I'm trying to find the truth."

"Then I think," she whispered, "you should find someplace to do it besides my office and my house."

Twenty-five

Twenty minutes later, Macon sifted back through the contents of the file once more, trying to ignore Jacob's hard stare and the sound of his even breathing. Charlie had diplomatically decided to let Jacob handle the situation on his own, and she had barely spoken two words to Jacob since she'd shown Charlie out the door.

"Are you going to talk to me?" he said, finally.

She looked at him, hurt. "I don't know what to say."

"I didn't lie to you, Macon."

She slipped the file back into the brown envelope and dropped it on the table. "Didn't you?"

"No." Jacob sat up on the couch. "I wanted to tell you this right from the start, but Quiver tied my hands. Surely you understand that."

"How could you do this to me?"

"I didn't have any choice." He stood up and started to pace the living room. "It was supposed to be so simple. I was supposed to just walk into your office and gain your support. In close proximity to you, I could take a hard look at Gordon's files, and once I'd proved he was guilty, I could bust him. In and out. Clean and simple." He met her with an anguished glance. "I wasn't supposed to fall in love with you."

"Do you still think Gordon is guilty?"

"I told you. I don't know. He could be."

"He's not."

Jacob let out a harsh breath. "Macon, what do you want me to do with all that evidence? Do you want me to just ignore it?"

"No." She leaned back against the sofa and closed her eyes, unable to look at him. "I want you to do whatever you think is best."

"But you're not just throwing me out of your office, are you?"

"No."

"You're throwing me out of your life."

She did open her eyes then, for fear she'd start to cry if she didn't. "Just this very morning you were pushing me toward him, Jacob. You practically begged me to deepen my relationship with him. Was that some kind of sick joke? Were you going to enjoy watching me get devastated?"

"No!" He walked over and knelt in front of her. "No. Honey, you promised you would listen to me."

She had, she realized, and she stared into his eyes, hoping to find some of the answers she sought. "I know."

"But you don't want to."

"No."

Jacob's breathing was ragged. "Macon, I'd never hurt you, not knowingly anyway. Surely you know that by now. Haven't you learned to trust me even a little."

She hesitated, torn. His features were haggard in the dim light, and she longed to smooth the worried lines off his forehead, almost as much as she longed to be convinced he hadn't betrayed her. "Please convince me, Jacob," she pleaded as two tears slipped down her cheeks. "I want to believe you."

He sighed and sat down on the couch, not asking her permission before he lifted her onto his lap. "Until I spoke with Gordon on the phone, I really believed he was guilty. I told you that."

"Yes." She nodded, finding odd comfort in the steady beat of his heart against her ear.

"This has been tearing me to pieces, Macon. I didn't know what to do. I was falling in love with you, but I knew there was every opportunity you might hate me when this was all over."

"Why did you push me toward Gordon?"

He let out a ragged sigh. "I don't know. Lots of reasons. Family is on my mind a lot, for obvious reasons. After I talked to Gordon last night, I knew how torn up he was. I didn't want you to miss the opportunity to have a relationship with him."

"Even though you think he's a criminal?"

"I don't think he's a criminal. I don't know what to think. I began to suspect that Peter Quiver was not what he seemed almost as soon as I returned to Washington. We've never gotten along, it's true, but Quiver was irrationally interested in this case. He seemed furious that the Service had recalled me from Thule without consulting him. At my request, he didn't even know I was in Greenland. The director had bypassed him on my last set of orders. It's unusual, but not unheard of, and Quiver's reaction was way out of line."

"You told me that first day that you suspected U.S. government corruption."

"That's right. I was talking about Quiver. He's been pushing too hard, too much. He's determined to pin this on Gordon, and I believe he's trying to protect himself."

"But?"

"But, there has to be someone else. Quiver has the power to make Customs and the Service look the other way, but he can't control the Washington policy makers. He needs someone on this side of the fence."

"Someone like Gordon." She shivered.

Jacob rubbed his hand down her spine. "Someone. The evidence against your stepfather kept mounting. Quiver was really pushing me to step up the investigation. After they found Eddie's body, Charlie said Quiver went ballistic. He wants me to set up a sting and use you as the bait."

Macon sat up and stared at him. "He wants me to help you arrest my stepfather?"

Jacob nodded. "That's when I decided this had gone far enough. There was no way I was going to involve you in that. Quiver warned me, through Charlie, not to talk to you. He's going to try to personally persuade you to agree."

"There's nothing he could say that would make me agree to that."

"He'd probably lie. If that didn't work, he'd probably threaten you. If he wanted to, and if he's in this as deep as I think he is, he could possibly pin some of it on you."

"What?"

"He's gone to extraordinary lengths to make Gordon look guilty, even if he isn't. He could do the same thing to you."

Macon moved off Jacob's lap and took the seat next to him, wrapping her arms around her middle. "I feel sick."

"I know." He smoothed her hair off her forehead. "This is dirty as hell, and you shouldn't be involved in it. I'm going to do whatever I have to to protect you."

"But you're still going to continue investigating Gordon?"

"That's part of what I have to do, Macon. If there's even the slightest chance that he's guilty, I can't let you get pulled into that."

She looked at him, aching inside. "Jacob?"

"Yes?"

"What you did today, telling me this, I mean, it could be the end of your career, couldn't it?"

"Yes."

"What's the worst thing that could happen?"

He shrugged. "I don't think we should talk about it."

"You could go to prison, couldn't you?"

"If Quiver sets me up, then yeah, I guess so."

"Could you get killed?"

"Macon—"

"Could you?"

He hesitated. "Yes. I suppose so."

She felt the tears start to flow in earnest. "This is what you meant when you said you'd go to whatever lengths to protect me, isn't it?"

He nodded. "Yes. I'm not going to let you get hurt."

She met his gaze. "Even if it means you lose me in the process?"

"Would I?" he asked.

Macon fought for control, torn between her desire to throw herself at him and beg for his comfort, and the desire to demand he leave her life. "You're asking me to betray my stepfather. He's all the family I have."

"No, Macon." He cupped her face and wiped

away the tears with his thumbs. "I might have asked you to do that in the beginning, but I won't now. I couldn't do that to you."

"But you already have. You've already gotten enough information from me to build a case against him, haven't you?"

"Macon, please listen to me—"

She wiped at her tears with the back of her hand. "How am I supposed to forgive you for that?"

"I'm not going to do anything until I'm absolutely sure Gordon is guilty."

"He's not guilty," she wailed.

"Macon—"

She pushed his hands away. "I can't take this any more, Jacob. I trusted you. I trusted you like I haven't trusted anyone in a long time. The whole time, you were lying to me."

"No."

"Yes." Macon looked at him and caught her breath on a sob. "All that talk about caring for me, was it just part of the game, Jacob?"

"No!" He stood up. "No. I love you. I want to marry you. I asked you to think about your relationship with Gordon because I knew there would only be a chance for you and me if you weren't afraid to give your heart."

Macon laughed a bitter, half-laugh. "Well, thank you, Jacob. It was a lesson well-learned."

"Macon, please."

"I think you should leave now."

"Macon, you have to listen to me."

"I'm through listening."

"Damn it, don't do this."

"Do what? Protect myself? Not let you hurt me

anymore? Not let you use me to advance your career?"

His eyes turned dark. "It's never been about that. You know that's not true."

"Do I? How can I believe anything you've told me?"

She saw the hurt register in his gaze and ached to take the words back, but she couldn't. Jacob had hurt her too deeply. "Like I said. I think you should leave now."

"If I walk out that door, I'm not coming back until you ask me to. I've told you the truth. I can't do anything else to make you believe me."

"I understand."

"Please don't do this to us."

She steeled herself against the plea in his voice and the way it pulled at her heart. "I think you should leave, Jacob."

He walked out without saying another word. In the ensuing silence, she was sure she heard her heart break.

Twenty-six

Jacob's fingers shook when he opened the folder Charlie had dropped on his desk the next afternoon. It had taken him less than an hour to clear his belongings out of Macon's office. He'd felt like his life was ending. She had refused to speak to him since the previous afternoon, letting the answering machine and May screen all her calls. Only the sympathetic look he'd gotten from Maylene Porter had given him any hope. He stared at the folder, unable to look inside.

"Go ahead," Charlie prompted, lighting a cigar and taking the seat across from Jacob's desk. "It isn't going to bite you."

"You got this from Raines?"

"Yeah."

Jacob flipped open the folder and picked up the first item. A photo of Elliot, a pretty young woman, and an infant. "Who is this?"

"His family."

Jacob looked at him in surprise. "I thought he wasn't married."

"Not anymore he's not."

"There's a child?"

"Yeah, and are you ready for this? The kid's name is Elliot Macon Raines. Our Ms. Stratton is his godmother."

"Oh God."

"It gets worse. The kid is nine years old and has Down's Syndrome. Soon after the baby was born, Elliot's wife left him for another man. Seems she couldn't bear the thought of spending her life taking care of a child who didn't meet her high standards."

Jacob was starting to feel sick. He picked up the next sheet of paper and studied the form. It was an admission paper for the Sheffield School for the Mentally Challenged, in Cary, North Carolina. A picture of Elliot's son was paperclipped to the top. "He's in school?"

"Yeah. It's a boarding school where they deal with the special problems of children like Elliot."

"It says here he was admitted by special permission from the schoolmaster."

"Sheffield has one of the best programs in the country. Expensive too. Their waiting list is miles long, and Elliot had to pull some major strings to get the kid in."

"Macon did the pulling?"

"Not exactly. It seems Macon and Elliot go back a long way. She's known him since she interned on Capitol Hill nearly fifteen years ago. Despite their differing political opinions, they've remained close friends. After his wife left him, Raines knew he couldn't care for the kid on his own."

"Couldn't he have hired a live-in nurse?"

"Probably. But he wanted the best education money could buy. That's why he decided on Sheffield. He goes down there almost every weekend and takes the kid out of school. Raines owns a beach house where they spend their weekends and all summer during non-election years."

"Where does Macon fit into all this?"

"First of all, she's one of a handful of people who knows about Elliot's child. Elliot has gone to extraordinary lengths to protect the kid from the media."

"Nobody but the tabloids would make a big deal out of this would they?"

"They would if they knew who the kid's mother really was."

Jacob's stomach started to turn. "What do you mean?"

"Elliot was married to the former Miss Colleen Dumont, of the Rhode Island Dumonts."

"Senator Carlton Dumont's daughter."

"And perpetual scandal maker. Everything Dumont or his family does is prime media and tabloid fare. Elliot knew if the media, especially something like the North Carolina media, got wind of the fact that Colleen Dumont couldn't stand the sight of her own child, the kid's life would be hell. To protect him, he lied about the boy's parentage."

Jacob picked up the last piece of paper and stared at it. Elliot had signed the admittance form as father of the child. The mother's signature was clean, neat, precise. It was Macon Stratton. "Why would she do this?"

Charlie shrugged. "I don't know. It probably didn't seem like a big deal at the time. Gordon is a huge benefactor to the Sheffield school. He had a younger brother who had Down's Syndrome and who went to school there for several years."

"The brother is dead?"

"Died at age thirty-two. Down's Syndrome children don't generally live to full life expectancy.

Anyway, as part of Gordon's compensation for his generosity, and he is very generous, any relative of his is guaranteed admittance into Sheffield. My guess is that Macon decided to put her name on the papers to guarantee that Elliot's son would be admitted. Look at the rest of the pictures. She and the child appear to be quite close. She might as well be his mother."

Jacob pulled out the picture envelope and flipped through the snapshots. There were several pictures of Macon with the little boy playing on the beach, standing in front of the school, and hugging each other. "No one knows about this?"

"The headmistress of Sheffield is smart enough to know that crossing a member of Gordon's family is probably not in her best interest. When she was told that no one was to know who the child's parents were, you'd better believe she took it seriously."

"This certainly explains Macon's defense of Elliot Raines."

Charlie dropped a report on Jacob's desk. "It also explains where Raines' money is going and coming from."

Jacob picked up the paper. "What's this?"

"It's a detailed accounting of how Elliot is being blackmailed and Gordon Stratton is giving him the money to pay them off."

Jacob's breath came out on a low hiss. "Gordon is doing it to protect Macon."

"So it seems. Elliot has paid all of it back, but it's tough for him to keep up with the black-mailer's demands when his business' cash flow is down."

"That would explain what he was doing at all

those Republican fundraisers where Macon spotted him in the slides."

"That's right. Elliot never accepts a client who's running against one of Gordon's chosen few political allies. In all those cases, he was checking out potential opposition to his existing clients to ensure that Gordon's backers weren't already on board. He'd have withdrawn, or so he claims, as the campaign consultant if they had been."

"Do you think Gordon is threatening him?"

"No. I just think the guy has high morals."

Jacob arched an eyebrow. "I can't believe I'm hearing this."

Charlie shrugged and took a long draw on his cigar. "I'm starting to come around. I spent an hour and a half with Raines. He was almost in tears when he told me he was worried this would leak to the press."

"Did he tell you who was blackmailing him?"

"Said he didn't know."

"Did you believe him?"

"No. He's just scared to death. I don't think we could even get that information out of him if we subpoenaed him."

Jacob leaned back in his chair and studied Charlie. "This case is falling apart."

"Unless Macon is right."

Jacob nodded. "Unless she's right."

"Are you going to tell me what you have now?"

"Not here I'm not."

"Afraid the walls have ears?"

"Wouldn't you be?"

"Yeah." Charlie looked over his shoulder before he returned his gaze to Jacob. "Are you sure about this, Jake. I mean dead-on sure."

"I'm sure."

"Then I want to help you roll the guy."

"It could mean the end of your career, Charlie. It could get political."

Charlie shrugged. "When I first became an agent, I did it because I wanted to do something valuable. I wanted to end corruption, change the world, you know, the usual."

Jacob smiled. "Yeah. I know."

"Well, maybe we won't change the world, but we sure as hell have a chance to clean up our corner of it. I couldn't live with myself if I turned my back on this, Jake."

Jacob scooped up the folder. "All right. Let's go."

"Where are we going?"

"To pay a call on Gordon Stratton."

Twenty-seven

Macon leaned back in her chair and studied the view out of her office window. Even with the pressing demands of her election-year schedule, the office seemed quiet, eerie, without Jacob bursting in on her. She laid her pen down and walked over to her balcony, staring out at the street below.

Three times, she had forced herself to resist telling Gordon what she knew. He had come by her office that day, and the concern in his eyes, the grim look on his face, had warned her that something was not quite right. Despite her unshakable confidence that Gordon was not guilty of the things Jacob suspected, he was clearly not himself. Somehow, the memory of one dead Secret Service Agent named Eddie kept her from telling Gordon what had happened.

"Macon?"

She turned to see Maylene standing in the doorway holding a vase full of irises. Macon frowned. "Are those from Jacob?"

"How many people know irises are your favorite flower?" May asked, plunking the vase down on Macon's desk. "You have a visitor in the front lobby."

"I don't want to see him."

"It's not a him. It's a her."

Macon frowned at the grammar gaffe. "He . . . she . . ." She stifled an exasperated sigh and looked past May's shoulder. "Who—" She stopped at the sight of Little Dove's concerned face.

"May I come in, Macon?"

Macon managed a slight smile. "How can I resist a woman with such fine grammar skills? Hello, Little Dove."

May slipped past Jacob's mother and shut the door. Little Dove drifted farther into the office, indicating the flowers on the desk. "Those are very nice."

"They're from your son."

Little Dove nodded. "When in doubt, trust a cliché. That's his motto."

Macon felt some of her tension leave her at the warm note in Little Dove's voice. She crossed the room to her side. "Would you like to sit down?"

Little Dove nodded and sank down on one of the soft, buttery leather chairs in Macon's office. Macon took the seat opposite. "I'm not here to pry, Macon," Little Dove said. "You've done so much for Jacob and for me, I just thought perhaps I could help you in return."

Macon sighed. "It's very complicated, Little Dove."

"Love usually is."

"Did Jacob tell you he was in love with me?"

"He did, yes, but he didn't need to. I knew it when I saw the two of you together at that party."

Macon leaned back in her chair. "I'm glad you and Jacob were able to work some things out."

Little Dove tipped her head and studied Macon in the bright light that flooded her office through the balcony doors. "He hurt you very much, didn't he?"

Macon nodded, fighting a fresh burst of tears. "Yes."

"You're in love with him too, aren't you?"

The tears started to fall. "Yes."

Little Dove pulled a tissue from the box on the coffee table and handed it to Macon. "I think you will feel better if you cry awhile first. I'll sit here until you're ready to talk."

It took two hours and two pots of coffee before Little Dove left. Macon felt oddly restored after her visit. Jacob's mother had filled in many of the details of Jacob's past, and Macon was beginning to understand why honesty and loyalty were so important to him. His father had been cheated by a dishonest banker, and Jacob had never fully recovered from the ordeal it had caused for his family. The fact that Jacob's relationship with Kristen Ager had ended just days before he'd begun working on his current case, had helped focus Jacob's attention almost exclusively on the unfolding evidence. He hadn't meant to use Macon. It had been second-nature for him.

In the course of the conversation, Macon had been forced to admit that Jacob was at least partially right. She'd wanted an excuse to end her relationship with him. She'd lost everyone she'd ever loved, and she wasn't sure she could risk loving Jacob. Little Dove had pointed out that Macon seemed to have no choice in the matter. She'd already fallen in love with him.

After Little Dove had left, Macon had spent a long time at her desk, staring at the irises. Only

Jacob could have found the summer blossoms so late in the year. She touched one of the satiny soft petals and accepted the truth. Jacob had not really betrayed her trust, he had merely kept his promise to go to whatever lengths necessary to protect her. Resolutely, she turned her attention to her work.

She didn't really feel any better, just too exhausted to cry. She decided to start with her phone messages. By the time she worked her way down to Nat's phone message, she had managed to restore some semblance of order to her office. She picked up the message and stared at it. May had marked it urgent. Macon's fingers trembled when she looked at Nat's name.

She had not spoken with him since the party and, oddly, when news of her accident had gotten out, Nat had not been among her well-wishers. She stared at the message, turning over the things Nat had told her about Jacob in her mind. Something bothered her, something she couldn't place her finger on. What had he said or done that was causing this strange sensation to trip down her spine. Slowly and systematically, she replayed in her mind the conversation at the Memorial with Nat. Greenland. That was it.

Jacob had told her that Peter Quiver hadn't known he was in Greenland until his return to Washington. Nat had said almost the same thing. She remembered him telling her he'd been following Jacob's activities in Europe when he'd lost track of him and he'd disappeared for over two weeks. The similarity niggled at her like a bad tooth. Nat's concern had been more like anger. He'd hounded her about her involvement with Jacob, but surely he couldn't be involved.

She shivered at the notion that he just might be. What if Nat was the man Jacob was looking for? Didn't Nat have the right credentials, the right contacts to pull enough strings of his own in Washington. He was a member of the media, for God's sake, the most feared entity in the entire city. She stared at the message slip again and contemplated what she should do.

The fact that Jacob didn't have any suspicions about Nat made her skin crawl. It would be too easy for Nat to blind-side him. With Nat's contacts among the Washington press corps, he would be invaluable to someone like Peter Quiver. He could start rumors among the journalists, keep tabs on suspicions and allegations, and worse, frame someone—someone like Jacob—to take the fall for Peter Quiver. She stood up and reached for her coat. Whatever game Nat was playing, she wasn't going to allow him to hurt Jacob.

Twenty-eight

Jacob shrugged into his coat and picked up the file on Elliot Raines. "Are you ready to go, Charlie?"

"Do you think going to talk to Gordon Stratton is such a good idea? I mean, what's he going to say?"

"Elliot Raines had a lot to say."

"Jake, what if he's guilty? You have to consider that."

Jacob sighed. "I know. I have, but I have to give him the benefit of the doubt. We don't have enough to convict, and short of manufacturing evidence, I don't think we're going to. I have to trust my instincts, Charlie."

"What instincts?"

"That whoever is blackmailing Elliot Raines is also blackmailing Gordon Stratton."

"Do you think Gordon would be willing to pay a blackmailer just to keep his business about Raines' kid silent. I mean, I know he's lending Elliot money, but that's not the same as paying himself."

Jacob shook his head. "I think Gordon is being blackmailed over something else. I should have seen it before."

"What are you driving at?"

"If we're right, and what we suspect is true, somebody needs a hell of a lot of money to pull this off. Gordon is a damn good source of quick cash. He just paid over a half-million dollars."

"So the blackmailers are using the money from Raines and Stratton, and whoever else, to buy the counterfeit money and put it into circulation."

"That's right."

"But we've checked every nook and cranny in Stratton's background. What could a blackmailer be using against him?"

"It's just a hunch I have. Come on. I'll brief you in the car." Jacob's hand was on the doorknob when his unsecured line rang. He hesitated. It might be Macon. "Hold on, Charlie," he said and reached for the receiver. "Macon?" he said.

"No," the male voice said, "but it's reassuring to hear that hopeful note in your voice, young man."

"Who is this?" Jacob demanded.

"This is Gordon Stratton. I've just gotten off the phone with Maylene Porter. I think we should talk."

Jacob let out a harsh breath. "I was just on my way to see you, Senator. I'm bringing my partner along."

"That will be fine. I'll see you in fifteen minutes."

Jacob hung up the phone and looked at Charlie. "Let's go. That was the senator. He wants to talk."

Macon tapped her foot on the pavement and glanced down at her watch. Nat had been visibly shaken when she'd arrived at his office an hour before. He'd refused to talk to her, however, begging her to meet him after work at the Lincoln Memorial. She'd grudgingly agreed. It bothered her that he was late. She didn't like not knowing where he was, especially when she didn't know where Jacob was either. When she finally spotted Nat's slim figure hurrying across the grounds from the Vietnam Memorial, she took a deep breath and sagged against a pillar.

He glanced over his shoulder before he stopped in front of her. "All right, Macon. I'm here. What do you want?"

"You were the one who called me this morning, Nat. Maylene said it was urgent."

"It was. It was." He took her elbow and led her farther into a shadow. "I heard about what happened after the party the other night. I warned you that Blackfort might get you hurt."

Macon jammed her hands down in the pockets of her coat. "It was just an accident, Nat. I think you're overreacting."

He shook his head. "I'm not. You've got to stay away from this guy. He's big trouble."

She studied the angled planes of Nat's face =id fought an inward shiver. She didn't like the haunted look in his eyes or his haggard appearance. He was normally high-strung, it was true, but something was seriously wrong. Her suspicions increased tenfold. "Nat, I wanted to talk to you about that."

"About what?"

"About your suspicions regarding Jacob Blackfort."

"Just stay away from him, Macon."

"But there's something I don't understand. From the file, I mean."

"What?"

"You said you'd talked to Dom Petrie and that he told you Jacob had muscled him out of his firm in Cheyenne."

"That's right."

"But I spoke with Dom just this afternoon, and he told me he was in ill health and had sold it willingly."

Nat's eyes darted back and forth in momentary panic. Macon watched as he appeared to shrink into his jacket. "So maybe I read between the lines and got the wrong message," he said, his voice sounding breathless, strained. "So big deal."

Macon knew then, knew from her conversation with Jacob in her office the evening he'd told her about his special arrangement with Dom Petrie, that Nat was lying. Nat had never spoken to Jacob's friend. He had gotten his information straight from Peter Quiver. She saw the sharp look in his eyes and felt a trickle of apprehension work its way through her blood. She also knew that he knew. "Well," she said, hoping she didn't sound frightened, and wondering where on earth she could get in touch with Jacob at that hour of the night, "you must have. I guess you know by now it's over between me and Jacob."

Nat's eyes narrowed. "Really?"

She nodded. "Yes. He moved everything out of my office this morning. I don't even know where he is."

Nat didn't flinch. "I'm glad to hear that."

"Do you know where he is?" At Nat's sharp glance, she hurried to clarify, "I mean, you're the one whose been keeping tabs on him for me."

Nat shook his head. "No," he said, and she

knew for sure that he was lying. "I don't have the first idea where he is."

She forced a smile. "Oh. Well, maybe he's left town. Gone home to Cheyenne or something."

"Maybe."

"I guess I should have exercised more caution, shouldn't I?"

Nat shrugged. "Yeah. You should have."

"Well, anyway, I just wanted to let you know that you didn't have anything to worry about." She was beginning to feel more and more nervous as the sky darkened and the monument grounds became isolated. There weren't many people about, and the sharp look in Nat's eyes was making her shiver. "I was on my way home, Nat. I just wanted to say thanks."

"You're going home?" he asked.

She nodded. "Yes. I still tire easily. The concussion and all."

Nat nodded and stepped away from her. "I'll see you around then. And, Macon?"

"Yes?"

"Be careful who you trust next time."

She barely kept herself from running to her car.

Twenty-nine

Jacob stared at Gordon Stratton. "Are you sure about this, Senator?"

"Well, hell, son, of course I'm sure. A man doesn't make a mistake like this."

"Why didn't you tell the police you were being blackmailed?"

Gordon shrugged and leaned back in his chair. The Capitol Dome was visible in the fading light through Gordon's window, and Jacob wondered if Gordon had positioned his chair in front of the window to achieve just that portrait of power—the senator, framed by the soaring white marble dome. Gordon cleared his throat. "It didn't seem like an option. Why would I want the police to leak something to the press instead of waiting for this slimeball to do it?"

Charlie put his hands on Gordon's desk and fixed him with a hard stare. "Do you know who's blackmailing you?"

Gordon shook his head. "No. If I did, I'd tell you. As soon as Jacob told me about Macon's accident, I knew—I knew none of it mattered." He indicated his office with a sweep of his hand. "Keeping all of this a secret used to seem very important to me. I couldn't imagine not being a senator."

Jacob narrowed his gaze at the older man. "You never told Macon the truth just so you wouldn't create a scandal?"

Gordon released a long breath. "No, not really. I wanted to protect her. I knew what her mother had told her, and there never seemed to be a right time. It was always too hard to face."

Jacob swallowed and looked at his watch. "Senator, I have to tell you something, and then I'm going to walk out of here. I have a case that is demanding my attention, and I can't waste anymore of it on you."

He took a deep breath. "You might hate me for this, but frankly, I'm not sure I care. I'm in love with Macon. I want to marry her, but right now, she's not even speaking to me because she thinks I used her to bust you in this case. It's true there were times I thought you were guilty. Now, I'm not sure what to think, but I do know that she loves me. And in spite of that, she's refused to let me into her life because she's defending you. You want to talk about 'hard'?"

Gordon shifted nervously in his chair. "You're right. Of course, you're right. That's why I called you. After I talked to Maylene this afternoon, I knew I had to go to her house and tell Macon the truth. I don't care anymore what it does to me. I can't stand the thought of her losing you on account of me."

Charlie took a long draw on his cigar. "Raines's story is that the blackmailer confronted him at the Capitol Hilton the night of Macon's accident. That's where the cuff link came from. But I still want to know how your prints got on that box with the dead rat, Senator."

Gordon blanched and looked at Jacob. "You

have to believe me. I don't know anything about that. It could be anything, anyone. I handle thousands of pieces of mail a day. If someone on my staff handed me a package, or I got something out of the supply closet—I don't know." He spread his hands. "But I didn't have anything to do with that box. I swear it."

Jacob studied him for several long seconds. "I believe you."

Gordon exhaled a deep breath. "You're a good man, Blackfort, and all I wanted was for Macon to be happy."

Jacob fixed him with a hard stare. "I hope you make good on that, Senator."

"I will. I swear I will. In fact, I'm on my way there right now, I just wanted to talk to you about it first. I thought you might like to go with me."

Charlie leaned back in his chair and let out a low whistle. "What are we going to do about Quiver?"

Jacob looked at Gordon closely. "Quiver's not our only problem."

"What do you mean?" Charlie said.

"Whoever is blackmailing the senator and Elliot Raines is Quiver's accomplice. We have to get this guy."

"Do you have any idea who it might be?" Gordon asked.

Jacob nodded. "Yeah. I think it's Nathaniel Baldwin."

Gordon gasped. "Oh my God!"

"What's wrong?" Jacob asked, suddenly alert.

"Maylene. She told me this afternoon that I wouldn't be able to catch Macon until later because she was on her way to meet with Nat Baldwin."

Jacob didn't wait to hear the rest of the conversation. He grabbed his coat and raced for the door.

"Why are you in such a hurry, Macon?"

Macon froze, her fingers on the door handle of the rental car she was using while her car was being repaired from the accident, when Nat Baldwin's hand curled around her elbow, and his smooth voice sounded in her ear. She forced herself to look at him. "I just remembered that I have an appointment. Did you need something else, Nat?"

He stared at her for several seconds. "You know. Don't you?"

Macon swallowed, hoping she didn't look as panicked as she felt. She was suddenly very aware of how quiet and deserted the monument grounds had become. "Know what?" she asked.

Nat growled beneath his breath. His fingers tightened on her arm. "Damn you. You weren't supposed to get involved, Macon. I told you. I warned you."

"Nat, I don't . . ."

"Shut up." He looked around once, before he fixed her with another glare. "You've ruined everything. Everything."

"Nat, please calm down. I'm sure we can work this out."

His short laugh was harsh. "That's a joke. Get in the car, Macon."

"What?"

"I said, in the car. You're involved now whether you want to be or not."

"Nat—"

"Get in the car." He bit out each word between clenched teeth.

Macon studied his hard profile and wavered on indecision. If she got in the car with him, she'd be helpless. Nat was scowling at her, but there was something, fear maybe, in the depths of his cool gray eyes that gave her hope. "All right, Nat. I'll get in the car, but only if you'll agree to talk this over with me."

"I never wanted to hurt you, Macon."

"I know you didn't. You still don't have to."

He shook his head. "You don't understand."

"Then explain it to me."

Nat nodded. She saw the defeat in his gaze and unlocked her car door. Nat walked around to the other side to slip in beside her. "Let's go to your house."

Macon hesitated. She didn't want to be alone with him. "Maybe we should just go to Old Ebbitt Grill, or F. Scott's. It would be closer."

His expression turned hard again. "No. It's too late for that. Let's go to your house."

She fought down a wave of panic and started the car. "Are you sure, Nat, I—"

"Damn it, Macon, I'm sure. Just drive."

Macon backed the car out of her spot and worked her way through the parking lot. The blood was roaring in her ears, and she swallowed several times to ease the sensation. Nat fell into a brooding silence as Macon eased her way into traffic. She waited until she was on the highway before she tried to broach the subject again. "Nat, don't you want to tell me what's wrong?"

He snorted. "What's wrong? You want to know what's wrong? Why don't *you* tell *me*, Macon? Why don't you tell me what you and lover boy have been talking about in bed at night?"

"That's not fair, Nat. I'm not having an affair with Jacob Blackfort."

"Yeah. Right."

She reached over and put her hand on his arm. "You and I are friends, Nat. We've been friends a long time."

"You know everything, don't you?"

She decided she'd better tell him the truth. "I know that you're in something maybe a little over your head. I know that a guy named Eddie Gilani is dead, and I know that Jacob and I almost got killed the other night. I want to believe, that you didn't have anything to do with it, Nat."

He looked hurt. "You were never supposed to get hurt."

"Did you have anything to do with Eddie Gilani's death?"

"We had to kill him. We had to. He knew everything. I didn't find out until the last minute that Gilani was part of a sting. All along, we thought it was Blackfort."

"Is the other person you're referring to Peter Quiver?"

Nat shuddered. "Yeah. You know about that too?"

Macon nodded and turned off the George Washington Parkway. "Jacob knows, too. He's suspected Quiver all along." A sudden thought occurred to her and her fingers tightened on the steering wheel. "Jacob told me Eddie Gilani's code name was Red Arrow. Jacob is Black Arrow. Like arrows in the quiver," she muttered.

"Quiver kept telling me he had everything under control." Nat was starting to sound rattled.

"We were supposed to make one more sale. Just one more. It was going to set us up for life and then I was getting out. I didn't think Quiver had control anymore. He was getting weak."

Macon swallowed. "Nat, surely if you told the authorities, I'm sure Jacob could—"

"Told them what? That I've helped Peter Quiver buy, print and distribute millions in counterfeit money all over the world. That I've blackmailed people to get the funds for—"

"Blackmail," Macon said. "You were blackmailing Elliot Raines, weren't you?"

Nat groaned. "Yes."

"And Gordon, too. You've been blackmailing my stepfather."

"Yes."

"But what could possibly . . ." She stopped a-a red light and looked at Nat. "I can't believe this, Nat. Why would you do this? What would make you do this?"

He raised tortured eyes to her. "It was the money. At first I just wanted the money. Do you have any idea what it's like to live on seventeen grand a year and move around Washington with all these consultants and senators and power-brokers who are raking in the millions?"

Macon shook her head. The light changed and she pressed her foot on the accelerator. "You sold your soul for money? It couldn't have been worth it."

"It didn't start that way. I met Peter Quiver one night at the Hawk and Dove. He was in a rage, a real first-class temper, about how you politicos rake in all the money. I found out later that some senator's son had just gotten a promotion in the

Service and Quiver was sure it had resulted from influence peddling."

He paused and wiped the sweat off his forehead with the back of his hand. "Anyway, we were talking, just talking, and I told him who I was, and what I did, and how I had to deal with you guys all the time."

"We're not the enemy, Nat."

"It seemed like it sometimes."

Macon sighed. "What happened?"

"Nothing happened at first. Then Quiver called me one day and asked me if I'd like to make a quick two thousand dollars."

"Weren't you suspicious?"

"Yeah, and I told him so too."

"What did he tell you?"

"He said it was all legal. He needed a courier to take something downtown for him, and the guy, some Arab guy, was willing to pay two thousand dollars to ensure safe delivery."

"Good grief, Nat, Washington couriers charge fifty bucks to take something all the way to Rockville. Why didn't you suspect anything?"

"He made it sound like we were duping this rich guy. He was with the Secret Service, Macon. Why should I suspect anything?"

She sighed. From the corner of her eye, she could see where Nat's fingers had relaxed against his knee. He seemed to be calming down the longer he talked. "So you took the package?"

"Yeah. It was a piece of cake. I handed the guy the package, and he handed me an envelope with two grand in it. Soon, there was another delivery, and another, and another, and before long, I was going once, maybe twice a week."

"You were carrying counterfeit bills," she said, turning into her subdivision.

"I didn't know that until later. By then, Quiver told me I was in too deep. I'd have to choose between going to jail and making two or three million dollars." He snorted. "What would you have done?"

"You could have called the police, Nat."

He shrugged. "By then, I don't think I wanted to. Two million dollars is a lot of money."

She was starting to feel sick to her stomach. "I thought I knew you better than that."

It had been the wrong thing to say. He tensed beside her and waited until she pulled into her driveway. "What do you know about it? You drive your fancy car and live in this huge house. Did you ever see where I lived before I started working with Quiver? It was a rat-infested hell hole. Nobody can live like that."

She heard the bitter note in his voice and shivered. "So what are you going to do now? You've killed Eddie Gilani."

"I didn't kill him. Quiver did."

"You knew about it, Nat. It's the same thing."

He blanched and reached for the door handle. "I think we'd better go inside."

Macon struggled to remain calm. Perhaps if they went inside her house, she could slip away from Nat long enough to call the police. She was fairly certain she could handle Nat, but she had to make sure Jacob was safe from Peter Quiver. "All right," she said quietly, and walked with Nat up the sidewalk to her house.

He waited, tense and agitated while she fumbled with the lock. Her fingers were trembling and she couldn't get the key to turn. Finally, Nat reached over her shoulder and gave the key a hard turn. The door swung open.

Macon stepped into the dark interior of her house and reached for the hall light. Before she had a chance to flip the switch, Nat was forcing her into the house, up against the wall of the foyer. "Nat!" she gasped, seconds before his hand wrapped around her throat and pinned her to the wall.

She felt something hard and unforgiving pressing into the sensitive spot between her ribs. Nat's eyes glittered in the dim light from the outside lamps. "I'm sorry, Macon," he said. "I'm sorry. You know everything. I have to kill you. I have to."

She sucked in a breath when Nat waved the pistol he was holding so she could see it. "You don't want to do this. You don't have to."

He pressed the barrel back into her rib cage. "Yes I do," he said. "If you'd listened to me, if you'd stayed away from Jacob Blackfort, I wouldn't. But you didn't leave me any choice. Peter Quiver is going to kill Jacob Blackfort, and I'm going to kill you, and we're going to get away with the whole thing."

She closed her eyes and swallowed a lump of fear that had lodged itself firmly in the back of her throat. She felt Nat's hot breath on her neck, and she sucked in several shallow pants, unable to breathe deeply because of the pressure he was exerting on her throat. Nat's breath was hot on her face, and she smelled the hint of licorice and tobacco and alcohol that laced his own harsh gasps. In those few fleeting seconds, she thought of Jacob. No one would warn him about Peter

Quiver. No one would tell him that Quiver already knew, was already planning to kill him.

Jacob thought he was one step ahead of Quiver, but Macon now knew he was wrong. She sent up a brief prayer that he would somehow survive. That he and Charlie would learn the truth before it was too late. She thought of Little Dove and how stricken she would be. Of Jacob saying that he loved her. Of the pain she'd seen on his face when he'd walked out of her house the last time. Of Irises. Of aquamarine eyes. Of Jacob touching her face and telling her she had given him hope. She had pulled him out of the pit. "Oh, Jacob," she whispered, when she felt Nat push the barrel of the pistol deeper between her ribs.

Jacob heard Macon whisper his name and decided he didn't give a damn whether Nat Baldwin confessed to the counterfeiting or not. They already had him on attempted murder. Damn if it was going to be murder one. He swung around the darkened corner from Macon's living room and leveled his pistol on Nat Baldwin the exact instant that Charlie flipped on the lights. "Put the gun down! Put the gun down right now!" Jacob yelled.

Nat looked like a small animal caught in the headlights of an oncoming train. He stared at Jacob a few, crucial, incredulous seconds while Jacob advanced just enough to kick the pistol out of Nat's hand and send it flying across the room. It shattered the hall light before it landed in the kitchen, clattering to a stop against the refrigerator.

Jacob pounced on Nat the instant the gun left

his hand. He had him away from Macon and pinned against the wall in seconds. Jacob landed two solid punches to Nat's midsection before Charlie pulled him off.

"Take it easy, Jake."

"Let go of me, Charlie," Jacob bit out, aching to grind his fist into Nat's face.

Charlie spun him around and made him look at Macon where she sagged against the wall. "Direct your energy that way. I'll take care of this."

Jacob heard, rather than saw, Charlie thrust Nat at one of the waiting policemen. "Are your guys ready to pick up Quiver now?" Charlie asked.

"I already called it in, Mr. Darrow."

Jacob tuned out the ensuing conversation and crossed to Macon's side in two quick strides. Across the crowded foyer, Nat Baldwin was staring at her with a haunted expression. She couldn't seem to look away from him. They put the cuffs on him, and Jacob heard the police officer begin reciting Baldwin's rights. Macon was staring at Nat, her eyes stricken. Jacob looked from one to the other and barely restrained himself from attacking Baldwin all over again.

Suddenly, as if pulled from his silent reverie by the commotion around him, Nat's expression changed to a hate-filled mockery. He threw back his head and laughed. The foyer fell silent. Nat fixed Macon with a caustic glare. "Bye-bye, babe," he chanted, his voice an eerie singsong. "Off to prison."

Macon's voice came out on a stifled sob, and Jacob decided he didn't care whether she wanted him to hold her or not. He needed to. He pulled her into his arms and crushed her against him. "Get him out of here now," he barked over his shoulder, threading a hand into Macon's hair. "It's all right, Macon. He's gone," he said, hearing the tremor in his ice.

"How could he?" she asked, rubbing her face against Jacob's coat.

"I'm not sure he knows that himself, honey. Are you sure you're all right?"

She nodded. "Yes. Yes. Oh, Jacob, he told me everything. He was blackmailing Gordon. He was . . ." She shivered.

He hugged her closer. "I know. I know. It's all over. All of it. They're on their way to arrest Peter Quiver right now."

Macon shuddered. "He would have killed you. He would have killed you."

"Macon!"

Jacob heard Gordon's voice from the doorway and stiffened. He was not yet ready to surrender his hold on Macon. His arms ached from the force of the adrenaline rushing through his blood. Macon lifted her head from his chest. "Gordon?"

Gordon hurried across the foyer. "Oh God! Are you all right?" He looked at Jacob. "Is she all right?"

"I'm fine, Gordon," she said, her voice wavering only slightly. "Jacob was here."

Gordon's face was pale, and Jacob took a deep breath before he released Macon. She practically fell against Gordon Stratton. He wrapped his big arms around her and held her close. "I was so afraid, Macon," Gordon said, rubbing a hand through her hair. "I would have died if anything had happened to you."

She clung to him. "I knew it wasn't you, Gordon. Right from the start. I never doubted it."

Jacob could feel her slipping away from him. He watched, helpless as Gordon walked with Macon to the living room. "Here Gordon said, guiding her toward one of the large chairs. "Why don't you sit down?"

She looked up and caught Jacob's gaze. "Jacob?"

He watched her for several seconds. "I have to go down and file the reports, I—" he paused, wondering if she possibly knew what was happening in his soul, the turmoil she was causing. "You and Gordon have a lot to talk about."

"Jacob, please," she held out a hand to him.

He couldn't stay. He'd be lost if he did. "I'll call you later, Macon. I'm glad you're all right. I'm sorry I couldn't have prevented this." And he walked out without looking back.

Thirty

Macon shivered and leaned back against the couch. It took another twenty minutes before Charlie had everyone cleared out of her house, and she and Gordon were seated alone in the living room. When they were finally settled, each with a cup of coffee, she looked at him with a weak smile. "So," she said, "how was your evening?"

Gordon released a pent-up breath on a shaky laugh. "I've never been that scared in my life, Macon."

"Me either," she said softly.

Gordon shuddered and placed his cup down on the coffee table. "I have something I want to tell you, Macon. I should have told you a long time ago, and I hope you'll just accept an old man's folly when I tell you I never meant to hurt you."

She frowned. "Does this have to do with how Nat Baldwin was blackmailing you?"

He nodded. "Yes. Baldwin was blackmailing both Elliot Raines and me. Elliot was paying to keep his son's identity a secret."

Macon shook her head. "I can't believe Nat would do this, Gordon. He was my friend."

Gordon sighed. "I honestly don't think he meant to hurt you."

Macon took a sip of her coffee. It was bitter and strong, and she winced when it burnt her tongue. "What about you, Gordon? How was he blackmailing you?"

He watched her for several seconds before he took a deep breath. "When your father died, Macon, Cornelia let you believe certain things."

Macon felt an unfamiliar curdling sensation begin to roil around in her stomach. She watched as the steam from her coffee curled upward in a steady spiral of mist. "Things like what?" she asked.

"Things about their relationship."

"She loved him very much," she said.

Gordon shook his head. "No, Macon. She wanted you to believe that. The truth was, your mother was quite," he paused, "promiscuous. She was an alcoholic, and she had a tendency to lose her head at times. Cornelia was a beautiful woman, and there were plenty of men willing to pay her court."

Macon stared at him. "What are you trying to tell me, Gordon?"

"Your mother actually worked for me before you were born. I had just been widowed, and she was young and beautiful, and I was lonely. We had an affair, a brief one, and then she left Raleigh, and I didn't see her again until years later."

Macon stared at him. "Gordon—"

He held up his hand. "I think this will be easier if I get it out in one shot. When Cornelia came to me the second time and told me she wanted a job, I refused. I didn't want her in my office. I was afraid of the scandal. I had no intention of hiring her. But then she told me about you. As soon as I knew, Macon, I tried to get her to marry me."

Macon nodded. "I remember you were always coming by the house. Mama was always telling me you'd proposed, and she'd turned you down."

"She told me she didn't want to be tied down again so soon. She put me off and put me off until you got sick and she needed the money. Finally, she agreed to marry me. I tried to make her happy, but she wanted more and more from me. She had already forced a wedge between me and Tommy."

"I don't really remember much about what happened after Mama and I came to live with you. I was sick so much of the time."

Gordon sighed. "Tommy hated your mother. My first wife died when Tommy was twelve and I don't think he ever recovered from it. My relationship with Betsy was . . . strained, at best, and I'm sure Tommy must have heard the arguments. He accused me one day of driving Betsy to drink. She was killed in an automobile accident when she drove her car off the road."

"Like Tommy."

"Like Tommy." Gordon drew a haggard breath. "What Tommy didn't know was why Betsy and I fought so much. I was young and ambitious when I met Betsy, and I believed she would make an excellent political wife. It was a business agreement from the start. She was supposed to support my career, and I was supposed to look the other way as long as her indiscretion didn't threaten to cause a scandal."

"She cheated on you?"

"Constantly. It wasn't supposed to matter, though. I wasn't supposed to care. Trouble was, I fell in love with her." He shook his head, his eyes filled with hurt. "I couldn't stand it anymore. I couldn't stand knowing she was with all those other men. I couldn't stand knowing she was laughing at me behind my back." He paused and looked at Macon. "I couldn't stand knowing the baby she was having wasn't mine."

Macon gasped. She'd had no idea, had never suspected. "Tommy wasn't your son?"

"He couldn't have been. There was no way Betsy could have been pregnant with my baby."

"Oh, Gordon."

"I couldn't tell Tommy. How could I tell him? Then when he was so angry at me for marrying Cornelia, the situation just seemed to go from bad to worse. That's one reason I adopted you right away. I was afraid she'd try and take you away from me. I'd lost one child. I couldn't lose another."

"If Mama had left you, she would have taken me with her."

"No doubt. I couldn't risk that."

"Gordon, it couldn't possibly have been worth it. If Mama put you through all that you claim, if it was so difficult, so trying, why did you put up with it."

"I tolerated Cornelia, Macon, because I loved you. You'll never know what it did to me when you started to pull away after her death. Soon after Tommy's accident, I knew I was losing you. You became more and more absorbed in your school work and your activities, and by the time you went to college we were little more than polite friends."

"I thought I was a burden to you," she said. "I couldn't imagine that you wanted to be stuck with me after Mama died."

He shook his head. "No. No, it was never like that. Cornelia didn't want you to know the truth, and I didn't tell you. I should have. Oh God! I should have. None of this would have happened."

She met his anguished gaze, her heart pounding. "Fred Baker wasn't my father. Was he?"

Gordon shook his head. "The irony was, Macon, Tommy never forgave me for being his father and you never forgave me for not being yours." A tear slid down his face. "But I was. I am. You're my daughter, Macon, and I would have given Nat Baldwin all the money I had to keep him from hurting you."

He paused and fixed her with an anguished look. "Now you've turned your back on Jacob Blackfort, and it's my fault."

Macon sucked in a deep breath. "No, Gordon. It's nobody's fault but my own."

Thirty-one

Macon stared at the newspaper article. Emery major newspaper in the country had carried articles about Jacob's success in arresting Peter Quiver and Nat Baldwin. In the wake of their arrests and subsequent confessions, nearly a dozen government officials and law enforcement officers had been indicted, and the Justice Department hadn't even begun investigating racketeering charges against several other prominent figures. Before all was said and done, experts were predicting between forty-five and sixty upper-level officials would be implicated.

Jacob had been commended by the president for his work on the case, and had been offered Peter Quiver's job. It still hadn't been announced whether or not he had accepted it. Macon had pored over every article, listened to every radio report, watched every news show, and remained glued to her television during all the press conferences and Senate hearings. Jacob had become a national hero almost over night, and miraculously, her name had been kept completely out of the press. True to his promise, Jacob had protected her to the last.

She had been riveted by the strong sound of his voice, and the way he handled the press all through the long media circus. Piece by piece, Jacob had revealed the story behind Peter Quiver's arrest. Six months before his return to Washington, Jacob had begun to suspect Quiver's involvement in the case. Already in Paris on assignment, Jacob cabled one of his superiors in the Secret Service and voiced his suspicions. Peter Quiver was taken by surprise when Jacob returned to Washington.

As evidence against several Washington key players mounted, Jacob and Edward Gilani, working directly for Peter Quiver's superiors, laid the trap that would eventually prove Quiver's guilt. During the many press conferences that followed the arrests, Jacob had expressed genuine remorse over Eddie Gilani's death, and Macon had read several articles about all he had done to help Gilani's widow relocate and begin a new life for her family. There had been pictures of Jacob standing next to Katherine Gilani during the funeral, his arm around her shoulders, offering comfort, offering strength. Every report had glowed about Jacob's abilities and integrity, and the public had responded with an outpouring of love and adoration to the handsome man who'd given so much to his country.

But this particular article was different. It was the picture that captured her attention. It showed Jacob standing next to his father on a small pier, holding aloft the biggest trout she'd ever seen. Jacob was smiling, a broad, genuine smile, and there were no traces of the haggard lines of fatigue she remembered around his eyes. She picked up Her scissors and started to cut out the article.

"Macon?" It was May's voice on the intercom.

"Yes?"

"Gordon's on line one."

Macon smiled. With everything finally in the open between them, her relationship with Gordon had flourished. The campaign trip they'd made to Raleigh in the first week of October had given them hours to spend putting old hurts behind them. She picked up the receiver. "Hey there, Senator."

She heard him smile. "Thanks to you it would seem. Have you seen the polls?"

"Yes, sir. One day until the election, and you're twenty-three points up. Don't do anything between now and tomorrow morning to screw it up."

"Don't worry. I've got the very best campaign advice in the business."

She leaned back in her chair and smiled. "You do, at that."

Gordon laughed. "And she's very modest too."

"Washington's most politically powerful woman doesn't have to be modest." Macon picked up the article and studied the expression on Jacob's face. *She just has to be lonely,* she added to herself.

"I just wanted to know if you think you're going to make it down for the victory party tomorrow night," Gordon was saying.

Macon sighed. "I don't know. I'd like to, but I'm not sure I'm up to the trip."

There was a long pause. "At the risk of sounding like I'm prying . . ."

"You're my father, you're supposed to pry."

She heard him smile. "Are you going to mope about that man forever, or are you going to do something about it?"

"You are definitely prying."

"It's in my job description."

Macon laid the article down on her desk and propped her forehead on her hand. "I'm not sure what I'm going to do. He's still in Wyoming as far as I know."

"What if I told you I have certain inside information that he's returning to Washington as we speak."

She frowned. "What?"

"Jacob left Cheyenne this morning. He's on his way back to Washington."

"How do you know that?"

"I called his mother."

"You talked to Little Dove?"

"We're partners in crime. Both of us want grandchildren before we're too old to spoil them."

"Gordon!"

"I'm an old man, Macon. I'm supposed to be eccentric."

She smiled in spite of herself. "You're not old."

"Close enough. So what are you going to do about it?"

"I don't know. I don't know that there's anything I can do."

"Can I give you a piece of advice?"

"I'm open to suggestions, I suppose." She swiveled her chair so she could look out the window of her office. It hadn't stopped raining since Jacob left town, and now, miraculously, the sun was beginning to fight its way through the clouds. She had a sudden memory of sitting at his kitchen table and listening to him talk about prophetic signs and dreams. She sighed. "What did you have in mind?"

"About twenty years ago, a scrappy little tow-headed tomboy came to live with me."

Macon felt a smile start to tug at the corner of her mouth. "The best thing that ever happened to you no doubt."

"No doubt. Anyway, I caught her one night sitting on the roof outside her dormer window."

"That wasn't a roof, that was a marble parapet."

"Oh, sorry. I think the shingles threw me off."

"It was an understandable mistake. What did she tell you?"

"She said she was waiting for her prince."

"I think I've heard this story. What kind of horse did he ride?"

"A palomino."

"Any self-respecting handsome prince rides a white charger," she said. "Everyone knows that."

"Not this one. It was definitely a palomino."

"Did he ever show up?" Macon asked quietly.

"Oh yes. I saw him a number of times."

She did smile then. "You did?"

"Yep. He used to scale the walls of the castle, I assume we're talking about a castle and not a Greek-revival mansion?"

"Definitely a castle."

"I thought so. He would scale the walls of the castle and consult with my little princess at all hours of the night."

Macon nodded and shifted the phone to her other ear. Outside her window, a bird had settled on her balcony railing and was staring at her. "He was a good man, that prince," she said absently.

"Do you remember what he used to say, Macon?"

She sat up in her chair and looked at the picture of Jacob, laughing on the pier with his father.

"There's a whole world waiting outside your bedroom window."

"I think it's probably still good advice, punkin."

Macon stared at Jacob's expression and felt her throat start to constrict. Her palms were sweating, and her heart was racing, and she was fairly certain she was going to have a heart attack if she didn't do something about it. Her fingers tightened on the receiver. "Gordon?"

"Yes?"

"Will you forgive me if I don't make the victory party?"

"If it's for the reason I think it is?"

"It is."

"It's about time," he mumbled. "I was starting to panic."

Macon laughed. "You know me. I have to wait until the last minute to do everything."

"Is there anything I can do to help?"

She paused. "Yes. Yes, there is." Macon grinned at the bird on her balcony railing, feeling better than she had in a long time. "Do you have any contacts with the phone company?"

"Sure. You remember Josh Chambers. He's a senior V.P. with Bell Atlantic in Northern Virginia. He's a big contributor to my campaign."

"Do you think he'd mind if I called and asked him for a small favor?"

"Macon, what are you up to?"

"I need to borrow a utility truck and a cherry picker."

Thirty-two

Jacob looked at Charlie as he tossed the last folder in the cardboard box on his desk. "I think that does it, Charlie."

Charlie leaned back in his chair and took a long draw on his cigar. "I can't believe you're turning down this job, Jake."

Jacob shrugged. "I want to spend some time getting my life in order. I'm not ready to give another four or ten or twelve years of my life to Uncle Sam. I've got my eye on a piece of property in Cheyenne. I might even work with Dad on the ranch for a while."

Charlie's gaze narrowed. "Don't you think it's going to get mighty lonely out there?"

Jacob looked at the box on his desk. It held all that remained of his career with the Secret Service. "Maybe."

"Hell, Jake, aren't you even going to call her?"

Jacob shrugged. "It's election day, Charlie. She's probably not even in town."

"And it's damned convenient of you to show up on the one day out of the year when you can bank on the lady not being here. It's not her that's screwing this up, Jake, it's you."

"She. It's she," Jacob said, the response to Charlie's grammar goof almost second-nature.

Charlie grumbled something under his breath that sounded suspiciously like "damned idiot." Jacob ignored him and walked to the window. From his fifth-floor office, he had an excellent view of the city, but his mind was on Macon. A loud rumbling noise broke his concentration, and he frowned in the direction of the sound. A yellow utility truck was barreling down the street, and the driver was leaning on the horn.

Jacob was about to comment on the fool, when something caught his eye. There was someone standing in the basket of the cherry picker. "Charlie," he said.

"Yeah?" Charlie walked over to join him at the window.

"Is the phone company scheduled to do any work on our building?"

"I don't think so. You know they always let us know in advance so we can shut down the secured lines. Why?"

Jacob pointed at the truck. "That truck is headed straight for this building."

The truck drew closer and Charlie frowned. "What's that damned fool driver doing laying on the horn like that?"

"Other than stopping traffic, you mean?"

"Yeah?" Charlie puffed on his cigar. "And what's that fool doing riding in the basket of the cherry picker?"

Jacob felt a smile start to tug at the corners of his mouth. "You'd better take a good hard look at the fool, Charlie."

Charlie stared a second longer before his mouth dropped open. "Oh my God! It's Macon."

Jacob shoved open the window and waited until the truck was directly in front of the building.

Macon signaled the driver, and the basket began
a slow ascent toward his window. He was vaguely
aware that his office was rapidly filling with curious staff members, and that the street below was
quickly becoming congested by a throng of onlookers. He leaned on his elbows and grinned.

Macon was wearing the most ridiculous outfit
he'd ever seen, and damn, she looked wonderful.
She had on a pair of fitted black pants that
hugged every curve and disappeared into a polished pair of knee-high brown boots. Her white
blouse billowed around her, lifted by the faint late
fall breeze. A black cape, full-length, complete
with a red satin lining completed the bizarre cos-
tume.

By the time she was close enough for him to
clearly see her face, he caught the determined
glint in her eyes, and watched in avid fascination
as her honey-gold curls ruffled in the breeze and
caressed her forehead. She looked for all the
world like she belonged on the deck of a clipper,
brandishing a saber and shouting. "Off with their
heads!"

Jacob leaned farther out the window as he
waited until the basket was parallel to his office.
Macon was holding something red. She tossed it
to him. "What's this?" he asked.

"It's a red sweater. I figured you need that a
whole lot more than you needed red roses. Put
it on. It's cold out here."

He raised an eyebrow before tugging the
sweater over his head. "To what do I owe the
privilege of this visit, my lady?"

"I see your grammar has improved at least.
That's a start."

He was starting to feel warm all over. Macon

motioned the driver of the utility truck, and the basket immediately swung closer to the building. "Might I be so bold as to ask what kind of start?"

Macon studied him for several seconds. Her cape was billowing around her, and Jacob had to forcibly restrain himself from reaching for her. "I've been thinking."

"I'm glad."

"I've been thinking that perhaps you were right, and you do need saving. If I don't do it, I'm afraid you might not make it."

"I could have told you that."

She indicated the truck below. "This was as close as I could get to a palomino."

Jacob felt a rush of relief like he'd never known flood through his body. "Are you my princess here to rescue me from the witch's castle?"

She nodded, her expression suddenly serious. "Jump," she said, "and I'll show you the world outside your window."

"Do you think the world out there is better than the one I already live in?" he asked, while his heart was pleading words of its own. Say it, Macon. Just say you want me and I'll take whatever risks you want. He looked at her, hoping she saw it in his eyes.

"To begin with, there's a lot more color," she said, pointing to the red sweater.

He rubbed his hands on the sleeves. "You think my life is too monochromatic?"

"That sweater's just a start."

"You're threatening to make my world bigger," he said, repeating the same objection she'd used the night in her office when she'd first told him about her imaginary prince and his palomino.

"Would that be such a bad thing?"

"It might work."

"We'd both have to give up a lot."

Jacob smiled at her. "I don't think it would require giving up, so much as it would being flexible."

She hesitated. He saw the indecision in her eyes and knew she was afraid. God, how could she not know. How could she not know he'd give the world for her. "Jacob?"

"Just ask me," he said, this time aloud. "Take this one risk, Macon."

"What if you say no?"

"What if I don't?"

She wet her lips and held out her hand. "Are you going to marry me or not, Jacob?"

He grabbed her fingers and squeezed tight. "Move over," he said. "I'm coming in."

Macon gasped when Jacob climbed out the window and slipped into the basket with her. He pulled her into his arms and smiled down at her. "I love you, Macon Stratton."

Macon started to laugh, and cry, and laugh some more. She wrapped her arms around his waist. "I love you, too. Oh, Jacob, I'm so sorry."

He shook his head and tipped her chin so he could look at her. "There's nothing to be sorry for, honey. It wasn't you who drove us apart, it was me."

"I," she said. "It was I."

He grinned at her. "Thank you for admitting your guilt. I knew you were big enough not to let me take all the blame."

She looked momentarily stunned, but Jacob didn't have time to measure her reaction. He crushed his lips down on hers in a consuming kiss, and as her cape swirled in the wind and wrapped them together, the crowd below, and the assembled personnel in his office, broke into applause.

And Jacob decided the top of the world was a damned fine place to be.

Epilogue

"Hello," Jacob snatched up the phone in the utility room on the third ring.

"Hey there, handsome," Macon drawled. "What took you so long?"

He grinned and slammed the washer shut, jumping up to sit on top. "I was throwing in a load of wash."

"What's Trevor doing?"

Through the doorway, Jacob could see their two-year-old son systematically removing all the Cheerios from the box and crushing them on the kitchen floor with his heel. "Playing in the kitchen," he said.

He heard Macon smile on the other end of the phone. "I have something to tell you. Are you sitting down?"

"Yeah, but I want to guess first."

"Okay."

"You're going to be Washington's Most Politically Powerful Woman again?"

"Well, that's part of it."

Jacob laughed. "I knew it. It had to be a foregone conclusion after you did the presidential campaign last year."

"Well, you never know."

"I knew. I'm so pleased."

"Yeah, I'm pleased, too. Actually, there's something else."

"Okay, let's see. The president and first lady are coming to dinner tonight."

"How did you know that?"

"It's Tuesday. Gordon and May come to dinner every other Tuesday."

"Jacob, I don't think you should make light of this. Not everybody gets to have the president and first lady over for dinner twice a month."

"Not everybody gets to watch his two-year-old spoiled rotten by doting grandparents."

"Speaking of which, did you order the tickets today?"

"Yeah. We're booked on the four o'clock flight to Cheyenne a week from tomorrow. Macon?"

"Um-hmm."

"I have something to tell you, too."

"What?"

"I sold my book today."

She squealed. "Oh, Jacob! Why didn't you tell me right away? How long have you known?"

"I just got off the phone with Jack. I was going to call you as soon as I added the fabric softener." Jacob leaned back against the wall and watched as Trevor trailed Cheerio crumbs all over the kitchen. Life was very good, he decided. When he and Macon had gotten married, they'd decided to live in Washington so she could continue running her business. They'd bought the property he'd chosen in Cheyenne and used it for a vacation home.

Jacob had started working on a mystery novel, thrilled with the prospect of working out of his home, and Macon had spent the first year of their marriage making him learn about color and light and family. The birth of their son Trevor had been the only remaining element he needed to be the happiest man on earth, and everything else was just icing on the cake.

"Jacob?" Macon said.

"Yeah, hon?"

"Isn't it almost time for Trevor's nap?"

He checked his watch. "Fifteen more minutes."

"Perfect. He'd better be asleep when I get there. I have plans for you."

"You're coming home early?"

"I'm Washington's Most Politically Powerful Woman. I can do any damn thing I want."

Fifteen minutes later, Macon walked in the front door and found Jacob standing in the foyer, wearing nothing but a pair of fly-button jeans, with the top two buttons undone. He leaned against the wall and smiled at her. "Trevor's out for the count." He spread out his arms. "My body's all yours. Have your wicked way with me."

Macon set her briefcase down on the bottom stair and surveyed him with a slight smile. "All that for me? I'm not sure I'll know what to do with it."

"I think you can probably figure it out, sweetheart. I've always admired your brain, you know?"

When Jacob slipped inside her heated sheath thirty minutes later, Macon sighed and hugged him close to her. They'd been married nearly three years, and she never failed to be stunned at the effect their physical intimacy had on her.

"Jacob," she said, her mouth pressed against his ear.

He grunted in response.

Macon smiled and stabbed the tip of her tongue in his ear. He was starting to move within her, and she locked her thighs around his hips. "Hold still a minute."

He raised his head from her shoulder and looked at her, his expression strained. "You're not serious?"

She stifled a giggle. "Just for a minute. I have one more thing to tell you."

His eyes widened. "Now?"

She nodded. "Right now." She arched her hips against his, and he groaned again. "While we're like this."

Jacob sucked in a ragged breath. "You'd better hurry, sweetheart."

She smiled at him. "I saw Doctor Raddigan today."

Jacob stilled, much of the tension leaving his body. "And?"

"And, I think it's very good that we're going to see your parents next week. They'll want to know we're going to have another baby."

An enormous shudder coursed through his body, and he finished what he'd started, calling her name all the while. When her heartbeat finally slowed to a manageable pace, and she felt like she could breathe again, she draped one leg over his thighs and tipped her head to smile at him.

Jacob was collapsed back against the pillows, one arm thrown over his eyes. She reached up and traced a finger over the curve of his upper lip. "Are you in there?" she asked.

He moved his arm. "Barely."

Macon's smile broadened. "Congratulations. On the book, too."

He grinned at her. "Are you trying to kill me, or what?"

She shook her head and trailed a hand down his chest, stopping just above his groin. "I can't get rid of you. You're too useful."

"Even if I have bad grammar?"

"Uh-huh." Her hand moved lower.

"Even if I use too many clichés?"

"I've learned to adjust."

"What if I tell you I forgot to add the fabric softener to the laundry that's in the washer, and it's your underwear in the load?"

She wrapped her fingers around his solid length and squeezed. "I could probably be coerced into forgiving you for that."

Jacob choked out a small laugh and rolled her quickly to her back, coming down on top of her. "All right, Kemosabe, before you get carried away with my other uses, I want to know just when this bundle of joy is due."

"Seven months."

He smiled. "Just in time for spring."

"And the spring thaw."

"And our trip to the mountains."

"And our anniversary."

"I love you," he said.

Macon smiled up at him, feeling the unexpected sting of tears in her eyes. She wanted to believe her pregnancy was making her more emotional. She wanted to believe she never would have found his declaration, the one she heard so often and cherished so much, could still make her cry, but as she looked at Jacob's strong face in the late afternoon sun, she knew, knew, it would always move her heart and touch her soul that he was hers and she was his and together, they had found their way through so much and climbed so high.

Jacob still claimed that the ladder in his dream had been prophetic, that Macon had saved him from the dark hole of his past and his fears, but she knew better. She'd never tell him, lest his ego soar completely out of control, but Jacob had been the one doing the saving all along.

Dear Friends,

Some books write themselves. Others are a little more trying. RESTLESS was that kind of book. Having grown up in Washington, I was in love with the setting of this book. I wanted to convey what I enjoyed about the political world in which I once worked, without losing the majestic flavor of the nation's capital. The setting wasn't the problem.

Jacob and Macon were the problem. These two really gave me fits. Somewhere in the back of my mind it's because I believe these events really happened. I still find myself checking the papers for Macon's name around election time. I still wonder if Jacob has managed to secure the world's money supply for another year. Their characters were the type authors love to meet. They were, by turns, obstinate and lovable, wounded and strong, and irresistibly romantic. I hope you enjoyed meeting them.

As many of you know, I also write historical romance as Mandalyn Kaye. RESTLESS is my first contemporary romance, and I loved working on it so much that I'm proud to announce A PLACE CALLED HOPE, a contemporary romance with two incorrigible ghosts, is a May 1997 Pinnacle release. You'll find a teaser for A PLACE CALLED HOPE at the end of this book.

Thank you again for reading RESTLESS. Please write me and let me know what you thought. You may write to me at: 101 E. Holly Avenue, St. 3, Sterling, VA 20164.

Sincerely,

Neesa Hart

Neesa Hart,
aka Mamdalyn Kaye

P.S. A special thanks to Kim, Chris and Debbie who had to put up with me during the writing of this book. Y'all are the best.

A Place Called Hope

One

Maggie had never felt more alone than she did standing near gate 19 in the crush of the 7:00 A.M. crowd at the Dallas/Fort Worth airport.

The terminal had a dense, air-conditioned feel, despite the slight coolness of the normally stifling outdoor temperature. A late November mist shrouded the airport in a glove of dismal fog. The beginnings of the holiday crowds paced among duffel bags and backpacks. Hundreds of business travelers, made anxious by the weather and delayed flights and congested traffic, huddled over laptop computers, cellular phones and morning papers. The sloshing sounds of burnt, bitter coffee punctuated the terse conversation and boarding calls. The unmistakable scent of polystyrene and disinfectant contrasted with the smell of stale cigars and cheap cigarettes. She was surrounded by people, strangers. And she'd never been so alone.

Maggie set her, briefcase on the concrete floor. She sank down on one of the padded benches, her gaze drawn, involuntarily, to the drama unfolding at gate 19.

A young woman, no more than twenty-four or twenty-five, stood near the gate, clutching with one hand the fingers of her small daughter and with the other a tiny American flag. It was a familiar scene. Mother and daughter, clad in matching red, white and blue sweatshirts, and holding American flags and yellow ribbons, could only be waiting for a serviceman, husband and father, returning from a combat assignment. The woman's tension, and the eager, unsettled movements of her child, suggested that this was no ordinary homecoming. This one probably followed months, perhaps even a year or more of separation and worry. Maggie had witnessed dozens such homecomings dozens of times. She had even participated on occasion in other times and other places when her own husband had been among the returning heroes.

She knew the tension of the final moments before the plane landed. She knew the rush 'of joy and relief, generally accompanied by uninhibited tears. She knew the feel of her husband's arms, warm, secure, safe, after months of tear-soaked pillows and anxiety-driven fatigue.

Feelings she would never know again. Maggie felt as if there were a hard, relentless band clenched around her throat. Tears threatened to flood over the pathetic resistance of her eyelashes. She swallowed, unable to tear her eyes from the mother and child. Their excitement was palpable, a tangible thing in the crowded terminal. All around her, Maggie felt, rather than saw, passengers begin to abandon their isolated existence, setting aside tempers and frustrations, to step into the growing circle of warmth near gate 19.

The young mother paused, only briefly taking her eyes from the closed door at the gate, to adjust a yellow bow in her daughter's strawberry blond hair. And then the waiting resumed.

The young woman clutched her child's hand, while an airline employee spoke in low, calming tones, gently doing his best to hold the two of them behind the white line on the floor. It seemed an eternity before the door finally opened.

Mother and daughter leaned forward, flags held high, necks straining, their toes as close to the forbidding white line as possible. The child began to fidget. She pulled anxiously on her mother's hand, and when passengers finally began to stream through the massive door, she let out an excited squeal that immediately summoned the attention of the other passengers in the terminal. No one moved. To Maggie, the events seemed to unfold in slow motion. She felt isolated in the sea of curious onlookers.

One by one, weary travelers, laden with garment bags and carry-on luggage streamed through gate 19. Every eye in the southwest end of the Dallas/Fort Worth airport remained riveted on the door. Seconds became minutes, minutes dragged together, time slogged forward with the slowness of Southern molasses, and the young woman and her daughter strained against the confining line as they eagerly searched the disembarking passengers for a glimpse, a first look at their returning hero. Maggie felt the first tear spill over her lower lashes.

Finally, when it seemed there couldn't be room on the plane for even one more passenger, when the burgeoning crowd had grown so large, and the wait had dragged on so long, a young Marine, resplendent, handsome, full of life, wearing his

dress uniform, stepped through gate 19. Mother
and daughter flew forward, no airline regulation,
or white line, or barrier on earth able to restrain
them. The young Marine dropped his duffel bag
and lifted his daughter in the air, pausing only
to wrap his other arm around his crying wife.

The passengers in the terminal broke into
spontaneous applause, peppered with cheers of
"welcome home," and an occasional muffled
sniffle.

Maggie's focus blurred as tears filled her eyes,
and pain filled her heart. She was unable to watch
the scene any longer, knowing there would never
be another scene in another airport with another
Marine who held her close and promised all
would be well. She grabbed her briefcase and ran
for her flight.

Scott Bishop stretched his long legs as he wig-
gled his toes inside his worn boots. He leaned his
head back against the padded rest of seat 3-A.
The hard rain that pelted the small window of
the aircraft suggested yet another delay. His 5:00
A.M. flight had already been canceled, due to haz-
ardous runway conditions. The only remaining
seat on the seven o'clock flight was in first class.
At least, he thought, flexing his shoulders, he
wasn't crammed in a center seat back in coach.
With his six-foot, five-inch frame, flying coach was
usually a challenge. With any luck, the added
space and a quiet and uneventful flight to Boston's Logan airport would allow him to catch up
on his sleep.

Any thoughts of a few quiet hours were quickly
dashed when he caught sight of the young woman

making her way down the aisle. At the combination of her tear-filled eyes and an expression so
mournful, so tragic it spoke of volumes of pain
and sorrow, Scott felt his insides clench into a
hard ball. It hadn't been so long ago that he had
felt the same hopeless anguish he now saw in the
young woman's face. He recognized that particular kind of pain, even from a distance. Even in
the face of a stranger.

As she slipped past the stewardess, her choco-
late-brown eyes darted briefly across the seat
numbers. Scott saw the tiny lines around her full
mouth, the telltale crease in her forehead, and
had to restrain an irrational impulse to reach out
and take her hand, offering comfort.

She stopped at his row. He had the briefest
glimpse of whitened knuckles clutching the handle of a burgundy briefcase, before she mumbled
an apology beneath her breath, then slipped past
him. She dropped into the window seat. She
brushed a long wave of pale blond hair behind
her ear, and began searching through her briefcase while tears spilled down her face and
dripped onto the burgundy leather. Scott slipped
his hand into his back pocket and pulled out a
clean white handkerchief. He extended it to her
without comment.

She glanced up, startled, before her fingers
closed onto the soft cotton. "Thank you," she
mumbled, wiping her eyes with the handkerchief.

Scott nodded briefly. "My pleasure."

She sniffled, pausing to blow her nose. "I must
look like an idiot." She hiccuped once, her
breathing still punctuated by an occasional sob.

Scott felt another twinge of sympathy. "No, you

don't. I've felt about that miserable in my life. There's nothing idiotic about it."

She met his gaze again. Scott was struck by the notion that her eyes were the softest brown he'd ever seen. "I . . ." She paused, wiping her cheeks again. "Thank you. For being so kind."

Scott hesitated only slightly before summoning the flight attendant. There was no point in pretending he wasn't already involved in this woman's problem. He couldn't possibly ignore her distress during the long flight to Boston.

The stewardess had been watching them, keenly interested in the small scene. At Scott's gesture, she hastened over to his side. "Is there anything you need, sir?" Her eyes darted to the crying woman in the window seat. "Anything I can do?"

Scott nodded. "I'd like two aspirin and a glass of water." He squeezed his seat mate's elbow. "Unless you'd prefer wine?"

She shook her head. "No, no. Water is fine."

Scott gave the stewardess a brief look. "And aspirin." She hurried away, to return within minutes with a small package of Tylenol and a glass of ice water. Scott thanked her as he tore open the package. He shook the two white tablets onto his hand, before offering them to the young woman at his side. "Here ya go. This should help."

She accepted the pills, and swallowed them with a long sip of the water. Leaning her head back against the seat, she gave him a grateful, if watery, shadow of a smile. "Thank you. You're being very kind about this."

Scott studied her in the dim, artificial light. There was pain in her gaze that reflected the same bone-deep kind of agony he remembered so well. The memories were still too fresh for him to simply ignore that kind of hurt in a fellow human being. When he'd lost Annie, he'd felt the same empty, clawing grief he saw in the velvet brown of this woman's gaze. "Let's just say I recognize the symptoms."

She tipped her head and sniffled. "I'm sure a hysterical seat mate isn't your idea of an ideal 7:00 A.M. flight."

He shrugged. "Is there any such thing as an ideal 7:00 A.M. flight?"

That won a small, tentative smile. "I guess not."

Scott wiped his hands on his thighs. She looked even more vulnerable when she smiled. He felt like his heart had dropped through the bottom of his boots. "My name is Scott Bishop," he said. "And I'd say you're a long way from hysterical."

She waved the handkerchief at him. "Not so long, I don't think. Are you always so chivalrous, Mr. Bishop?"

"Only to ladies on the verge of hysteria." He gave her a conspiratorial wink. "I find it helps turn the tide in a more favorable direction," he indicated his shoulder, "and saves me money on dry cleaning bills. Handkerchiefs are less expensive to clean than suits."

She sniffed. "This time, you might be right." She held out her slim hand. "My name is Maggie Connell. It's nice to meet you."

He briefly shook the hand she offered. He liked the firm, slender feel of her handshake. "I'm glad I could be of assistance."

"I'm not usually so emotional, it was just . . ." she trailed off as her voice slightly wavered on a fresh flood of tears.

Scott studied her in the dim, artificial light.
Something about the entreaty in her eyes, or perhaps it was the curve of her mouth—a curve he
suspected would be more comfortable laughing
than it was with the tiny lines of fatigue pulling
at the corners—beckoned to him. He wanted to
talk to this utter, vulnerable stranger about the
answering ache in his own heart, the one he'd
grown so adept at hiding beneath a ready smile
and a quick wit. "You don't have to explain anything, Maggie Connell," he said softly.

The plane had begun to fill more steadily, and
Scott shifted closer to Maggie when a passenger
brushed past him with a large garment bag. He
caught the faintest scent of Maggie's light perfume and fought the urge to lift her hair and
find its source. "Although," he said, dragging his
thoughts back where they belonged, "I'd be glad
to listen if you'd like to talk about it."

She gave him a curious look. "Are you willing
to risk the very real possibility that I might dis-
solve into tears all over again?"

Scott nodded. "I'm a brave man. I feel com-
pelled to warn you, though, that I've given you
my last handkerchief."

Maggie dabbed at her eyes once more. "I . . .
it was the scene in the airport, with that young
Marine lieutenant. I suppose you didn't see it?"

He shook his head. "I boarded early."

She swallowed. "His family was meeting him at
the plane and I," Scott waited while she fought
back a fresh surge of tears, "there were a lot of
memories for me."

His gaze slid to the third finger of her left
hand. "Did you lose your husband?"

Two tears spilled over her spiky lashes and she

nodded. "Yes. Mark was a captain in the Marine Corps. He died in a training exercise in Saudi Arabia about a year ago."

Scott felt something inside his heart, the heart he thought had turned to stone long ago, tighten into a hard fist. "A year ago?" he asked.

Maggie nodded. "He was killed December twenty-third."

His breath came out in a long whoosh, powered by some spring of longing deep inside his being. "I lost my wife to cancer last year," he said quietly. "December twenty-first."

Maggie reached out and touched his arm in an offer of comfort that seemed compulsive. "I'm so sorry. I—I'm sure you loved her very much."

How many times in the months following Annie's death had he heard trite, if well-meant, offers of sympathy and advice? How many times had he listened to condolences with a heart too numb, and a spirit too exhausted to do more than shrink back into its own dark corner of sorrow? A hundred? A thousand? Yet no one, not in the days or weeks or months since Annie died, had ever so knowingly put their finger on the source of his pain like this virtual stranger in seat 3-B. "I did," he said.

"I know," she whispered.

Scott felt suddenly drained, like a ship cast adrift by a dying breeze. His memories of Annie rushed in with the force of a great winter wind and consumed every space, every facet of his emotional and mental energy. "Would you like to tell me about your husband?" he asked. He wondered if his voice sounded odd to Maggie.

She paused. "It's an ordinary story. It's only extraordinary to me. He was a pilot, and he died when his FA/18 Hornet went down over Saudi Arabia."

Scott shook his head. "That's not what I meant. I don't want to know how he died. I want to know how he lived."

Maggie's gaze registered her surprise. She studied him for a minute. Then a ghost of a smile touched her lips. "I would like very much to tell you that, Mr. Bishop."

Scott tipped his head back and closed his eyes. The sound of her voice was like a warm breeze, and he found comfort in it. "Start at the beginning," he said.

The aircraft engines roared to life. The plane began a slow taxi away from the gate. Even through the din, he was sure he heard Maggie's soft sigh. "The first time I met Mark," she said, "I was sitting on the porch swing outside my dorm, and he was walking to class, eating an apple."

Two

There were times when Mark Connell really hated being a ghost. As he watched his seven-year-old son Ryan prepare for a penalty shot that would be the winning point in his pee-wee league hockey game, he decided it was definitely one of those times. Across the empty expanse of ice, he met Ryan's gaze and admitted to himself that only his son's willing acceptance of his father's unworldly existence made the whole thing bearable. He smiled at Ryan, then skated across the ice to join him beside the puck.

With arms that ached to hold, and hands that ached to touch, Mark skated next to Ryan as he circled the puck. Ryan looked at him with a bright grin. The bruise on his eye was already starting to purple. Mark knew he'd soon be sporting the full effect of the illegal hit that had earned him the penalty shot. Mark winked at him.

The fact that only Ryan could see or hear him had long since ceased to bother Mark. Instead of agonizing over what he couldn't seem to change, he'd concentrated his efforts on building a relationship, no matter how strange, no matter how different, with his son. Besides, , he thought, glancing at Ryan's coach where he stood tensely gripping the boards, none of the other dads got to offer on-ice coaching. That was a privilege reserved for fathers of the invisible variety.

With a slight smile, Mark leaned forward and braced his hands on his knees. "Are you ready son?"

Ryan turned his gaze to the goalie. He gave Mark a brief, no-nonsense nod. "Ready," he said beneath his breath.

"Have you been practicing that lift shot?"

Ryan nodded again.

On instinct, Mark reached out, wanting to touch, wanting to give a reassuring squeeze to Ryan's shoulder, but his fingers, devoid of substance, met only the cool air of the ice rink. He forced back the disappointment. "All right," he said. "Give it your best shot, and remember, no matter how it turns out, I'm proud of you, Ryan."

Ryan pulled his protective mask over his small face. His gloved fingers clenched and unclenched on the grips of his stick. As Mark had instructed him, he circled twice around the puck before he started his charge on goal.

Mark watched from his spot at center ice. His shoulders shifted slightly with each of Ryan's movements. When Ryan neared the goal, Mark clenched his hands together and leaned forward in anticipation. He knew the instant that Ryan released the puck from his stick that it would sail past the goalie's left shoulder and lodge in the net.

The small crowd went wild when the shot registered on the scoreboard. Mark threw his hands up in the air with a loud whoop. He could not have been more exultant had Ryan just won the Stanley Cup. Ryan pivoted to an abrupt stop on the ice. He met Mark's gaze across the frozen expanse. His grin was broader than before, his eyes sparkled, a flush had settled in his cheeks. Mark gave him a victory salute.

For an instant, Ryan ignored the clamor of his teammates, who were now pouring onto the ice. He lowered his head and began skating toward Mark, picking up speed as he crossed the ice. Mark waited, anticipating. When Ryan drew within a yard of Mark's spot on the ice, he scrunched his little body into a tight ball and skated directly through Mark's image.

For the barest of seconds, Mark felt the slight touch of their souls, as fleeting and tender as a fluff of down on a summer breeze. He closed his eyes, savored, then willed himself to Maggie.

Seconds later, he settled back in the comfortable first-class seat across from Maggie's row on the plane. He pulled a Granny Smith apple from his pocket and took a bite. It took him several moments to realize that the attractive young woman with light brown hair and pixie-like eyes in the seat next to him was staring at him. Disconcerted, he stared back. When her gaze didn't flinch, he threw a quick glance over his shoulder. He was relieved to find she was actually focused on the view from the aircraft window.

He returned his gaze to Maggie. She'd been crying, he realized. He decided to move closer so he could eavesdrop on her conversation with the tall, blond stranger—the stranger who was sitting far too close to Maggie for Mark's piece of mind.

He moved to lever himself out of his seat, then stopped, shocked, when his hand encountered the very real, very warm flesh of the young woman next to him, and his foot made sound contact with her shin.

"Ow!" She rubbed her leg and glared at him in temperamental protest.

Mark jerked back his hand, and stared at her. "Can you see me?" he asked.

She smiled at him, a slight, enigmatic smile. "Ever since you dropped into that seat." She extended her hand. "My name's Annie. Annie Bishop. I guess you're Mark."

Mark wiped the apple juice from his lips with the sleeve of his faded Marine Corps sweatshirt. "How do you know that?"

Annie inclined her head toward Maggie. "That's my husband, Scott. Your wife has been telling him about you for the last half-hour."

Mark blinked. When he opened his eyes, she was still beside him. "Can you—I mean, are you—"

"A ghost?"

Mark nodded. She shrugged and tucked her feet beneath her long, gauzy skirt. "I guess, although, I stopped thinking about it a long time ago. No one can see me. No one can hear me. I can't do anything. I just follow Scott around."

Mark looked across the row again and studied the view of Maggie bent close in conversation with Scott Bishop. "Maggie can't see me either." He stopped and glanced back at Annie. "But Ryan can."

"I suspected that," Annie said.

Mark frowned at her. "What do you mean?"

"Your wife mentioned that your son is seven, and that he claims he talks to you. She believes he's having trouble accepting your death." She made a small gesture with her hands. "I wondered if perhaps you were like me. Here, but not here."

"I didn't know there were others," Mark said. He pushed up the sleeves of his sweatshirt. "You're the first one I've ever seen."

She nodded. "Me, too."

Mark closed his eyes for a minute. "I can't imagine what it must be like for you. Ryan is the only thing that makes this tolerable for me."

Her gaze turned wistful "He sounds like a wonderful boy."

Mark's eyes opened again and he nodded. "Yeah. He's seven and a half. Smart as a whip, too, and the absolute spitting image of Maggie." He watched Maggie's animated expression for a few seconds. "When Ryan was born, I couldn't believe how much I loved that little guy. Maggie handed him to me the first time in the hospital, and it was like my whole inside exploded."

"Do you think Maggie's right? Is he having trouble accepting that you're gone?"

Mark nodded. "I've tried to explain to him that I'm not real. He knows he can't touch me, but he knows he can see me and hear me. It's a lot for a kid to take in. What hurts the most is how sad he is. He was never like that," Mark said. "One of the things that makes Ryan easy to love is the way he smiles at you."

Annie threaded her fingers through her hair. "Perhaps he needs you so much, he's willed you to be visible to him."

Mark frowned and studied the slender young woman next to him. After nearly a year of his solitary existence, a year made tolerable only by the comforting, if odd, reality of his relationship with Ryan, he wasn't sure what to make of this new development, or her probing questions. "Do you think," he asked cautiously, barely daring to voice the question that nagged him almost daily, "that we'll ever get out of here?"

Annie looked over her shoulder, and studied Scott. "I don't know. I guess I almost started to believe this is what happens when you die. You're just stuck here."

Mark's gaze strayed back to Maggie's profile. She was laughing, ever so slightly, at something Scott Bishop was telling her. Mark watched as she tucked a strand of pale blond hair behind her ear, and smiled at Scott. He remembered those smiles. What the hell was she doing passing them around? "The worst part is being with Maggie, and not being with her all at the same time."

Annie's eyelashes fluttered briefly. "Did you have a chance to say good-bye?"

"No. I left for Saudi Arabia in August. I was supposed to be back the fifteenth of January. Maggie even promised to stall Christmas." He smiled sadly. "We never even thought about the fact that I wouldn't come back. It was supposed to be a routine training mission. Not coming back wasn't an option. What about you and Scott?"

"We said good-bye. I had to make Scott say good-bye. I was afraid he'd hold on forever if he didn't."

Mark studied her. "How did you—go?"

"Cancer." She rocked back and forth slightly, swinging her legs over the side of the seat. "I was diagnosed a year before I died, though, so I had time to prepare Scott."

Mark glanced back at Maggie. "Nothing could have prepared Maggie."

"What about you?"

The question took him by surprise. "What about me?"

"Were you prepared?"

"To die, you mean?"

Annie nodded. Mark thought the question over. "No," he said. "You never think about dying. You just fly each mission, go on each tour, do what you're supposed to do. I guess it's always there, at the back of your mind, but you never think about it."

Annie smoothed a hand over the hem of her pink sweater. "Missing Scott is the hardest part. I know how much he hurts sometimes. It makes me feel bad."

"I know. Maggie is having a rough time. She's trying so hard." He felt his chest constrict as he watched her pull a picture of Ryan out of her briefcase to show to Scott. "She really wants to move on. Sometimes I feel guilty for hanging around Ryan, like I'm keeping him from recovering or something."

"Why don't you leave?" she asked, her voice quiet.

"That would be like dying all over again."

Annie's breath came out on a long sigh. She looked once at Scott, then back at Mark. She pulled at a string on her sweater, and unraveled part of the hem. "Do you think maybe this is what was supposed to happen all along?"

"What?" he asked, not sure he liked the grave note in her voice. He stuffed his apple core into the seat pouch in front of him, then crossed his long, jean-clad legs. He was glad Maggie was flying first class this trip. He hated it when she flew coach and his knees were crammed up under his chin.

"This," she said. She indicated Scott and Maggie over her shoulder. "Do you think this is what we're supposed to be doing?" At his confused look, she leaned over to place a slim hand on his forearm. The contact felt odd. He could tell by the way she was staring at her fingers against his skin that she was thinking it too. "I haven't touched anyone in so long."

"Neither have I. What do you mean we're supposed to be doing this? Doing what?"

She met his gaze. "I can't help but wonder if we're here," she glanced over her shoulder, "with them, for a reason."

Mark leaned back in his seat. "Do you think we're supposed to do something?"

"I hope so," she said. "I really, really hope so."

She could hardly wait to get started.

If you liked this book, be sure to look for the June releases in the Denise Little Presents Line:

DANGEROUS GAMES (0-7860-0270-0, $4.99)
by Amanda Scott

When Nicholas Barrington, eldest son of the Earl of Ulcombe, first met Melissa Seacourt, the desperation he sensed beneath her well-bred beauty haunted him. He didn't realize how desperate Melissa really was . . . until he found her again at a Newmarket gambling club—being auctioned off by her father to the highest bidder. So, Nick bought himself a wife. With a villain hot on their heels, and a fortune and their lives at stake, they would gamble everything on the most dangerous game of all: love.

A TOUCH OF PARADISE (0-7860-0271-9, $4.99)
by Alexa Smart

As a confidence man and scam runner in 1880s America, Malcolm Northrup has amassed a fortune. Now, posing as the eminent Sir John Abbot—scholar, and possible discoverer of the lost continent of Atlantis—he's taking his act on the road with a lecture tour, seeking funds for a scientific experiment he has no intention of making. But scholar Halia Davenport is determined to accompany Malcolm on his "expedition" . . . even if she must kidnap him!

GREAT GIFT IDEAS FOR THAT
SPECIAL SOMEONE!

DEAR GRANDMA, THANK YOU FOR . . . (0-7860-0253-0, $5.99)
by Scott Matthews and Tamara Nikuradse
Hundreds of heartwarming, funny, loving reasons to thank Grandma
for being there in her special way. This sweet book will say it all, ex-
pressing appreciation for Grandma's care. You can thank her for letting
you break the rules, telling stories about Mom, always saving you the
last piece of cake, and of course, for her gentle laughter and wisdom.

THE BRIDE'S LITTLE   (0-7860-0149-6, $4.99)
INSTRUCTION BOOK
by Barbara Alpert & Gail Holbrook
Forget the bridal registry or that casserole dish. Give her something that
she'll be able to use before and after the wedding. This nifty little treasure
trove of lighthearted and heartwarming tips will make her laugh when
she needs it most: while making the wedding plans.

DAD'S LITTLE INSTRUCTION BOOK   (0-7860-0150-X, $4.99)
by Annie Pigeon
This funny and insightful look at fatherhood is from the author of the
popular Mom's Little Instruction Book (0009-0, $4.99). From "learn
how to make balloon animals" to "know when to stop tickling," and
"it's okay to cry when you walk your daughter down the aisle" to "it's
also okay to cry when you get the catering bill," here's lots of wise and
witty advice for fathers of all ages.

MORE FROM LOVE'S   (0-7860-0107-0, $4.99)
LITTLE INSTRUCTION BOOK
by Annie Pigeon
Just like the previously published LOVE'S LITTLE INSTRUCTION
BOOK (774-4, $4.99), this delightful little book is filled with romantic
hints—one for every day of the year—to liven up your life and make
you and your lover smile. Discover amusing tips to making your lover
happy such as—ask her mother to dance—have his car washed—take
turns being irrational.

*Available wherever paperbacks are sold, or order direct from the
Publisher. Send cover price plus 50¢ per copy for mailing and
handling to Penguin USA, P.O. Box 999, c/o Dept. 17109, Ber-
genfield, NJ 07621. Residents of New York and Tennessee must
include sales tax. DO NOT SEND CASH.*